'This debut novel from a gentle and perceptive new voice in Australian fiction is deeply evocative of a bygone era . . . This is a story we live through on every page which underlines the painful reality of history repeating itself through generations but delivers a powerful and cathartic final message.' *The Australian Women's Weekly*

'Affecting, heartwarming and devastating . . . a brilliant insight into family relationships, history repeating itself through the generations and the unparalleled bond of siblings.' *Herald-Sun*

'Well-written and very evocative, this poignant novel examines the complexity of motherhood and the powerful bond of sisters.' *Canberra Weekly*

'The two sisters are vividly contrasted and other characters add colour and sensitivity to the story . . . It's an engrossing read to follow their fortunes and tragedies.' *Good Reading*

'Allan's insights into a family's patterns, particularly those that damage its members is present in sharp characterisation, Ida's reflections and the vivid depiction of the context of both the time and the landscape.' *Otago Daily Times*

'The characters . . . are well drawn and the complex relationships between the women perceptively observed.' *The Listener*

LOUISE ALLAN is a debut author from Western Australia. This manuscript was awarded a Varuna residential fellowship in 2014 and shortlisted for the City of Fremantle–TAG Hungerford Award. Louise grew up in Tasmania but has since moved to Perth where she lives with her husband, four children and two dogs. She is a former doctor and has a passion for music.

The Sisters' Song

Louise Allan

ALLEN&UNWIN
SYDNEY·MELBOURNE·AUCKLAND·LONDON

Allen & Unwin
83 Alexander Street
Crows Nest NSW 2065
Australia
Phone: (61 2) 8425 0100
Email: info@allenandunwin.com
Web: www.allenandunwin.com

A catalogue record for this
book is available from the
National Library of Australia

ISBN 978 1 76052 997 0

Set in Adobe Garamond Pro by Bookhouse, Sydney
Printed in Australia by McPherson's Printing Group

10 9 8 7 6 5 4 3 2 1

I dedicate this book to the memory of my grandmother,
Olive Ivy May Allan.
12.6.1910–19.2.1984

She and Ida have a lot in common.

There are some women not meant to have children,
and there are others born to do nothing else.

Ida Bushell, 1947

Part I

For all women were girls once,
with dreams of their own.

Chapter 1

My memories of my father are scant and faded, and I have only two photos of him. The first was taken by Uncle Vernon with his Box Brownie when we were on a picnic at Ben Craeg in 1924. It's a distant shot of all of us sitting on a tartan blanket in a paddock. Above us arches a clear Tasmanian sky, and behind us is Ben Craeg, the mountain, covered in trees almost to its summit.

Mum and her sister, Aunty Lorna, sit on one side, all smiles under hats that burst with petals and leaves. Dad's in the middle, smiling at the camera and sitting with his legs outstretched. Nora, my younger sister, perches on his knee, fair curls framing her cherubic face. I'm next to them. I would have been six at the time, and my face is almost completely covered by a white cloche hat, as if I'm trying to hide. I'm clutching Frances, my doll, and my other hand rests on Dad's arm, so he wouldn't forget I was there, too.

The other photo is of Dad and Mum, just the two of them, and neither of them is smiling. Mum's hair is pinned and curled, her cheeks are smooth and her lips are tinted pink. She's sitting as straight as a doll, stretching herself as tall as she can, but she still looks tiny beside Dad.

He stands behind her and he's solemn, as well. His chin is long, and he's all bones and angles so his suit hangs from his frame, as if he's just a skeleton. He's changed since the first photo—he was already sick when this second one was taken. That's why they sat for it. Mum wanted a photo of them together before he died, so they dressed up and visited the studio.

I remember when I found him behind the chaff shed, red-flecked vomit on the grass at his feet.

'Don't tell Mum,' he said, and kept repeating it until I promised I wouldn't.

Stomach cancer, I heard Aunty Lorna tell Mr Clarke after mass one day. Each night, we knelt around the statue of Our Lady on the mantelpiece and counted Hail Marys on our rosary beads in the hope that he'd get better. That was all we could do—pray and wait.

We didn't see Dad much after that, we weren't allowed. But sometimes I'd sneak along and, if the bedroom door was ajar, I'd peer in. The blind would be drawn and he'd be propped up on pillows, his cheeks and eyes sinking back into his head as if he was already hollow, the rest of him a thin ridge under the sheets. I barely recognised him.

Once I saw his arm up in the air, skinny and yellow, waving about as if it didn't know where to go. Another time, when the doctor left the room, I stood in the doorway and called to him.

'Dad . . . Dad . . .'

His eyebrows shot up and his eyes darted around the room as if he was searching for me. I kept calling to him until he found me and then his eyes didn't move. He didn't smile, but he kept looking at me. He tried to lift his head off the pillow and his mouth opened, as though he was trying to talk.

Then the doctor returned, closed the door as he entered, and that was the last time I saw Dad alive.

We weren't allowed to go to Dad's funeral.

'Why can't I come?' I asked.

'Because you're seven years old,' said Aunty Lorna, the blooms in her hat jiggling.

'Eight,' I said.

'A funeral is no place for a child,' she said.

'But he was my dad.'

She drew in a breath and released it again. 'Ida, can't you just do as you're told for a change?'

I swallowed hard and said no more, and swatted at an insect flying past.

'Why do you want to go anyway?' asked Nora after Aunty Lorna had gone.

'You're only six,' I said. 'You're too young to understand.'

So on the day of the funeral, Nora and I were sent to Molly Bryant's house, and while our father was laid to rest, we played with dolls, hung upside-down from the verandah rails and ate iced cupcakes for afternoon tea.

Everything changed after that. Mum refused to open the curtains and the house was dim and silent. Even the weather seemed to echo our grief. I remember the first time it rained after Dad's funeral. I parted the curtain and peeked out, but I couldn't see Ben Craeg, the mountain, because of the low sky. It wasn't stormy or pouring, just a thin drizzle that trickled in lines down the glass—enough for me to worry about Dad being out in it all alone. I wanted to slip out of the house, run down to the cemetery and lay a blanket over him.

The first Sunday we went to mass after Dad died, people swooped on Mum, and Nora and I were caught in the middle. I glanced up, past shadowy legs and drab coats, to doleful faces and shaking heads.

As soon as I could, I took Nora's hand and pushed my way through the legs and coats, out into the air.

'Come on,' I said, and headed down the gravel path at the side of the church.

'Where're we going?' she asked.

'To see our father.'

We walked past the three firs that marked the boundary of the cemetery and along the rows of headstones towards the newer graves at the back. When I saw the mound of fresh soil, my footsteps slowed. I wasn't sure I could go any further. I didn't want to see him in the ground like that.

We reached the pile of chocolate earth and stood at the foot. A piece of tin poked from the ground. Scratched onto it was a number and Dad's name, Edward Parker.

'Where is he?' asked Nora.

I pointed at the grave. 'In there.'

'In the ground?' she said.

'Yes.'

She let go of my hand and walked around to one side, blonde curls bouncing as she went. 'I want to get in there.'

I wanted to get in there, too. Climb in under the dirt and pull it over me like a cover. I stood there in my shiny Sunday shoes, beholding my father's grave, wanting to burrow down in that earth and be with him again.

It was 1926. Mum was as old as the century and already a widow.

'You are in mourning,' Aunty Lorna reminded us whenever we laughed or asked to go outside.

I did my best to act mournful. I put on a long face and spoke in a low voice as much as I could, but I just wanted to be normal again. I resented the fact our father had died, but, even more than that, I resented that we had to act like it. Sometimes I ducked under the drapes, just to peer out the window and glimpse our old life alive on the other side of the glass. The sky and the grass and Ben Craeg on the horizon.

I'd suck on my plait and let the sun warm my face while I remembered the minty smell of the outside and our picnics at Ben Craeg. We'd ride in the back of Uncle Vernon's ute over a dirt track, and Dad would lean out and pluck the leaves off the wattle as we passed. We'd eat sandwiches and blackberry pie for lunch, and Mum would tell me off for staining my dress. Nora and I would race each other through the spiky grass to the trees and sit in the crook of their branches. Sometimes, we'd just lie on the ground and gaze up at a sky filled with clouds that looked as if they'd been painted there with an artist's brush.

I remembered, too, our trips with Mum into the township of Ben Craeg. We'd trudge after her, following her from the post office, where she'd collect her parcels of felt, to the bakery, where Mrs Monteath would cut the crusts off the day-old bread for us. In the butchery, Mr Slater would stand in front of his carcasses and smile despite his missing thumb, and at the grocer's, Mr Douglas, would always give us a candy cane at Christmas.

Because I was daydreaming, I wouldn't hear Mum calling my name, and I'd jump when the curtain rustled behind me. She'd swipe the plait from my mouth and say, 'Stop sucking your hair. It looks like rats' tails. And there's no time for absent-mindedness.'

So I'd save my wishing until night time, when I could lie in bed and suck my hair and pretend we were a normal family again. I imagined what we might be doing: sitting on Dad's lap and giggling as he bulged his muscles; watching Mum by the fire, steaming felt for a hat she was making and barking at us if we got in the way; or listening to Dad sing in a language we couldn't understand.

Take anything of mine, I'd pray, *an arm, a leg, whatever you want. Take it if it will bring Dad back, healthy and warm.*

Mum began to spend more time alone in her room. One day I heard her in there, banging on the wall. When I looked in she was nailing a charcoal-grey blanket over the window with a hammer.

'What are you doing, Mum?' I asked from the doorway.

'It's too light and I can't sleep.'

'That's 'cos it's day . . .'

She swung around and let the hammer fly from her hand. It whirled across the room, spinning wildly in the air. I jumped as it hit the doorframe next to me and clunked to the floor.

Mum stood trembling by the half-hung blanket, fists at her sides. 'Get out!' she screamed. 'Get out!'

I turned and ran down the hall, away from her screams. Her moods and her harshness hadn't seemed so brutal when Dad was alive. But now there was no one to make us smile or laugh, no one to cushion her blows.

After that, Aunty Lorna started coming every day. She was older than Mum and her kids were grown up. All afternoon, she and Mum would sit in Mum's bedroom, talking in low voices, while Nora and I tiptoed around in the gloom. Aunty Lorna was the only person brave enough to enter Mum's room, except I had to venture in to fetch Mum's chamber pot. I'd brace myself before entering, then whip in and out as fast as I could without spilling any.

Towards evening, Aunty Lorna would warm the pot of soup she'd brought. Nora and I would wait by the kitchen table while Aunty fetched Mum. I'd smell the warmth of the bread and soup and struggle to keep my hands by my sides because I wanted to tuck in.

Mum would teeter along the hallway, still in her nightdress, her face flushed from the eiderdown. She'd stand in the doorway and put a hand over her eyes to protect them from the dying rays of sunlight that angled through the window.

'Close that curtain,' she'd say. 'How many times do I have to ask?'

I'd draw the curtains, and we'd all sit and eat in gloomy silence. I couldn't stand it and I'd wriggle in my seat or pull faces at Nora or pinch her knee under the table.

'Ouch!' Nora would say.

'How can you do this to me?' Mum would snap. Then her voice would falter and her face would crumple. 'How can you be so dishonourable to your father's memory?'

I'd stop pinching Nora's knee and my shoulders would slope in shame.

Each day as she left, Aunty Lorna would caution, 'Be good, Ida.' She'd catch my elbow and pull me towards her so I'd feel her breath against my ear and smell the floral scent of her perfume. ''Cos if you aren't, your mother will be in the asylum and you'll be in the orphanage.'

One day not long after that, Mum didn't get up at all. Aunty Lorna came and went. An hour or so later, she returned with Uncle Vernon, Dr Crocker's car following discreetly behind.

Nora and I stood on the front verandah, our toes poking through the railings. The morning frost had cleared, but we could still see our breath in the air. We watched Uncle Vernon as he carried Mum out to the doctor's car. She looked tiny in his arms and the blooms in her hat jiggled all the way down the path. The doctor held the door open and Uncle Vernon slid her onto the back seat.

'Where're they taking Mum?' asked Nora, after the doctor had driven off. Her green eyes were wide and frightened.

'To a place where she can rest and get better,' Aunty Lorna said.

'Is it an asylum?' I said.

'Stop asking questions, Ida.'

'Are we going to the orphanage?'

'No. You're going to live with your grandmother for a while.'

'Grandma?'

'Yes.'

'But Mum doesn't like her.'

'There's no one else to take you. Uncle Vernon and I don't have room in our house for children,' she said.

'We could stay here until Mum gets back.'

'Don't be ridiculous. Now come inside and wash.'

I was quiet as she wiped my face, scrubbed my hands and nails, and made me dress in my Sunday best.

'Lace your boots and keep yourself tidy while I pack the suitcases.'

I bent on one knee and began to tie my laces. 'Will Mum get better?'

'That's up to God,' she said.

I took my doll, Frances, outside and sat on the steps of the verandah. Nora came and sat next to me. We both gazed out at the green countryside and the familiar houses on the hillsides. I inhaled it all, the smell of the grass and the forest and the cow pats, so I wouldn't forget it while we were away.

When Aunty had finished bundling our clothes into the suitcases, Uncle Vernon loaded them onto the back of the ute, along with a couple of boxes. Then it was time to leave. I brushed the dirt off my hands, ran down the steps and climbed in beside Nora. Uncle started the engine and we bumped down the driveway, past the wooden gateposts, and onto the road.

Then I remembered. 'Frances . . . I forgot Frances.' I spun around and looked out the back window. Our house was already receding, the blinds down like closed eyelids. At the top of the steps, I could just make out Frances' curved shape.

But Uncle didn't stop. Aunty stretched her fingers over my head and wrenched it back to the front.

'Don't look back, Ida,' she said. 'You'll just make it harder on yourself.'

As soon as she let go, I twisted around to look out the window again, but our house was out of sight. All I could see was the dark green of the forest stretching right to the horizon, where Ben Craeg stood, small and lonely, and getting further and further away.

Chapter 2

Grandma was our father's mother and she lived in Tinsdale, the main township of the northeast. Her house was on a street lined with picket fences and rhododendron trees. It was only twelve miles away, but it felt as if we'd crossed to the other side of the world.

I barely remembered Grandma. She and Mum didn't get along, so we hardly visited.

When we arrived, Aunty Lorna lined Nora and me up on the front verandah and inspected us from head to toe. Nora stood tall and looked straight at Aunty. Her curls were still neat, her dress prim and unsoiled. Whereas my hair was a frizz, my clothes streaked with dust and my palms smeared with dirt. I was also still annoyed about leaving Frances behind.

Aunty praised Nora, then turned to me and shook her head. 'Oh, Ida, how do you always manage to get so dirty? Can't you act your age?' She brushed my dress down, smoothed my unruly hair, then spat into her hanky and wiped it over my palms. They felt sticky afterwards and I rubbed them against the front of my dress to wipe off her spittle.

She clipped me over the ear.

'Now, Ida,' she said. 'Remember that your grandmother is a lady, so for the Lord's sake, can you act like one, too?'

We stepped into Grandma's lounge. Nora clung to me so tightly I thought our legs would tangle. The room smelt old and stuffy, as if it had been closed for a long time. Maroon drapes hung long at the window, and the room was cluttered with old-fashioned furniture. It was the opposite of the sparse, bare home we'd just left. The chairs were covered in velvet and the tables strewn with trinkets. A piano stood against the wall, its lid closed. Sitting upon it, in an ornate silver frame, was a photo of a grave looking man with a bushy, white beard that reached as far as his bow tie. From somewhere in the house I heard the deep tick of a clock.

'Ah! You're here.' The voice was slow and came from the other end of the room, where an old lady sat on a chaise longue next to the fireplace. She looked like a photo I'd seen of the elderly Queen Victoria. Her mouth was turned down, and her hair was parted in the middle and pinned in a bun on top of her head. She wore a long, ink-coloured skirt and high-necked blouse.

'Come along now,' she said.

Being the eldest, I took the first step. Nora clutched my hand and stayed so close behind me I could feel her breath on my neck. I trod deliberately, lest I bump a table and send a trinket crashing. Slowly, we made our way towards the straight-backed figure by the crackling fire.

'You have your mother's beauty and your father's height,' she said to Nora. 'And you are the image of him,' she said, turning to me. She reached out and pulled me closer. Her lips felt hard and dry against my cheek, and her fingers dug into my shoulder. I could smell her old skin and see the dandruff powdering her collar, but I liked that she held me—no one had done that since Dad had died.

When she let go, she pulled a hanky from her sleeve and dabbed at the wet lines on her chalky cheeks.

Nora and I shared a room. That night, after we'd slid under the covers, Nora started to cry. I rolled closer to her in the bed and slipped my arm under her head.

'I know you wish we were back in our old house,' I whispered, 'with Mum and Dad. The way it used to be.'

She didn't answer.

'But you still have me.' I stroked her hair and let it curl around my fingers. 'You'll always have me.' Her breath blew warm against my cheek. When it became as regular as a slow-ticking clock, I slid my arm out from under her, then lifted my plait to my mouth and cried. I, too, wished we were back in our old house with Dad alive and Mum happy, all of us a family again.

Grandma was already dressed each morning when we woke—we never saw her in her night clothes, nor glimpsed any part of her skin apart from her head and hands. In the mornings, she tied an apron over her dress and hummed to herself as she swept and scrubbed the house. We had our jobs, too—fetching the still-warm eggs and collecting kindling for the fire.

After lunch Grandma would prepare dinner, and the smell of stewing onions and roasting vegetables would creep through the house. Then she'd remove her apron and change into her 'afternoon dress', which wasn't a dress at all, but a long skirt and a tight, high-necked blouse that squashed her bosom so it looked big and round. After that she'd spend time in the garden, or sit on the chaise and hum while we played cards on the mat in front of the fire.

The mat was so thin that the cold from the floor seeped through, freezing the cheeks of our bums until they turned numb. The house was always cold, but we could only have a small fire because the wood had to last the winter. We'd inch ever closer, jostling for its measly warmth and complaining if the other was 'hogging it'.

'Now, now,' Grandma would say. 'It's time we had a song.'

We'd jump up and join her around the piano. We'd forget about the cold as she played songs we knew and some we didn't. She'd tell us to make up a song, so we'd sing about kangaroos and lions, and zoos and jungles. Grandma would play the notes, finding them slowly with her right hand, until her left hand could join in, too. Note by note and chord by chord, she'd build it up until her old hands were bouncing over the keys, transforming our songs into music.

Even back then Nora's voice stood out as clear as a stream, and sometimes I stopped singing just to listen to her.

The days were short and overcast, as if the night was never far away, but lingering, waiting to creep back in. Some days the mist didn't lift. I'd gaze out the window in the late afternoon, at the hanging fog and the grass still wet with dew, convinced the weather understood our sorrow.

Before dinner, Grandma would drink a sherry, sometimes two. One night, she drank three and pointed to the photo on the piano, the one of the stone-faced man with wavy, silver hair and a beard so bushy his lips were barely visible. She told us he was her father, and he'd been a Member of Parliament and very dignified. Stern but dignified. When Grandma and her sister, Florence, would hear the gate click and his heels on the path, they'd race down the hall, straight to their seats at the dining table. He'd stride in and sit at the head without a word, expecting his dinner in front of him.

'He didn't like my choice of husband,' she said. 'But I was in love. And I didn't realise what I was giving up.' She cast her eyes down and cleared her throat. When she looked up again, she was smiling. 'That wood has to last the winter, mind, so off to bed.' She called each of us over for a kiss. 'Oh, you are a bonny delight,' she said as she squeezed our cheeks. 'Doing your mother and your dear, late father proud.'

At night I'd lie in bed with Nora's arm across my chest while I sucked the end of my plait. It tasted like stiff straw and wasn't very comforting anymore. Out in the lounge, Grandma's sherry glass would tinkle. Later her door would click shut, and the bed would creak as she climbed in.

We'd passed another day. That's what we were doing—passing the days. Rising each morning, going to our new school, then coming home and waiting for the night to blow back in.

As soon as the winter frosts began to clear, Grandma showed me how to prune the roses and trim the ivy. We prepared the soil for the vegetable garden, digging the ground and stirring in the manure.

'Dig the soil deeply and turn it well,' said Grandma, as she hacked the dirt with a hoe, 'to keep it in good heart.'

We put soil in pots, made holes with our thumbs and planted seeds. Grandma labelled each one so we'd remember what it was—carrots and cucumbers, lettuce and parsley—and set them on the windowsill.

'Allow the water to warm in the sun before you sprinkle it on the seedlings,' said Grandma. 'Or you'll startle them.' So I'd sit the jug on the sill beside the tiny plants until the water was warm and gentle enough not to alarm them.

I kept asking when they'd be ready to plant.

'They need to be a bit sturdier yet,' Grandma would say, 'or they'll perish. They need nurturing until they can survive on their own. Just like children.'

A few weeks later, we finally planted them in neat rows with pegs and string, and I was proud of our work.

Mum joined us at Grandma's one Friday in spring. It had only been three months since I'd seen her and six months since Dad's death, but it felt like years since we'd been a real family. As soon as I heard the putt-putt of Uncle Vernon's ute, I shot out the door and down the steps two at a time, Nora close on my tail.

Aunty Lorna was the first to alight. 'Mind your mother, now,' she said, the sunflowers in the brim of her hat bouncing as she bent down to open the passenger door.

I squinted and craned my neck, trying to glimpse Mum through the opening. Finally, she stepped out and gawked about as if dazed. Her hair was curled and brushed, and she had a dusting of powder on her cheeks. She looked smaller, more fragile.

I felt my heart rise in my chest. I wanted to race over, throw my arms around her, and tell her how much I'd missed her. To say how sorry I was for my behaviour and for causing her to go to the asylum. Instead, I stood straight as a fence picket, smiling and squinting into the sun. Nora stood slightly behind me, as if she was hiding from Mum.

Aunty Lorna took Mum's elbow. 'I've got you, Alice,' she said. 'Easy now. Careful with that case, Vernon.'

'We've been good,' I called. 'Very good.'

Mum stopped and looked over. I stood taller and puffed my chest, hoping to show her how much I'd changed. 'You don't have to be leaving us again,' I called. 'I'm well behaved now.'

'Shhh,' whispered Nora.

Aunty Lorna nudged Mum's elbow and together, they stepped forward.

'I'm much better than before. Truly,' I went on. 'Grandma says I'm doing you and our late father proud.'

'Shhh,' whispered Nora again.

'Ida,' said Aunty Lorna and fixed me with a glare straighter than her eyebrows. 'Hush! Don't be upsetting your mother.' She nudged Mum's elbow again and they kept moving. 'Mind the puddle, Alice.'

They walked up the muddy path, the grass either side blunt and sparse from the winter frosts. Uncle Vernon trailed behind with the suitcase.

'Watch your step,' said Lorna as they climbed the stairs to the verandah.

Grandma waited by the door, already in her afternoon dress although it was only morning. Mum stopped when she reached her. Grandma took Mum's shoulders and pulled her close, just as she'd done to Nora and me on the day we arrived. She kissed Mum's cheek.

'You can have Edward's old room,' she said.

Mum's back was to me so I couldn't see her face and I didn't hear what she said.

'No need to thank me,' Grandma said. 'You're family and welcome to stay as long as you need.'

Mum and Aunty Lorna disappeared inside, and Grandma turned to us. 'Just wait outside, girls, until we get your mother settled.'

So Nora and I sat on the front steps, plucking onion weeds and sucking on their stalks. Every now and then, one of us would peer down the hall at Mum's closed bedroom door and will it to open. We waited all morning, glancing up each time Aunty or Grandma stepped into the hall. But they'd just disappear into the kitchen and reappear a while later carrying a tray or a bottle of medicine, or a bowl and towel. We watched with envy each time they entered Mum's room without us.

I stood and kicked at a plank on the verandah. 'This is stupid.'

Nora didn't answer, but plucked another stem of weed and began sucking. She looked as unhappy as me.

'This is not how it's meant to be,' I went on. 'Mum's meant to be back to normal, and we're meant to be a family again.'

Nora looked up at me, her eyes sad, curls tumbling around her six-year-old face. 'I don't think she likes us very much anymore,' she said.

Later, Grandma called us inside for lunch, and as we sat down to our sandwiches, she said, 'Now, girls, you're not to pester your mother, mind.' She finished tying her apron, then ran water into the sink and collected a couple of spuds from the hessian bag behind the kitchen door. 'She needs to rest.'

'Can't we see her?' I asked.

'Give her a day or two to adjust.' Grandma began to scrub the spuds.

'But she might have missed us,' I said. Nora looked up at me and put a finger to her lips, before picking up the sandwich from her plate.

Water dripped from Grandma's hands as she carried the potatoes to the table and placed them on a board. 'No doubt she has.' She smiled, then picked up a spud and gouged an eye with the knife.

'Can't you ask her if she wants to see us?' I said. Nora glanced at me again, frowning and shaking her head.

'We won't pester her just yet, eh?' said Grandma. She began to peel the potato. The skin coiled and fell to the board in a spiral. She sliced the potato into halves and then quarters. Each time, the knife crunched hard against the board.

Throughout the afternoon, the smell of stewing onions and carrots crept through the house but, for once, it didn't warm me. At dinnertime, Grandma took Mum's food in to her on a tray while we ate on our own in the kitchen. Although steam rose from our plates, the food tasted cold.

That night in bed I slid under the blanket and wept into the mattress. Mum was back, but it wasn't the same. There was no laughing, no cuddles, no joy.

Nora rolled over. 'Why are you crying?' she whispered.

'I just want to be a normal family again,' I said.

'Crying's not going to bring Dad back.'

'I know but I can't help it,' I said.

'You've got to be good, Ida.'

'I'm trying,' I whispered.

'You'll have to try harder. Or Mum will go away again.' She rolled back to face the other way. 'And she mightn't come back.'

'Don't say that,' I whispered. I felt my chest tighten at the idea of losing Mum. Then we would have lost everything—our home *and* our parents, both of them.

Mum didn't get up the next day, or the next, or the one after that. I tried to be good and not pester Grandma, but each day I asked if Mum was ready to see us yet. Each day Grandma's response was the same: 'Just have patience.'

On the fifth day I asked again. 'Why can't we see her?'

Grandma was setting up the meat mincer on the kitchen table. 'Be patient.'

'Is she dying, too?'

Grandma stopped and regarded me with her kind blue eyes. 'Of course not, dear.' She wiped her hands on her apron then patted my shoulder. 'Wait here.'

Nora and I waited outside Mum's room while Grandma went in.

'Alice, your children would like to see you,' Grandma said.

The sheets rustled and Mum muttered something inaudible.

'They've already lost their father. They can't lose their mother, too.'

There was silence for a while, then the door opened and Mum stood in the light. She was pale and dishevelled and wobbly. Nevertheless, she was standing and trying her hardest to smile.

'See, she's fine,' said Grandma, smiling, too.

Chapter 3

From then on, Mum started coming out of her bedroom in the afternoon.

'Good afternoon, Alice,' Grandma would say each day.

But Mum wouldn't answer—she'd just sit in the chair by the fire and stare at the rug by her feet. She seemed to be fading away before our eyes, and I didn't like seeing her so still and silent. One day, I inched my way across the rug until I was right by her shoes. I wriggled about until I was in her line of sight, and when she didn't move, I called to her in my softest whisper. 'Mum . . . Mum . . .'

Her face twitched and she turned. Her eyes found mine. I smiled and said, 'It's good to have you back,' in the gentlest voice I could make.

She didn't return the smile, but I tried again the next day.

'I'm good now,' I said. 'I help Grandma in the garden. I squash the caterpillars before they eat the spinach, and I collect the eggs.'

Each day I told her something new and nice in the hope of sparking her to life again. It didn't seem to help much, but at least she noticed me.

❧

After a couple of weeks of Mum's silence, Grandma decided to set up one of Mum's old hat blocks by the fire. Next to it she laid a large piece of felt and Mum's sewing basket. As soon as Mum saw it, she stopped.

'I thought you might show me how to make a hat,' Grandma said quickly. 'You used to make beautiful hats.'

Mum kept looking at the dome of wood, the firelight shining over its surface.

'I don't have the faintest idea what to do,' Grandma went on. 'Would you explain it to me?'

Mum turned to her chair and picked up the felt lying across it. She sat, placing the felt on her lap. Slowly, she ran her fingers over it, spreading and smoothing it. It was a wide circle of fabric, a couple of feet in diameter and the colour of dark mushrooms.

'I'd need a kettle and a flat iron,' she said, her voice cracking. She cleared her throat and she sounded stronger when she spoke again. 'And a good rag and some drawing pins.' She looked up, and although her skin looked sallow and her eyes looked pained, she smiled. 'Yes, I'll show you how to make a hat.'

It cheered us all to see Mum perk up again—to watch her fingers massaging the wet felt, stretching and smoothing it over the wooden block. Her eyes lost their distance and became intent as she steamed and measured and trimmed. The room smelt of warm wool, the sweetest smell in the world.

Mum's health improved over the summer, and she began getting up earlier and staying up longer. After a while, it felt like nearly all of her had come back, except that she hardly smiled and we never heard her laugh. Each afternoon when she sat with us making her hats, her mind still seemed to be in another place.

Mum had always been prone to moodiness, and we were used to her snapping at us if we got in the way. All of that sharpness returned, and more. Sometimes, she was as brittle as a dry twig. No warning, just snap, and my ear would be ringing. Like the time I asked her what she did with Frances.

'Who?' she said.

'Frances. My doll.'

Her hand clipped the back of my head. 'How am I meant to know what happened to your doll?'

There was no Dad to buffer the hurt anymore.

As Mum came back to life, Nora grew quieter. It was as if she was frightened to speak lest she say something that might upset Mum.

Nora also started wetting the bed. Mum began waking her in the middle of the night to use the potty, and when that didn't work, she stopped Nora from drinking anything after dinner. But that didn't help either, and most mornings I woke to a wet mattress and the smell of pee.

Mum would take to Nora's behind with the switch and make her haul the mattress outside to the verandah, where it's tea-coloured stains told everyone walking past that Nora, at six years of age, still peed the bed.

'Can't you stop it before it leaks out?' I said one morning.

'Please don't tell,' she begged. 'I don't want Mum to leave again.'

So we'd pull the bedcovers up before Mum spotted the wetness, and at night we'd climb back between the still damp sheets that reeked of ammonia.

Each wash day, when Mum found the mouldy sheets, Nora and I would both cop the switch on our behinds—Nora for peeing the bed and me for lying about it.

However, no amount of walloping stopped Nora's bladder from leaking. Mum took to punishing her by bolting her in the chaff shed, where she had to sit on her own amongst the dust and Grandma's old furniture. The sun was usually setting before Mum would unbolt the door and let her out, but Nora never complained.

I used to feel sorry for Nora, alone in the shed without anything to eat or drink. One lunch time I slipped some bread and dripping onto my lap, waited until Mum left the room and snuck outside.

'Nora . . . Nora . . . It's only me,' I said as I peered into the keyhole. I squinted until I spotted her sitting against an old chest next to a bassinette, drawing pictures in the dust. 'I've brought you some bread and dripping,' I whispered.

I checked Mum wasn't in sight, then I crouched on all fours, my cheek against the ground so I could smell the dirt and wood. I slipped the bread through the gap. Nora's boots came closer until I could have touched them on the other side of the door. She picked up the bread and sat down again by the chest.

After that I started taking bread and dripping to Nora every time Mum bolted her in the chaff shed so at least she wouldn't go completely hungry. After a few weeks of this, one day when Nora had been hauled out to the shed yet again, I overheard Grandma and Mum talking in the lounge.

'I don't think it's right to be punishing a child for wetting the bed, Alice,' said Grandma.

'Well, I can't be washing sheets every day,' said Mum.

After a pause, Grandma cleared her throat. 'Belting her and locking her up isn't going to make her stop.'

'I don't know what will then.' Mum's voice was shrill.

'Time. Time and patience. And letting her grieve her father's death.'

Mum sniffed. 'I'm grieving, too.'

'I know.'

Another pause.

'I just don't know how to keep going without him.'

'You have to,' said Grandma. 'We both have to, for the girls.'

The mantel clock chimed and they said no more. A minute later, Mum opened the door. I pretended I was rearranging the trinkets on the hall stand and didn't notice her red face or watery eyes as she strode past and into her bedroom.

Later, when I took bread and dripping out to Nora in the shed, I stayed crouching by the door.

'I don't reckon Mum'll lock you up again,' I said into the gap, and I told her about the conversation I'd overheard. 'Grandma said to give you time to get over our father's death.'

We were both quiet for a while, then Nora said, 'I don't remember him much anymore.'

'I'm frightened I'll forget him, too.'

'I remember his voice when he sang,' she said. 'So deep it made the floor tremble.'

'I remember his muscles. I'd try to make mine big like his and he'd say, "Like a pimple on a pumpkin," and I'd think that was really big.' I felt my lip quiver. 'Every night before I sleep, I imagine having our family back as it was.'

'I just want Mum to love us again,' she said.

Then I heard Mum's voice. 'Get back inside, Ida, or I'll put you in there, too.'

I scrambled to my feet, brushing the dirt off the side of my face and my dress. 'Just collecting more kindling.'

A short while later, Mum unbolted the door and let Nora out. I don't remember Nora wetting the bed again after that.

About a year after Dad died, in the autumn of 1927, ladies began calling in to be measured for Mum's hats. Mum started advertising in the local newspaper and Mrs Flanagan even began selling them in her millinery shop in the main street. Soon, the women of the district were wearing Mum's hats to church and to the races, and Mum became known for her beautiful millinery.

At home she'd tell us if she was expecting someone for a hat fitting, and she'd say their name as if she was announcing royalty. They were usually from farming families, far richer than us. I remember the day the doctor's wife came. Mum swept the front verandah and ran around the house with the duster. We were banished to our room and told not to make a sound. At the knock on the door I heard Mum say, 'Good morning, Mrs Crocker,' in a voice far posher than the one she used with us.

Mum talked a lot to these ladies, too, more than she did to us, telling them about our great-grandfather who'd been Speaker of the House, and about how there was a castle named after our family in England, which I think she just made up because to this day I've never heard of Parker Castle.

After the ladies had gone, the house would go quiet again, and I'd venture in to see Mum. She would be holding a damp cloth and wetting the felt stretched over a wooden block while the flat iron heated up in the coals nearby. I'd ask if she wanted me to hold the drawing pins or fetch more felt, but she'd bark at me to leave her alone while she worked, so I'd reluctantly slink back out.

I didn't want to leave because I liked watching Mum work. She'd always been skilled with her hands—she could knit or sew or craft anything, big or small. She made all of our clothes, bedlinen and tablecloths. She'd embroider the edges with dainty flowers in canary yellow or cornflower blue, and their leaves in mint-green.

I used to watch her hands as they formed the stitches, the needle and cotton pushing in and out, in and out, in tiny, delicate strokes. When she knitted, her fingers flicked the wool like levers and the needles clicked faster than I could blink.

One day I asked her to teach me how to knit. She shook her head, then looked up and seemed to change her mind. 'All right. I suppose you've got to learn some day.'

I sat between her legs, and felt the warmth of her arms around my shoulders and the softness of her hands over mine. She showed me how to loop the wool over the needle, then slip one stitch through the other and slide it off. I wanted to stay there forever, enveloped in her arms. But I wasn't very good at knitting and Mum soon tired of teaching me. Still, I kept trying, just so I could sit on the chaise beside her. We didn't speak, but were close enough so our arms and legs touched and our needles nearly clicked in time.

Although our family was never the same again, our lives did settle. We got used to the routine of school and chores, prayers and Sunday mass. I didn't always like it, but I was learning that there are things in life we have to bear whether we want to or not. Things like mass on Sundays, dreary days in winter and the death of a father.

Still, there were things I didn't dare voice, not to anyone. Malicious thoughts that if I'd told the priest at confession, he'd have made me say rosaries for a week. But I had thoughts I couldn't help thinking and feelings I couldn't help feeling. Unkind thoughts towards kids in my class, whose parents were still alive. Kids like Beth Prosser. She was my best friend, yet each week when she stood in front of me at mass with her mother and her father, I glared at her back for the whole hour. Sometimes I even willed bad things to happen to her, to all of her family.

I never told a soul about these fantasies.

At least there was the garden. While I was there, all my anger and grief seemed to melt away. I spent the afternoons outside with Grandma, deadheading the roses, their scent still faint on the air. We turned the soil in the vegetable patch out the back and fertil-ised it with chicken poop, and we trimmed the strawberries and the fruit trees. It felt good to come inside at the end of a warm after-noon with dirt under my fingernails and my face freckled by the sun. I was excited when we could pick the strawberries and enjoy their sweetness, and I felt proud when I looked out the window and saw the hollyhocks and marigolds in bloom.

It wasn't the easiest of childhoods, but it wasn't all bad. We were fed and we were clothed, which was more than I could say for some. And scattered amongst the bleakness were moments of peace and kindness, which I held onto.

May was the month of Mary. Her statue stood on the mantel and, ever since I could remember, each day in May Mum made us kneel below it and say the rosary. Mary's skin was pearly white and she gazed down at us with benevolence. She wore a blue cape trimmed in gold, which draped softly over her arms. Under this, her cream dress fell to her feet, where a snake coiled, its fangs visible in its open mouth. Every time I spotted that snake, I marvelled at Mary's serenity and how she didn't appear afraid.

It was the second year after our father had died, and Grandma told Nora and me that she'd buy us each a set of rosary beads once we were good at saying our Hail Marys. But reciting the same prayer over and over bored me. As the words marched from my mouth, I'd start scratching at my knees, or gazing out the window, or pursing my lips and blowing air at the candle beside Mary until it flickered.

Nora was good at praying, though. She'd kneel next to Mum, close her eyes and bury her nose in her hands. She recited each Hail Mary as if she truly meant every word. It was no surprise when Grandma gave her a string of mother-of-pearl rosary beads blessed with holy water from Lourdes. I coveted those beads. Each time Nora brought them out to pray and I saw their dainty shimmer against her skin, I wanted them.

Nora kept them under her pillow, and I used to sneak into our room and slide them out. I'd finger each bauble and, sometimes, I'd even sling the beads around my neck like a necklace. If I heard someone coming, I'd slip them off and hide them back under the pillow as quickly as I could.

But one day I didn't hear the approaching footsteps, or the door opening, and Nora caught me.

Her green eyes flashed. 'Take them off!' she cried, her voice a screech. I tried to pull them over my head as quickly as I could, but Nora's hands were grabbing at them, tugging on them, and they were cutting into my neck. 'They're mine. Not yours. Give them back!'

With all the wrenching and pulling, they snapped, and the crucified Jesus fell into my lap. I picked him up and held him out to Nora, the three beads for the Hail Marys and the one for the Our Father still attached.

Nora really began screaming then, one blood-curdling shriek after another, as if I'd crucified Jesus Christ myself.

'I'm sorry. I'm sorry,' I said.

Mum came running in, followed closely by Grandma. 'What on earth is going on?' Mum cried.

I slunk off the bed, still holding the broken beads and saying, 'I'm sorry. I'm sorry.' I stood by the window while, between shudders, Nora relayed the story. 'They were my favourite things in the whole world, and she's broken them.'

I was whacked good and proper for that—not just for coveting Nora's rosary beads, but for being so sacrilegious as to wear them around my neck.

I stayed in our room for the rest of the day, my head buried in my pillow until it became wet and cold with my tears. I wasn't crying for the walloping but because I couldn't help myself but behave badly. I hadn't meant to break Nora's rosary beads; I just couldn't resist playing with them even though I knew I shouldn't.

As the twilight deepened, the bedroom door opened, but I didn't look up.

'Ida, are you joining us for dinner?' It was Grandma.

I shook my head.

The door shut softly and the mattress sank as she sat. Then I felt her hand on my cheek, stroking it gently, as if it was made of butter that she feared she might dent.

'Do you know why I didn't buy you the rosary beads?' said Grandma.

I kept my head down, hidden by the pillow. 'Because I'm bad?'

'Because I don't think you really want them.' She paused. 'You don't seem to like praying much.'

I slowly shook my head.

'Your Dad didn't either. He always played the fool during the rosary, pulling faces and distracting everybody.' She was quiet for a while. 'You remind me of your Dad.'

I lay still.

'Every time I look at you, I catch my breath because I see him. And you have mischief in you, too. Just like him.'

I turned to face her. 'I'm sorry I'm so bad.'

'You're not bad, Ida. You're a child, that's all.'

I rolled over. 'But Nora's so good. She never does anything wrong. I don't even know why she goes to confession—she never sins, and Mum sends me in with a list of mine.'

Grandma paused. 'If you could choose a present, what would you like most of all?'

I pushed myself up to sitting. I knew my answer straight away. 'A doll. Like Frances.'

Grandma repaired Nora's rosary beads and bought me a doll that I named Polly. She was a proper doll—a bride doll—more elegant than Frances, with long hair and a ribbon and a dress of white lace.

I played with her behind the chaff shed, alone—Nora wasn't interested in playing with dolls. Besides, I didn't want anyone to see my pretend games. I used to imagine she was my child and we had our own house. I made her a bed out of twigs and leaves, with a rag for a blanket. Whenever I tucked her in, I kissed her goodnight, like Mum and Dad used to do to us.

I took Polly to school with me and every lunch time, Beth Prosser and I clambered over the fence with our dolls, making a beeline for the river. We knew it was out of bounds, but we'd found a shady hollow next to a fallen log. It was quiet and private, and no one knew we were there.

Not until the day Sister Xavier spotted us climbing the fence and followed us. When she dragged us back, we got the yard rule on our behinds, ten hard ones, for absconding.

During the first year we lived with Grandma, she started teaching me how to play the piano. She sat beside me, demonstrating how to run my fingers up and down the notes.

'C-D-E-F-G. G-F-E-D-C.'

I tried to copy her, but I couldn't make my fingers move one after the other over the keys. Before long, I grew bored and started wriggling and gawking about. As soon as my time was up, I slid off the stool and ran outside. I couldn't make up my mind which I liked less—praying or piano practice.

Grandma began to teach Nora, too. Even though she was two years younger than me and only seven-years-old, from the first day she sat on the stool and placed her fingers on the keys, she could make music. I used to watch her through the window. She looked so pretty, sitting straight backed, her hands on the keys, eyes squinting at the yellowed page before her. Grandma would stand close beside her, tapping and counting. The sight of them together, bringing the faded dots on the page to life, was like a picture from a storybook.

I used to sit with Polly on the verandah outside the front window and pluck buzzies from my socks as I listened. How I wished I could do it, too—read those notes and make music from them. But each time I sat, I couldn't remember the names of the notes and my fingers wouldn't go where they were meant to. In the end, Grandma told me I didn't have to do the lessons anymore, and while I can't say I was disappointed, it didn't stop me wishing I could play.

Nora continued her music lessons with Grandma over the next few years. She sat at the piano for hours while her hands chased each other up the keys and back down again. She practised the same pieces over and over until her fingers were skipping and running, and going anywhere she wanted them to. She made music like I thought only possible in stories and movies and dreams.

Grandma said she had 'a gift' and hardly needed a teacher.

Chapter 4

It was never explicitly stated that Grandma's bedroom was out of bounds, but we knew from the way Grandma always kept the door closed that it was private. As tempted as I was, I'd never dared set foot inside.

After we'd been living there for a couple of years, one afternoon I noticed the door was open a crack and, from within, I heard Grandma's voice. 'I think you'd like these.'

I peered in. The room smelt musty and old, with a strong odour of camphor, like the inside of a wardrobe that hadn't been opened for years. I could see a tasselled mat and a velvet chair draped with Grandma's clothes. I nudged the door further, and a knobbly four-poster bed covered in a lumpy satin quilt and cushions came into view.

Nora sat on the other side of the bed, facing away from the door. She was watching Grandma, who was bent over next to her, rustling something I couldn't see. Grandma straightened, holding a soft bundle wrapped in tissue paper. She dusted off the package and unwrapped it, letting the paper float to the quilt. In her hands were the shiny folds of a sapphire-coloured gown. As she held it up, it tumbled to the floor and the light rippled across it in waves.

'I wore this at the opening of Parliament in 1892, when Father was sworn in as Speaker of the House,' Grandma said as she draped the dress over the bed beside Nora.

Grandma continued unwrapping the garments, holding each one and its memory in her hands for a moment before letting it glide to the bed.

'I wore this to a dance at the Albert Hall,' she said as she let an emerald-coloured taffeta gown with a tight bodice and tiered skirt drop to the quilt.

'And this,' she said holding up a red satin dress, 'I wore to see Dame Nellie Melba.'

'You saw Dame Nellie Melba?' said Nora.

'Yes. In 1903. At the Theatre Royal in Hobart. The tickets cost a guinea, and we sat in the Dress Circle. The Premier and the Governor of Tasmania were there, too. I'd never seen so many people in one place. More than four thousand. When I leant over and saw all the people below, my heart leapt into my mouth. Then the curtains parted and Melba stepped onto the stage. I couldn't believe I was actually there, seeing her in real life. I clapped so hard my hands were stinging before she'd even started. Oh, her voice—it sounded as if it was coming from heaven itself. How I'd dreamt of being a singer like her . . .' She stopped, still gazing at the red satin in her hands. Then she shook her head and draped the dress on the bed with the others.

Nora's hand reached out and caressed the satin. I could imagine its softness under my fingers.

'And I mustn't forget to show you these . . .' Grandma stood beside a cedar dresser on the far wall. The top of the dresser appeared cluttered, but I could make out an ivory-handled brush and mirror, a dainty figure of a shepherd boy and his dog, and an oval portrait of a beautiful young woman with the same eyes as Grandma.

She reached towards the back, picked up a rectangular silver box and swivelled to face Nora again. 'Here,' she said.

I stepped further into the room so I could see.

Grandma held a long string of pearls in one hand and the silver box in the other. The lid of the box was open. Inside were coils and clusters of gold and pearls and gems. Nora gingerly took the pearls from Grandma's hand and draped them over her head. She fingered a bead, her eyes wide and her lips apart. She was barely breathing. Then she stood and picked up the red satin dress and held it against her.

'May I try it on?' she said.

Grandma nodded.

Nora whipped off her serge dress and slid the red satin over her head. It fell down over her body, and when she straightened again, she'd changed—she looked taller, older, and not at all the ten-year-old child she'd been a moment ago. I thought she looked beautiful. She smoothed the dress's creases, then held it out with her hands, twirling one way and then the other. When she looked up again, she was smiling.

'I never want to take this dress off,' said Nora. She whirled right around, tilted her head back and laughed.

Grandma laughed, too. 'I used to feel like that when I wore it.' They both sounded breathless. 'But we will have to pack it away now.'

'Can I wear it another day?' she asked.

Grandma eyed the silks and satins draped over the bed. With a smile on her lips, she nodded.

'You promise?' said Nora.

'Of course.'

Grandma began to fold the dresses, wrapping each one in tissue paper as gently as swaddling a baby, before tucking it back inside the box.

Nora picked up the silver jewellery box from the dresser and closed the lid. 'Estella Rose,' she said, reading the name engraved on the top. She glanced up at Grandma. 'Who's that?'

'That was me,' Grandma whispered. 'Once upon a time.'

'I want to be an opera singer, like Dame Nellie Melba,' said Nora.

'You have the talent and dedication to be anything you want to be, young Nora,' said Grandma.

'What about me?' I said. They both looked up, surprised to see me. I stepped further into the room. 'Can I be an opera singer, too?'

Grandma tilted her head and smiled sympathetically. 'Ida, dear, I suspect the Lord has different plans for you.'

I glanced at Nora standing behind Grandma, looking elegant in the red satin dress. I looked at her hands, still holding the silver box—those hands that joined in fervent prayer and those fingers that made music, beautiful music. I tried to smile, but had to gulp hard to swallow the bitter taste that had risen in my throat.

After that, Nora would sometimes dress in Grandma's clothes and jewellery when she played the piano. Grandma didn't mind, but Mum would shake her head and mutter under her breath, 'Giving her ideas beyond her station.'

One Sunday afternoon, when I was in the chaff shed spreading the onions on the mats to dry, I heard Nora calling for me. When I emerged, she was standing on the back step, wearing Grandma's red satin dress and beckoning with silver arms. I dusted off my hands and knees and followed her inside.

Nora ushered me into the lounge, which now smelt of camphor. Grandma was already seated on the chaise, so I sat on a fire chair with Polly, my doll, on my knee.

Nora stood in front of the window, silhouetted by the afternoon sun. She swivelled one way, then the other, and the light shifted across her gown.

'I'm going to give a concert. Today I will play . . . Where's Mum?' she said, and glanced towards the door.

'Your mother's busy,' said Grandma. 'She'll pop in if she gets a moment.'

'Today I will play "Für Elise" by Ludwig van Beethoven.'

Nora walked towards the piano. She was already nearly as tall as me, and she'd pulled her hair up in a knot. She unwrapped the fur stole from her neck and slung it over a lamp table. Slowly, she peeled the silver gloves from each of her arms and draped them, too, across the table. Even at her tender age, she could already do things like that and look elegant. Finally, she sat on the worn tapestry of the stool and tucked her shimmering folds under her. A blonde ringlet had escaped and was coiling down her neck.

Then she began to play. Her fingers crept over the keys and from them came the tune I'd heard her practising. It was simple and pretty and familiar. As she played, she began to sway and move with the music. Her face changed and she looked transformed, as if the music was coming from inside of her. As if she was inside of it. As if the rest of the room had disappeared, and there was just the music and her.

I felt it, too—the music in the air around me and inside of me. I glanced at Grandma, who had shifted forward on the chaise, her eyes intent on Nora, and I could see she felt it, too. I began to feel warm and my throat was dry. I clenched my teeth and waited for it to end.

As soon as she'd finished, Grandma clapped her hands. 'Oh, Nora, that was exquisite!' She looked across at me, a big smile on her face. 'Wasn't it so, Ida?'

I held my lips together and nodded, but I couldn't bring myself to clap.

'Next I will sing "Bist Du Bei Mir" by Johann Sebastian Bach,' said Nora.

'I think Mum wants me,' I said and stood to leave.

'Oh, stay and listen, Ida,' said Grandma. 'It's so nice to have an audience.'

I flopped back in the chair, looking at my lap rather than Nora, not even trying to hide my reluctance.

Nora began to play and then to sing.

Bist du bei mir

My body stilled at the sound of her voice, but I kept my head down, determined not to look up.

Geh ich mit Freuden

Her voice sounded like a tiny bell. I wanted to glance up, but I kept my eyes on my hands, clasped together in my lap.

Zum Sterben und zu meiner Ruh.

I couldn't help but glance up. Nora was swaying back and forth as she sang, her hands rising and falling over the keys. I quickly averted my eyes.

Ach, wie vergnügt wär so mein Ende

I tried to hold myself rigid, but her voice kept coming, tender, like a caress.

Es drückten deine schönen Hände

Mir die getreuen Augen zu.

She was still trying to come in, through my skin and my ears, and in the end I covered them with my hands. I didn't let her in. I didn't hear the last lines of the song, and I didn't know she'd finished until I looked up. Grandma and Nora were staring at me. I uncovered my ears and stared back at them.

'Aren't you going to clap?' asked Nora.

I glared at her, hoping my hands might jump up and clap all by themselves. But they didn't.

'Didn't you like it?' Nora's brow was furrowed.

I kept eyeing her and then, even though I didn't mean it, and even though I knew it was the most unkind and vicious thing I could do, I shook my head.

Nora's face dropped. She blinked; she was on the verge of tears. I could feel Grandma's eyes boring into me.

I jumped up and ran out, slamming the door after me.

Behind the chaff shed, I sat on my haunches and cried while the chickens clucked and pecked at the ground around me. 'Shut up,' I said, shooing one away. 'Just shut up!' Music, beautiful music. I wanted to make it, too, but it was just dots and lines on a page that I couldn't read. The keys might as well have been sticks for all the sound I could create. As for singing, my voice couldn't have made a melody even if I'd had lessons from Dame Nellie herself.

I couldn't make music. I couldn't do what Nora had done, and I'd never be able to.

That night at dinner, I didn't meet their eyes, and later when we went to bed, I kept to my side and she to hers.

Each year before Christmas, our school held a concert. It was the highlight of the year, and because every child performed, all of the parents came. Every seat in the hall was filled. The most sought-after role, given to the best singer in the school, was the solo at the end. Over dinner one night, Nora announced that she'd been chosen to sing the solo.

Grandma sprang out of her seat and shot around the table to kiss her. 'Oh, I knew they'd pick you! I'm so proud.'

'But you're only eleven,' I said. 'It should be my turn before yours.'

No one heard me, and Grandma kept talking about what a wonderful opportunity it was and how she knew Nora would go far. 'One day, we'll be sitting in the audience watching you on stage at Covent Garden.'

I bowed my head and tried to cut my omelette, but it had become all watery.

'Covent Garden?' said Mum.

'Yes, there's no stopping her,' said Grandma.

'Stop filling her head with ridiculous ideas,' said Mum.

'What will I wear?' asked Nora.

'We need to buy a dress for such an occasion,' said Grandma.

'No, we don't,' Mum snapped. 'It's just a school concert. Besides, I don't have the money.'

'But I do—' said Grandma.

'I said no,' Mum cut in. 'I'll make one. If I have time.'

'Mum,' said Nora, lowering her voice. 'Could you please? I'd really like a red dress. Satin, like Grandma's.'

'We'll see,' said Mum.

I couldn't stay and listen to it anymore, so I placed my knife and fork together on my plate and left the room. I kept my head down because I didn't want anyone to see my tears, but I don't think anyone noticed me leave even though I hadn't excused myself.

Later that night as Nora and I lay in bed, we heard their heated voices coming from the kitchen.

'Prodigy?' said Mum. 'Prodigy? What would you know?'

'I know more than you think,' said Grandma. 'And I know, too, that there's nothing wrong with a girl having dreams.'

'Dreams?' Mum cried. 'We can't afford them. We can't afford singing lessons or to go to London. We can't even afford a new frock for a concert. We can't afford dreams.'

The kitchen went quiet.

'You're living in the clouds,' said Mum, her voice quieter. 'Someone around here has to keep their feet on the ground.'

Nora and Grandma practised every day, while I sat behind the chaff shed and tried not to listen. But her voice still found me.

Sleep in heavenly peee-eace. Sleee-ep in heavenly peace . . .

'No portamento, Nora,' Grandma would say. 'And remember your consonants.'

Nora sang it over and over until it became a beautiful, continuous line.

'Bel canto!' cried Grandma. 'Lovely singing!'

One afternoon, Mum sewed a floral cotton frock on the treadle machine, but when Nora saw it, she burst into tears.

'I asked for a red dress. One like Grandma's, red and shiny.'

'You're eleven years old,' said Mum. 'You're too young to wear red satin.' She held up a cotton frock decorated with blue magnolias. '*This* is much more appropriate.'

Nora pressed her lips together, but they quivered as she nodded.

When the rehearsals at school began, I wanted to run away. I stood with the rest of the school in the choir stands while Nora walked to the centre of the stage. She held her shoulders back and her head erect, and she looked like a different person—more confident, radiant even. She seemed to relish being in the spotlight, as if it was where she was meant to be. Before she'd even sung a note, she'd drawn the attention of everyone around her. Everyone had stilled, even the kids in the choir stands.

Alf Hill stood next to me in the choir. He was in my class, the son of a local sawmiller and built as big as a gum tree. But he was quiet and gentle, not like the other boys. He never teased or chased us girls; he even seemed to enjoy playing with us. He took the other end of the skipping rope if Beth Prosser or I asked, and every girl wanted to be his partner for dancing lessons because he remembered the steps and did them properly.

To tell the truth, I quite fancied him, but Alf only ever had eyes for Nora. As soon as she took to the stage, he didn't stop staring at her, even when we were meant to be watching Sister Veronica and her baton.

I elbowed him in the ribs. 'You're meant to be watching Sister,' I whispered.

He tried to drag his eyes away, but each rehearsal they were glued to Nora. His ribs must have been bruised from my prodding.

'We're so proud of Nora,' said Sister Veronica to Mum after mass. 'Does she get it from you?'

Mum shook her head. 'From her father, I believe.'

Then Sister spotted me and tilted her head. 'It's amazing how two sisters can be so different, isn't it?'

The night before the concert, Grandma washed Nora's hair and set it in rags. On the day, Mum hummed as she ironed Nora's frock. The house thrummed and everyone, including Mum, seemed excited about the concert.

While the others readied for the big night, I closed the curtains and slipped between the sheets of the bed. When Mum came searching, I told her I was sick.

She felt my forehead. 'You do feel a bit hot.'

Uncle Vernon and Aunty Lorna arrived to pick the others up. Jittery heels tapped down the hall and the door clicked shut. The ute puttered off down the street and silence settled over the house.

I got out of bed. For the first time in over a year, I picked Polly up off the dressing table and took her into bed with me. I'd grown out of playing with her, but I needed her that night. I lay with her and sucked my plait while the shadows lengthened and deepened and gradually turned into night.

It wasn't fair, I thought. Why could Nora create something beautiful and I couldn't?

The house was quiet and still as a graveyard. I lay in the darkness, wishing for sleep to come to dissolve the wretchedness I felt inside me. But it didn't.

Much later, I heard the rattle of the ute outside. Footsteps pattered up the path and the door clicked open. Voices and laughter burst into the house, and I buried my head deeper into my pillow. I tried not to hear them talking about how well Nora had sung and how beautiful she'd looked in her frock.

When Nora slipped into the bed beside me, I lay motionless and pretended I was asleep. I was still awake long after I heard the steady sounds of her sleeping beside me.

At lunch the next day, Grandma said, 'It's a pity you missed your sister last night, Ida. She was the star of the show.'

Without taking a bite, I pushed my sandwich aside. 'I'm still not feeling well,' I lied. 'May I be excused?'

It was a chilly December day and Mum had lit the fire in the lounge. I sat by the hearth, clutching Polly to my chest and feeling sorry for myself. The pale sun darted in between the drapes, landing on the wood of the piano and the sheet music sitting on the ledge. I stared at it, but there was no point in me even trying to understand it—I couldn't make music. I only made noise.

I stood Polly up on my lap and jiggled her about. 'I'm Nora Parker and I'm the best singer in the whole wide world,' I said in a fake, high-pitched voice.

I took Polly over to the piano and stood her on the stool. 'Today I'm going to play "Für Elise".' I turned her towards the piano 'Plonkety-plonk-plonk,' I sang as Polly punched the notes with her hands, then bashed them with her head.

'Now I'm going to sing "Silent Night". *Silent night, Holy night.* I cleared my throat and deliberately sang off tune. *All is calm, all is bright.*

I kept going, dancing and singing Polly around the piano. The door opened and Nora stood in the doorway, but I didn't stop. I was enjoying myself now.

'Nora,' I said in a slurred, crackly voice, pretending to be Grandma after she'd had a few sherries, 'remember your conshonants.'

Nora looked stricken. She pivoted and ran, but I continued with my song. I heard the footsteps up the hallway, and I saw Mum in the doorway, but still I sang, loudly and out of pitch.

Round yon virgin, mother and child . . .

Mum knocked me so hard, I swear I was airborne.

'How dare you?' she shrieked.

I lay on the floor, my cheek against the frayed fringe of the floor rug, not daring to move.

Polly lay next to me. Mum bent and picked her up. She shook her. 'How dare you?' she repeated. 'You are so mean, Ida Parker. Your father would be turning in his grave.'

I lay still.

Mum tightened her lips, then regarded Polly. 'You're too old for a doll.' She spun around and stomped over to the fireplace. Nora stood in the doorway, Grandma behind her, their eyes on Mum.

The screen scraped as Mum shifted it aside.

'No!' I cried, pushing myself to sitting. My heart was banging in my chest. 'I won't do it again, I promise.'

Mum stepped closer to the fire and held Polly out over the glowing coals.

'No! No!' I screamed as I jumped up and ran towards her. 'Don't! Please, Mum! Don't!'

Polly's auburn locks dangled tantalisingly above the flames. I tried to reach her.

'Don't hurt her!'

Mum's eyes moved from me to Polly. Her fingers began to loosen and Polly fell lower, closer to the flames.

'No!' I screamed.

'Alice!' Grandma stepped into the room, her voice was shrill and high. 'What are you doing?'

'She's too old for a doll,' said Mum.

'But there's no need to burn it.'

'She can't poke fun at her sister like that,' said Mum. 'She deserves to be punished.'

'But not by burning her doll.' Grandma didn't move.

Mum looked at Polly, then eyeballed me. One by one, she let her fingers uncurl.

'No!' I screamed.

Polly landed on the log with a soft crunch.

'No!' I lunged for Polly, believing for a moment I could save her, but Mum caught my shoulders and pulled me back.

The flames skipped around Polly and her face glowed. With a fizz, her auburn locks caught fire and sizzled. The stench of burning hair filled the room.

'Let me get her! Let-me-get-her.' I tried to wrench Mum's fingers from my shoulders, but I couldn't break her grip.

The flames leapt all over Polly and the fire crackled as she fed them. I smelt her burning—her hair, her clothes, her body—and I felt the heat from her on my cheeks. Her face greyed, then blackened.

Mum loosened her grip, but there was nothing I could do. I watched Polly become stringy blackened shreds and her face turn the colour of soot. Slowly, she slid down the front of the log and onto the red coals, which shifted as if to make room for her. Another flame burst up and her eyes melted and disappeared. All that was left was a hollow, blackened, mask-like head.

I faced Mum, but I couldn't speak. My nostrils flared and my breathing became shallow and fast.

'That'll teach you to be disrespectful,' Mum said, glaring at me.

I wanted to hit her. I wanted to pummel her for what she'd done to Polly, but I just stood there, trembling and shaking.

'It's time you grew up,' said Mum.

'Alice!' Grandma was shaking. 'I have no words!'

I ran from the room and spent the rest of the afternoon in our bedroom, thumping the mattress and pelting the pillows. In the end,

I lay on the bed, closed my eyes and sobbed. I felt as if I'd lost my only child.

It's not fair. Nothing is fair.

I could hear the dishes clattering in the kitchen and smell the stew cooking, but no one came to get me for dinner. I'd missed lunch and I was hungry. Slowly, I walked into the kitchen.

'Before you sit, apologise to your sister,' said Mum. 'And to your grandmother.'

I couldn't meet Nora's gaze as I whimpered my way through the apology. Then I turned to Grandma, but before I started she took my hand. Her skin felt dry, but her touch was comforting.

'Never mind about me,' she said, but there was a quiver in her voice. 'Let's just put it all behind us and forget it ever happened.'

That night, Nora brushed her hair in silence, our eyes meeting in the mirror on the bureau. We climbed into bed and lay stiffly beside each other.

Each night after that it was the same—we prepared for bed without speaking and kept to our own sides in the pitch-black darkness. During the day, we avoided each other, too—we stood on opposite sides if we were in the same room and didn't make eye contact. If we happened upon each other in the hall, we averted our gazes and kept our elbows by our sides as we passed.

The ghost of that day hovered in the air between us for the next two years we shared a bed together. A shadow had been cast that neither of us knew how to lighten. Every day as Nora's voice grew stronger and brighter and rounder, my feelings of resentment only deepened.

Chapter 5

When I turned fifteen, I left school and started work. I'd found a job in Launceston, with an English family, the Godfrey-Smiths. Mr Godfrey-Smith was a surgeon and his wife was a doctor, too. They needed a live-in housekeeper and carer for their two young daughters.

'What is the world coming to?' said Mum, as her knitting needles clacked. 'A woman doctor! What sort of an example is she setting for her daughters?'

They picked me up from the railway station in Launceston in a motor car. A motor car! I'd only ever ridden in Uncle Vernon's old ute, but the Godfrey-Smiths' car was shiny and smooth and smelt of leather.

We drove past drapers, grocers and chemists. Past trams and cars, and ladies in stylish clothes and men in suits. Then we passed the park with its neat lawns and hedges, and swept around the bend onto the High Street.

The Godfrey-Smiths lived in a brick house—two-storeys with a shingle roof and tall chimneys. I'd never seen a house as grand before, let alone lived in one.

Mum asked me all about the house on my visit home, and her eyes widened as I told her. 'An upstairs balcony? With iron lace?'

I nodded. 'Yes, and I can see right out over the valley to the mountains, nearly to Ben Craeg.'

'Oh, Ida, you've done well! Mind you watch your p's and q's.'

'I do.'

She observed me for a moment, and then she shook her head. 'You never were one for that.'

It wasn't just the fancy house and car that made the Godfrey-Smiths different—everything about them was refined and genteel. Their coats were soft and fine, not scratchy and harsh like mine. As I hung them in the wardrobe, I wanted to bury my nose in all the gentleness hanging in there. Their hands were smooth and creamy, not red and chafed like Mum's and Grandma's. Their English accents were clear as glass, but their voices were muted and kind, never raised, not even to their children.

They knew about everything—not just doctoring, but also about literature and art and music. I listened to their conversations with each other and with their girls. They'd discuss Twain and Rembrandt and Mozart, and I wondered how they remembered all that they knew. Living with them was like being transported to a different land— as if I'd been whisked out of a cold, harsh place to one of warmth and kindness.

My job was to care for their girls—Elizabeth, who was six, and Mary, who was four. They were just like the girls I'd read about in storybooks. Girls who wore pretty dresses and played with dolls and tea sets.

Each morning, I made their breakfast and dressed them— Elizabeth in her school blazer and tunic, and Mary in a white dress. I untied the rags from their hair and looped the blonde ringlets around my fingers before tying them up in pastel ribbons. Then we pulled on our hats and coats and walked Elizabeth past all the majestic houses and down to Methodist Ladies' College on Elphin Road.

The school was a huge mansion, stately and imposing, and bigger than any building I'd ever seen. It even had a turret and ivy creeping over its walls. Mary and I didn't go inside the building but waved Elizabeth off from under the huge oak tree on the lawn, waiting until her tiny figure had disappeared through the door.

On the way back, if the weather was accommodating, Mary and I detoured via St George's Square. We giggled as we ran along the paths, the leaves of the elm and oak trees crunching under our feet. We sat on the grass and made daisy chains for our hair, or blew on dandelion seeds and made wishes, or hung upside-down from branches and let our hair swirl in the dirt. Sometimes, we flopped on our backs and watched the clouds being scuttled by the wind, just like Nora and I used to do.

At home, we dressed dolls in velvet frocks and put them to bed in cradles with satin covers. Then we pretended to drink tea from a china tea set painted with flowers.

In the evenings, I prepared the children's dinner with the best cuts of meat because Dr Godfrey-Smith said children's brains needed the protein. We ate beef or lamb, or even chicken, every day and not just on special occasions. Roasts sizzled in the oven every Sunday and we had thick rump steaks for dinner.

One night, Mr Godfrey-Smith brought home two crayfish in a bucket. I'd never seen anything so red and crawly before, but the girls were excited. We watched as he boiled them over the fire until they stopped moving, and then he cracked their shells for the meat. I had to pretend I wasn't disappointed by their rubbery taste.

I washed the dishes while the family sat in the formal lounge and Mr Godfrey-Smith played discs on their shiny gramophone. Every evening their house sounded like a concert hall.

At night I climbed under the covers of my bed, weary but happy in a way I hadn't ever been before.

Each morning I sprang out onto the cold floor and dressed quickly. I lit the fire in the kitchen and watched the sun rise over the peaks of the Eastern Tiers, Ben Craeg nestled in amongst them. By the time I woke the girls, the house was warm.

On Saturdays the girls had their baths, and I'd wash and dry their hair. Afterwards, we'd sit on the upstairs balcony, from where I could see over the river valley to the Tiers, long and blue on the horizon. As I brushed the girls' hair, I'd look at the mountains and think of home. Of Grandma on the chaise; of Mum making her hats; of Nora singing. Of everyone's life going on out there without me.

One evening as I was doing the dishes, I heard the gramophone start to play. It was a familiar melody and as soon as the singing started, I stopped with my hands still in the suds.

Bist du bei mir, geh ich mit Freuden

I'd heard that song before and sung just as sweetly, and I felt a sorrow building in my chest and a pressure behind my eyes.

Zum Sterben und zu meiner Ruh.

I gazed out the window, towards the east and the dark ridge of the mountains, and my heart twisted with homesickness and tears spilled down my cheeks.

Ach, wie vergnügt wär so mein Ende

I didn't hear Dr Godfrey-Smith coming, not until she was in the kitchen. I brushed my tears away with the back of my hand, which just made my cheeks wetter. I pulled my apron up and wiped my face again.

'I'm sorry, I got distracted. I'll have the tea ready soon,' I said as I went to the stove to pick up the kettle.

'Ida, you're upset.'

I took the kettle to the sink and twisted the tap. 'I'll be all right.'

'Has something happened?' Her voice was behind me and she smelt of lavender.

I shook my head as the water trickled in. 'No, nothing's happened.'

The music still drifted down the hall.

Es drückten deine shönen Hände
Mir die getreuen Augen zu.

'Are you unhappy here?'

'No, not at all. You're very kind to me.' I finished filling the kettle and placed it on the sink, then I turned to face her. 'It's . . . it's just the music. It's making me cry.'

She smiled, then reached for me and pulled me close. 'Ah, Ida. You recognise beauty.'

I let my head rest against her shoulder, and I wanted to stand there all night in the kitchen, feeling the softness of her against my cheek while the music played.

The following night, Dr Godfrey-Smith invited me to join them in the lounge when they listened to the gramophone. I sat on the edge of my chair, my knees together, my back straight and my hands on my lap lest I mark the brocade.

'We're going to listen to Dame Nellie Melba,' said Mr Godfrey-Smith.

'Oh, my grandmother saw her when she sang in Hobart,' I said.

Mr Godfrey-Smith raised his eyebrows as if he was impressed. He set the needle on the record and the sound hissed and crackled for a few seconds. Then came the notes of a piano, then a violin, and, finally, Melba's voice.

Ave Maria, gratia plena,
Dominus tecum, benedicta tu in mulieribus,
Et Benedictus fructus ventris tui, Jesus.

Even though I'd recited these words over and over every May while kneeling before the statue of Our Lady, at that moment, sitting with the Godfrey-Smiths in their lounge and listening to that prayer in song, I realised for the first time how beautiful it really was.

Sancta Maria, Sancta Maria, Maria

Ora pro nobis peccatoribus,

Nunc, et in hora, in hora mortis nostrae.

Amen! Amen!

Grandma was right—listening to Melba was like glimpsing heaven itself.

Each night after that, I sat with the Godfrey-Smiths. We listened to symphonies and concerti by composers such as Johann Sebastian Bach, Ludwig van Beethoven and Edward Elgar. Although I liked the swelling sound of the symphonies, my favourites were the operas. Dr Godfrey-Smith always explained the story beforehand and I nodded as she talked, but I didn't need to know the story—I was impatient for the music to start. Besides, I could tell if the characters were falling in love or had been forsaken, or if they were ill or dying, even without knowing the story or the language. I could hear it. It was all there in the music and in their voices.

As I sat with the Godfrey-Smiths in the lounge each evening, I had to pinch myself that it was me, Ida Parker, sitting on brocade in a posh room with educated and genteel people, and listening to a gramophone. I knew this life wasn't really mine, though, none of it. Each time I returned to the shabby cottage at Tinsdale and sat with Grandma on the faded chaise or lay in the bed beside Nora, I was reminded of the true Ida Parker.

Except when I listened to Nora singing. Her voice was as good as any I heard on the Godfrey-Smiths' gramophone. She wasn't like the rest of us; she deserved to be in a far grander place than Grandma's old lounge.

One day I realised that I didn't mind hearing Nora sing anymore; it didn't worry me how good she was. I had made my own life, outside of the family, and it was a good one.

Towards the end of 1935, when I'd been working for the Godfrey-Smiths for about two years, one evening after dinner we listened to Enrico Caruso and Dame Nellie Melba sing 'O Soave Fanciulla' from *La Bohème*. When it finished, Dr Godfrey-Smith tapped me on the knee.

I startled.

She laughed. 'Ida, you were entranced.'

I blushed. 'I love that duet.'

'It's one of my favourites, too.' She paused before speaking again. 'Ida, Mr Godfrey-Smith and I were wondering if your sister, when she finishes school, would like to teach piano to our girls. Elizabeth will be eight soon and will need a teacher, and we were wondering if Nora would like the job.'

I wanted to shake my head and say, *No! She can't come here. This is my place, not hers. You'll see how beautiful she is and how good she is at music, and you won't want me anymore.*

'You seem troubled, Ida,' said Dr Godfrey-Smith when I just stared at her and didn't speak.

I rubbed one hand over the other. 'Would she replace me?'

'No, no.' Dr Godfrey-Smith laughed and laid her hand on my arm. 'Darling Ida, you're irreplaceable. No, Nora would come and live here, too. You would both live here.' Her hand still rested on my arm and it felt reassuring. 'Ask her next time you go home.' She nodded and sat back, her attention already on the next aria.

But I didn't hear the rest of the opera. I spent the remainder of the evening twisting the ends of the tie around my waist into knots.

I brought it up when I next went home. 'Nora . . .' I said, setting my spoon in my soup bowl and clearing my throat.

She was about to take a mouthful but stopped, surprised I'd spoken to her.

'Dr Godfrey-Smith was wondering if you'd like to teach Elizabeth piano.' I spoke quickly and without emotion.

Nora's hand wobbled and some soup spilled from her spoon onto the tablecloth.

'Teach piano?' said Mum. 'I hadn't thought of that.'

Nora was stone-still, the spoon still in the air.

'I think not,' said Grandma. She wiped the sides of her mouth with her napkin and shook her head. 'No. After school Nora should continue her singing with a good teacher, and then in a couple of years she'll be ready to enter a conservatorium.'

Mum's eyes locked with Grandma's across the table, both of their faces icy and stern.

'And where would the money for that come from?' asked Mum.

Grandma tilted her chin. 'From me.' She spoke firmly.

'No,' said Mum. 'Definitely not.' She shook her head vigorously. 'No. She'll go to work for the Godfrey-Smiths. It's a good job, too good to refuse. I've made up my mind.' She stood to start clearing the table.

Nora set her spoon down in her full bowl. 'I'm not going.'

Mum spun around. 'Yes, you are.'

Nora shook her head. 'No, I'm not.' She inhaled. 'I've always done exactly what you've told me, and I've never been a disobedient daughter. I've never asked for anything before, ever.' She pressed her lips together and swallowed. 'Until now. And Mum . . . I want to sing.'

'Get your head out of the clouds, girl. You can't go to a conservatorium. Your grandmother shouldn't be putting such a grandiose idea into your head . . .'

'It's not grandiose . . . I can do it.' Nora's voice was pleading.

'You can't. You have to work. I'm not arguing with you anymore.'

'Mum, please . . . please . . .' And then, softer, 'It's the one thing I want to do more than anything. Please, can I sing?'

Mum shook her head again. 'No, I'm not wasting good money on singing.'

Nora stood. 'It wouldn't be a waste . . . I could be good, Mum. I could be like Dame Nellie.'

'Don't be silly. Forget your stupid dreams.'

Nora began to cry. 'But I want to sing . . .' Her voice trailed off.

'Nora, when will you learn that dreams like that aren't for people like us. You are a Parker.' She said those words slowly. 'Not a Godfrey-Smith. And this is a good job. Too good to give up. My mind is made up.' Mum's cheeks, ears and neck were red and blotchy. She turned back to the sink.

Nora ran from the room and her footsteps hurried up the hall to the lounge.

It didn't take Grandma long to speak. 'I disagree wholeheartedly with this decision, Alice. Wholeheartedly. And I beg you not to do it.'

Mum turned around, shaking now. 'How dare you? How dare you fill her head with wild fantasies?' With each word, her jaw clenched tighter so her teeth were gritted. 'Might I remind you she is fifteen years old and she is *my* daughter. *I* make the decisions for her until she is of age.' She turned back to the sink and braced her arms either side. Her shoulders heaved up and down, and her breaths were audible.

Grandma stood and left the room. Her footsteps followed Nora's up the hall to the lounge. I got up from the table to help Mum with the dishes. Low voices drifted from the lounge, along with the occasional thud and rustle of paper. When the dishes were dry and stacked away, I crept along to the lounge. The door was open a crack and I peered in. Nora's music littered the floor—a carpet of crumpled sheets and books of Bach, Beethoven and Tchaikovsky—but the room was empty.

I went in. I picked up a copy of Mozart's 'Eine Kleine Nachtmusik', as well as a book of Beethoven sonatas, and began ironing out the creases with my fingers. I gathered up all the music that was strewn on the floor and tried to smooth it. Some of the pages were torn and I joined them as best I could, then I packed all the books back inside the stool. It was only then I noticed Nora's singing music wasn't there—all of her songs were gone.

I waited up for Nora, but she didn't return, so I went to bed alone. The room felt thick and black. I lay listening to the Tasmanian devils fighting and the possums scampering over the roof. Much later, the door creaked open, and Nora's dim shape slipped in. She changed out of her clothes and the bed dipped on her side as she climbed in. I could hear from her breathing that she was facing away from me.

'I'm sorry, Nora,' I whispered. 'I really am.'

'No, you're not.' Her voice was muffled, and she whimpered before continuing. 'You probably arranged it just to stop me singing.'

'No, I didn't. Dr Godfrey-Smith asked me . . .'

'You've ruined my life, and I'll never forgive you.' Her voice was a growl.

I kept facing away from her. I wanted to turn back time, back to when we were younger. Back to when Nora was a child and I could hold her and comfort her, and feel her breath against my cheek. But it was too long ago, and too much had happened since, things that couldn't be repaired. So I kept to my side of the bed, and eventually I drifted off. When I opened my eyes, the room was grey with early light, and Nora was already dressed.

'What time is it?' I whispered.

'Shhh!' she said, her finger to her lips. She bobbed down, and the suitcase scraped as it slid from under the bed.

I sat up. 'What are you doing?'

'Shhh!' she said again. She turned and opened the drawer.

I was breathing faster. 'Are you running away?'

She spun around, her finger over her lips and her face stern. 'Would you shut up? You'll wake the house.' She hissed the words through gritted teeth, and the whites of her eyes gleamed.

She packed her clothes into the suitcase, then came over to the bed and slid her hand under the pillow. The pearly rosary beads shone even in the dimness. They jangled softly as she placed them on top of her clothes.

'Don't go, Nora!' I whispered.

She shut the lid and clicked the latches closed, hoisted the case off the floor and shuffled out. I hesitated a moment, then climbed out of bed. The floor was icy against my soles.

Out in the hallway, Nora lugged the suitcase silently down the hall, past Mum's room, then Grandma's. At the door, she pulled on her coat and hat.

I caught up to her. 'You can't just leave.'

She lifted the case and twisted the door handle slowly until it clicked, ever so faintly.

'Where'll you go?'

She shook her head. 'As if I'd tell *you*.' She pushed the door open until it was wide enough for her to squeeze through, then peered back at me through the gap. Her eyes were puffy and she looked as if she hadn't slept all night. Then she pulled the door closed.

I barely paused before I opened it and followed her outside. The air felt brisk through my nightdress. The verandah was in semi-darkness, the moon still visible just above the horizon. Nora was already walking towards the gate, slim and fragile in the half-light. I hurried down the steps and along the path after her.

'Nora!'

She reached the gate and pulled it open.

I caught up to her. 'I'm sorry . . . It's all my fault . . . I'm sorry I was horrible to you. I shouldn't have been.'

She turned and her eyes held mine. A few coils of blonde hair had escaped from under her hat. She sighed and her shoulders hunched forward. 'Ida, it's not your fault. Mum will never let me sing, no matter what, but I have to do it, so I must go.'

I reached out and pulled her to me. Although she held herself rigid, I could feel her bones through her coat, and she felt slim and fragile. When I let her go, she wiped her nose with the back of her hand.

'I'm sorry you have to go,' I said.

'I'm not sorry.' She adjusted her case. 'I'll be all right. I can look after myself.'

'Write to me,' I said. 'Let me know where you are.'

She turned quickly and stepped onto the footpath. Her feet almost criss-crossed as she trudged up the street in a straight line.

'Good luck,' I called.

I watched until she turned the corner, but she never looked back.

Chapter 6

The wind felt cold through my nightdress. I turned away from the empty street and the lightening sky, and walked back inside the house. I gently pressed the front door shut so I didn't wake anyone, and crept back down the hall to our room. The note on the pillow caught my eye as soon as I opened the door. I unfolded it and read the neat lines of Nora's handwriting.

Dear family,
I am sorry to leave like this, however I have no choice. I cannot go to work for the Godfrey-Smiths. If you knew me, you would understand why, but you do not know the dreams I have inside of me. They are so important that I would rather die than give them up.

This is something I must do. I will write to you again when I get where I am going.

Mum, I hope that one day you will understand. Grandma, thank you for everything.

I will miss you all.

Nora.

I heard a creak, and when I turned Grandma was standing in the doorway.

'I didn't mean to make her leave,' I said. 'I really didn't.'

Grandma took the note. Her chin trembled as she read.

'I tried to stop her. Oh, Grandma, I'm so worried. What's she going to do? Where's she going to live?'

Grandma was quiet until she finished reading, then she closed her eyes and sighed. 'We will find her. Don't worry.'

In the kitchen, I was quiet as Grandma lit a fire we both knew wouldn't warm the air. 'I really did try to stop her,' I said.

She blew out the match. 'My dear, no one could have stopped her.'

Mum's face turned ashen as she read Nora's note, and it fluttered slightly in her hands. When she'd finished, she tossed it on the table. 'She'll be back before nightfall,' she said.

'I don't think so, Alice,' said Grandma.

At lunch, Nora's empty seat was pushed tightly against the table, and later, when we sat in the lounge, the piano lid was closed, the stool vacant and the music still stacked away.

I sat on the woodbox facing the fire, watching the hot coals and the flames, listening to them sizzle and hiss. Grandma sat on the chaise, Mum on the fire chair opposite. We were all silent and the air felt full, as if something heavy was about to fall.

'What on earth's she going to live on?' said Mum.

No one answered.

'Why didn't you stop her?'

I kept my head down.

'Why didn't you stop her?' she repeated, her voice more shrill.

I raised my eyes. Mum was staring at me, her eyes full of tears and her face twisted.

'I tried,' I said, my voice small.

'You didn't try hard enough.' She leant forward and shook her head. 'Why didn't you wake me? Or your grandmother?'

'Alice,' Grandma's voice was sharp and she fixed Mum with a glare. 'Leave her be.'

Mum turned towards her. 'You . . . You . . .' She pointed at Grandma. 'I blame *you* most of all.' She shook her finger at her, the tendons in her neck standing out. 'Feeding her dreams. Giving her false hopes, and now look what you've caused.' She was shaking when she'd finished.

Grandma's head bobbed and her lip trembled. She looked down for a moment and took a few breaths. 'I think we're all feeling a little repentant right now.'

Mum stood and left the room.

I returned to the Godfrey-Smiths', but on my first night back I didn't hear *La Traviata* as it played on the gramophone. As the soprano's voice spiralled around the room, I kept biting my lip and rubbing my nose, hoping the Godfrey-Smiths wouldn't notice I wasn't concentrating. I could only think of Nora and wish she'd come with me to work for the Godfrey-Smiths. At least then I would have known she was safe.

I tried to keep busy so I wouldn't think of Nora.

The Godfrey-Smiths employed a piano teacher for Elizabeth—Miss Gertrude Hart. She was an imposing lady, almost as old as Grandma but taller and stiffer, with iron-grey hair, rimless glasses and a string of pearls around her neck.

Each Wednesday afternoon, Elizabeth and I dressed in our coats and hats, and we walked down the steep hill to Miss Hart's house in Frankland Street. There was a short, swept path to the front door, and we waited under the iron lace of the verandah as the previous student's piano notes tumbled from the front room.

At half past three precisely, Miss Hart would open the door. A boy would race out and Elizabeth would trudge in.

'Come,' she'd say, and Elizabeth would look pleadingly at me before following Miss Hart into the front room, clutching her books to her chest. I'd wait on a spindly chair in the narrow hall outside and listen to Elizabeth's slow, leaden notes coming from behind the closed door.

'No, no, no,' Miss Hart's clipped voice would say. 'Like this.' The notes that followed would be flowing and melodic.

Elizabeth would try again, the notes even more hesitant.

'No, no, no,' Miss Hart would say again. 'Watch carefully.'

Each week as Elizabeth left her lesson, Miss Hart would raise her finger and admonish, 'You must do more practice.'

Elizabeth's eyes would dull, her shoulders slope, and her footsteps drag. On the way home, we'd stop at the swings in the square. I'd push, and Elizabeth would say, 'Higher, higher.' I'd push harder. By the time she climbed off, her cheeks would be pink, her eyes bright and she'd be smiling again.

At home, Mary and I would sit with her while she practised. Her fingers moved like caterpillar legs over the keys. Away from Miss Hart, they didn't trip but hit the notes and created a melody. As she played, Mary and I would sway and dance, and when she finished, we'd clap.

'I wish I could play like that in the lesson,' she'd say.

I'd sigh and pat her shoulder. 'It will come in time.'

Yet each Wednesday afternoon as we neared Miss Hart's, Elizabeth's grip on my hand would tighten and her step would slow. Every week she'd play the same songs in the same lifeless manner, while Miss Hart tapped her cane and repeated, 'No, no, NO! You must COUNT! One-and-two-and-three-and . . .'

Afterwards, I'd take Elizabeth's hand and squeeze it as we walked up the hill to the square. 'Higher!' she'd say. 'Higher!' And I'd push her so high on the swing I thought it might go around in a full loop.

I was waiting out in the hall during one piano lesson when Miss Hart's voice came screeching through the door.

'No, no, NO. You are *not* counting.'

The notes came again, faltering and muddled, followed by an almighty clash and a sob, then hurried footsteps towards the door. I stood as the door flew open and Elizabeth ran out, straight into my belly. She stretched her arms around me and clung tightly.

Inside the room, Miss Hart sat primly on her chair next to the empty piano stool and stared at us. She sighed, then stood. 'Tell her mother that I can't teach her anymore.' She gathered Elizabeth's music books off the piano ledge and came to the doorway. She stood stiffly, a vein pulsing at her temple. 'And that she hasn't a musical bone in her body.'

I held myself rigid and took the books from her hands.

'See yourselves out.'

I pinched my lips together as I dressed Elizabeth in her hat and coat. I tucked her hand in mine and went to open the front door, but I turned back.

Inside the lounge, Miss Hart was replacing music books on her shelves.

'You are wrong,' I said from the doorway.

She turned, lowering her chin and eyeing me over her glasses. 'I beg your pardon?'

I swallowed and went on. 'It's not true that Elizabeth hasn't a musical bone in her body. She just plays badly in front of you. Because she's afraid of you.'

Her eyes widened and a flush spread up her neck. 'She's afraid of me?'

I nodded. 'Yes. When she plays at home, she plays beautifully.'

She raised her eyebrows. 'And you would recognise beautiful music?'

When I didn't answer, she turned back to her music books. 'Be gone with you,' she said, with a flick of her hand.

'Stupid woman,' I said under my breath as we set off.

'I'm not musical,' said Elizabeth.

I crouched down and placed my hands on her shoulders. 'You are musical. Don't pay any attention to her.'

'But, she said—'

'She hasn't a clue what she's talking about.'

Back at the Godfrey-Smiths', I hung up my hat and coat, and went straight to Dr Godfrey-Smith's office. The door was ajar, and I could see she was on the telephone.

'I'm sorry Elizabeth's not up to your standard,' she said into the receiver. 'We were hoping she would improve . . . Yes, yes . . . Offensive? Ida? My apologies . . . Did she? . . . I'll speak with her . . . I'm sorry that's how you feel . . . It's probably for the best then . . .'

I crept back to the kitchen and started whisking the eggs, my stomach churning like the yolks in the bowl. It wasn't long before Dr Godfrey-Smith came in.

'Ida, may we talk?' Her voice was steady.

I set the bowl down and wiped my hands on my apron. 'I'm really sorry. I know I was disrespectful. I'll write and apologise . . .'

'Ida . . .'

'I'm so sorry to have embarrassed you. My mouth runs away without me sometimes.'

'Ida, I want to thank you—for standing up for Elizabeth.'

I exhaled and let my shoulders relax. 'I tried to keep my lips zipped because she's an old lady and a piano teacher. She knows music and I'm just a girl from the country who can't play a note. But when she scolded Elizabeth and told her she had no musical talent, it was too much. I thought no one should say things like that to a child, especially when I see how Elizabeth plays at home when she's with Mary and me. It's not her fault she gets to her lesson and plays badly because she's so frightened of that woman. I had to tell her . . .'

Dr Godfrey-Smith came around the table to where I stood. 'Thank you, Ida. Thank you for caring for Elizabeth. For both of my girls.'

She bent and kissed my cheek. She felt as soft as cheesecake and I caught her lavender smell again.

Not long after that, a letter arrived from Mum. Nora had written home. She'd found a place to live as well as a job, and she said things were working out. She didn't say where she was, not even if she was still in Tasmania, and Mum said the postmark was smudged so she couldn't read it. But at least she was safe, and I could tell from Mum's letter that she was relieved about that, too.

Chapter 7

Dr Godfrey-Smith hired a new piano teacher, Mrs Higgins, who was nicer and didn't use a cane. Her piano room was cluttered with furniture and books. Not only did she teach Elizabeth how to play the piano, but she taught her about the composers, too. About their lives, their lovers, and even their pets. I used to sit close by so I could listen to the stories as well.

The girls were well into their schooling by this stage. Sometimes, as I shelled the peas and chopped the onions for dinner, I heard them talking with their mother in her office. They discussed things like Ancient Greece and the planets and how we evolved from apes. I used to shake my head as I listened—if Sister Xavier had taught us any of this, I certainly couldn't remember it. All I could recall were the lists of mortal and venial sins and being whacked for mispronouncing my Latin.

When I dusted Dr Godfrey-Smith's office, I saw the big, heavy books on her desk. I tried to read the long medical words and understand the drawings of the insides of people's bodies, but I couldn't. I couldn't imagine knowing all of that.

But I'd never had much of a brain for learning.

Returning to Tinsdale wasn't the same after Nora left. A pall hovered over the tiny house, and it felt almost as grey as it did after Dad had died. The piano sat unplayed against the wall, the sheet music neatly stacked on top. It all seemed to hold the ghost of the girl no longer with us.

Mum barely spoke to Grandma, so I tried to fill some of the emptiness when I sat with them in the lounge. I told them funny anecdotes about the Godfrey-Smith girls, but they didn't smile, and I felt as if I was just talking to myself.

My visits dwindled, and each time I returned, I felt more like a stranger and less like I was going home.

One day, Dr Godfrey-Smith walked into the kitchen and held up a ticket. 'I've arranged for someone to mind the girls so you can come with us,' she said.

She placed the card on the table:

Dorothea Schwarzkopf in Concert

Princess Theatre

Circle A18

7.30 p.m. Saturday 28th November, 1936

I couldn't wait to visit home and tell Grandma.

'Oh, Ida!' she said, her hand flying to her chest. 'How wonderful!'

'May I borrow one of your dresses? One of those in the box . . .'

She hoisted herself from the chaise, and with joints creaking but a bounce in her step, she left the room. When she returned, she peered down the hall, then shut the door behind her. She put a finger to her lips as she came towards me, her eyes bright and a playful grin on her face. She looked almost young again. Instead of the big box of dresses, she carried a small wooden box and key. The lock was old and she fumbled with it, but when she opened it up, it was filled with wads of neatly folded banknotes.

'Oh, Grandma!' I said, my hands on my cheeks.

'Shhh!' she said. 'Or your mother will hear.' She unrolled the notes, counted out three pounds and held them out to me. 'Here!' Her face was lively, and I thought she was about to giggle. 'Go and buy yourself something nice.'

My mouth gaped. 'I can't take that,' I said, shaking my head. 'You need your money. I'll just wear one of your frocks.'

Her face changed and she looked stern. 'Dear Ida, you can't possibly go to the Princess Theatre in a dress from last century. Here, take it.' She shook the fistful of notes at me.

'No. You need it.'

Turning, she bent and placed the box on the small mahogany table behind her, before straightening again. She caught my hand and thrust the notes into my palm. Then she pressed my fingers around them. 'Ida, you might never get another chance to do something like this. Take the money and enjoy. Nothing would please me more.' She wrapped her hand over mine and it felt warm. 'Just don't tell your mother.'

When I looked up, she was grinning.

I bought a dress of blue chiffon. On the night of the concert, I hitched my nylons to my girdle and slipped on a petticoat. I brushed my hair and pinned the side to hold it. Then I stepped into the dress. It felt weightless and tissue thin and seemed to float around me. I felt transformed, as if I was a princess. When I stood in front of the dresser and surveyed myself in the mirror, I almost didn't recognise the wide-eyed stranger who stared back at me. I finally understood how Nora felt when she wore Grandma's frocks.

The Godfrey-Smiths were already waiting in the foyer when I walked down the stairs. Mr Godfrey-Smith inhaled and let out a whistle. 'Wow, Ida!'

'You look lovely,' said Dr Godfrey-Smith.

I lowered my eyes and felt myself blush, and as we drove down the hill towards the lights of the city, all I could think was, *How can someone like me, Ida Parker from Tinsdale, be going to a grand concert to listen to a real, live opera singer?* It was the highlight of my nineteen years.

We walked through the glass doors at the entrance to the theatre, over the parquetry floor, and through the crowd of shining gowns, thick furs and dinner suits. The carpet on the stairs was thick and soft under my feet, and a circular recess at the landing held a huge vase of blue gladioli and purple hydrangeas. At the top of the staircase, I peered out over the balustrade at the pearly lights that hung over the milling heads below.

Then we entered the theatre through thick wooden doors and took our seats in the front row of the Dress Circle. Inside, it smelt of wood and carpet and paint. The curtains hung thick and heavy over the stage. Above us arched a dome of pressed tin, painted blue with gold leaves. Around me, everyone was chatting and smiling as if they attended grand concerts every week.

Then the lights dimmed and the audience hushed. I could feel excitement in the air, as if something magical was about to happen.

The curtains parted and the audience applauded. I sat forward. A black grand piano stood alone on the stage, its lacquer reflecting the lights like a mirror. Then Dorothea Schwarzkopf glided on. She wore a long silver dress that looked as if it was made of liquid and had been poured over her. It rippled as she moved, and her matching gloves glinted in the lights. Her skin was as pale and delicate as the white of a soft-boiled egg. Her hair was blonde and parted on the side and fanned out to a mass of yellow curls. It looked like bottled sunlight. Her eyelashes were thick and dark, and her eyebrows appeared to have been drawn on over her eyes.

I thought she looked beautiful.

She moved to the centre of the stage, bowed low and waited.

The accompanist began to play—long slow notes. Dorothea inhaled, and I waited for her voice to come. I couldn't hear it at first, and if someone had asked me when the note started, I couldn't have answered, because it had no beginning. It was as if it came from nothing. A long, thin line of a note, which grew and kept growing, and became louder, slowly, slowly, until it opened into a clear, unimpeded sound.

Ombra mai fu

Her voice made its way through the shadows of the theatre.

Di vegetabile

She stood beside the piano, her silver hands reaching out towards us.

Care ed amabile

A part of me began to stir, a part of me that had been asleep, that had perhaps never been awake before and had been waiting for her to wake it up and breathe life into it.

She sang the slow, sad notes and my thoughts drifted to my father. I could feel him beside me in the theatre and I could hear him, singing in my memory. She was singing my father's song. Dorothea's eyes found mine, and I knew she understood. She knew. She wasn't just singing for herself, but for me as well.

Her voice rose. It crept up, up, to the final note of the song.

Soave più.

She held it there, long and hanging, until it diminished into silence. Then she lowered a gloved hand and stood without moving, her other hand still out, still reaching. Towards me.

The audience began to clap, and Dorothea placed a hand on her breast, as if surprised they would clap for her. But I didn't move. She had sung my father's song. Her voice had reached into my mind and found a memory I didn't know I had, and given it life.

All evening she sang to us, one song after the other. At times, her voice was rolling and strong, like a giant wave, rising and carrying us with her on its crest. Other times, it was high and trilling, as light and lacy as birdsong in trees. All night, she showered us with her crystal sound, taking us with her everywhere she went.

When her final song ended, I clapped so long my palms were stinging. Some people stood and others called out, 'Bravo. Bravo!', and Dorothea had to keep returning to the stage and bowing, each time with a hand humbly upon her breast.

I knew I'd just witnessed perfection. She'd taken me to a place I hadn't known existed until that night. And I knew I'd never be the same again.

When the concert was over and I was walking down the stairs, I spotted a familiar shape in front of me.

'Nora!' I cried.

I pressed my way through the crowd towards her. 'Excuse me . . . Excuse me,' I said as I pushed my way down the stairs, nearly tripping over my frock. I felt the glares as I elbowed my way past, but I had to reach her. 'Nora . . . Nora.'

At the bottom of the stairs, I could still see her—a full head taller than every other woman in the foyer, her blonde hair swept up in a roll, a few stray curls escaping down her neck. She was carried by the crowd towards the doors, and I kept calling to her. 'Nora . . . Nora.' Then she disappeared outside.

'Excuse me . . . Excuse me.' I kept pushing forward until I reached the doorway. I stepped out onto the footpath, now slicked with rain. I glanced up and down the street, but there was no sign of her. Rising to my tiptoes, I still couldn't see her. I stepped off the footpath and into a puddle in the gutter. I crossed the street to the other side of the road, where the crowd had thinned. I glanced all around, but she wasn't there.

She'd gone.

I waited for the Godfrey-Smiths and, with my head down, I followed them back to the car. It had been two years since I'd last seen Nora and she would be seventeen now. I'd missed her.

As we drove off, Dr Godfrey-Smith asked me what I thought of the concert. I was about to respond when, through the window and the raindrops, I saw her again. She wore a red satin dress, and was walking with an older lady whom I didn't recognise. I wound down the window and the cold, wet air swept in.

'Ida . . . Ida . . .' Dr Godfrey-Smith was calling, but I kept winding the window. The breeze whipped about my ears as I squeezed my head out and looked back.

'Nora,' I called.

But all I could see was a line of parked cars, and the lights shining in the wet road.

Later that night, I lay in bed and thought of her. At least she was safe, and I could tell Mum and Grandma. And she was here, in Launceston. Then I thought of the concert and I knew Nora, too, would have been swept away by the magic of the night.

With that thought, I rolled over and let sleep lay its quiet breath over me.

Chapter 8

'Oh, Grandma, I wish you could have heard her. I've never heard or seen anything like it before.'

She smiled and patted my hand.

'And Nora was there, too.'

Grandma's hand stilled and she appeared to hold her breath as she looked at me.

'I tried to reach her and talk to her, but she disappeared too quickly.'

She nodded and gave my hand one last pat. 'I'm glad you got to hear Miss Schwarzkopf sing.'

About six months after the concert, I'd returned from walking the girls to school and was leafing through a copy of *The Examiner* when an article caught my eye.

MONDAY, 10TH MAY, 1937
LAUNCESTON COMPETITIONS

Praise For The 'Exceptional Talent'

The Competitions Association has been praised for the exceptional talent on display at the musical and literary competitions at Launceston. Musical adjudicator, Mr Max Curnow, yesterday said it was the fifth time he had adjudicated at Launceston and noted the talent was always of such high quality it belied the fact Tasmania was an island state of sparse population.

'I very much look forward to returning to Launceston each year,' he said. 'It is a highlight of my adjudicating calendar.'

Sacred Solo

The judge awarded first place in the Sacred Solo to Miss Hazel Clutterback for her rendition of 'The Lord is Mindful of His Children' (Felix Mendelssohn), and second place to Miss Nora Parker who sang 'A Slumber Song of the Madonna' (Samuel Barber).

He commended both singers, awarding the winner by only one point. He said that both Misses Clutterback and Parker had sung with sincerity and musical skill but without making the song doleful, something to which sacred song can fall prey.

Nora Parker. It was Nora! She had come second. She was singing!

I found the scissors and carefully cut out the piece, keeping it to show Grandma and Mum. After that, each day I searched for more news from the Competitions. A few days' later, my heart raced as I read:

THURSDAY, 13TH MAY, 1937

LAUNCESTON MUSICAL AND ELOCUTION COMPETITIONS

German Lieder

The adjudicator, Mr M. Curnow, announced Miss Nora Parker as the winner. He said that in lieder the poem and the music were equally important, and that Miss Parker's performance of 'Gretchen Am Spinnrade' (Franz Schubert) was most intelligently done. It was an ambitious choice and she had interpreted the mood of the piece well.

Song by Female Composer

The adjudicator awarded Miss Nora Parker first place for 'Liebesfrühling' (Clara Schumann). He commented on Miss Parker's attractive voice and said she had once again given an artistic performance. He awarded her 92 marks, the highest score in the vocal section at the competitions so far.

Grand Champion Solo

The last section of the Competitions will be held Saturday night, 15th May, with six contestants vying for the women's prize and five for the men's. The winner of the women's grand champion solo will receive £10 and the second placegetter £2. The winner of the men's will receive £15 and the second placegetter £5.

The lucrative prizes, made possible by a donation from the State Government, have attracted entrants from the mainland.

The programme will be as follows:

Women's operatic aria: Misses Betty Quinn; Emmie Bennett; Ruby O'Bryan; Nora Parker; Hazel Clutterback; and Enid Hay.

Men's operatic aria: Messrs. Clement Barry; Kenneth Murray; Albert O'Toole; Mervyn Findlay; Bernard Singline.

Dr Godfrey-Smith granted me the night off to go and watch. I prepared the girls' dinner early, then headed out. Although it was only May, the evenings were already cold, and I rugged up in a woollen coat and hat. I set off down High Street, past the new maternity hospital. Then I cut through the greenery and colour of the City Park, towards the Albert Hall. As I neared, I began to feel a bit queasy in my stomach—*What if Nora didn't want me there?* I stopped by the rotunda and considered turning back. But then I looked at the grand hall ahead of me and thought, *No, I want to see her. She's my sister and I don't want to miss this night.*

I walked up the steps, through the arched door and into the foyer. I paid a shilling for my ticket, then I stepped into the Great Hall. It was huge, and I felt my heart race and my palms moisten. A wood-panelled ceiling arched overhead like the upside-down hull of a ship, and a gold mezzanine balcony ran around three sides of the hall in a curved 'U'. Row upon row of chairs had been set out on the floor, right to the back of the hall. Most of them were already taken, and my mouth became drier and my palms even more sweaty at the thought of Nora singing in front of so many people.

I walked down the aisle, searching for a vacant chair. I'd nearly reached the back of the hall when I spotted one, but as I was about to sidle in, further back, just inside the door, I glimpsed a familiar hat. It was adorned with flowers, and the owner's head was lowered. The seat beside her was empty.

My step picked up as I headed towards her. I slid along the row, bumping knees and bags and programmes in my haste. When I sat down next to her, she glanced up.

'Oh!' said Grandma, 'What are you doing here?'

'I read about it in the paper,' I said. 'How did you know?'

She hesitated. 'I read it in the paper, too.'

The lady next to her leant forward.

'Ida, this is a dear friend of mine, Mrs Barrett.'

I nodded and we exchanged courtesies, but there was something familiar about her that I couldn't place. Maybe she knew the Godfrey-Smiths?

I turned my attention to the stage as the first contestant was announced. Her name was Betty Quinn. She walked on in a gem-coloured gown and sang a song from *Carmen*. She stood rigidly in front of the gold pipes of the organ and sang well, but I was fidgety and not really concentrating because I couldn't stop thinking about Nora, behind the stage somewhere, waiting to come on.

While the other contestants performed, I kept glancing at Mrs Barrett's profile out of the corner of my eye, trying to remember where I'd seen her before. Barrett? The name wasn't familiar.

Finally, it was Nora's turn and we sat straighter in our seats. I held my breath as she walked onto the stage and stood in the centre. Her shoulders were back, and her arms and hands looked relaxed at her sides. Her hair was coiled up and shone gold in the light, a few stray curls in front of her ears. She wore the same red satin dress she'd worn the night I'd seen her at the Schwarzkopf concert. It hugged her body right up to her shoulders, which were exposed. She didn't look nervous at all but confident, as if she was in the exact place she was meant to be.

She nodded towards the accompanist, who began to play, then she lifted her chin and gazed directly out at the audience.

O mio babbino caro

I took Grandma's hand. Nora's voice had changed so much I wouldn't have recognised it. It sounded richer, thicker and more polished, and she sang with an Italian accent, not an Australian one.

Mi piace, è bello, bello.
Vo'andare in Porta Rossa
A comperar l'anello!

Her voice grew even more in volume and strength as she sang the next few lines. Her hands rose in front of her, her fingers outstretched as if she was pleading. I felt her plea and it made me want to cry. I swallowed and closed my eyes, but I couldn't stop the tears. They squeezed out between my lashes and dripped down my cheeks.

Sì, sì, ci voglio andare!
E se l'amassi indarno,
Andrei sul Ponte Vecchio,

Ma per buttarmi in Arno!

For it wasn't just her singing that was making me cry, it was everything: her struggle, Grandma's struggle, our struggle. Yet, here she was in this beautiful hall, singing for us all.

Mi struggo e mi tormento,
O Dio, vorrei morir!
Babbo, pietà, pietà!
Babbo, pietà, pietà!

The final note was a fluttering wisp of sound that trailed off into nothingness. She bowed but I couldn't clap—I didn't want to move and break the spell. I wanted the sound to stay in my head, in the air, in the hall. She'd taken me to another, more beautiful, world. There was nothing I'd heard before that matched it, not even Dorothea Schwarzkopf. I turned to Grandma, and both she and Mrs Barrett were dabbing at their eyes with their hankies.

Then I realised where I'd seen Mrs Barrett before—with Nora on the night of Dorothea Schwarzkopf's concert at the Princess Theatre.

At the end of the night, the Minister for the Arts invited the adjudicator, Mr Curnow, to announce the winners.

Mr Curnow cleared his throat, then swivelled so he faced the minister. 'I note with surprise that the Government used to give fifty pound towards these Musical and Elocutionary Competitions,' he said, 'but this year decided to halve that sum and contributed only twenty-five pound.' He cleared his throat. 'Twenty-five pound is a paltry sum, especially when you compare it to the large grants made by Government to sporting enterprises. Art is an essential part of people's lives, as it lifts persons from the humdrum groove of existence, and Government should realise that music and the arts play an important role in the welfare of the people.'

He waited, still eyeing the minister. The audience shifted and rustled, and a few people clapped politely. Mr Curnow exhaled, then turned his attention to the audience.

'Moving on to the main event,' he said. 'The awards. I will announce the winner of the women's grand champion solo and then the men's. I was most impressed with the display of talent tonight . . .'

He went on to describe what he was seeking in the contestants—quality of voice, intonation, artistry. He then announced the winner of third place, Miss Enid Hay of Hobart. Second was Miss Hazel Clutterback of Launceston, both of whom he thought gave well rendered performances and showed potential.

'In announcing the winner,' he said, 'I believe I've discovered a remarkably good voice, one of exceptional quality and vitality, yet with almost perfect control and intonation. In fact, I've rarely seen better on the professional stage. So, without further ado, I announce that the winner of the women's grand champion solo is . . . Miss Nora Parker.'

I stood, we all stood, and clapped. Nora came onto the stage again, a hand on her chest. She shook the adjudicator's hand, then accepted the trophy, cheque and a bouquet of flowers. Arms laden, she turned to face the audience. Her cheeks glowed and she smiled as everyone continued clapping. Her eyes roved the crowd until they found Grandma. Her chin and lips trembled and her eyes were glassy.

After we sat down, Grandma pulled out her hanky again.

It was a clear night outside and the air carried the warning of a morning frost. Already we could see our breaths. I stood under the streetlight at the bottom of the steps with Grandma and Mrs Barrett to wait for Nora. Grandma slid her fingers into her gloves as people chatted and streamed past us down the steps.

'I know what you've done,' I said. 'I saw Nora and Mrs Barrett together at the Dorothea Schwarzkopf concert.'

Mrs Barrett looked up at the mention of her name.

Grandma sighed, her breath puffing in the cold. 'Oh, Ida. I'm sorry I couldn't tell you. I was worried you'd let something slip and . . . I couldn't risk your mother finding out.' She finished pulling on her gloves and hitched her handbag into the crook of her arm. 'And at the time, you and Nora weren't getting along terribly well.'

'It's all right. I understand,' I said.

'And I had all that money tucked away doing nothing, when it should have been going to good use. So I paid for Nora to have lessons with Olga.' She nodded at Mrs Barrett, who smiled. 'Olga and I used to sing together when we were girls.' Mrs Barrett nodded again. 'You see, Ida, I know what it's like to give up something you love.' Grandma put her hand to her breastbone. 'It's like being buried alive.' She kept looking at me.

I nodded. I understood why she'd supported Nora and kept it a secret. And although I hadn't experienced it, I also understood what it would feel like to have to give up a dream.

Then Nora appeared in the light from the doorway and looked about. She wore a grey, woollen coat over her dress, and carried her bouquet and trophy in one arm and her purse in the other. As soon as she spotted Grandma, she hurried down the steps, straight to her. They clasped each other. I stepped away from the three of them, feeling like an intruder.

'I knew you'd win,' said Grandma, laughing and patting her back. 'No one else even came close.'

Then Nora embraced Mrs Barrett. 'Thank you,' she said. 'I couldn't have done it without you.'

'It's been my pleasure, Nora. I knew you could do it. You have what it takes.' Mrs Barrett smiled.

'Congratulations, Nora,' I said, and stepped forward.

Nora turned, and when she saw me, she stiffened. 'Ida—'

'You were splendid.'

'Thank you.' She tilted her head and frowned. 'What are you doing here?'

'I saw it in the paper and wanted to come. I wouldn't have missed it, in fact. I've been reading about your success all week.'

Nora nodded, and we stood in silence. Then Grandma shivered and said, 'We should be going home.'

Grandma took the bouquet of flowers, and they gathered themselves. I watched the three of them head down Tamar Street towards the gasworks, a sprightliness in their step. I'd already turned and started walking in the other direction, back towards High Street and the Godfrey-Smiths', when I heard my name being called.

Nora was hurrying towards me, her heels clipping the pavement and echoing in the clear air. 'Would you like to come back to Mrs Barrett's?'

'I'd love to.' I checked my wristwatch. 'But it's getting late, and I have to work in the morning. I'm sorry.' My voice trailed off.

She nodded. 'I understand. Shall we meet some other time?'

I wanted to hug her. 'Yes, that would be lovely.'

She nodded, and we both waited.

'I really am pleased for you,' I said.

She nodded again. 'The adjudicator told me to audition for the Melba Scholarship. It's to study at the Albert Street Conservatorium in Melbourne. It's worth over a hundred pounds a year.'

'Oh, Nora. That would be wonderful!'

We arranged to meet the following week, and before going our separate ways, we embraced.

Back at the Godfrey-Smiths', I lay in bed and thought of Grandma having to give up her music. I thought of Nora, too, at the piano, day after day, playing the same scales and the same pieces over and over until she got them right. I remembered her dressing in Grandma's frocks and giving us concerts. I remembered her running away from home so she could sing. I remembered, too, my jealousy at Nora's talent and how it had kept us apart. That night, I resolved that I'd never be jealous of Nora again.

I had no idea what it felt like to yearn for something so much you'd give up everything to do it, and part of me wished I did.

Chapter 9

Nora and I met up at a dance a couple of weeks later at St Ailbe's Hall, on the western side of the city. The hall was decked with streamers and balloons, and a three-piece band played on the stage.

Nora had twisted her hair up in a French roll and wore a strapless gown in sapphire blue with a matching evening jacket. As soon as we entered, the men turned, their eyes drawn to her as if by magnets. She was taller than me—she was taller than everyone, even most of the men. She crossed the hall with her head erect and her eyes straight ahead, seemingly unaware of the spellbound gazes upon her.

Almost as soon as we sat down, a burly fellow began making his way towards us. He was in a hurry, swerving around the tables and bumping people as he passed. He was as big as a boar, his face square and his shoulders as wide as a bridge. His eyes didn't stray from Nora and when he reached her, he was panting.

'Nora. It's Alf, Alf Hill. From school. Do you remember me?'

She tilted her head. Her brow creased as she thought for a moment, and then she nodded. 'Yes, I think I do.'

I remembered him—that he was a good dancer and that all the girls, myself included, had adored him. I remembered, too, that he'd only ever had eyes for Nora.

'Would you like to dance?'

She removed her jacket. He led her onto the floor, and placed his hand on the small of her back. She looked up at him—one of the few men taller than her—and rested her gloved hand on his shoulder. The music started and the two of them began to skim across the boards, their feet lightly touching the floor before lifting again. It was like watching swans on a lake, gliding towards each other, criss-crossing and drifting apart again. Back and forth, back and forth, their eyes not straying from each other as they coasted around the room.

I was interrupted by a tap on my shoulder. When I turned, a small, wiry fellow was smiling down at me. He cleared his throat. 'Would you like to dance?'

I felt myself blush as I nodded.

His name was Len Bushell and we danced the Pride of Erin. We stepped back and forth, together and apart, and spun around. Every time I glanced at him, he was still gazing up at me. I kept blushing and my legs got in such a lather they became tangled and I stumbled. He caught me and I apologised, but he went on spinning me around as if he hadn't noticed. When the music stopped, he kept dancing, twirling me under one arm and then the other, whirling me about so fast my feet barely had time to touch the boards. By the time we stopped, smack in the centre of the dance floor, we were the only ones left. I felt dizzy and out of breath, and it wasn't just from exertion.

He didn't let me go and we danced the next one and the one after that, and by the end of the evening, I felt like a yacht with the wind in its sails, and I never wanted to stop sailing around that dance floor.

We ate a supper of sandwiches and cream puffs, and pineapples set in jelly.

Nora leant in towards me. 'Looks like you've found yourself a beau.'

I felt myself blush and my hand went to my cheek. 'And you.'

'Grandma confessed to Mum last week,' she said.

I gasped. 'Is she angry?'

'Apparently not. She wants to see me again.'

'She wouldn't stop you singing now, would she?'

'No, she wants to *apologise*.'

'Oh? That would be a first.'

Nora raised an eyebrow and nodded.

'Take it while you can get it,' I said.

I looked forward to the dance the following week, and when Len took me onto the dance floor again and placed his hand in the small of my back, I felt its familiar warmth and my chest stirred.

Len worked as a labourer at the wharf, but his main love was fishing. His older brother, Fred, owned a car and, of a weekend, Fred and Len and their younger brothers and sisters would pile in and drive out to a river or lake.

One day, after we'd been courting a few months, Len took me with them. We went fishing up the Ringarooma River. We turned off along a boggy road, dipping and bobbing in and out of potholes. The bush was so close we could reach out and touch it as we passed, and it reminded me of our family picnics at Ben Craeg when I was a child.

The day was cloudy and the water was brown and still, occasionally eddying noiselessly around a protruding rock. Len and Fred set up their tackle boxes and tied flies onto their lines. They waded out, flicking their rods back and forth. Downstream, the kids swam, while I stayed on the bank—I'd never learnt to swim—and set up the picnic blanket. When I'd laid out the sandwiches and scones, I sat on a rock by the edge of the river and watched them all dipping and diving and yahooing in the water.

Mavis, Len's youngest sister, who was seven or eight at the time, had been splashing about in the middle, having fun, but then her head went under. She surfaced, gulped at the air and disappeared again.

'I'm coming, Mavis,' I called, running towards the water, pulling my shoes off as I went.

I waded out and the water crept up my calves and then up my thighs. My dress was pulling against my legs and getting heavier, but I kept trawling through the water.

'I'm comin' . . . I'm comin' . . .'

Mavis's head bobbed up and her arms splashed, then she gulped and disappeared again.

The water was up to my waist, then my chest, and my dress was dragging. I was nearly there. I could almost touch her. If I could stretch another couple of inches. Then the bottom slipped from beneath me and I went under. All I could see was murky water, brown like onion soup. I couldn't touch the bottom, but I could see the light at the top and Mavis's legs moving about just in front of me. I reached for them, but I was sinking and they were getting further away. I swept my arms about, straining and stretching and trying to reach her, but my clothes were heavy and dragging me down.

I can't hold on much longer, I thought. *I need to breathe. Both of us are going to drown.*

Then Mavis's head was under the water and coming towards me. Her eyes were wide, staring into mine, and I held out my arms. I was running out of air and I wanted to open my mouth and breathe—I wasn't sure how much longer I could last. Mavis was close. Her arms swept through the water and she grabbed my hand. We moved upwards through the brown towards the light.

Then it was all light and my head was out of the water and I could breathe. Someone caught my other arm and hauled me towards the bank and laid me down on the stones. I coughed and vomited and couldn't stop the tears.

'What sort of stunt were you pulling?' said Len.

I turned towards him, about to explain that I thought Mavis was drowning and I was running out to save her.

He stood a few feet away, one hand on Mavis's elbow, shaking her. The water was streaming from the crotch of her knitted bathers, which had stretched down the inside of her legs, and she was crying.

'Ida nearly drowned,' he yelled at her. His face was red and he was shaking. I'd never seen him angry before. 'I should put you over my knee, young lady, so you'll never pull a stunt like that again.'

Mavis held her face in her hands and her shoulders shook.

'Len . . .' I tried to get up on my elbow, but the stones cut into my arms. I was coughing and panting, too, so I couldn't get enough voice. 'Len . . .' I tried again, louder.

He turned, still holding Mavis's elbow.

I shielded my eyes from the sun. 'Don't hit her.'

'She needs to be taught a lesson.'

I took a deep breath. 'I reckon she's learnt her lesson. No need to hit her.'

'But she nearly caused you to drown.'

I sat up properly and leant on one hand. 'You've learnt your lesson, haven't you Mavis?' I was still puffing.

Mavis howled. 'I didn't mean to. I didn't know you couldn't swim.'

'She was just mucking about, Len.'

He studied Mavis with squinted eyes.

'Please don't hit her,' I said. 'I couldn't abide a kid being hit because of me.'

He looked at me and then at Mavis, and he let her go.

I lay back on the stones and closed my eyes, letting the sun warm my face.

Len made a fire to boil the billy and I stood close, drying off and warming up. He slipped a blanket around my shoulders and stood next to me. I felt his arm slide across my back and, because I was slightly taller, it felt awkward. But he was warm, and as I leant into him, I could smell the salty scent of his skin.

'Ida, I've never seen anyone risk their life for a kid, then stick up for them like that,' he said. A breeze blew and ruffled his hair. His eyes were the colour of chocolate. 'And that's the type of woman I'd like as my wife.'

When I next went home, over a lunch of poached eggs on toast, I told Mum and Grandma that I was getting married.

Mum's face softened like a dawning sky. 'Oh, Ida. That's glorious news.' She came around the table and kissed me. As she sat back down, my hand went to my cheek and touched the spot where her lips had been. I couldn't remember the last time she'd kissed me. She felt softer and warmer than she looked, and she smelt of Pond's face cream and hairspray.

I told her I wanted to get married at Ben Craeg, then I cut into my egg. The yolk oozed over the toast, and I cleared my throat. 'Nora's going to audition for the Melba Scholarship.'

'Yes,' said Mum. 'So I hear.' She picked up the bottle of Worcestershire sauce and shook a couple of drops onto her egg.

'It would be marvellous if she won,' I said.

'Yes, yes,' she said, and picked up her knife and fork. 'Although I hear it's dangerous over there, on the mainland.'

'She can look after herself,' I said. 'She's proven that.'

Mum glanced at me. 'It's a lot different over the other side. You've just got to read the papers. She could get murdered. Or worse.' She took a mouthful.

'She won't. She'll be too busy singing.'

Mum finished chewing. 'Oh well, she's got to win it first.' She took another mouthful.

'She'll win it,' said Grandma, and sniffed.

Mum threw down her knife and fork so they clanged on the plate. Grandma and I jumped. 'I know I don't have a say in it,' she said, glancing from one to the other of us. 'You don't need to worry that I'll try to stop her. I won't. I've learnt my lesson. But that doesn't mean I like it. I don't like any of it. But, I'll let her go, if it comes to that.'

I returned to my food. 'She'll appreciate it, Mum.'

Mum picked up her knife and fork and resumed her meal, too. She sighed audibly. 'Well, at least I have a wedding to look forward to.'

On 11th June 1938, the day before my twentieth birthday, Len and I married in the church at Ben Craeg, the same church in which my parents had wed, and next to the cemetery in which my father lay at rest.

I took Mr Godfrey-Smith's arm and we walked through the door of the church. The building smelt familiar—of wood and dust and candle wax—although the building itself had wearied over the years. The organist played Handel's *Water Music* as Nora led us down the aisle, past Len's younger brothers and sisters. Past Dr Godfrey-Smith and the girls, and past Mum and Grandma, who were holding hankies to their noses.

At the altar, Mr Godfrey-Smith took my hand and, before he passed me to Len, he kissed my forehead. I felt his lips through my veil and closed my eyes. For a moment, I felt my father's presence, giving me his blessing.

The priest married us in the ancient language of the church. He laid his hands upon us and anointed us with oil, and we became joined, husband and wife.

A few months later, Nora won the Melba Scholarship to the Albert Street Conservatorium in Melbourne.

TUESDAY, 8TH NOVEMBER, 1938

LAUNCESTON GIRL WINS MELBA SCHOLARSHIP

MELBOURNE

Launceston girl, Nora Parker, has been awarded the prestigious Melba Scholarship to the Albert Street Conservatorium of Music. The scholarship is worth upward of £100 per year, and is the most valuable scholarship ever made available in Australia for singers. The sole adjudicator, Dr E.A. Lloyd, commented that Miss Parker showed talent and great possibility for further development.

Nora and I caught the train out to Tinsdale to say goodbye to Mum and Grandma. Grandma was blooming with smiles and laughter. She kept waving her arms about as she spoke of the heights to which Nora was destined.

'You're on your way, young Nora,' said Grandma. 'Nothing can stop you now.'

Mum was quieter. She kept her head down and was fidgety. As we left, she cleared her throat and said, 'I'm proud of you, Nora.'

'Thank you,' said Nora quietly. 'It means a lot to hear you say that.'

Mum smiled.

'You might even get to see me on a stage one day,' said Nora.

'One step at a time,' said Mum.

Chapter 10

After we married, Len and I rented a house in Pearson Street, Launceston. It was down the street from the wharf where Len worked, and built on a swamp, so it was like living on jelly—every time a truck rumbled past, the ground wobbled beneath us. The house was weatherboard with steps up to a bull-nosed verandah lined with iron lace and geraniums in pots. Inside there was a narrow hall with two bedrooms either side, then down past the lounge and another bedroom, to the kitchen and bathroom.

The kitchen was small, with a wood oven and wooden bench tops, and cabinets I painted cream. We bought a second-hand Kelvinator fridge and a dresser with leadlight in the doors, which we set against the far wall.

I wasn't a fancy cook—nothing French or anything like that—just plain meals like shepherd's pie and lamb casserole, or fried fish if Len had caught any. After he'd eaten, Len would mop his plate with bread until the floral pattern was the only thing left on it, then hand it to me and say, 'That was beautiful, Ide.'

My favourite place, though, was the garden. I pruned the rose bushes by the front fence and struck more from cuttings, like Grandma had taught me to do. I tended the geraniums in the verandah boxes, and they grew thick and rich. I planted hydrangeas, daffodils and irises, and scattered a few marigolds amongst them to keep the bugs away. Out the back by the fence, I prepared a vegetable garden and planted all sorts of winter and summer vegetables, as well as a rambling strawberry patch. I set up a trellis for tomatoes and climbing beans. There was an apple tree, too, and when they were in season, the house smelt of stewed apples and cloves.

We ate at the tiny table by the kitchen window from where I could see my garden. As I ate with my husband, overlooking the veggies and the flowers, and the clothes flapping on the line, I felt content with my life.

It didn't take long for me to fall pregnant, and I had to stop working for the Godfrey-Smiths. The girls were nearly in high school by then, so Dr Godfrey-Smith just employed a housekeeper after I left. On my last day of work they gave me a pram made of white wicker and chrome that gleamed in the sunlight.

'Please visit, Ida,' said Dr Godfrey-Smith. 'And bring the baby.'

'I will,' I said. 'I'll never forget you, any of you. You've taught me more than I ever learnt at school.'

Mr Godfrey-Smith drove me home, and Dr Godfrey-Smith and the girls came out to see me off. As the car headed down their driveway for the last time, I told myself that even though I had to leave them, it was better to have known generous people than never to have met them at all.

Len's cousin gave us their old bassinette. I sanded down the wicker and painted it white, and set it up in the room opposite the lounge. I sewed a white cotton coverlet and embroidered it with teddies, and bought some fine, white wool and knitted a shawl, booties, mittens and a jacket.

Each Saturday, I lay in the bath and ran my hands over my growing belly. Then I began to feel the baby moving, its touch as soft as a whisper, like a goldfish swimming around inside. It grew bigger and started to kick and tumble as if it was somersaulting. One night in bed, I lay with my belly pressed against Len's back and the baby kicked. Len rolled over and rested his hand on my tummy as it kept kicking.

He leant over and kissed me. 'Ide, this is the most exciting thing that's ever happened to me. I don't care if nothing else ever happens after this.'

I kissed him back. 'You just want someone to take fishing.'

Len fell asleep, but I lay awake with my hand on my belly, feeling the life we'd created tumbling around inside. Here I was, an ordinary woman and nobody special, yet within me, a new life was beginning.

Just before midnight on 18th February, 1939, six months into my pregnancy, my waters broke. At first it was a slow trickle and I thought I'd wet myself. Then the contractions started.

Len ran to our neighbour, Stan, and he raced us to the Queen Victoria Maternity Hospital in his plumbing van.

They tried to stop the baby coming, but he was born at twenty to five in the morning. He came out and didn't take a breath. I lay with my feet still in stirrups, craning to see him.

'No, Mrs Bushell, don't look,' they said as they wrapped him in a towel.

'What is it?' I said. 'A boy or a girl?'

'A boy.' They whisked him out the door before I even saw him.

I lay on the starched sheets in the maternity home for ten days, listening to the nurses wheeling crying babes to their mothers every four hours. I lay there wishing it was my baby they were bringing to me.

Every morning when the nurse came in and flicked the blind open, I gazed out at the circular driveway and the bluestone fence, and beyond, to the city below where everyone was getting on with their lives, unaware I'd just birthed a dead baby.

Dr Godfrey-Smith visited me in the hospital. She said stillbirths weren't uncommon and given my good health and youth, there was no reason I wouldn't have a successful pregnancy next time.

But going home without a baby hurt. Sometimes, I went into the baby's room to check the bassinette really was empty. It was hard to believe it had even happened—that after carrying him inside me for all those months, feeling him moving and tumbling, I didn't get to keep him after all.

'It's not fair,' I cried to Len each night.

He stroked my arm. 'We'll try again, Ida. We'll have a baby one day.'

Meanwhile, Nora sent me letters from Melbourne.

12th March, 1939

Dear Ida,

I'm having the most joyous time! I feel as if I've finally found my home. I get to wear gloriously outrageous costumes and wigs, and stand on a stage and sing the most dazzling music! I feel as if I've come to life!

I'm working hard to learn everything I must know. I have four lessons each week in singing and two in piano. As well as lessons in Italian, French, German, musical history and musical analysis. There's so much to learn: all the techniques, the language, the theory and I'm gobbling up as much as I can.

I love performing, Ida. And I'll tell you a secret: I adore applause! I feel incredibly vain to say that, but my Italian tutor keeps telling me, 'Norrra, God has given you a gift, like he has given the flowerrrs theirrr petals. He doesn't want you to hide yourrr beauty. He wants you to blossom and sharrre yourrr gift with the world.'

So I tell myself it's what God wants and I'm morally bound to keep singing! But I couldn't stop it anyway.

With love,
Nora xx

P.S. Mum wrote me about your miscarriage. I'm terribly sorry for you, but I'm sure you'll have good news soon.

Her letters were a respite from my grief and I looked forward to seeing her neat cursive on an envelope in my letterbox. The letters gave me a glimpse into another life, a life filled with music and theatre, a life I could barely imagine.

21st May, 1939

Dear Ida,
Everyone here is so knowledgeable and I feel like such an ignoramus, but I'm doing my best to catch up.

My Italian tutor, Marco, grew up in the same town in which Giuseppe Verdi was born. Marco learnt music like we learn to read. Imagine that!

I think I was born in the wrong country, Ida. I should have been Italian. Maybe I was born in the wrong century, too. At least I know now where I'm meant to be and what I'm meant to be doing. And that is singing. I need it like other people need bread and water. Or even air.

With love,
Nora xx

10th September, 1939

Dear Ida,

I have a beau. He's my Italian tutor and he's lovely. His name is Marco, I might have mentioned him before. You'd laugh at his accent and the way he says things back to front. He's so different from anyone I've ever met and says things other men never say. He's always calling me 'belladonna' and telling me I'm beautiful.

The only thing we daren't discuss is food. He refuses to eat anything I cook, says it's tasteless. He won't drink tea because it tastes like dishwater! He cooked for me last week and it was divine—spaghetti but not out of a tin! With a creamy sauce, not tomato. My breath smelt of garlic the next day and the other chorus members kept a wide berth!

Don't tell Mum, but I've been missing mass. We have to go to parties and sometimes I don't get home until dawn. But, oh, what a time I'm having!

With love,
Nora xx

P.S. I hope you and Len will have some news soon!

Less than a year after the first stillbirth, I had another one. Another boy. He came early, too, blue and lifeless. I'd knitted him a layette and a shawl, which I folded and set on the shelf in the wardrobe next to his brother's.

At least now the doctors could give me a diagnosis: cervical incompetence. Dr Godfrey-Smith explained that the neck of my womb was weak and as my babies grew, I couldn't hold them in anymore.

The medical staff told us to try again, and this time, as soon as the pregnancy was confirmed, they stitched my cervix closed. I was confined to bed and didn't leave. I lasted longer, over seven months, and this baby was breathing when they took him from me. I saw him, silent but alive, before the midwives bundled him in a towel and hurried from the room.

'Leonard,' I called. 'His name is Leonard, after his father.'

They cleaned me up and wheeled me back to my room, and I waited for them to bring him to me for his feed. I heard the other babies crying as they were taken to their mothers, and towards evening, as tight and sore as I was, I pulled myself out of bed, slid into my dressing gown and walked down the corridor to find him.

As I passed the matron's office, I overheard her saying, '. . . and Baby Bushell has just died.' I stopped in the doorway. She clicked the phone back on its cradle, then looked up and saw me.

She startled and her face blanched before she pulled herself together and smiled. 'Mrs Bushell, I didn't see you there.'

I lifted my chin and stared at her from my full height. 'I want to see him.'

She rose from behind her desk. She was pale, almost transparent. Her face, her long veil, her dress all blended into one and melded into the cream wall behind her. I could barely see her as she glided towards me, as translucent as ice.

Then she cleared her throat. 'Come back to bed now, Mrs Bushell.' Her voice came from the air, and a cool hand reached out and caught my elbow. 'It's late. Doctor will see you in the morning.'

'No,' I said, and pulled my arm away. I raised my head higher and pressed my slippers into the floor as if to cement myself there. My mouth felt dry and my breath came faster. 'I want to see my baby.'

My other babies had been whisked away as soon as they took their lifeless bodies from me. I never saw them, not a glimpse. Never saw the colour of their hair or who they resembled. In the back of my mind I'd always wondered if maybe they'd got it wrong. Maybe they'd mixed up my baby with somebody else's. Maybe my baby was still alive and out there somewhere, in another mother's arms.

I stayed where I was. 'Take me to him.'

She reached for my arm again, but I shook it off. I spun around and took off down the hallway towards the nursery as fast as my soreness would let me. My dressing gown splayed open and my slippers swished against the linoleum of the corridor.

Matron's heels stuttered behind me and her voice echoed around the empty space. 'Mrs Bushell . . . Mrs Bushell . . .'

I kept striding down the hall.

'Mrs Bushell . . . Come now . . . Don't do anything rash . . .'

I reached the nursery and glanced through the window. Nurses with veils like yacht sails leant over the rows of babies in their cribs.

I threw the door open.

They turned towards me and their veils lifted as if caught by the wind. One headed towards me, shaking her head, her arm outstretched. 'You can't come in here . . .'

'Where is he?' I said, and stepped in further. 'Where is he?'

They didn't answer.

I moved closer to the lines of cribs. 'I want to see him . . . Where've you put him?'

'Call the doctor!' Matron cried from the doorway. 'I think she's hysterical.'

I began to dash up the row of cribs, reading each label and peering into each baby's face. Some were sleeping, some were howling. None were him. I moved further along the row, searching for the one who could be mine, the one named 'Leonard'.

'Where is he? Where've you put him?'

The nurses were still now, and I could feel them watching me as I passed along the rows, inspecting each baby, willing one of them to be him. When I reached the last crib, I stopped and looked around.

The nurses stared back at me.

My breath came fast. 'What've you done with him?'

Their eyes darted about under their lashes, glancing at each other and at Matron.

'Where've you put him?' My voice was high and harsh. 'I'm not going anywhere 'til I've seen him.'

Matron held out an arm and stepped towards me. 'Calm down, Mrs Bushell. This is not good, upsetting yourself like this.'

'I will not calm down until I've seen him. He's mine.'

There was silence, then Matron said, 'I'll take you.'

I strode towards her and when I reached the door, she said, 'Really Mrs Bushell, I don't think this is wise.'

'I don't give two bloody hoots what you think. He's my baby and I want to see him.' My chin trembled, but I didn't break her gaze. I didn't move.

She led me, heels tapping, down the corridor to the doctor's office at the end.

I followed, slower, muted.

Matron entered the unlit room and pulled the cord to the electric light. It clicked on and a circle of light fell on the doctor's desk.

I lingered at the doorway, in the shadows.

Matron shifted around the desk and over to a crib which stood alone against the wall on the other side.

I stepped carefully into the room, as if the floor might give way. It was cold. I walked around the desk and towards the crib.

I could see him—a tiny mound under the sheet, completely still. I lifted the sheet and uncovered his head. There he lay. Eyes shut. Cheeks smooth. Lips pursed. Small, just like any other sleeping baby.

My baby.

I leant down until my cheek touched his mouth. I waited, hoping to feel his breath, hoping to hear him. Hoping it was a mistake.

But there was nothing. No swish of soft breath. No warm air against my cheek.

As I lifted my head, my nose brushed his, but he didn't flicker or twitch. I lifted my lips and kissed his cheek. He was cold and still.

I raised my head and shivered. 'He's cold,' I said. 'Can you get him a blanket?'

Matron nodded and left the room.

I lifted him into my arms. He felt weightless. I stroked his skin and burrowed my head into him and inhaled. He smelt of soap. And of birth. And of me.

Matron returned with a blanket, a blue one, and draped it over him. I gathered it around him and tucked it under. We stayed like that and I held him while the clock on the doctor's desk ticked.

Matron waited until I looked up and then she took him from my arms. I let him go. She placed him back in the crib, folded the blanket in half and spread it over him.

I read the label at the head:

> Baby of Mrs L.D. Bushell
> b. and d. 17th September, 1940

There was no mistake.

Chapter 11

At twenty-two years of age, I had to accept the fact I'd never birth a living baby and it was a bitter pill to swallow. For the first time in my life, I understood the meaning of yearning.

I tried to keep going. Each day, I lifted my body out of bed, and dressed and washed and ate. But the food had no taste, the house had no warmth and the days had no joy. Most of all, my arms held no baby. The days kept blending into night and becoming day again. The spring inched towards summer and I felt nothing except emptiness.

Nora's letters dwindled after the last stillbirth and in my grief I didn't notice. One morning in early November, Mum arrived on my doorstep unannounced.

'I need to speak with you,' she said, businesslike.

I took her down to the kitchen. She arranged her handbag on her lap and sat upright on the chair. 'Nora's getting married.'

'Oh, that is news!'

Mum fidgeted with the handles of the bag. 'To Alf. Alf Hill.'

'Alf Hill? From school? The sawmiller?' I shook my head. 'What about Marco?'

Mum kept her face as straight as a poker player's. 'The wedding's at Ben Craeg. December 13.'

'But it's already November.'

She nodded. 'Yes, and it's Advent, but it was the only day available. We had to hurry it along.'

I felt the air rush out of me as it dawned, and I could barely even whisper the words, 'Is she pregnant?'

The answer came with Mum's silence.

'What about her singing?'

'Oh, Ida, you know how I feel about that, how I've always felt about that. It was all your grandmother putting ideas into her head.'

'But she was so happy.'

'Evidently not enough.'

'Is it what Nora wants? Does she love Alf?'

'That's not the point,' said Mum, and she filled me in on the details. A month ago, when Mum was delivering some of her hats to the store, Mrs Flanagan asked if she'd wait. Nora was going to telephone because she wanted to speak with her. So Mum sat on the chair by the front counter and waited for the phone to ring. She thought maybe Nora had won another competition or had a lead role in an opera. She didn't think for a minute that she'd be calling to tell her she was pregnant. And worse. That when the director of the conservatorium had discovered the affair with her tutor, he'd called her into his office and told her she was unworthy of the scholarship and it would be withdrawn.

I couldn't speak as Mum talked and kept myself busy making the tea. My eyes didn't leave the kettle until it had boiled. I poured it into the pot and watched it steep.

'She was already four months along,' Mum continued. 'So I had no choice but to tell her to just come home. There was nothing else could be done. And everyone in the shop had stopped to listen, so

I tried to keep a straight face and pretend that the stuffing hadn't just been knocked out of me.'

I took the pot and cups over to the table.

'When I got home,' Mum went on as I poured our tea. 'I remembered Alf used to be sweet on Nora. So I wrote to him and told him of Nora's predicament. He replied straightaway, said he loved Nora, that he didn't care whose child she was carrying and that he'd marry her if she'd have him.'

I sat. My mouth felt dry. When I spoke my voice was so soft I wasn't even sure Mum could hear. 'I would have taken her baby.'

Mum picked up the cup I'd placed in front of her. 'Not your sister's bastard child, Ida.' She sipped, then shook her head. 'No, this is for the best. He's given her a lifeline, that's for sure. I told you the mainland was dangerous.'

After Mum left, I circled the house in a daze. I felt the heat of anger and jealousy as sharply as vinegar on raw flesh. I knew she'd carry this child to term. I knew her womb would nourish and nurture. I knew I'd see her with a babe in her arms, while my own ached with emptiness.

And I knew that, just like after Dad died, I'd have to watch someone else enjoy what I didn't have: a family. But this time, I was determined to hide my bitterness and not tell a soul.

I didn't see Nora until the day of her wedding. The church bells rang as she walked down the aisle on Uncle Vernon's arm. She wore white lace and looked like a model from a magazine. No one else would have noticed, but I spotted the barely detectable bump under her gown.

Uncle Vernon gave her to Alf and they promised to love and cherish and honour and obey—Alf standing tall and brimming with pride, and Nora speaking in a soft murmur.

Mum's eyes didn't move from Nora the whole ceremony. She sat bolt upright, as if she was frightened Nora might run away again.

Grandma didn't watch any of it. Not once did she raise her eyes to see her granddaughter wed.

There was a reception tea at the hall after the ceremony. We stood around drinking cups of tea and eating lamingtons and sponge cake.

Alf's father and brothers came. They were all built like Alf—sturdy and square. Their suits strained across their backs, and their hands smothered the porcelain plates and dainty cups they held. They laughed a lot and loudly, tilting their heads back as they did.

'Welcome to the family, Ida,' they said, their faces creased and beaming. As they kissed me, rough bristles of their chins scratched my cheek and they smelt of Old Spice.

'Good to meet you,' they said to Len and shook his hand, squeezing it tightly before letting it go. 'Ida's a good sort. You've done well.'

Len smiled and nodded, but raised his eyebrows at me and shrugged, unsure what to make of these exuberant giants.

Alf and Nora went around the hall, greeting their guests. When they came over, Alf's brothers' grins spread wider. They engulfed their brother in their arms and clapped him on the back. But when they saw Nora, they seemed overcome. I thought they might genuflect, such was their reverence. One by one they silently took her hand in theirs as one might a just-hatched chicken they feared they might harm.

When Alf and Nora reached me, I kissed them both and said, 'Congratulations'. Nora nodded and quickly averted her eyes.

'I'll take good care of her,' said Alf.

'I know you will,' I said, and tried to smile.

After they'd moved off, Len shifted closer and took my hand. 'He *will* look after her, Ide. He seems like a good bloke.'

'It's not that, Len.' I wanted to tell him everything I was feeling—not just my sorrow at Nora losing her dream, but also the deep wound of once again watching Nora do something I couldn't. But in the end, I just sighed and said, 'It doesn't matter.'

Later I found Grandma and sat down next to her. 'I don't know what to say.'

''Twas never meant to be,' she said.

'But you must be disappointed,' I said.

She patted my hand. 'Don't worry, my dear, I've survived worse.'

After the wedding, Nora and Alf moved to the northeast, where Alf's father had a sawmill. I tried to keep myself busy, so I didn't have to think about Nora and the baby. As it was summer, I spent long days in the garden, deadheading the roses and tying up the gladioli and hollyhocks. I gathered the seeds from the border plants and dried them in the shed. I sowed a few straight away and kept the rest for spring. The apple tree and strawberry runners needed thinning, and I took up the onions and laid them out to dry.

I deliberately wore myself out, yet there were still nights when I couldn't sleep. I'd get up and creep into the spare room, tiptoeing in as if it actually held a sleeping baby. I'd stand by the bassinette, running my fingers over the twists in the wicker and over the teddies on the coverlet I'd sewn and embroidered. I knew every thread even though it had never been used.

Sometimes I'd sit in the rocker in the corner and watch the moonlight dart in around the edges of the blind. It streaked the room and glinted off the white and chrome of the pram.

There was only one thing I'd ever wanted in this life: a family. It had been taken away from me in childhood, and now it had been taken away again. I felt betrayed by God and by life.

At times, the hole I carried inside me felt too big, too gaping, its edges too raw. Sometimes it seemed as if it was growing, enlarging and taking me over. I felt as if I was becoming less like a person, and more like an outline around a big, empty hollow. No longer solid but a shell. The remains of a mother.

I felt them in the room sometimes, as if they were present. The ghosts of my children. The bassinette wasn't empty—they were just sleeping under the coverlet. And when I rocked the pram, I could feel their weight in it. If I closed my eyes, I could hear them, too. Their gurgles and their cries. As I rocked back and forth, my arms against my chest, I could feel them. I could even smell them. On those nights, I could dream them up, alive again.

But I'd open my eyes and my arms would be empty. The room would be cold and silent, and I'd be shivering in the darkness, alone. They weren't there and they never would be.

One night, the door creaked open and Len's face appeared.

'What're you doing?' he asked, his voice as soft as clean sand.

I shrugged.

His bare feet pattered on the boards as he crept over to the bassinette, just as I'd done.

'We'll keep trying,' he said.

'No.' My voice had an edge. 'You heard the doctors, Len. It's not going to happen. We're never going to have a baby of our own.'

'We don't have to do it straight away . . .'

I shook my head. 'I couldn't go through it again. I couldn't face losing another one.'

There was silence, then his voice came softly. 'We could adopt?'

I rocked slowly in the chair, then shook my head. 'I could never take a child from its mother.' When I looked up, his face was twisted. 'Oh, Len . . .'

He covered his face with his fingers.

I went to him and slid my arms around his neck as he cried. I kissed his wet, salty cheeks.

He pulled his hanky from the pocket of his pyjamas and blew his nose. Then he straightened. 'We tried and it's just not meant to be. Don't worry about me. I'll be all right. There're some things in life you just gotta accept, and this is one of them.' He tried to smile.

I kissed his cheeks again.

'At least we have each other,' he said.

'And that's more than some,' I said.

Every payday, Len went to the pub for a beer or three on his way home. One night when it was raining and I knew he didn't have his coat, I took it around for him. I didn't go inside—pubs weren't for women—but waited outside by his bike, which was leaning against the wall. Eventually the pub door opened and Len emerged in a burst of light and noise, holding a box under his arm.

'What're you doing out in this weather, Ide?' he said when he spotted me under the umbrella. His words were a bit slurred. 'You'll catch your death.'

'You'll catch it yourself,' I said. 'I didn't want you walking home in the wet without your coat. Quick, put it on.' I could smell the beer on his breath as I helped him slide his arms into the sleeves, shifting the box from one arm to the other as he did. 'What's in the box?'

'I won a camera in the raffle. I had a choice between a side of beef and a camera, and I chose the camera.' He held it out as if it was priceless.

'What do we want with a camera?' I said. 'We could've eaten the beef.'

'Ida!' He stopped still and looked shocked. The rain ran off the brim of his hat onto the footpath, and his face was wet so it shone in the streetlights. 'Don't say that when I've just won us a time machine.'

'Give it here or it'll get wet.' I unbuttoned my coat and wrangled it inside, then attempted to button myself up over it. We set off, Len pushing his bike as I walked alongside, trying to hold the umbrella over both of us.

The next day he took the camera out of its box and held it up for me to see. It was black and smaller than I'd expected, with a round lens that jutted out at the front and 'Leica' written on the side. When I saw the knobs and lever at the top, I said, 'Are you sure you know how to work it?'

''Course I know.'

He opened up the back and hooked up the reel of film, then took me outside by the veggie garden, where he told me to pose and smile. I felt as if I was the Queen of England as he fiddled and clicked. Then I grew bored and tired of smiling into the sun, so I started mucking around, pulling silly faces and pouting with my hands on my hips, not trusting the camera would even work.

'Stand still,' he said.

When he'd finished, he handed the camera to me to take a photo of him, but I didn't dare. 'No,' I said. 'I don't know which bit's which and I might break it.' So he asked Stan, the plumber who lived next door, to take a photo of us out in the street under the power pole.

The film took a couple of weeks to develop and cost most of Len's pay. When he came home with the yellow Kodak envelope, I stood behind him, waiting for him to open it. He pulled out his packet of Drum and started rolling a cigarette.

'Hurry up. Hurry up,' I said.

'Hold your horses.' He lit his smoke then shook out his hanky and wiped his hands, including between each finger, before he slid the photos from the envelope. There, on the top of the pile, was me in my pastel dress with the lace-edged collar, standing by the fence and its ragged palings. I was smiling wanly, as if I was afraid of the camera. I laughed and so did Len.

He slipped the photos out one by one and I gazed at us caught in the moment. We nearly split our sides at the photo of me, hand on my hat, tilting my head like a movie star and pouting at the camera. We marvelled at how it worked. How the light captured the moment somehow, and there it was on the glossy card in front of us, never to be forgotten.

'Don't bother explaining it,' I told Len when he started. 'I'll never understand.'

I reached for the photo of Len and me by the power pole—Len in his slate-coloured trousers and white shirt, and me in my pale dress, taller than him but trying to hide it—but Len tapped my hand away.

'Don't touch them with your dirty fingers.'

I went back to the sink, humming and smiling as I finished the wiping up, while Len rolled a smoke and looked at the photos all over again.

Just before Easter 1941, Alf was called up to the Army. He didn't want to leave Nora, because the baby was due, but he had no choice. After a few weeks of training he was sent to Darwin and the War.

The day after he left, on 11th April, 1941, Nora gave birth to a boy. She named him Edward, after our father.

I put off visiting the maternity hospital, but after a week, I knew I could delay no longer. I wrapped the layette and shawl I'd knitted during my first pregnancy and caught the tram up to the Queen Victoria Maternity Hospital.

As the tram rounded the curve of the hill, I saw the hospital again, set back from the road, all long and sprawling and antiseptic white. The tram stopped and I climbed off. It dinged and rattled and went on its way, but I waited in the middle of the road, too afraid to move. I made myself cross the road, but my feet slowed with each step. I stopped at the bluestone fence, unsure if I could go in there again after all. Then I took a breath, put my head down, and walked down the circular driveway and through the doors.

Inside, the smell of wax and disinfectant were crushing reminders and the memories came flooding back. The stab of heat in my breasts at the sounds of the babies crying. The searing pain in my womb as they trundled the other babies to their mothers. The never-ending nights when I lay waiting for sleep to swallow me so I was spared a few hours of knowing my baby was dead.

I wanted to drop to the floor right there in the middle of the foyer, curl up into a ball and disappear. But I held my breath and pressed my hands against my chest, and I kept pressing until I'd tucked it all away again, deep inside where it had to stay.

I inhaled and stepped forward to the front desk. 'Nora Hill's room,' I said.

'Second floor, room five.'

I took the stairs and opened the door into a recess. Around the corner, the pastel corridor stretched, broken every now and then by a low light just above the skirting board, its beam shining dully onto the waxed linoleum.

I kept my eyes straight and didn't glance to the sides, walking in a straight line down the middle of the corridor and trying to ignore the smell of starched sheets and hygiene. I reached the doorway to Nora's room. It was pastel yellow, with matching curtains, and she lay facing the window. I stepped into the room, my heels soft on the lino, and headed towards her slim figure lying motionless under the sheets.

It took a while before she heard me and looked around. As soon as she saw me, she turned away again. But I'd glimpsed her—her face colourless and grief-stricken, her hair tangled, and her cheeks wet with tears. I sat down on the chair by the bed.

She wiped her cheeks with the heel of her hands and cleared her throat. Without turning she said, 'I don't want to see anyone.'

'Do you want me to come back another time?' I said.

'Don't come back,' she said. 'I don't want to see anybody.'

I seized the chance to escape, then I remembered the parcel in my bag. 'I've brought you a present.' I delved into my bag and extracted the brown paper package. 'It's a shawl and some clothes for the baby.'

She sniffed but didn't look.

'I'll just leave it here.' I set it on the bedside cabinet beside a jug of water.

She didn't move.

'I'll go then.' I stood and took a few steps towards the door.

'Thank you,' she whispered. I waited, but she didn't say any more, so I left.

I was managing all right until I passed the nursery and saw them behind the glass, tiny mounds of white lined up in rows like graves, except they were breathing. Some were sleeping, some crying—I could hear their muted cries through the glass. I wrung my hands together and for a moment, a brief moment, I wondered if anyone would stop me if I strode in and took one.

I moved closer to the window and found him—at the back, a blue card with 'Baby Hill' pinned to the bassinette above his head. He was asleep, his tiny fingers curled under his nose. His skin was fair, as was his hair, thick and swept up like a wave on his scalp.

My empty breasts ached at the sight of him. *Edward*, I mouthed. I stood with my hand on the glass just staring at him and I didn't want to leave. I glanced towards Nora's room and back at her baby. Then I spun around and walked back the way I'd come.

She was lying as I'd left her—on her side, facing the window.

'Nora . . . Nora . . .' I said as I entered the room and hurried towards her bed.

She didn't move. 'I told you I don't want to see anyone.'

'I won't stay. I just wanted to tell you that, if you want, you could come and stay with Len and me when you leave hospital. You and . . . Edward. Len wouldn't mind. At least then you wouldn't be on your own.'

Part II

She dug in the soil,
a garden.
And she saw in the flowers,
her children.

Chapter 12

They moved in and the milky smell of newborn crept throughout the house. Nora was tired and spent much of the time in bed, but at least I was there to help. I did the washing—boiling, soaking and bleaching the nappies on wash day, and pegging them on the line. Each time I glimpsed them through the kitchen window, strung up and flapping in the wind, my chest fluttered.

Every morning I filled a small tub with warm water. I set it on the kitchen table, along with a towel, a fresh nappy and singlet, and the baby powder and comb. Then I waited for Nora. She'd drag herself out of bed and down the hall with Ted curled against her shoulder. She bathed him as efficiently as if she was scouring a pot, and then rubbed the drops of water from his skin as if she was polishing Grandma's silver.

'Gentle,' I'd say as I hovered by her side, my arms loose with uselessness, watching while she treated him as if he was a rag doll. But it made no difference.

When she'd finished and shuffled back up the hall, I'd wipe the dots of baby powder from the tabletop. As I pegged the towel out to dry, I could still smell the scent of him in its fibres.

I couldn't help but creep in and out of his room when he was sleeping. He lay so still, and my heart would thump until I saw the rise of his chest or felt his milky breath against my cheek. Sometimes I stroked his cheek with my finger, just to make him twitch and reassure myself he was alive.

One morning he stirred, so I lifted him out. He fitted into my arms as if we were two pieces of a jigsaw puzzle. His head turned towards my breast and his mouth jerked open and shut, hoping for milk. He started to cry, so I loosened his swaddling and sat in the chair next to the fireplace and rocked him back and forth, back and forth, as he sucked on his fist and kept crying.

As naturally as if I was his mother, I unbuttoned my dress. He seemed to sense what I was doing and quietened, waiting. The blind was down and the room was dim; it was just the two of us together in the quiet. I lifted my breast from my bra and brought my feeble nipple to his lips. I felt his warm, wet mouth around it and the tug as he took it to the back of his throat. His fingers stretched across my skin and he sucked—once, twice.

I held him closer and smoothed his hair with my hand and, for a moment, I wondered if I might be able to do it—feed him and be a mother to a living child. But then he opened his eyes and looked at me. He let go of my nipple and screwed up his face and wailed, because there was no milk and I wasn't his mother.

But just for a wee while I'd felt what it was like to be a mother with a child.

Nora was still in bed when I took him to her. He was howling with hunger, and she hoisted herself up and untucked her bulging breast from its coverings. She took him and positioned her nipple in his mouth. He suckled, his fair head against her creamy skin, content.

She sank back against the pillow and closed her eyes. Her face was gaunt and her skin grey with weariness.

'Would you like me to bathe him when you've finished?' I said.

Her eyes stayed closed and she nodded.

I filled the tub and set it on the kitchen table. After he'd fed, I lowered him into the water. He smiled and gurgled as I trickled it over his honey-coloured hair and skin. Afterwards, I dried him and wrapped him in the towel. Then I picked him up and nestled him against me. His hair was wet and curly, and he smelt of soap and wind-dried towel.

Each morning after that, I'd pick him up when he woke and take him into Nora for his feed. I sat in a chair next to them, watching his tiny jaw chomp and listening to him wheeze, feeling his wispy curls brush against my arm.

When he'd finished feeding, I'd take him into the kitchen, where it was warm and light, and burp him until the blue disappeared from above his lip. After I'd bathed him, we'd sit by the stove and I'd stroke his hair and forehead until his eyes closed. I'd hold him in my arms while he slept, all the while admiring the fineness of his skin, the feathery veins over his lids and the milk spots across his nose.

Sometimes we stayed like that for hours. I told myself it was because I didn't want to disturb him but, really, the feel of him was a comfort to my otherwise empty arms.

I began to look after him more. Nora spent most of each day in her room, lying in bed with the blind drawn. I took her breakfast and lunch into her, and she only came out for dinner or to go to the outhouse, trudging about with her shoulders hunched.

'How much longer's she gonna get about looking like death warmed up?' Len asked one night.

'Shhh,' I said. 'Give her a chance to adjust.'

She didn't improve. One night a few weeks later, when she was sitting at the table toying with the sausage and mash on her plate, Len set down his knife and fork, and cleared his throat.

'Nora,' he said. 'Isn't it about time you pulled yourself together?'

'Len!' I glared at him. 'Don't!'

Nora gaped at him, her brow creased. 'How can you say that?'

'We've all got to accept things we wish were different,' he said. 'Ida and me did, and you have to as well.'

'Len, be quiet,' I said, and turned to Nora. 'Pay no attention. He doesn't mean it.'

'Yes, I do. She's a mother now and—'

I kicked him under the table.

Nora determinedly picked up her plate and took it to the sink, then hurried from the room.

'Len,' I said, standing. 'How could you? How could you be so insensitive?'

'She mopes around as if something really bad has happened, when it hasn't. She's had a baby, Ida. A baby. No one's died.'

'For godssake, Len!' I spun around and left the room.

Nora didn't answer when I knocked, so I opened her door. She was lying on the bed, facing the closed blind, and didn't look up.

'Len didn't mean what he said.'

She rolled over to face me. Her eyes were red and puffy. 'I can't stay here, Ida. Not where I'm not welcome.'

'Don't leave. Please, Nora . . .'

'As soon as I can find another place.'

'Don't leave because of what Len said. He's a bloke and he doesn't understand.'

'No, he doesn't understand and he shouldn't have said it.'

'He won't do it again. I'll make sure he doesn't. I promise.'

She sat up straighter and ran a hand over her hair. I noticed the bones of her wrist and how much she'd thinned and hollowed. She looked at me, her face pinched. 'Do you know what it's like?'

'I think so,' I said, my voice fading.

'You were allowed to grieve.' She closed her eyes and I thought she might cry, but she swallowed and opened them again. 'But I'm not.' Her forehead creased as she told me the story of what had happened.

'I was so happy in Melbourne. I'd never been so happy. I was doing what I'd always dreamed of doing—on the stage, singing—and I was good. Everyone said so. Dr Lloyd, the director at the con, said I could go to London or Milan or New York when I finished my studies. And I had Marco. He treated me like I'd never been treated by a man before, by *anyone* before. As if I was beautiful and special and had a gift. I got a flutter in my chest whenever I saw him. I couldn't help it, and even though I knew I shouldn't . . . I would have done anything for him. Anything. I tried to tell myself it wasn't wrong because we were in love.' Her voice lowered and she spoke slowly. 'But when I told him about the baby . . . that's when he told me he was married. I didn't know what to do. Then the Faculty found out and Dr Lloyd . . . and that was the end of it all.'

She ran her hands over her legs under the blanket.

'I've never felt so ashamed in my life,' she went on. 'Sitting on that chair while Dr Lloyd loomed over me from behind his big, heavy desk and told me I wasn't worthy of such a prestigious scholarship and that I'd brought the shame all upon myself. Then I had to tell Mum, and all she kept saying was, "What will people think?" And all I wanted to say was, "I've lost everything, Mum. I don't care what people think." Then she said, "Of course, if you'd done what I wanted and got married in the first place, you wouldn't be in this predicament. And with an *Italian*, no less." But the hardest part was when she went quiet because I knew I'd let her down more than I'd ever let her down before.' She looked up at me. 'Not even when I ran away. I had to try to fix it, so when Alf said he'd marry me, I . . . What choice did I have?'

She looked at me. 'But I've made a terrible mistake, Ida. I'm here and I'm alone. I have a baby I don't want, a husband I don't love, and no chance of ever being happy again.'

I didn't know what to say. I let a minute or two pass before I sat on the bed beside her and took her hand. 'You *can* be happy. You have a beautiful baby and a husband who loves you. You have more than most.'

She tried to withdraw her hand. 'I knew you wouldn't understand.'

I held it tighter. 'I do understand, Nor. I know what it's like to want something really badly, and to get it and then have it taken away.'

Nora stilled, leaving her hand in mine. 'There are only two things I've ever wanted. Singing and Marco. I risked everything to get them, and now I've lost both.'

'Don't you dare say anything like that to her again,' I said to Len that night as we lay in bed.

'She should just make the most of it. Like we all have to.' He reached for my hand under the covers, but I rolled away from him. 'She's a mother now. She needs to start looking after her son and stop expecting you to do it.'

I was quiet for a while, then I said, 'I don't mind, Len. In fact, I quite like it. I want to look after him.' I could hear his breathing behind me. 'You don't understand what it's like. You think you do, but you don't.' Inside my chest, I felt the ripples stir as I spoke. 'I carried them. They were inside me. I felt them moving, tumbling, kicking. I felt them and they were *alive*. And now they're not. Every cell in my body knows it, every day of my life. They're not here and they never will be. It's as if I have a big hole inside me where they lived. When I'm with Ted, that hole isn't as big and it doesn't hurt as much. And sometimes . . .' I swallowed. 'Sometimes, it almost disappears.'

He reached for my hand and I let him take it.

'Don't you ever do anything that might make her take him away from me again.'

'I really am sorry.' His voice was a whisper.

I rolled over to face him, and I could just make out his shape in the dimness. 'It's not me you should be apologising to.'

He stiffened. 'I'm not apologising to her. I meant every word.'

I pulled my hand from his and rolled away from him again.

We were quiet for a long time, then I heard him sigh. 'All right. I'll say I'm sorry. But I'm only doing it for you.'

After that, things were tense between Len and Nora. Whenever she saw him, she lifted her chin and looked away. For the whole time she and Ted lived with us, I don't think Len and Nora ever spoke directly to each other again.

Nora's unhappiness didn't improve, but apart from the night Len told her off, I never again saw her cry, nor heard her discuss what had happened in Melbourne. That conversation was the only time she allowed me a glimpse of the real Nora, the one who'd been humiliated and hurt. From that night on, even though she never brought it up again, I felt as if we shared a bond we'd never had as children and that we now understood each other's shattered dreams.

Mum and Grandma visited regularly after Nora and Ted moved in. Each time they came, they bore gifts: a teddy bear Mum had knitted in blue wool, or an embroidered baby towel or a smocked jumpsuit.

Mum would smile and chat to Nora as if nothing was awry. She'd enquire about Alf and how he was getting on in Darwin, and ask about Ted. She wanted to know how many ounces he'd gained, about his sleeping habits, and when Nora intended to introduce solids and start toilet training him. Everything had worked out how Mum wanted it to, and it was as if her memory of the events leading up to Ted's birth had evaporated.

Grandma always sat quietly at the table, sipping her tea and not saying much. When Ted woke and I carried him out, Grandma and Mum would take turns at holding him in their arms.

'Everything happens for a reason, doesn't it?' Mum would say as she held Ted and made clucking noises at him. But Grandma never commented, just watched him silently as his fingers curled around hers.

Nora never said much either. When she answered Mum's questions, she was always cordial and never unfriendly, but she seemed to be holding a part of herself back, like she always had.

Ted was an easy baby. He didn't cry but sat watching, always watching, with eyes so dark and deep they appeared infinite. And knowing.

His first word was my name, and when he said it I called Len out to the kitchen. I pulled Ted from his high chair and sat him on the edge of the table. His knees dimpled as he kicked his legs.

'C'mon, say it again,' I said.

He reached for the rattle on the floor. 'Da,' he said.

I clapped my hands and picked up the rattle. 'See, he can say my name.' He took the rattle and began to suck.

Len ruffled Ted's hair as he passed. 'You know how to please her, mate.'

Then Ted learnt to sit and stand, and one day when he was nearly one, he let go of the chair and took off. Two, three, four wobbly steps before he tumbled onto his cushioned bum.

Nora was in the bath, so I banged on the door. 'Nora! Nora!'

'What?' she called as she hurried out, a towel wrapped around her and water droplets still shining on her skin.

'Watch,' I said.

I propped Ted against the dresser and called to him. 'One, two, three, four, five, six,' I counted as he stepped. 'Six steps.' I picked him up and kissed his curls and his olive cheeks. 'Aren't you a clever boy?'

'Oh, Ida, don't get carried away. They all learn to walk at some point.' She left to finish drying herself.

'Well, at least Aunty Ida's excited,' I said to Ted after she'd gone.

Once he was up and about, I had to follow him everywhere in case he tumbled or banged his head. Our trips to the shop became long meanderings as he poked a stick into every puddle and examined every snail and slug. If we spotted a bird, we had to follow it, and he cried big, globular tears when it flew away.

At home, Len trailed him with the camera. He took a photo of him in the garden with a caterpillar on his hand, and another of him climbing the front steps carrying some roses. My favourite was the one of the two of us on the verandah, Ted sitting on my knee, his feathery curls almost covering his face as he studied a picture book.

When Len wasn't looking, I slipped that photo inside the box I kept on top of our wardrobe. It already held a flower I'd pressed from my wedding bouquet as well as the two layettes and babies' shawls I'd kept. I put the photo of Ted and me on the top, replaced the lid and slid the box back in its place.

Chapter 13

As Ted grew, he started doing the usual things kids do, like venturing too close to the fire or crying when he had to get in the bath. Nora would give him a tap on the hand or a whack on the bum. Sometimes, she lost her temper.

The first time I saw her rage at him was one rainy Monday when I was hanging the washing over the clotheshorse by the fire. The lounge room smelt fresh—of Velvet soap and wet cotton. Ted had just turned two, and was playing at my feet, crawling in and out between the shirts and pillowcases as if they were a tent.

'Ted!' Nora screeched from the hallway.

We both stilled. Nora's footsteps echoed as they hurried up the hall and the door flew open. Ted cowered amongst the whites, as if he hoped the wet linen might hide him, but she streaked across the room and squatted in front of the clotheshorse. She reached in, past one of Len's shirts, and grabbed him by the arm.

Ted started screaming.

'What's going on?' I said, still holding Len's singlet in my hands. 'Nora . . .'

She yanked him out, her fingers tight around his arm so his skin blanched. Then she bent and slapped his bare leg. The sound was as wet as the laundry in my hands. Ted screamed and she slapped him again.

'What's he done?' I said. 'What's happened?'

She didn't answer. Her eyes were on Ted, her mouth set, her jaw clenched. Even the muscles of her neck were taut. She pulled a lipstick from her dress pocket and held it about two inches from his face. The top was broken and squashed flat, and its gold case was smeared red. 'You did this, didn't you?'

Ted glanced sideways at the lipstick, then turned away and covered his face with his hands. He was crying softly.

Nora shook him. 'How dare you take my lipstick and draw on Aunty Ida's wall.'

She shook him again and when she let him go, he crumpled to the floor. He curled into a ball, his cries muffled under his arms.

I flung Len's shirt on top of the washing pile and went to him.

'Leave him,' said Nora, as I bent.

'He's crying . . .'

'He's been into my lipsticks *and* drawn on the wall.'

'But he doesn't know that's wrong.'

'He's been told. He knows not to touch anything on my dressing table.'

Ted was still whimpering on the floor at my feet and I bent towards him again.

'Leave him, Ida. He's got to learn.'

I eyed her. 'That's not the way to teach him.'

'I'm his mother and I'll decide how he'll be taught.'

I stilled. My arms ached to pick him up, but I did as I was bid and returned to the washing in the basket.

She left the room, and as soon as she'd gone, I scooped Ted into my arms and pressed his head against my shoulder. He looked at me, his eyes glistening with unshed tears and his curls wet and sticking to his reddened cheeks.

'I know you were just playing,' I said, 'and you didn't mean to. But please don't do it again, Teddy, because I can't bear seeing her hit you like that.'

He settled and I set him down. I finished hanging the rest of Len's singlets, Y-fronts and socks on the rack, and shifted the clotheshorse in front of the fire to dry. Then I took Ted's hand. In the hall, Nora was on her knees with a soapy bucket of water beside her. She was scrubbing at the wall to remove the red streaks.

To me, Ted was just being a kid, but to Nora it was deliberate misbehaviour. Like when he took the butter off the table, and smeared it over the chair and table legs and a fair portion of himself. And when he tipped things out of their containers—marbles, pencils and a whole bottle of milk. He liked to copy what I did and plant things in pots about the garden—crayons, a library card and the front door key, which we couldn't find for weeks. One day he cracked half a dozen eggs because he was looking for the chickens inside.

Nora would lose her temper at him and the thwack of her hand against his skin made me recoil. I had to wrap my arms tightly around myself to stop from whisking him away. But as much as it hurt to witness, I couldn't leave him alone while it was happening. As soon as Nora left, I'd go to him. I'd take him outside and up the path past the clothesline, to the garden by the back fence. We'd pluck apples from the tree and let the air cool our cheeks. Sometimes, we went out the front and picked hydrangeas and roses. Back in the kitchen, I'd peel the fruit for him to eat and we'd arrange the blooms in vases. All the while, I'd keep telling him that I loved him and always would.

'It's not his fault,' I tried to tell her one day after she'd whacked him on his bottom for shaking the talcum powder all over the floor.

'It *is* his fault,' she said. 'He spread it from one end of the hall to the other. It looks like the frost has come inside.'

'I'm not meaning that.' I inhaled and slowly released my breath. 'I'm meaning it's not his fault you had to give up singing.'

Her face twitched, and she looked down and swallowed a few times. 'He's still done the wrong thing.'

That night, I whispered to Len in bed. 'I've tried to turn a blind eye to it because I know this isn't the life she wanted, but, sometimes, I'm not sure she loves him at all.' I hesitated before continuing. 'Sometimes, I think she even hates him.'

'She's his mother,' Len whispered back. 'Every mother loves their child.'

'Do they?' I said.

'At least *you* love him, Ide,' he continued. 'Let's just hope she'll be happier when Alf gets back.'

Meanwhile, Alf was fretting up in Darwin. He was homesick and wrote sad letters about how much he missed Nora and the bush. Eventually, Alf's father wrote to the powers that be saying they needed him at the mill, cutting wood, and as that was considered an essential wartime service, he was allowed to come home early.

'He's a bit soft if you ask me,' said Mum when she heard. 'It's that cleft in his chin.'

'Alf is not soft,' I said. 'He's built for log-cutting, not soldiering, that's all.'

He arrived late one afternoon towards the end of 1943. Through the window of the taxi, I glimpsed his slouch hat move forward and back again. Then the door opened and he climbed out. He appeared slimmer and taller in his uniform, and the sun behind him made his shadow long. He slung his swag over his shoulder, and as he began to walk towards us, his pace quickened until he was striding over the footpath and through the gate. He took the steps in one stride, up and onto the verandah. He dropped his swag and enveloped Nora in his arms, holding her as if he wanted to draw her inside of him and never let her go.

'I've missed you so much.' His voice sounded dry, as if it was coming from the back of his throat.

Nora's arms stayed by her sides, and then slowly one hand slid up to his shoulder.

Alf took her chin in his hands and looked her full in the face. 'You're a sight for sore eyes, let me tell you.'

She laughed, a low-pitched, awkward sound.

Then he pressed his lips against hers and closed his eyes for a long minute.

Ted was watching them. His eyes were wide, his face open and angelic, framed by his blonde curls. In one movement, Alf let go of Nora and crouched in front of him. Ted's fingers tightened around mine. Alf took off his hat and tucked it under his arm. His square face was smiling and friendly. 'By jeez, have I been itching to meet you.' He motioned with his hand. 'Come here, son.'

Ted hid his face in my skirt. 'It's all right,' I said as I patted the top of Ted's head. 'Go and say hello to your father.' But he gripped me even tighter.

Alf winked. 'It's all right. We've got plenty of time to get to know each other.'

The next day, Rex, one of Alf's brothers, came into town with the truck. I waited with Nora and Ted on the verandah while Alf and Rex loaded the suitcases onto the back of the truck.

'Tarney's Creek,' Nora said. She was wearing sunglasses and I couldn't see her eyes. 'Alf and Rex have bought their father's sawmill and a lease on a plot of forest there.'

'Tarney's Creek?' I said. 'I didn't know there was anything there.'

She shook her head and her lips quivered. 'Some huts, apparently. But they want to make the most of the war, with all the building that's going on. Then we'll be able to buy a house.'

'We're ready when you are,' Rex called from the truck.

I squeezed Nora close as we embraced. She felt spindly, as if she was hollow and might break. Briefly, her arms pressed against my back, before she let go and stepped away. She pushed a finger up under her sunglasses and wiped her eyes. Then she fixed her handbag over her elbow and said, 'I'll be in town each month.'

'And I can visit you,' I said. 'It's not like when you were on the mainland.'

'C'mon, Ted,' she said. 'We've got to go.'

He squinted up at his mother. I bent down and pulled him towards me, holding him so my cheek was against his. So I could feel him and inhale the soapy scent of his curls and the milky fragrance of his skin. I knew they were waiting, but I couldn't let him go. The past couple of years had been the happiest of my life. I wanted to keep holding him until the light waned and the shadows crept forward and hid us, and we could escape and never have to part.

'C'mon, Ted,' Nora said again.

I let my arms drop and straightened. Without looking back, I turned and ran up the steps and into the house. I was already sobbing before I'd closed the door. I leant against it and felt the house judder as the truck rumbled and clanged its way up the street and took him away.

After two and a half years of having a child in the house, just like that it was empty again. I wandered from room to room, trying to find something to do or dust, but all I could hear was the sound of my own feet. I wouldn't have believed our tiny house could echo, but it did. I think I cried more about them leaving than I did when I lost the babies.

⟨∾⟩

I spent the daylight hours outside, trimming the ivy before it took over the whole house; getting stuck into the weeds and ripping them out with the hoe; raking fertiliser into the soil; and planting bulbs and perennials. Each night at dusk, I stood on the back step and surveyed my day's work—the churned soil, the vibrant blooms and the verdant green. I saw all that I'd created, yet I felt empty.

In the evenings, Len and I sat in armchairs by the fire. He smoked and read the newspaper, while I sat opposite and kept myself busy. I knitted a sky-blue jumper for Ted, a grey cardigan for Nora and a rust-coloured jumper for Len.

At the end of the following month, Nora and Ted came into town with the log truck to do the shopping. By nine o'clock I was out on the wicker seat on the verandah waiting for them. The day was already warming up—puffy clouds in a light-blue sky, birds singing in the trees on the verge and the smell of the geraniums in my nostrils. Every now and then, I wandered down to the gate to check the street.

Then I felt the shudder as the timber-laden truck rounded the corner, and I dashed to the gate and peered out. When I saw its peeling and rusty face as it clanged and hissed its way down the street, I felt as if I was greeting an old friend.

They pulled up outside. Ted was sitting on Nora's knee, squinting out of the cabin window. His face burst into a smile when he spotted me. Nora couldn't get down from the truck fast enough, and Ted scrambled out and into my arms. He was heavier and his limbs were longer. His hair was thicker and his eyes were darker. But he was in my arms and, once again, my world felt complete.

'I'll be back about four,' Rex called, as the truck rattled off.

Ted and I waved until he disappeared, while Nora brushed herself down. Despite living in the bush, she looked smart in a grey linen jacket and pleated skirt. 'You've no idea how much I've been looking forward to this.'

We went to town and bought flour and butter, Velvet soap and Ajax, and four ounces of cheese from the store. Nora bought some fabric and I purchased more wool. Finally, we visited the lolly shop for Ted, where Mr Gourlay in his starched white apron slid humbugs into a brown paper bag before spinning its ends so they looked like ears.

Then we sat down in the tea rooms, at a table with a chequered cloth and a sprig of lavender in the centre. All around us customers chatted and clanged cutlery, and the place smelt of pumpkin soup and toast.

'Did you see that lady in McKinlay's wearing slacks?' said Nora.

I shook my head and lifted Ted onto my knee.

'I wish I could be that adventurous with fashion. Lots of women in Melbourne wear trousers . . .' She fell silent and picked at a thread on the tablecloth. 'I'm finding it hard.'

Ted wriggled on my lap and I held him closer.

'We don't even have running water. I have to fetch it from the creek with a bucket. And there's just a camp oven over a fire to cook with, and I have to do the laundry by hand . . .' She spread her fingers to show me the ulcerated skin over her knuckles.

'Oh, Nor, take care that doesn't get infected.'

She clenched her hand and covered it with the fingers of the other. 'It's never-ending, the work. Cooking and cleaning. Alf keeps telling me it's not forever, that we'll move to a proper house soon, and Rex keeps telling me being busy is good, that it'll make the time pass quicker.'

I let my chin rest on top of Ted's curls. I could smell Velvet soap in his hair.

'The highlight of my week is mass. Father Piper comes out and says it for us. He's very nice and it's terribly good of him to come because it's such a long way. We set up the kitchen table outside in the clearing for an altar. It's not a real church, and it's not the same . . .' She shrugged. 'But it's better than nothing. And I thought I might sew a dress to wear . . .'

Our soup and bread arrived. I cut off the crusts and tore up the bread, and dotted it on top of the soup. It was tomato, warm and familiar. I blew on it and fed a spoonful to Ted. He opened his mouth for more.

Nora inspected her bowl but didn't lift her spoon. Her top lip twitched. 'I don't know how much longer I can do it.'

I kept feeding Ted. As soon as he'd swallowed one spoonful, his mouth was open for more. 'It won't be forever, Nor.'

'Marriage is.'

'Alf's a good man,' I said. 'He'll look after you.'

She sat a while longer, eyeing her bowl with glassy eyes, then picked up her spoon.

We were quiet when we returned home. I kept an eye on the clock and felt heavier with each passing minute—I wanted to send those hands back the other way until it was morning again. But the crockery on the dresser soon started clinking as the truck rumbled down the street. Outside, Rex honked the horn and it was time to go.

I carried Ted out on my hip. Nora came through the front door, grappling with her hat and bags. I kept walking down the steps, my feet slowing and growing heavier. When I'd unlatched the gate, I turned.

Nora was still at the front door, trembling and shaking her head. 'I can't. I don't want to go back out there.'

I wanted to close the gate and say, 'Stay. Both of you. Stay.' But already she was striding forward again, down the steps onto the path and through the gate. I followed and with each step, Ted's knees pressed further into my midriff. When we reached the truck, Nora set her basket on the grass and held out her arms. Ted clung to me, his knees gouging my waist and his fingers pinching my shoulders.

'C'mon, Ted. We've got to go,' said Nora. She gripped his waist and pulled.

His fingers dug in deeper, and he shook his head and started to cry. I wanted to glue him to me and run back inside so she couldn't take him. Instead, I hitched him closer on my hip and brushed a curl away from his ear. With my mouth against his pink, wet cheek, I whispered, 'Go to your Mum. So you can come back next time.'

He quietened, the tears in his eyes like morning dew.

'Go, Teddy,' I said.

Nora caught him by the waist and he let go of my shoulder. He twisted and watched me as she hoisted them both up and into the truck. I bent and retrieved her basket, wiping under my nose before straightening and handing it to her. She shut the door of the truck and Ted squashed his face against the window. His fingers blanched against the glass, his eyes dark. He stayed pressed against the window as they jostled up the street and the ground under me quivered. They reached the corner and stopped. At a break in the traffic, they were off again, a red rag swinging back and forth, alone on the empty tray, until they disappeared.

I walked back through the gate and ran up the stairs and inside. I kept going, down the hall and out the back door to the garden. When Len came home from work, I was still outside, hacking at the ground with the hoe, hoping to bury my ache.

A few months' later, as I stood at the kitchen bench cutting orange cake for afternoon tea, Nora told me she was pregnant again. I swallowed and said, 'That's great news.' I kept my back to her and my eyes on the cake until my face had time to settle. I cut slowly, a couple of pieces each, and arranged them elegantly on the plate. By the time I turned, I was smiling.

But Nora wasn't. She was looking at me with terror in her eyes. 'The last thing I want to do is take another child to that godforsaken place.'

I joined her at the table and took her hand in sympathy, but as she talked I could feel the pressure percolating and rising like steam inside me.

At the end of the conversation, she pulled herself taller and exhaled. 'I've made my bed and in it I must lie.'

After Nora had left, I headed outside to water the bulbs I'd just planted, but as I passed the baby's room, I stopped. I turned the handle and stepped inside. The room was in half-light, and the bassinette stood silhouetted by the window. Before I'd reached it, my tears were already flowing.

Each time Nora came to town, she was paler and skinnier and lagged further behind her swollen belly.

'Take it easy. Take it easy,' Rex would say as he helped her down from the lorry. He'd hold her gently as he lowered her to the ground, as if she might break. He kept holding her, walking with her, until he was sure she had her balance.

As her date of confinement neared, her belly protruded further and her walking slowed. She took the verandah steps slowly, then stood at the top, hand on hip, while she caught her breath.

'Why don't you wait here and rest while I go to town for you?' I said when I saw the dark arcs beneath her eyes.

'I've got an appointment with the doctor. But it'd be nice to go on my own for a change.'

So Ted and I waved from the gate as Nora's slim back plodded its way up the street towards the tram stop on the main road. We spent the morning in the garden picking ripe tomatoes. We ate them on the verandah with a sprinkling of salt, smiling at each other as the juice dribbled down our chins.

Later, we sat at the kitchen table. I sharpened the pencils with a vegetable knife and Ted asked me to draw birds with pretty wings.

As I was drawing a colourful rosella, he said, 'Can I live at your house again?'

'Oh, Ted, you make my heart do somersaults.'

'Like an acrobat?' he said.

Just after two o'clock, the front door clicked open and Nora bumped down the hallway, her arms laden with bulging bags.

I took the bags and set them down by the dresser. 'You shouldn't be carrying those.'

'They weren't going to walk themselves home.' She removed her hat and held the back of the kitchen chair as she eased herself into it. 'The doctor said I shouldn't be lifting things. Apparently, it can make the cord wrap around the baby's neck.'

I stilled. 'Oh, Nor . . .'

She stripped her gloves from her hands and rubbed at the bandage between the knuckles of the fingers of her right hand. 'But who else is gonna cart the water? Alf's gone all day and when he's home, well, he can't do the laundry or cook or any of the other things that need to be done . . .'

I sat next to her and took her hand. It felt dry and chafed. 'Nor, I'm coming out to help.'

Her lips quivered. She withdrew her hand and reached up her sleeve for her hanky. 'Thank you.' She sniffed and wiped under her nose. Her eyes were red and puffy. 'I think I'm getting a cold.'

I rubbed her shoulders and, even pregnant, she felt thin and bony and like a fragile bird.

I told Len that night after dinner.

'How long will you be gone?'

I shrugged. 'She's got no one, Len. Mum and Grandma can't get out to Tarney's. There's no running water or electricity and the doctor's told her she's not meant to be lifting.' I leant in closer and deepened my voice so it sounded grave. 'I don't think either of us could live with ourselves if another baby in this family died.'

He sighed, then nodded.

Chapter 14

At three o'clock the following Thursday afternoon, I was packed and waiting for the truck. Rex always brought the timber into town, while Alf and his other brothers kept working at the mill. Rex looked like a giant behind the wheel, filling all the space from the roof to the floor. I climbed into the cabin and found a spot for my feet amongst the twigs and bark. It smelt of wood and diesel.

We drove up past the City Park and onto High Street. Past the stately homes, including the Godfrey-Smiths', then out through St Leonard's, where the houses became smaller and more sparse. The road grew narrower and more convoluted, then we were in amongst trees and ferns and the patchy light of the forest.

We wound our way over the Sideling Range. Rex let the truck build up speed on the downhill sections, so it could chug its way to the top of the uphill ones. My hands gripped the seat as we lurched around each bend, and Rex honked the horn in case another truck was coming from the opposite direction. There was no railing, nothing to stop us going over the edge, and my knuckles stayed white until we were through.

Then the farmland and hills rolled out before us. Paddock after billowing paddock, folding and criss-crossing, all shades of green and yellow, some fallow and red. It was even more vivid than I remembered.

'Looks like patchwork,' I yelled over the jangling of the truck.

Rex leant forward and peered out the window. He nodded, as if he'd not noticed it before.

We drove through the town of Tinsdale, and on further. Past farms with gracious English trees clustered about the gates, past cows with bursting udders and past fences crawling with blackberries. Then I spotted her—a small, grey peak rising from the horizon and shrouded in cloud.

'There's Ben Craeg!' I cried.

I was still moved by the sight of her, striking and majestic against a sky lit by the lowering sun. She kept disappearing behind a hill or the trees. But she was still there, always there, and I felt as if I was coming home.

Rex slowed and changed gears, and we veered northeast off the main road onto gravel. Our jaws juddered as we bounced over the ruts. I laid my forehead against the glass and felt the vibrations through my bones. I gazed up, right up, past the pale trunks to the branches and leaves.

'The trees are so tall,' I said.

'That's mountain ash. She grows pretty big out here. Tallest in the world, they say. Well, I've never seen anything like it anywhere else.' He was quiet for a while before adding, 'Never been anywhere else, though.'

The road narrowed even more, and branches and ferns clawed at the sides of the truck. Then we emerged into a clearing that looked as if a hand had reached down and scooped out the forest. Rex cut the engine and pulled up the handbrake.

'Home sweet home,' he said.

I looked around. Five or six huts, a chain or two apart. Nora had been right, they were huts, not houses. No bigger than sheds, wooden, with brick chimneys and tin roofs. At one end was the mill, which was just a few sheets of tin over a steam engine and a long bench with a saw. On one side, the hewn boards were stacked neatly and, on the other, the logs lay lined up like corpses. Next to them was a pile of sawdust and another pile of off-cuts. To the side of the huts, fenced off by chicken wire, were a couple of milking cows and hens.

All around us the eucalypts rose, hundreds of them, like a battalion of protective troops. They were straight and almost bare right up to their tops, where their leaves clustered, swaying in the wind.

It was the last place on earth I could imagine someone like Nora.

Alf opened my door. He was neat and clean in a crisp shirt and trousers. I stepped down from the truck, and he squeezed me to his chest. He smelt of soap, and under that I could smell the wood and sap ingrained in his skin.

'Careful,' I said, 'or you'll wind me.'

'Good to see you, Ide.' He grinned, and I noticed new lines around his eyes.

I followed him towards the huts, watching my feet as I trod over the twigs and bracken and the lumpy ground. The air was sharp and stinging, and I pulled my collar up against the cold. I could smell the tang of the forest.

We stepped under cover of the eaves—a rusty sheet of tin held up by a couple of wooden posts—of one of the huts. Alf levered off his boots and set them next to the woodpile, then held the door open for me.

The inside smelt the same as outside—of the forest and the sharp air. Then I spotted him and my heart leapt into my throat. I didn't notice anything else after that, not the cold, or the starkness, or Nora beside him. There he was, sitting in a chair, blonde curls around his face, as he fed himself with a spoon.

He jumped down when he saw me, and my words stuck inside my throat as I scooped him up and kissed his curls and his pumpkin-streaked cheeks. For the second time that day, I felt as if I'd come home.

Nora was slow to rise and held her belly as she stood. Her face was pale and long, and she had dark shadows under her eyes. I hugged her and felt the bulge of her fertile womb against my barren one. She didn't smile as she sat back down slowly, like a ship coming in to berth.

I sat with Ted on my knee. Alf lit a roaring fire, and the air crackled and smelt of burning eucalypt. Then he lit the kerosene lamp and the room filled with light. The hut was spartan but still managed to look dishevelled. The grey mat by the front door was muddied. The table, the shelves, the dresser were in disarray and covered in dust. The only decorations were the statue of the Holy Family on the dresser and a picture of Pope Pius XII that hung from a nail on a wall stud.

I scrubbed a pot and cooked dinner—spuds boiled over the fire, and some silverside and bread I found in the meatsafe—and we ate at the table in the centre of the room. Alf closed his eyes, brought his hands together and said the grace, and we thanked the Lord for all the goodness he'd provided for us that day.

Nora toyed with a potato on her plate. In the firelight, the shadows under her eyes seemed darker. She barely ate a morsel.

'You all right, Nor?' I said.

She glared at me. 'This isn't how I envisioned my life, Ida. None of it is.'

I winced, but Alf's face gave nothing away. It was as if he'd heard it before.

'You'll feel better when the baby's here,' I said, trying to sound reassuring. 'Not long to go now.'

'The baby's not going to fix things,' she said without lifting her eyes.

The fire hissed and popped, and outside a gust of wind rattled the roof. 'The wind's coming up,' said Alf. 'Rain might be on the way.'

I nodded. Alf and I chatted about the wet weather and tried to keep the mood light. But each of us stole glances at Nora, who sat in silence and barely ate.

I cleared up when we'd finished eating, while Nora sat at the table. Then I readied Ted for bed and buttoned him into his pyjamas. After I'd kissed him goodnight, Nora took him into the bedroom. While she was gone, Alf made up the camp bed.

When she returned, I said, 'You look tired. Why don't you retire, too?' Arm-to-hip, she lilted towards the bedroom and the door closed behind her like an exhalation.

I made a pot of tea, and when we sat at the table, I pulled out my knitting—a layette for the new baby in fine white wool.

'I know it's not much, living here,' said Alf. 'And I know it's hard on Nora. But I've told her we won't be here forever. I have plans, Ida. Big plans. That's why I'm working hard.' He lit a cigarette. 'One day I'm going to build her a house, a proper house, a really nice one. So she can live how she should, like what she deserves. Surrounded by nice things. Nice furniture and pictures. And a piano she can play. And maybe she can even sing again.'

Outside, a possum scuttled across the roof.

'I'll do my best to take care of her, Ida. And the rest of our family as they come. I promise.'

I nodded. 'I know you will, Alf.'

'Rex and I have to work tomorrow. Fell as much as we can before the rain sets in. So I'll say goodnight.' He stood. 'It's good of you to come.'

''Night.'

After Alf had left the room, I swilled the last of my tea and wound up the wool. Then I changed into my nightie and turned down the wick on the kerosene lamp until the light disappeared. The room was black except for the winking firelight. The sheets felt like ice as I climbed between them and the pillow smelt of sawdust. I pulled the blanket and quilt around my chin, before rolling over to face the hissing embers.

Outside, the wind rushed through the treetops, and the hut creaked and moaned. An owl hooted in the distance and some Tasmanian devils screeched nearby.

I hoped Alf was right, that Nora would be happier in a nice house closer to town. But the disquiet I felt didn't abate and the embers had faded before I fell asleep.

Chapter 15

The rain fell against the tin all night, and the next morning a westerly was still blowing the rain across the roof in sheets. The bedroom door creaked and Alf crept in. He was unshaven and his hair stuck up, making his face appear even more square. He padded past me, almost soundless on the floor.

He scrunched up some newspaper and gathered kindling from the basket. The twigs crackled alight and he set a log on top. Soon, I could smell the burning eucalypt—a minty, clean smell. He straightened and rubbed his hands together. 'Soon be warm,' he said, and slipped back into the bedroom in silence.

He returned dressed in his singlet and trousers, braces swinging, a towel over his shoulder. He scooped water from the bucket into an enamel bowl and slipped outside. I climbed out of bed, the blanket around my shoulders, and opened the curtain over the sink. The window was foggy and I cleared a gap with my hand. Outside, the weather was blustery and grey. Alf was under the eaves, leaning over the bowl on the stump and scooping water into his hands. As he lifted them to his face, the water streamed from between his fingers, and when he shook his head, the droplets sprayed around him, some of them caught in the wind. He pulled the towel from his shoulder and wiped one side of his face, then the other, before raising his face towards the sky.

I let the curtain drop before he noticed me watching, then filled the kettle and hung it over the fire. Alf was shaved and dressed when he returned and ate the eggs I'd boiled. He pulled on his oilskin and turned the collar up. I watched him through the window as he loped across the clearing towards the mill, the rain pelting down on his hat, and the smoke from his cigarette curling upwards until it disappeared into the mist.

Nora hadn't been up long when she began rubbing her belly. 'It's just those false labour pains you get a couple of weeks before the baby's due,' she told me when I looked worried.

Outside, the trees hurled about like dancers, tossing and turning in the wind. Rain battered the roof, drumming and pounding the tin. In the distance, the steam engine at the mill clanked and hissed, and its saws droned as they buzzed through the wood.

I kept my eyes glued to Nora as I swept. When she started holding her belly and breathing through pursed lips, I said, 'I think I should get Alf.'

'Stop panicking, Ida,' she said.

A minute or two later, she gripped the edge of the table as she breathed through a contraction.

'I'm fetching Alf,' I said, but she was too busy breathing and clutching her belly to answer.

I threw my coat over my head and ran out into the pelting rain. The wind was blowing and the rain was teeming. In the distance, I could see Bill, Alf's brother, shovelling wood into the furnace at the mill.

'Bill! Bill!' I called as I ran, but he couldn't hear me over the racket of the engine and the saws. I kept calling. 'Bill! Bill!' At last he glanced up, red-faced and sweaty.

'Nora's having the baby,' I called as I puffed and panted. 'Fetch Alf!'

He spun around and ran straight out into the teeming rain, not stopping for his jacket or hat.

Back at the hut, I collected Nora's suitcase and helped her into her coat. We were waiting with Ted by the door when Alf returned. Rivulets of water ran from his hat and oilskin, pooling on the floor. He took Ted in one arm, Nora's case in the other, and ran out to the truck.

Nora and I followed more slowly, clasping our hats to our heads and trying to shield the rain from our eyes. I led Nora by the elbow, pulling her towards the truck as the rain swept across the yard.

Alf had climbed in with Ted and leant across to open the passenger door.

'C'mon Nora, in we go,' I said.

'I can't!' Her voice was shrill.

'Yes, you can. Just put your foot on the step.'

She gripped the door of the truck and didn't move. The rain streaked over her and a puddle formed at her feet. I couldn't tell if it was the rain or her waters breaking.

'You can't have the baby here,' I said.

'Aaargh!' She clutched the door, breathing in and out through tight lips.

The contraction passed. I pushed her from behind while Alf pulled her by the arm until she was up and in the truck.

I climbed up next to her and took Ted on my lap. Alf started the engine and put his foot on the accelerator. The wheels spun but we didn't move. He released the pedal, then pressed down again. I twisted around to see mud spraying like a chocolate fountain behind us, but we stayed where we were.

'C'mon,' said Alf, and tried the pedal again. 'C'mon . . .'

The wheels whirred and the mud splattered, but we didn't move.

Nora was breathing in and out through drawstring lips.

Alf pressed the accelerator once more, but it was no good—we were bogged.

'I'll get Bill,' he said, and jumped out into the wind and blustering rain.

'It's all right, Nora,' I said, patting her hand. 'We'll get you to the hospital.'

She didn't answer but gripped my hand and squeezed as she let out a groan. 'Aaargh!'

Bill and Alf came back with a couple of planks. They poked and prodded at the back of the truck, then Alf climbed in just as Nora started screaming.

I squeezed her hand again. 'We're on our way now, Nora. Just hang on for a bit.'

'No, the baby's coming,' she screamed. 'Aaargh! I need to shit!'

'Hold tight,' I said, as she squished my fingers between hers

'I can't. It's coming . . . Aaargh!' She was spreading her legs.

'Alf, this baby isn't going to wait,' I said. 'We'll have to deliver it here.'

He blanched.

Nora screamed again, then gasped, 'Take Ted inside. He can't see me like this.'

Alf took Ted and sprang out onto the mud, shutting the door behind him. With Ted tucked under his coat, he took off through the rain towards the hut.

Nora was panting. Her hair was stuck to her forehead and rainwater trickled down her face. 'Don't leave me, Ida.'

'I'm here,' I said.

Righto, I thought. *I'll have to deliver this baby on my own.* I blessed myself—I needed all the help I could get. The rain pounded on the metal of the truck and the wind howled around us, whistling through the gaps. We were sheltered, at least, in the dusty cabin. The two of us. Two about to become three.

Nora lay across the driver's seat, her head back, her belly a tight hillock between us.

'It's starting again,' she said. 'I can feel it . . . its head.' She began to spread her legs. 'Aaargh!' A guttural noise, coming from deep within. The noise that comes when words can't.

The contraction eased, and when her breathing settled, I pushed her further towards the driver's side.

'We'd better get your pants off, Nor,' I said. I slid my hands under her dress and either side of her bum, grabbed her knickers and tugged them down to her ankles. I lifted one leg out and bent it up on the seat, then I lowered the other leg onto the floor, amongst the leaves and twigs.

'I'm gonna take a look at what's happening,' I said, trying to catch her eyes, but they were closed. I lifted the hem of her dress and peered between her legs.

There it was—the opening, stretching and thinning around a small patch of dark.

'Oh, Nora,' I said. 'I can see it coming. The baby's on its way.'

'I know it's on its bloody way . . . Aaargh!'

'You're doing good,' I said. 'Just keep breathing.'

'Aaargh!' She lifted her head from the seat, set her chin on her chest, and pushed. 'Aaaargh!'

I kept my hand on her thigh and rubbed and patted, rubbed and patted. 'You're doing great. You're doing great.' I kept repeating those words because I didn't know what else to say. 'We're gonna have a baby soon, Nora.'

In between contractions, I glanced over at the hut where Alf and Ted waited inside.

'Aaargh!' she cried. 'You won't leave me, Ida?'

I grabbed her hand. Her fingers gripped mine tight as a mangle. 'I'm right here,' I said.

'Aaargh!'

I looked between her legs again. The dark patch was bigger. 'It's coming,' I said again. 'Keep pushing . . .'

'Aaaaaaaaarrrrrghghghgh!' Her skin stretched, thinning so it became almost transparent. I reached out, my hands ready to take the baby that was coming. With each contraction more of it came, little by little, a dark oval shape, then out, out, more and more, until Nora opened up and there it was: the head. Face down. Swollen and purple, and streaked with mucus and blood.

'The head's out!' I cried. 'The head's out!'

'Where are you, Ida?' Nora called, her eyes shut, her head propped against the driver's door.

'I'm right here,' I said. 'I'm right here and you're doing a great job. This baby's nearly out. Keep going, keep breathing, keep going.'

'Aaargh . . . Aaargh!' she screamed.

'Breathe in . . . and out. That's it. One shoulder. And again. In . . . and out.'

Out came the other shoulder, then the body and the legs slipped into my hands in a whoosh of fluid.

A boy.

He was limp and purple and not moving. He lay across my hands, still attached to his mother. *Breathe*, I urged him. *Breathe. Go on, boy. Breathe.*

He opened his mouth and cried the soft, sharp cry of the newborn. He was alive!

I felt as wobbly as a half-set pudding. I lifted him up to Nora. She stared up at the roof, her eyes not moving, her hair stuck to her skin, her face sallow.

'Do you want to see what you have?' I said, and held him out.

She kept her eyes upwards. 'I don't care what it is,' she whispered.

'It's a boy!' I said.

She nodded and closed her eyes.

I brought him towards me and held him against my chest. I caught sight of the hut, still and silent in the squall. I wanted to jump out and run over with the baby and show Alf his son, show someone this baby. We had a baby!

I found a knife in the glove box and extracted a shoelace from my boot. I cut the lace in half and tied each piece around the umbilical cord, tugging the knots as tightly as I could, before I cut in between. The baby was free and breathing by himself. I unfastened my coat, took off my cardigan and wrapped it around him. Then I laid him on Nora's chest.

'Congratulations,' I said. 'You have another son.'

'The afterbirth is coming,' she said, and didn't move.

I took it when it came, heavy and thick with blood. I climbed out, leaving Nora lying on the seat with the babe on her chest.

The rain was easing now and the wind had settled. My hair stuck to my face, and the air blew cold through my dress. I walked into the bush and through the wet shrubs until I found a spot by a thick-trunked mountain ash. I knelt on the ground softened by rain and laid the afterbirth beside me. The blood trickled from it and mingled with the water and seeped into the thick soil. I scooped the mud with my hand and dug a hole deep in the ground—I could smell it, the thick, wet earth—and I placed the afterbirth in its grave and piled the soil back over the top.

We drove straight into town and to the hospital. Alf parked the truck outside and ran in while I waited with Nora and the baby. He came back out with a doctor and two nurses, one pushing a wheelchair. I slipped onto the footpath and watched while a nurse took the baby, still wrapped in my cardigan. She passed him to another nurse, who carried him through the doors. They helped Nora down from the truck and into the wheelchair, and pushed her inside.

I lingered on the footpath after they'd gone, just until I'd cleared the tears from inside me. Just until all those memories were back in their private place inside my heart.

Chapter 16

Ted stayed with Len and me while Nora was in hospital. On the first night, we invited our next-door neighbours, Stan and Doreen, and Len's brother Fred and his family over for dinner. I made a savoury casserole, using some of our ration coupons for the beef, and I pulled some parsnips and carrots I'd planted over the winter. We had to sit on apple crates because we ran out of chairs. Ted sat on my knee and Len took a photo of us all.

After breakfast the next morning, Ted and I watched Len ride off on his bike, one trouser leg in his sock, whistling as he pedalled up the street towards the wharf. We shrugged into our coats and set off down the street. The world appeared more colourful than usual—the sky more blue, the sun more yellow, even the green of the grass and the pinks of the roses were more vibrant. As I pushed Ted along the street in the pram, snug and tight, everything in the world seemed right.

On the first day, we caught the tram to the City Park and fed the ducks and watched the monkeys. The next day, we walked over King's Bridge and along the Cataract Gorge, and sat in the tea rooms while the peacocks strutted about. The day after that, Mum and

Grandma came in on their way to the hospital, and the following day, Ted and I went to town and borrowed some books from the library. Each day there was something different to do, and on the way home Ted would fall asleep in the pram. I'd lift him out and sit on a fireside chair in the lounge, while he slumbered on my lap. We'd stay like that for a couple of hours, just the two us in the quiet with the mantel clock ticking beside us.

Len kept asking when I was going to visit Nora in the hospital and I kept saying I was busy. Finally, on the fifth day, when I couldn't put it off any longer, I dressed Ted in his new check shirt and a jumper I'd knitted, and we set off. It was still brisk, and the cold darted up my nose and through my coat. I wasn't nervous as the tram rumbled past the Albert Hall and the City Park, but as soon as we rounded that bend and I saw that white building, the panic started rising in my chest. I grasped Ted's hand as we stepped down, and we made it across the road, but my legs slowed as I headed towards the driveway. I stopped.

'Let's sit,' I said to Ted.

We sat on the bluestone fence by the driveway and I pulled Ted onto my knee. I broke off some of the scone I'd brought with me and rested my chin against the softness of his curls as he ate.

'I used to live along there—' I pointed up High Street, past the hospital—'with the Godfrey-Smiths. Oh, they had a beautiful house, with an upstairs balcony. I used to stand on it and gaze out towards the river and the mountains. I could see almost to the forests where you live. Except when there was a fog.'

I kept talking and each time a tram passed, we caught the eye of a passenger and waved at them as if we knew them. After a while we turned around, away from the road. We watched the sparrows and twits in the bushes, the branches shivering as they flitted in and out. I told Ted to close his eyes and I closed mine, and we tuned out the other noises—the cars, the trucks, the passers-by—so only the birdsong could come to our ears.

When I opened my eyes again, Ted was asleep. I sat for a while, wondering if I should wake him. His dark lashes curled against his cheeks and his breaths were soft and regular. He was peaceful, oblivious to the traffic and the passers-by. I couldn't move him. I stayed there all afternoon, watching him slumber and enjoying his perfection. I just sat and listened to the birds and tried to forget there was a big, white hospital looming behind me.

The next day, Len minded Ted and I set off on my own. I walked all the way up to the hospital, keeping my eyes on the footpath, especially as I rounded the bend. When I reached the driveway I still didn't raise my eyes but kept them down as I walked straight on through the doors.

Nora was propped up on pillows, as pale as the sheets on which she lay. Dark crescents ringed her eyes and her curls were flattened on one side. I walked over to the bed and kissed her.

She was shaking.

'What's wrong?' I said.

She opened her mouth but couldn't speak.

'It's all right, Nor. I'm here now.'

'I can't stop it.' Her eyes filled and she breathed faster, then wiped her mouth with her hand. 'I can't stop fretting.' She picked at the sheet and began to twist it in her hands.

'I should've brought Ted,' I said. 'You're probably fretting for him.'

She shook her head. 'No, no. Ida . . . Ida . . .' She started crying. 'Don't bring him. I don't want him to see me like this.' I took her hand and she squeezed it. 'I can't do it, Ida.'

'What can't you do? '

'I can't go back out there. I can't keep living like this . . .'

I patted her hand and rubbed her arm. 'It's just the baby blues, Nor. You'll feel better soon.'

Her eyes didn't lift and she kept wringing and kneading my hand. I sat with her for an hour, until the nurse came and announced visiting time had ended. I went to leave, but Nora caught my arm. I sat down again and kept patting Nora's hand as her fingers gripped and twisted mine.

Outside, the day was dimming and night time was on its way. A nurse walked past and pulled up when she saw me. 'Oh, I didn't realise you were still here. Visiting hours finished ages ago.'

'I didn't want to leave her while she was so fretful,' I said.

'I'm afraid visiting time is up.' Her voice was clipped and efficient. I went to move but Nora's hand clutched mine.

'Can't I stay a bit longer?' I said to the nurse.

She shook her head. 'She needs her rest.'

'I have to go now, Nor.' I prised her fingers from my arms, but she kept reaching for me.

The nurse came over and took her hand. 'Come, come, Mrs Hill, what's all this nonsense? You can't get upset or you'll upset your baby, too.'

I stooped and picked up my bag, then stood. When I reached the door, I glanced back at her, alone and fretting in that sterile place.

I walked along the corridor. Past nurses carrying trays and pushing trolleys, and past dimly lit rooms whose occupants were preparing for the night. As I passed the nursery, I glanced through the window at the rows of babies in the light-filled room. But I didn't stop—I needed to get home to Ted.

⁂

Meanwhile at home, Len was enjoying Ted as much as me. He took him outside and snapped away with the camera. Each night after dinner, he poured some froth from his beer into a glass and made a cigarette out of a match rolled up in a Tally-Ho paper. He burnt the end so it looked like a real cigarette, and the two of them sat at the table with their beers and smokes. Len showed Ted how to tie fishing flies, and Ted's eyes never moved from Len's fingers as they worked.

The Saturday after my visit to the hospital, Alf came into town—Nora and Benedict, their new son, were ready to go home.

'She's better?' I said when he arrived to collect Ted.

'Better? Was she sick?' he said, his forehead creased.

I hesitated. 'She must be better now.'

I carried Ted to the gate, and when Alf leant down and held out his arms, I clasped Ted a little tighter. 'Are you sure you don't want me to keep him while you settle in with the new baby?'

'We'll be all right,' he said. His arms stayed outstretched. 'Come here, son.'

I held him out to his father and he didn't make a whimper as I let him go. My arms felt light and cold.

Alf hoisted him onto his hip and turned towards the street. He pointed at a shiny green Ford parked on the verge.

'I bought a new car,' he said. 'D'you reckon Nora'll like it?' His face beamed like a child's.

All I could feel were my empty arms at my sides. But I nodded. 'Yes, yes. Of course she will.'

'I reckon she will, too.'

Ted watched me over Alf's shoulder as they walked to the car. Alf opened the door and slid him onto the front seat beside him. Ted gazed out the window, twisting around so he could still see me as they took off up the street. I waved and kept a smile on my face as they drove off. I stayed outside by the gate long after they'd gone, staring out at the empty street. Then I turned and went inside.

❧

A week or so later, Len came home with a packet of newly developed photos. I picked up the one of Ted and me sitting on the apple crate on the first night he stayed with us. Stan's in the background pouring a beer and I have my arms around Ted, gazing at his face. Ted's peering into the camera, but he's not smiling. His head is tilted and his eyes are black and deep. He looks wiser than his years and, the closer I looked at the photo, sadder, too. I took that photo and stowed it with the others inside my box of keepsakes.

Chapter 17

Grandma passed away just over six months later, in March, 1945, at the age of seventy-two. Len and I made the sad pilgrimage out to Tinsdale for her funeral.

The church looked the same, and still smelt of dust and candle wax. Mum sat in the front pew, wearing a black hat and a dark-grey coat. She turned as we neared. Her eyelids were reddened and weary, her cheeks were no longer pink and round but pale and drawn, and she had deep ruts either side of her chin. As I slid in beside her, I noticed the tears in her eyes.

Nora slid into the pew opposite, followed by Ted and then Alf, with Ben in his arms.

Ben was seven months old and big and square like his father. His skin was pale and his eyes were the colour of the sea on a cloudy day. He had a covering of fine, dark hair, which stuck straight up from his scalp. He spent the service squirming on Alf's lap and sucking on a rattle.

Ted looked tiny next to Alf. He was nearly four and his features were even finer and more delicate than when I'd last seen him. His skin was tanned and olive, and his hair had thickened and deepened to a honey colour. It curled over his scalp and fell almost to his collar. He was dressed in shorts and a matching jacket and tie. His socks were pulled up and folded over evenly below his knees. He faced the front of the church and sat stock-still, as if he didn't dare move. His eyes were twitching and, at one point, he seemed to sense me staring and turned. I smiled, but he quickly looked away, glancing up at his mother to see if she'd noticed him gawking about.

Nora sat at the end furthest away. She kept her head bowed and her hands clasped below her chin. Her hat almost obscured her face, except for the peaks of her chin and nose and the jet-black of the pendant dangling from her ear lobe. The rosary beads Grandma had given her as a child were entwined around her chafed fingers.

Afterwards, we walked in a straggly procession over to the graveyard. As Grandma's coffin sank into the plot next to our father, the clouds felt so low I could almost taste them.

After the priest and the rest of the congregation had left, Nora stepped forward and stood by the grave. She closed her eyes and clasped her hands, the rosary beads wrapped around them, under her chin. She stood a long while in silent prayer. When she'd finished, she turned to Mum. 'She was the only one—' her chin trembled and her voice cracked—'the only one who understood.'

Mum shook her head and opened her mouth to speak, but closed it again without saying anything.

Nora began to walk off and Mum called after her, 'I understood, too.'

Nora stopped and half-turned so her head was in profile.

'I understood,' continued Mum, her voice low, her hands clenching and unclenching at her sides, 'but I just . . . I didn't want you to get let down.'

Nora sniffed. 'It didn't work.' Then she continued walking, her head bowed and her shoes scraping the gravel as she headed towards the pines that stood at the entrance to the cemetery.

Mum watched her leave, then Alf stepped forward and kissed his mother-in-law, before following Nora slowly up the gravel path. Ben sat in the crook of Alf's arm, still sucking on his rattle, while Ted held his father's hand. As they reached the pines, Ted glanced back, gazing at us with his dark, bottomless eyes.

Len, Mum and I waited silently in the heavy air. I went up to Grandma's grave and stood by the edge. I could smell the fresh earth and feel the rising coldness on my face. I peered down, past the clay-coloured sides and the tangle of roots, down to the bottom where, in the darkness, her coffin rested. It seemed tiny and far away. A wreath of roses sat on top along with some earth the priest had scattered.

'Thank you, Grandma,' I whispered. 'Thank you.' She'd been a good person, sometimes the only good person, in our lives. I never once heard her yell or say anything unkind and she never raised a hand to us. And she always, always forgave. She was the only person I knew who could see the good in everyone, even when they were behaving at their worst.

Mum returned to Grandma's house, but in the winter she took to her bed and didn't get up. There was only Len and me to look after her, so she came to stay with us. I prepared the front room overlooking the garden—I set a vase of roses on the dressing table, wound the clock on the mantel and lit a fire in the grate. Len carried her in and helped her slide under the crocheted bed cover. Her back was hunched and she held herself up with trembling hands. She looked small and gaunt, as if she was slowly crumbling.

'Have you been eating?' I said to her.

She didn't look at me. 'It's a bit hard when you're only cooking for one. And, quite frankly, I don't care if I live or die anymore.'

'C'mon, Mum, we'll get you going again.'

She rested in bed for a week, then two. I attempted to coax her out, but her arms and legs shook so much the bed wobbled. When the doctor came, he said to let her rest a while longer. So I waited and waited, but the weeks rolled on and still she didn't get out of bed.

The only things Mum could do for herself were eat and wash. Three times a day, I took her meals into her. Each night I fetched her a washbowl and flannel, and every morning and evening I emptied her chamber pot. Some days, her brass bell didn't stop tinkling.

If I was late to change her potty. *Tinkle, tinkle.* 'I thought you'd forgotten.'

And after I'd returned it. *Tinkle, tinkle.* 'Did you rinse the potty properly, Ida, because I can still smell it?'

Tinkle, tinkle. 'Could you make me a fresh cup of tea, Ida? This one's a bit tepid.'

Tinkle, tinkle. 'I can feel a draught. Would you move the door snake?'

In the afternoons as the weather warmed, she'd tinkle her bell for me to carry her out to the front verandah for her 'air', as she called it. She'd huff and puff as I lifted her, as if she was the one doing the heaving, and tell me off if I wasn't fast enough.

One day when we were sitting outside on the wicker seat, she came out with, 'It was those long, hot baths you took that did it.'

'Pardon?' I said.

'When you were pregnant,' she continued, not looking up from the pillowcase she was embroidering. 'Hot baths can cause a baby to come early. Elsie Green from number twenty-seven was telling me about her daughter-in-law. She miscarried after a bath.'

I kept knitting, winding the wool over the needles and sliding the loops over each other.

'And all that lifting . . .' She held out the pillowcase and examined the long, neat stitches she'd sewn to make the petal of an apple blossom. 'It causes the cord to wrap around the baby's neck.'

I set my knitting in my lap.

'But, really, I think it was the Lord's doing. You never set foot in a church . . .'

'That's quite enough, Mum.' I stooped to pick up my knitting bag and stood. I went to leave, then turned about. 'Don't you think I haven't gone over every minute of those pregnancies, examining them for something I did that caused what happened? Don't you think I would have prevented them if I could have?'

She kept her eyes on the pink of the apple blossom and pierced the fabric once again with her needle.

'I cooled my baths. I got Len to hang the washing and lift the cast-iron pots. I stopped scrubbing floors. I stopped gardening. I stopped everything but sleeping and eating. And praying. I prayed as hard as a whole bloody convent for my babies to live.'

She didn't look up as she pulled the thread through, then dabbed at the fabric with a finger.

'There's nothing you can tell me, Mum, that I haven't already berated myself for. I'm going inside and you can get yourself in.' I headed for the door and as I reached it, her bell tinkled.

Her head bobbed and her eyes looked wilted. 'I'm sorry.'

I sniffed, then nodded.

'And you're late with the tea,' she added.

Mum had her moments, that's for sure. There were times I rolled my eyes, times I wanted to drop that brass bell in the bin. Times I wanted to drop *her* in the bin. But then she'd say she was sorry and the heat of my anger would dissolve. She did nice things, too, like made me a tablecloth and linen teatowels and embroidered them with lavender. She didn't need to say it for me to know she was grateful.

I also felt grateful to her. I liked that she needed me, and I liked having someone to keep me company during the day. We talked a lot, especially while we knitted and sewed on the verandah in the afternoons. We discussed the weather and the neighbours, and we also talked about things closer to our hearts.

One day as we were sitting on the verandah, out of the blue Mum started weeping. I shifted closer to her on the wicker seat and put my arm around her shoulders. She took a while to settle, then I asked her what was wrong.

She took her glasses off and wiped her eyes with her hanky. 'There's no one who remembers your father anymore,' she said.

'I do. I was only young when he died, but I remember him. How tall he was and his beautiful singing.'

'That's not the same,' she continued. 'It was something your grand-mother and I did a lot—talked about your father. I don't think a day went by we didn't mention him. She told me stories from when he was a boy and I never grew tired of hearing them, even the same ones over again. She loved him as much as I did and now there's no one to talk about him anymore.' She wept again. 'It was the reason I never left your grandmother's. I couldn't leave the only other person on this earth who'd loved him as much as me.'

These words of Mum's moved me more than anything else she'd ever said to me before.

One job I never minded was washing Mum's hair. Each Saturday morning, I'd undo the pins and let the honey-brown skeins tumble down her back. Her hair was long, nearly to her waist, and, even though she was in her mid-forties, it wasn't grey. She'd lean back over the bowl and her hair would swirl about in the water. I'd rub flakes of Lux soap, which I'd grated, into her scalp until they frothed white. I'd massage it in with my fingers, around and around her scalp, and she'd close her eyes. Then I'd pour jugs of warm water over it all until the lather was all rinsed out.

Afterwards, we'd sit outside on the verandah while I towelled her hair dry and brushed it smooth, one long stroke after another. I kept brushing it, sliding the bristles through her hair longer than necessary, and then I'd reluctantly coil it back in its bun. I didn't like tucking it away again, hiding all that beauty.

Nora and the boys still visited with the truck every month, and Mum looked forward to their visits as much as I did. She painted on her lipstick and donned one of her bed jackets, then tinkled the brass bell she kept at her bedside to let me know she was ready. I carried her outside to the front verandah, and we both waited for the truck to appear at the top of the street.

Nora was reserved around Mum. She always sat with her body tilted slightly away from her and they never kissed. Mum would try and make conversation with Nora, and Nora would answer politely but in a closed kind of way that didn't invite further questions.

'How's Alf?'

'He's good. I'll pass on your regards.'

'And the mill?'

'The mill's doing well, thank you.'

'When will Ted be starting school?'

'Next year.'

At least there were the boys. Mum's face lit up when she saw them alight from the truck. She chatted with Ted, asking if he'd been good for his mother and father, and praising him for eating his slice of cake without dropping a crumb. She kept her eye on Ben as he waddled about, tapping my hand if he got too close to the edge of the verandah or into the garden. 'Catch him, Ida. Watch he doesn't put a snail in his mouth.'

After they'd gone, Mum and I would sit in the quiet. She'd giggle and shake her head and say, 'He's a scallywag that Ben.' We'd catch each other's eyes and laugh together, both of us with a flush to our cheeks and a sorrow to our voices because we knew it would be another month until we saw them again.

She seemed to enjoy them in a way she never did Nora and me when we were children.

At the end of January, 1947, Nora and Alf and the boys moved to Milaythina, south of Tarney's Creek, a mile or two closer to Tinsdale. Alf and Rex's business was booming with all the post-war building, and they'd bought the licences for fresh plots of thick forest in the area. They set up a couple of mills, and hired more loggers and a manager.

Then Nora announced she was pregnant again and I realised that watching her belly grow would never get any easier.

The baby was due in September, and because Ben had come early and quickly, Nora needed to be in town a few weeks before her due date so she was near the hospital. Nora and I talked at length about what to do. She thought about bringing the boys and staying at our house, but we didn't have a lot of space and Ted would miss school. In the end, we decided the best option was for Nora to come to our house on her own so at least she could care for Mum until she went to hospital, while I went out to Milaythina and and looked after the boys and Alf.

I put off telling Len and kept waiting for a good time but none came. A couple of days before Nora was arriving, I told him over dinner.

'What?' He looked up from his plate, his eyes wide.

'It's the only option,' I said, pleading with my eyes. 'They can't all stay here, not now Mum's here, too.'

He shook his head. 'What about Rex's wife? Or your Aunty Lorna? Why can't they look after the boys?'

'Beryl has her hands full with her own kids and Aunty Lorna's too old.'

He looked back at his dinner, then scratched his head. 'No,' he said. 'I can't do it.'

I sighed and wrung my hands. 'All right. If it's too much, I'll just tell them Nora can come, but Alf will have to manage with the boys on his own.'

'Ide . . .' His face was pinched.

I pushed out my chair and went to the sink.

It didn't take him long. 'If you want to go out and help, Ida, go. I'll stay here with your mother . . . and Nora.'

I turned around. 'Oh, Len, it would help everyone. Mum knows to be on her best behaviour. And I know you and Nora aren't each other's favourite people, but at least you'll be at work during the day, and you can come out to Milaythina at the weekend.'

He closed his eyes for a second and inhaled deeply. 'I'm only doing it for you, you know.'

A few days later, Alf brought Nora into town. As Len loaded my suitcase into the boot of the Ford, he asked, 'When will you be back?'

I shrugged. 'I'm not sure.' I kissed him, letting my lips linger on his rough skin. 'I do appreciate it, you know. I appreciate all that you do.'

'I hope so,' he said, and tried to smile.

As we took off up the street, I watched him through the back window. He stood on the verandah by the geraniums, gave us a wave, then turned and went inside.

Chapter 18

We drove over the Sideling Range and through the forest, between the hills and rolling paddocks, past Tinsdale and onwards to the tiny town of Milaythina.

'You can see her peak today,' said Alf when Ben Craeg came into view, her soft blues rising from the hills.

We drove along a sealed road and then a short dirt road before we pulled up at a house—a proper house, not a hut. Ted, who was now five and a half, and Ben, who'd turned two the month before, came hurtling out the door. They tripped down the steps, calling out to us. This was the first time I'd visited since they'd moved. Before my shoes had even hit the soil, they were jumping up and down around me, their little hands in mine. Then their legs were carrying me back towards the house. Their tongues were rattling, telling me about their books, their toys, giggling and laughing as their legs churned, running us up the steps and inside.

After dinner I watched from the back step as they played football in the back paddock with their father—they were all rubbery arms and legs. As the last of the sun's rays melted away and the air chilled, they came inside, cheeks red and noses running. They changed into their pyjamas by the fire in the lounge and then skittered along the hall to their bedroom.

I stood at the door, gazing at them cocooned in their beds, and I felt it. The pull of lives unlived. Little ghosts inside these two little boys.

Then I flicked out the light.

I slept on the couch in the lounge, and next morning the room was filled with a pearly light and the trills of waking birds. The floorboards creaked and the pipes clunked and clunked again as water gurgled down a drain. I peeled off the quilt, slid into my slippers and dressing gown, and opened the curtains to the unfolding dawn. The mountains were silhouetted against a pinking sky and, overhead, the flickers of the stars were disappearing into daylight. Everything was still, as if holding its breath.

The kitchen was cold and in shadow, but by the time Alf entered I had the fire crackling and the eggs frying. He ate quickly, before Rex arrived in the truck. Through the window I watched them walk over the frosted grass, their voices a low growl as they talked into their chests. They were both as solid as chimneys, their shoulders as broad as bridges and, from behind with their hats on, you could barely tell the two brothers apart. They climbed into the truck, reversed out along the dirt track and were gone.

The boys woke soon after and Ted readied for school, then Ben and I walked him up to the main road to catch the bus. We took our time walking home. Ben stomped in a mud puddle and poked it with a stick. Then he climbed a tree and sat in the crook of a low branch. Back at the house, I cleared a space at one end of the table and we sat to draw. I wrapped Ben's fingers around the pencil and held his hand while we drew a cat sitting on its curly tail, and a house with smoke puffing from its chimney. Then he wanted jungle animals—tigers with fangs and lions with manes—as well as ships and cars and trains and trucks.

Each morning after we'd waved goodbye to Ted, we'd sit by the kitchen fire and draw. The fire would hiss and crackle and our pencils would scratch across the paper.

One morning as we were drawing, I started humming and tapping my fingers against the table.

'Sing again,' he said when I stopped.

'That wasn't singing,' I said. 'That was just noise.'

'No, you was singing,' he said.

I shook my head.

'Go on . . . Sing again.' His eyes were lively.

I looked at our drawings of lions and tigers and trains and cars and, remembering Grandma's made-up songs around the piano, I started singing about a zoo where jungle animals drove trains and cars. Ben put his pencil down and sat straighter, not taking his eyes from mine until I'd finished. When Ted came home, Ben wanted me to sing it for him, too.

'I can't remember how it went,' I said.

'Doesn't matter,' said Ted.

So I sang it again, a bit differently because I couldn't remember it exactly.

Then Ted sang a song about a bird and a lion, and every day after that we sang. On the way to the bus stop and on the way home again. We sang the same song—well, pretty much the same song— and different songs. Songs we made up and songs we knew. We sang anything that came into our heads and we sang it from the bottoms of our bellies. The sounds of us rang through the air, shifting the trees and rustling the leaves. And we laughed.

Of a night, Alf and I sat by the fire. I knitted while he smoked. We spent much of the time in contemplative silence, but we also talked. Alf told me things I'd never known about him, like that his father and grandfather had been bullockies.

'The last of 'em,' he said as he leant forward and flicked the ash from his cigarette into the fire. 'I was afraid of the steers when I was a kid. But they were as patient as Job, all of them. Dad had names for them. He called the lead one Pavlova, after the ballet dancer, 'cos he reckoned she was light on her feet.' He laughed. 'She did whatever Dad wanted. She knew, just from the tone of his voice. He didn't need the whip.'

I let my knitting rest in my lap while I listened.

He told me how his father made sleepers for the railways and hewed all the wood himself, carving it with an axe and a gauge.

'In all the years he did it,' he said, 'the inspector never found a single mistake in his measurements.'

Another night he told me about when his father used to take him and his brothers up Ben Craeg. There was a mill about halfway up where Alf's father used to do business, and when he'd finished they'd walk up to the summit.

'It was bloody cold,' Alf said. 'And, by jeez, it could blow. But we didn't mind. On a clear day, you could see over the whole district, as far as the coast and Bass Strait. Other days, it was just clouds drifting all around.' He paused to puff on his cigarette. 'One day I said to Dad, "This is like Heaven." And Dad said, "There'd be no better place for a soul to go, son."'

We sat in silence for a while, and then he looked up. 'I reckon Dad's up there right now.'

I picked up my knitting and started clicking and looping again.

'I've never told Nora half of what I've told you this past week,' he said.

I glanced up. 'I like hearing your stories.' I smiled.

He didn't smile back but said, 'It's nice to have someone to tell them to.'

I lowered my eyes and kept on with my knitting. I felt my cheeks and the tips of my ears grow hot.

'You were always smiling.'

'I beg your pardon?' I said.

'At school. That's what I remember about you. And you and your friend used to ask me to hold the end of your skipping rope.'

'Beth Prosser.'

'Yes, Beth Prosser.'

I laughed as I remembered and looked up at him. 'We asked you because you were gentle and didn't try to trip us.'

He smiled and shook his head. Then he went quiet while he finished his cigarette. I kept on with my knitting. 'A lot of water under the bridge since then,' he said as he threw the butt in the fire.

I sighed and nodded. 'If only we'd known . . .'

'We might have done things a bit differently.' He held my gaze for a moment and neither of us moved. I felt my face flush again and looked down at my knitting.

He finished his smoke and stood. 'Good night, Ida.'

'Good night, Alf.'

I sat on the chair for a long time afterwards, gazing into the fire and rubbing my cheek, and contemplating a lifetime of what ifs.

Len caught the bus out the next morning and Alf picked him up from Tinsdale. As the truck pulled in, I flew down the steps and clasped him to me.

When at last I let him go, he tilted his head and scrutinised me. 'You all right, Ide?'

'Of course I am,' I said, and rubbed my hands up and down against his arms. 'I just missed you.'

'I brought my fishing rods,' he said, and pointed towards the tray of the truck, where a couple of rods, a tackle box and an ancient tin bucket sat. An hour or so later, we'd loaded a picnic basket and a couple of darned blankets in with the rods and the wood chips. Chocolate-coloured rainwater sprayed out behind us as we lurched and tipped our way down the driveway and up onto the main road.

I kept my face to the open window and let the wind whip my cheeks and knot my hair. I turned every now and then to check on the boys. They were sitting in the tray with their backs against the cabin, watching the road stream behind us.

Alf veered off at the river and drove along the gravel track past the swimming hole. He wound the truck further upstream, where the track narrowed and rutted. We dipped in and out of potholes, and the bush closed in around us. Branches scratched the sides and roof of the cabin and, in the back, the boys laughed as they ducked to avoid them.

Alf pulled up and we jumped down. The sky was almost hidden by the thick bush around us, and the air felt dull and damp. The path smelt of rotting leaves and mud. As we neared the river, the trilling of the cicadas grew louder until it was almost throbbing. Nearer to the river, the bush opened and the air lightened. A blue sky and fairy floss clouds arched overhead. We skidded down the riverbank, setting stones rolling, and I spread the blanket over the rocks and pebbles by the water.

I started unpacking the picnic basket while Len hooked up the rods. He handed a rod to Ted, the worm still writhing, and they scrabbled over to where the water lapped at the stones.

'Here, you hold it like this . . .' He took Ted's hand and wrapped it around the rod. 'And swing it like this . . .' He stood behind him and together they swung the rod back and forth. The worm and sinker swayed from the end like a pendulum. 'Just relax,' he said, and kept swinging. 'Then you unclip the reel, swing it back and throw . . .'

Whizzzzzz. Plop.

'And now you wait until you get a bite,' said Len.

Ted sat, his eyes not moving from the tip of his rod. 'How long will it take?'

'You gotta be patient, mate.'

Len set up a rod for Ben and himself, and sat a few yards upstream from Ted. Ben nestled in his lap, the rod in front of them. Alf lit a fire and put the billy on, and sat on a rock by the blanket. I kept my eyes on the still water and the kids and Len fishing.

'This is good, Ide,' Alf said.

'Yes, it is.'

We said no more. Around us the bush rustled and the water lapped. When the billy began to hiss, I made the tea and poured it into enamel mugs. I took it to Len and the boys at the water's edge, along with some egg sandwiches. While they were eating, Len took a photo of Ted with the rod in one hand and a sandwich in the other. I'd learnt how to use the camera by then, so I took a photo of Ben grinning as he sat between Len's legs holding the fishing rod.

Suddenly, Ted's line flipped into an upside-down 'J' and twanged back and forth. Len clambered over the rocks towards him, holding out the net and calling, 'Reel it in! Reel it in!' Alf and I ran down and joined them at the water's edge. Len stood behind Ted, his hands covering Ted's, and together they steadily wound the reel.

The water was dark and still, the line bobbing as they wound. Then there it was, a flash of silver below the surface. The water broke with a 'whoomp', and the fish flipped and flashed on the end of the line. It was as shiny as a newly minted coin, the water streaming from its skin. Ted kept winding, and the fish swung in the air, flipping and somersaulting.

Len was laughing and saying, 'Stop, stop!' as he followed it with the net, to and fro, trying to land the flapping fish. When he'd captured it, they looked up, and I clicked the camera and captured them, flushed and smiling with the sun glinting off the water behind.

Len unhooked the fish and plopped it in the bucket. The boys gathered around and peered in as it took its final gasps. Their heads lowered closer until they were nearly inside the bucket, then they jumped as the fish flipped again.

'It's trying to get out,' said Ben.

'I feel sorry for it,' said Ted.

With the sun sinking lower, Len showed them how to gullet the fish.

'This's where you start and you cut him like this . . . up to his gills . . .' he said.

Heads together, they watched.

'And we don't want these bits . . .' The boys' heads followed his hand as he flung the entrails into the river with a plip-plop, then turned back to the fish.

Alf and I walked back to the picnic blanket. 'They're never like this with Nora,' he said.

I didn't say anything and we sat back down.

'This is good,' he said softly.

We made our way home, the boys and their sun-kissed cheeks and noses peering into the bucket every now and then, smiling and chatting about what they'd do next time they went fishing with Uncle Len.

That night, I lay on the couch and Len lay in the camp stretcher alongside. I rolled towards him in the dark.

'That's exactly what we would've done if our boys had lived,' I said.

I rolled back. A moment later, I felt his hand fumbling for mine. I took it and slid out from under the blankets and lay alongside him in the camp stretcher. By the tender glow of the dying embers, I showed him how much I loved him.

Chapter 19

Early the next week, the telegram arrived and I propped it behind the sugar canister on the dresser. I tried to act bright and jolly and like it was any other day, but I felt its intrusion all day. As soon as Alf came in, I handed it to him.

He read it and grinned. 'She's had a girl! This morning at five minutes past three.' He lifted me up and spun me around, and kept swinging me around, dancing in the kitchen.

I put a smile on my face and kept it there even after he'd set me down. I had to pat my cheeks because they were flushing. 'That's great,' I said.

'It sure is. A girl!' He was still beaming when he scanned the telegram again. 'Yep. That's what it says.' He rapped it with his fingers. 'I can't believe it!'

I was happy for them, I really was, and I was surprised at the tears building behind my eyes. I turned away from Alf and called down the hall, 'Come on, boys. Your dinner's ready.' I didn't hear footsteps, so I walked out into the hall and called again, 'C'mon, boys. Dinner's on the table.'

I stayed in the hall and caught my breath. Each time Nora had a baby, it brought it all back. Reminded me of everything I didn't have. For the past week or so, the heavy void I carried had lightened like a balloon floating away with the wind. It had become so light I'd almost forgotten it was there. When I was with these little boys, I felt whole and solid again. I could almost believe this was where I was meant to be. But the reality always came crashing back, reminding me that this was Nora's family and I was just kidding myself.

I returned to the kitchen and, putting excitement in my voice because I really was happy for them, I said, 'Congratulations.' I reached up and kissed Alf's cheek.

He rubbed my back. 'Thanks, Ide.' His face turned serious. 'I don't know what we'd have done without you.'

Then I remembered and my hands flew to my face. 'Oh, dear,' I said, 'Mum'll be in a tizz. She's been sewing all blue.'

That night I lay under the covers in the still hours and felt a familiar sensation curdling inside of me. I could usually contain it within the walls of my mind but that night, I let it spill. I lay face down on the pillow and let out a long, guttural sound from the depths of my belly. Then I clenched my fists and thumped the pillow, and kept pounding it until my arms lost their strength. When I'd finished, I climbed out, straightened the twisted sheets and smoothed the blankets. I lay back under them, panting in the darkness. The sadness came, then, for everything I wanted but would never have.

At the weekend, Alf and I left the boys with Beryl, Rex's wife, and drove into town to see Nora. Alf looked awkward behind the wheel of the Ford in his suit and hat. I braced myself as we walked down the hospital's circular driveway towards the doors.

As we entered, Alf leant closer. 'I get all tongue-tied around doctors. Can you do the talking?'

I tried not to notice the smell of polished wood and antiseptic and how it fermented my insides. I walked over to the desk and asked for Nora's room. Alf followed me up the stairs and along the first floor corridor until we reached it. The other women in their beds glanced over at us standing in the doorway, but I couldn't see Nora. A pale blue curtain had been drawn around the remaining bed, and pairs of legs were visible below.

Then I heard a scream—Nora's. The legs shifted quickly and gathered at the head of the bed. The curtain swayed and bulged over rounded backsides, then fell straight again.

Nora's voice, 'Get away from me with that . . . Get away . . .'

Alf stood beside me, with his hat in his hands. He was silent, but there was fear in his eyes.

Nora kept screaming and I strained to hear what the voices were saying. My heart thumped each time I heard her shriek and saw the legs glide and the curtain quiver.

'Maybe we should tell them we're here,' I whispered. 'Maybe it would help her if she knew.'

Then it went quiet. The curtain whizzed back and a doctor in a white coat stepped out. He was tall and slender with dark, wavy hair. He turned to one of the nurses. 'I'll write up some more Phenobarbital,' he said in an elegant English accent. 'In case the hysteria continues. But we may need to try ECT.'

He walked straight past us.

'Excuse me, doctor,' I said.

He stopped and turned to Alf. They were the same height.

'Excuse me. I'm Ida Bushell, Nora's sister, and this is her husband, Alf. Alf Hill.'

Alf shifted his hat and extended his hand.

'Dr Ernest Williams,' he said as he shook Alf's hand and nodded at me. 'I'm looking after your wife. Things are not good, I'm afraid. Not good at all.'

Alf stood beside me with rod-like stiffness.

'What's wrong?' I said.

The doctor blinked and kept his eyes on Alf. 'Physically, she's fine and so is the babe. But I suspect she has some postpartum hysteria.' He cleared his throat. 'Does she have a history of this with her other pregnancies?'

Alf stared back at the doctor, unmoving, his eyes fixed and glazed.

I shook my head.

'Of any mental illness?'

I shook my head again.

The doctor nodded. 'I'm sure it will pass. A couple of days, a couple of weeks at the most. It's all right to visit her, but keep your visits short and quiet. We've just given her a tranquilliser, so she'll be a bit drowsy.'

'What is postpartum hysteria?' I said.

The doctor kept his eyes on Alf, as if he had asked the question. 'It's an hysteria that can occur following a birth. Your wife became unsettled yesterday, quite agitated and paranoid. Like I say, we should be able to get on top of it, but if she doesn't settle quickly we may have to send her for shock treatment.'

I gasped. 'That sounds serious.'

The doctor sighed and brought his Gladstone bag to the front. He clutched it with both hands. 'Don't be alarmed,' he said to Alf. 'It isn't as frightening as it sounds and it's very effective. She may not need it. We'll keep an eye on her and, in the meantime, keep your visits quiet and don't traumatise her any further.' He lifted the cuff of his white coat and checked the time on his gold wristwatch. 'I'm sorry, but I have to continue my rounds.' He nodded again and turned to walk off, then stopped. 'By the way, congratulations on your new daughter. And good luck—those redheads are a fiery bunch.' He smiled as he left, the nurses like a trail of gulls behind him.

Nora was lying back against the pillows. She wore a mauve silk bed jacket that Mum had sewn, and it gave her skin a bluish hue, like porcelain. Her hair was dull and hung limply around her face, flattened on one side. Her eyes were half shut, as if paralysed and unable to close properly.

I went to her, placed my hands on the starched cotton sheets and bent to kiss her cheek. Her skin felt soft.

'Hello Nora,' I said. 'It's me. Ida.' I stroked her arm.

Her eyes tried to open. 'I haven't shlept a wink,' she said, chewing each word.

I nodded. 'It's all right, you can sleep now.' I kept my hand on her arm and sat on the chair next to the bed.

Alf stood back, still holding his hat in his hands and running his fingers around the brim. He stepped forward, tentatively, jerkily, as if frightened. His suit coat stretched taut across his shoulders as he bent to kiss her, a bird-like peck on her cheek, before he stepped away from the bed again.

I scanned the room. The lady opposite looked older than me. She was sitting up, lipsticked and knitting something in pale blue as she chatted ninety-to-the-dozen about the importance of routines for a baby. A younger mother next to her listened intently.

Beside me, Alf waited, fidgeting and silent.

I pulled my handbag onto my lap, and from it I took a brown parcel and placed it on the side of the bed. 'These are in white, but I'll get some pink wool in town, now I know I'm knitting for a girl.'

Nora didn't move to pick up the package. The chatting mothers laughed and Nora's head rolled as she tried to raise it. 'Oh, for five minutes peash,' she called.

'Shhh.' I took her hand again. 'It's all right, Nor. It's all right.'

Her legs started agitating under the sheets. 'I can't do it anymore.'

I stroked her hand. 'Shhh. I'm here.'

Her leg still jiggled, so I shifted closer and laid my hand on her knee. 'I'm here, Nora,' I whispered in her ear. 'You'll be all right. Just go to sleep, now. I'm here with you.'

She didn't speak and her lids began to drift over her eyes. The women laughed again and Nora's eyes sprang open.

'It's okay. Shhh . . . Go to sleep now,' I said, and kept stroking her until her eyes closed and her breathing slowed. 'Go to sleep . . . It's all right . . .' I repeated the words as I patted her, until she was asleep. Slowly, I lifted my hands and waited until I was sure she wouldn't wake. She was still. Her eyes were shut and her face, for once, was unfurrowed.

Alf held the card against the window of the nursery and a dark-haired nurse in a crisp uniform found 'Baby Hill' in the back row. She lifted her out and set her in the crook of her arm, then carried her over to us.

I leant in, until my forehead touched the glass.

The baby was all red, her face scrunched up, her mouth wide and shuddering. She was screaming although we couldn't hear her through the window.

The nurse stood on the other side of the glass and smiled and swayed from side to side. She turned away from the window and spoke to another nurse. Their mouths moved like a silent movie. Absentmindedly, the nurse lifted the baby up over her shoulder, patting her back. We could see the baby's face, her mouth opening and closing as she kept wailing.

Alf tapped on the glass, smiling at his daughter. I smiled, too, but her crying was tugging at my heart. I wished I could walk in there and take her in my own arms and comfort her.

The nurse turned to face us, again cradling the baby in her arms. She pointed towards the bassinette, indicating she was taking her back. We nodded, and she carried the baby back to her crib. She tucked her in and left her screaming on her own.

Alf dropped me home and drove off to see a bloke at the lumberyard. I was about to open the gate when Len rode up Pearson Street on his bike. Before he'd come to a stop, I'd already started telling him the story.

'Oh, Len. She's not good . . .'

I filled him in as I followed him up our tussocky driveway and around to the shed. He set his bike against the wall and untucked his trouser leg from his sock, then straightened.

'It's nice to see you too, Ida,' he said in his gravelly voice. He took my shoulders in his hands and kissed me.

'I'm sorry. It's good to see you. It really is. But something's seriously wrong with Nora and . . .'

'I know you're worried,' he said, holding my shoulders firmly. 'But she's got a good doctor caring for her. I'm sure he knows his stuff and he'll look after her. Don't you go making yourself sick, too.'

'Len, I've got a bad feeling. As if she won't get better.'

'You've got to let the doctors do their job,' he said.

'I'll need to stay out there when she gets out of hospital.'

He let go of my shoulders. 'Oh . . . I was hoping you'd be home soon.'

'I can't leave them on their own, not with Nora sick.'

He winced and was silent a moment. 'I'm sick of you worrying about Nora. I want you home with me.'

I stared at him. The heat crept up from my chest and over my face, then I spun around and walked inside. My chest rose and fell with each breath as I filled the kettle at the sink and set it on the stove. The door opened and Len's boots tramped across the lino. He struck a match and I smelt the smoke from his cigarette. I picked up the teapot and ran water into it, then walked past Len without looking at him and took it outside.

I needed to be out at Ben Craeg with them. Nora needed me. The kids needed me. Len could look after himself and he'd just have to wait. I swirled the water around in the pot and poured it on the ground under the apple tree.

When I returned, Len hadn't moved and his eyes followed me across the kitchen. I pulled the tea canister down from the shelf and removed the lid.

'Sometimes I think you'd prefer to live with them instead of me.'

'They need me. I should be where I'm needed.' I spooned leaves into the pot.

He cleared his throat. 'I need you here, too, Ide.'

'Don't say that.' I replaced the lid on the canister.

'What am I meant to say? "Do whatever you want. Don't worry about me?" Because you will anyway, no matter what I say.'

I held the canister in my hands as I turned. 'You have me, Len. All the time. But I can't leave them on their own.'

He didn't say anything for a long while. 'Are you sure you're doing it for them?'

I threw the canister down and it shattered on the floor. Broken pieces of ceramic bounced high and the tea leaves scuttled across the floor like ants. 'Get your own bloody tea.' I strode past him, my footsteps heavy and fast, up the hall and into the bedroom. I yanked the dresser drawer open and wrenched out a cardigan. And another. I rolled them up and tossed them in my basket.

'Ida! Ida!' It was Mum calling out from her room.

I ignored her, opened the wardrobe door and unhooked a dress. As I tossed it on the bed, I heard Mum call my name again. I walked out and stood in the doorway to her room. 'I know what you're going to say.'

'He's right, you know,' she said at the same time I spoke. 'Your place is here.'

'Not you, too.'

'And I'm not just saying it because I want you here. But because I see the longing in your eyes, Ida, every time you're with those kids. I know how hard it is for you. Believe me. I used to feel it every time I saw a woman with her husband. But you have a husband, Ida, and your place is here with him. You've got to ask yourself . . .'

I put my hands up. 'Stop. Don't say any more.'

'. . . who are you *really* doing it for?'

'Mum . . .'

I heard Len clear his throat and when I turned, he was standing in the doorway.

I looked from him to Mum and back again. 'I can't.' I shook my head and my chest was heaving. 'I can't leave them. They need me.'

Len didn't speak.

'And I need them.' Tears smarted in my eyes. 'They're the family I couldn't have.' I started to cry. 'It's not fair, Len.'

His arms slid around my shoulders and his head was against mine as I cried. He patted my back and stroked my hair. I pressed my cheek against his and felt his whiskers and smelt his familiar smell—Drum tobacco and aftershave.

'You are who you are, Ide.'

I raised my head. 'I don't deserve you.'

'Yes, you do.'

Chapter 20

Nora was discharged after ten days. The medications must have worked because her postpartum hysteria settled without the need for shock treatment.

I'd been staying with them for three weeks. The night before Nora and the baby came home, Alf and I sat in the lounge by the fire for the last time. The house was quiet and Alf smoked while I knitted a jumper for Ted, swapping the needles every now and then as I braided a cable.

Alf rolled a cigarette and licked the paper to seal it. 'The kids will miss you when you go, Ide.'

I nodded and tried to keep knitting, but I couldn't see the stitches for the watery film over my eyes.

'We'll all miss you.' He struck a match and the smoke smelt sweet like incense.

My hands slipped as I twisted one band of the cable over the other. I caught the needle and tried again.

'I want to show you something.' He stood and left the room. A minute later, he returned carrying a piece of wood. 'Look at this.'

I set my knitting down on my lap and took it in my hands. The block was about a foot long and an inch and a half wide, a dull red-brown colour, with a dark wavy line like a watermark through it.

'Run your fingers over it,' he said.

It felt smooth, as if it had been powdered.

'Smell it.'

I held it to my nose. I had to inhale deeply because its odour was faint. It smelt like earth and mint mixed together.

'That's blackwood,' he said, as if its name was magical.

'It's beautiful.'

He nodded. 'It's that good they make fiddles out of it.'

He took the block of wood back and sat down in the chair again, turning it over in his hands. He drew back on his smoke so the tip glowed orange, then he exhaled.

'That's what I want to do. Buy a kiln and a planing mill and make furniture. Blackwood furniture. Real fancy furniture.'

'That's a lovely dream, Alf.'

'Then I wouldn't be just a sawmiller. I'd be a furniture maker.' He looked down. 'And Nora might . . . want that.'

'You're good enough as you are, Alf.'

He shook his head. 'No. I'm just a bloke from the bush. I don't have much to offer anyone. Not someone like Nora.'

'Yes, you do.'

His eyes stayed on mine. 'Sometimes I wonder if I married the wrong sister.'

I looked down at my lap, feeling myself blush and grow hot under my clothes.

'Forget I said that,' he said quickly.

I swallowed. 'It's forgotten.'

He was silent and when I glanced up he was running his fingers over the wood again. When he'd finished his smoke, he flicked it into the fire and stood. 'I'll call it a night.' He came over and I smelt the rough, woody scent of his body as he bent and kissed my fore-head. His footsteps up the hall were soft except for a creaking board.

I sat with the silence of the night around me. Along the hall were two boys asleep in their beds and a father lying in his. I let my mind fill with what-ifs, dreams almost real as I sat in that room. Until the clock on the mantel chimed eleven and brought me back to the present. I straightened the chairs, plumped the cushions and made up my bed on the couch.

The next morning I woke to a clear sky and a brisk September air. Alf dressed in his suit and tie, then he drove into Launceston to collect Nora and the baby. While he was gone, I scurried about tidying the place—checking the hospital corners on the beds, mopping under the mats and cleaning three weeks of ashes from the fireplace—while, one by one over the course of the morning, people arrived at the house: Beryl was the first to come with her kids, then Rex, then Bill. They crammed into the kitchen and I boiled the kettle and brewed pots of tea. All the while we listened out for the drone of the car.

Not long before midday, the green Ford rolled up outside, the sun glinting off its bonnet and windscreen. Beryl and her kids bowled out the door and down the steps. Ted and Ben held back, waiting with me by the front door.

'You can go, too,' I said.

They peeked up at me and shifted closer to my legs.

Nora stepped out and held her hand over her eyes to block the sun. Her coat gaped over her still protruding tummy. She saw us but didn't smile or wave. Instead, she swivelled back to Alf, who was carrying the bassinette, and said something to him. Alf removed his hat and held it over the bassinette to shade it.

They came towards the house. Beryl gushed over the baby, but Nora barely seemed to notice. As she came up the steps, I saw the pallor of Nora's face, the hollows under her cheeks and the fatigue in her eyes. She kissed her sons and turned to Alf. 'Quick, get her out of the sun.'

Alf hastened his stride up the stairs and as he drew near, I spied the bundle in the basket he carried. Her eyes were shut and her face was plump and peaceful.

'She's beautiful,' I said in a feathery voice.

Nora had already moved off down the hall, but Alf stood tall and grinned. 'She sure is.'

Rex, Beryl and Bill went home, and the boys and Alf padded down the hall and out the back door. There was just Nora and me left in the lounge room. The baby started to cry.

'I don't get five minutes . . .' said Nora.

I picked her up from the carry basket and she quietened. She felt weightless in my arms and I pulled her close. She was long, like our side of the family. Her eyes were a dark violet, the colour of a bruise. Milk spots dotted the crease in her nose, her eyebrows were fair and her scalp had a faint glow of red, like the eastern horizon just before sunrise.

I handed her over to Nora's outstretched arms and, as soon as I let go, she squeezed her face and her mouth opened. Her wail was heartfelt and plaintive, and I felt that familiar ache in my chest.

'She's a screamer,' said Nora.

'She might be a singer,' I said.

She was sucking on her fist, impatient for her mother's breast. Nora unbuttoned her blouse and held her closer. She latched on to the nipple and began to suckle. Her jaw moved up and down and her tiny hand grasped Nora's taut, pale skin.

I sat beside them on the couch.

'What's her name?'

'Grace. Grace Cecilia.'

'Grace Cecilia Hill,' I repeated. 'Very nice.'

Nora reclined against the couch and closed her eyes again. Her lips parted slightly, as if she was too tired to hold them together. I leant closer and brushed Grace's head with the back of my fingers. It was the softest thing I'd ever felt. I kept stroking her scalp as she suckled and I felt linked to her, too, as if through a phantom umbilical cord. It wasn't just Nora feeding Grace, but I was part of it, too.

'You're very lucky, Nora.'

She didn't open her eyes. 'I feel as if I'm in a living hell.'

That night at dinner, Ben asked me if we could sing afterwards.

'No,' said Nora before I had a chance to respond. 'You'll wake the baby.'

'Don't you want to hear their songs, Nora?' I said.

Nora turned to me, her face long and drawn. 'Can't I come home to some peace and quiet?'

Alf tried to smile. 'There'll be plenty of time for songs later.'

'I wish Mum hadn't come back,' said Ted as I sponged them before bed.

'Your Mum's tired,' I said. 'It's hard with a new baby. And she's been sick. She'll get better soon.'

'Will she?'

I nodded and smiled back.

Throughout the night, the baby's cries drifted in and out. I woke to soft footsteps and low voices outside the window. I climbed out of bed and rubbed my arms in the cold, then pulled back the curtain. Alf and Rex were on their way to the mill. They trudged over the muddy driveway towards the truck, their voices a growling hum. The clouds billowed wet and low in a sky tinged with early light.

I let the curtain drop and wrapped my dressing gown around me. As I stepped into the hall, I heard a cry. A faint cry. I stopped, ears pricked. It came again. Definitely a cry, little and weak, but not coming from Nora and Alf's room. It was from out the back. I tied my dressing gown and hurried down the hall towards the sound. At the back door, the crying grew louder. I opened the door and the cries were louder still. They were coming from the bathroom off the porch. I stepped out into the chill and opened the bathroom door.

She lay in her bassinette next to the copper. I hurried towards her, my breath puffing in the cold, the chilly air stinging my nostrils. She was swaddled as tight as an Eskimo, her face scrunched and red, her mouth open, her breaths serrated.

'Gracie! Gracie! What're you doing out here?'

At the sound of my voice, she stopped crying. Her eyes glistened in the dawn light and she hiccoughed. I picked her up and pulled her to my chest. I had nothing except my little finger, which she took to the back of her mouth. As she sucked, I could feel the roughness of her tongue and the ridges of her palate.

'Come on,' I said. 'Let's get you inside. By the fire.'

I carried her into the kitchen, rocking and bouncing her in my arms as she sucked on my finger. I found the honey and dipped my finger into the jar. She liked that, so I dipped my finger in again.

Holding her in one arm, I gathered kindling and lit the fire. I kept my finger coated in honey as I waited for the kettle to boil, then stirred a spoonful in a cup of hot water. I blew on it until it cooled and fed the sweet liquid to her, her fingers wrapped around mine. She drifted off to sleep. Her skin looked as fragile as porcelain, more delicate than the lacy garments I knitted. Her chest rose and fell, and I could smell her honey breath.

We stayed like that, just the two of us by the warmth of the fire in those soundless moments before dawn. Before the sky woke and the birds began their song. I didn't want the rest of the house to wake and disturb us; I wanted the silence to stay.

Then I heard Nora's bedroom door open and her footsteps shuffle down the hall. She stepped in, pale, with crescents under her eyes and her hair unkempt. She startled when she saw us.

I held Grace close. 'She was in the bathroom.'

'I put her out there so I could sleep.'

'She was hungry. And cold.'

'Ida, she's got to learn night time's for sleeping, not feeding. I can't get up to her every time she whimpers.'

'But she's a baby . . .'

'She'll soon learn, and when she can sleep through the night, she can come back in again.' She lifted the sleeping Grace from my arms.

I frowned at her.

'I know what I'm doing, Ida. I need *my* sleep, too. Remember I have two other kids to look after as well as her.' She left the room.

I sat for a moment by the crackling fire, mulling over what she'd said, trying to understand leaving a baby in a cold bathroom to cry. Then I pushed those thoughts aside and woke Ted for school. With comb lines in his slicked down hair, his shirt-tails hidden and his socks reaching his kneecaps, we set off over the frost-covered ground. I carried his case, and we walked in silence while he read his book. The grass licked his shins and the cold lashed at his face and pinked his cheeks, but he didn't seem to notice.

The bus arrived, and he barely glanced up from his book as he took his school case and climbed up. The bus pulled out, but I stayed, watching the empty road until the sound of the engine had died away and all I could hear were the birds calling and the wind rustling through the trees.

On the way back to the house, the clouds lowered and the sky darkened and the air around me thickened. I began to hurry when I felt the first drops of rain and the wind blowing hard through my dress.

When I returned, Ben was sitting at the kitchen table, a half-eaten bowl of porridge in front of him. The room smelt of boiled oats and warm milk.

'Spare us your fussing today, Ben,' said Nora. 'I've just come home with a new baby and I'm not in the mood.'

Ben glowered at his mother then at the bowl. Outside, the rain began to patter against the tin roof.

'I can feed him,' I said, and sat in the chair next to him.

'No,' said Nora. 'He's got to learn to do it himself.'

I clasped my hands in my lap to stop them from helping. The rain fell harder—tat-tat-tat against the tin—and silver streams stippled the window. The wind had begun to bray. Ben dug the spoon in, then lifted it out and stared at it. He set it on the table and climbed down from his seat. Nora picked him up and plonked him back on the chair, then pushed it hard against the table. 'Sit and eat.'

As soon as she let go, he slid off again. Nora caught him and sat him back down. 'Eat!'

He waited until she'd spun around then pushed the bowl away.

'I can feed him, Nora. Really,' I said, loudly so my voice carried over the thrum of the rain.

Turning back to the table, Nora caught Ben's hand and slapped it. Then she bent down so her face was close to his and there was only a sliver of space between them. 'Eat. Now.' Her teeth were gritted. 'I mean it, Benedict. You're not getting down from there until you've eaten that porridge.'

Sheets of rain swept across the roof as loud as a battle. The fire hissed and spat gobs of heat, trying to keep the warmth in the room.

I watched it happen as if in slow motion. Ben lifted the bowl off the table and, pivoting in his seat, hurled it across the room. It spun as it left his hands. I tried to catch it as it flew past, but it kept spinning towards the cupboard doors, gluggy porridge spewing in its wake. It hit the cupboard and fell to the floorboards upside-down, wobbled a few times and then stilled.

I jumped up and grabbed the cloth from the sink. 'I'll clean it up, Nora.' I could barely see through the window over the sink for the rain hammering the glass. I bent to the floor. The porridge dripped down the wooden door in thick, lethargic lumps. I started scooping it back into the bowl.

Ben sat motionless, staring at the porridge-strewn kitchen as if stunned. I tried to keep my eyes on what I was doing, but I was really watching Nora. She glared at Ben, her eyebrows low, then she clenched her teeth and pounced, catching him under the shoulders.

As she hauled him up and out, his leg wedged between the table and the chair. He shrieked and she slapped him.

I jumped up. 'Nora!'

She yanked him again but his leg was still caught. He cried louder.

'Nora! Careful!'

Nora kept tugging and Ben kept hollering. I held my breath, expecting to hear the crack of bone. The chair rocked back enough for his leg to escape, and Nora clutched him under his belly, pulling him against her. He was bent over her forearm, screaming as his arms and legs flailed. Nora slapped his thigh again.

'Stop!' I was trembling. 'Stop!'

She didn't look at me but kept slapping him. Slap! Slap! Slap! Ben kept screaming.

'Nora . . .'

She kept hitting him, one slap after the other. Slap! Slap! Slap! Sharp against his skin, like gunshots. Again and again. Outside, the rain pounded the roof, clobbering the tin. I stood by the sink, my fingers over my face, barely able to watch, all the time calling out, 'Nora! Stop! Calm down!'

Eventually, she set him down and he collapsed in a puddle on the floor, his tears spilling like rainwater.

She straightened. Her forehead was coated in sweat and strands of her hair stuck thickly to her skin. She was breathing heavily.

My lips and hands trembled, my whole body shook. 'How could you? How *could* you?'

Ben was slumped on the floor, weeping quietly, and I ran to him. 'Don't you dare pick him up,' said Nora. I glared at her and she shook her finger at me. 'He's got to learn.'

I kept glaring at her. 'You're not thinking straight.'

'Don't tell me what's wrong with me. It's him. If he ate his breakfast, I wouldn't have to punish him.'

I swallowed but held her gaze. 'This home has been peaceful for the past three weeks . . .'

She tilted her chin, her finger still raised. 'I can see what's been happening here while I've been gone. They've been allowed to run amok.'

'—with no hitting or crying or screaming . . .'

'I'm warning you, Ida. Don't you *dare* lecture me on how to raise kids.'

'—and no one being hurt.'

'Enough!' She lowered her finger, stood taller and glared at me. Her eyes flashed and her teeth were clenched together. 'You think because you've been here for three weeks that you're their mother now? Well, you're not. This is *my* house and *my* family, and you need to realise that. If you don't like the way I do things, you can leave.'

'You don't have to hit a kid to teach them right from wrong.'

'I'm warning you, Ida. Leave!'

I swallowed and shook my head. 'No, I'm not leaving, but I'm not going to shut up either. They're only little. Grace is just a baby. She doesn't know night from day. And Ben's just a child. Hitting him's not going to make him eat.'

'Get out!' Blotchy islands of red crept up her neck and clammy sweat streaked her forehead.

I shook my head. 'No.'

'Get out!' She loomed closer. Ben still lay on the floor between us.

'Don't act like this, Nor,' I said. Then I lowered my voice and spoke gently. 'You don't really want me to go away.'

She stared at me, her mouth gaping, while she inhaled and exhaled. Then she turned and left the room. Her feet clomped up the hall towards her bedroom and the door clicked shut.

I stood a while, shaking and grimacing. I was angry at her. For what she'd done to Ben and baby Grace. For not caring about her children. For not wanting to be a mother.

I crouched next to Ben and stroked his head. He turned to me, his face spattered with tears and streaked with porridge. I gathered him in my arms and carried him out to the bathroom. He smelt of milk and oats and the salt of his tears. I ran water in the basin, rubbed Velvet soap on a flannel and wiped his face clean, so his cheeks were fresh and pink.

Then I saw the hot finger marks on his legs, weals of burning redness. I brushed my hand over his skin in the hope my fingers might cool them. I held him close and whispered, 'I'm sorry, Ben.'

He turned and his eyes were grey and sad and lost. I set him down on the floor of his room with his toy soldiers. Pulling on my coat, I went outside in the rain and the wind, over to the wash-house. My feet squelched through the mud, and the rain pummelled my skin. I lifted my face to the air and let the water and the wind course over me in the hope it might wash away what had happened. I found a tin bucket, filled it from the tap over the trough, and grabbed the mop and a rag. Back in the kitchen I wiped the cupboard doors and mopped the floor in wide, wet arcs, back and forth, back and forth.

The rain beat down all day before it began to ease towards dusk. As I prepared dinner, I kept an ear out for Alf. As soon as I heard the hum and jangle of the truck, I wiped my hands on my apron and dashed down the hall. When I opened the front door, Rex was reversing out of the driveway, the headlights of the truck bouncing about as the tyres swished through the muddy potholes.

Alf was on the porch, bent over while he untied his bootlaces. He glanced up as I stepped out, pulling the door to behind me. He smiled but must have guessed from my face that I was upset. 'What's up, Ide?'

The truck took off up the road.

'It's not been a good day,' I said.

He nodded and straightened, supporting himself against the wall of the house as he removed his boots. He didn't seem surprised. 'What's happened?'

I told him about Ben. 'There's something wrong with Nora,' I concluded. 'She went right off the deep end.'

He stood in his socks and rubbed his chin while staring at the boards under his feet. His face was streaked with grime. 'I don't know what to do, Ide. I've tried to say things, get her to see a doctor, but it just makes her worse. She gets even angrier. It's always everyone else's fault, or if the kids would behave she wouldn't be like it. So now I say nothing—' he turned to me—'because it does no one any good. I just wait for it to pass. Which it always does, eventually.'

Nora was in the kitchen when we went inside. Alf bent to kiss her cheek, but she rolled her shoulder to block him.

We ate dinner in near-silence and after dinner, when everyone had left the kitchen, Nora sat at the table and breastfed Grace while I cleared up. I beat the soap dispenser under the hot water tap until the water was light and soapy, then I started washing and rinsing the glasses.

'I thought it'd be better here, in a proper house,' she said. She was staring at Grace, the rain a light patter above us. 'But it's not. I thought I'd be happier with running water and electricity.' She rocked back and forth as she spoke. 'I cried when we first moved in and I turned the tap and water ran out. And when I flicked a switch and the light came on. I laughed and kept flicking it, on and off, on and off. Alf laughed, too, because he thought I was happy. But he had no idea. No idea.' She kept rocking, back and forth, back and forth.

I started washing the cutlery, wiping the length of each knife and fork and spoon, and placing each one down softly on the stainless steel so it didn't clatter.

'I thought it'd be enough, too. I thought I could do it. Get married, have children.' Her voice rose and her words came faster. 'Feeding, nappies, bathing. Cooking, washing, dusting, mopping. Bush. Trees. More bush. More trees. Day in, day out and it's never going to end.'

I washed the plates and set them on the sink to drain. Nora was still rocking back and forth. I took the cast-iron pot and started scouring.

'It takes all my might to get up each morning and get through another day,' she continued. 'Married to someone I have nothing in common with. Every day the same. More cooking, more cleaning, more kids.'

The scourer scratched against the pot. Scratch, scratch, scratch.

'I feel as if I'm slowly going mad. It's *exactly* like Grandma said it would be—it's like being buried alive. I'm suffocating. I'm bloody suffocating.'

I set the pot down on the sink.

'I can't keep going,' she said. 'I can't. I just can't.'

The kids' voices drifted down the hall from the lounge. I picked up the frying pan and started scrubbing that.

Nora's eyes were on Grace as she rocked back and forth. 'But there's no way out. I have to keep going. It's too late now. I'm trapped. Too late. I'm trapped.'

I finished scouring while she kept rocking and repeating, 'Too late. I'm trapped. Too late. I'm trapped . . .'

I pulled out the plug and the water gurgled into the pipes. I wiped the sink and hung the teatowel over the edge, then I went to her. I stroked her hair as she sat and rocked. Its blonde colour was fading, but it still felt soft, just like it did when she was a child.

She leant her head against my abdomen. 'I know I'm a bad person, Ida.' Her voice was muffled by my clothes. 'I know I'm not a good mother. I'm not a good woman.'

I held her closer.

'Please don't leave me,' she said.

'No, Nor. I'll never leave you. I'm your sister.'

That night, I made up my bed on the couch in the living room, changed into my nightie and flicked the light off. The coals hissed softly and the mantel clock ticked rhythmically. In the golden light from the fireplace, I could make out the silhouette of the Holy Family on the mantelpiece.

Then I heard her shuffle down the hallway and open the bathroom door. The wicker squeaked as she set the bassinette by the copper and the door closed again. Her footsteps came back up the hall and her bedroom door shut. A soft rumble, a squeak of springs.

I lay there for a while, listening to the rain drip from the roof to the ground outside. Then I sat up and lowered my feet to the floor. I avoided the creaky floorboard beside the couch and crept across the room. I opened the door with barely a click and stole down the hallway to the bathroom.

Grace was swaddled tightly and asleep in the bassinette. She didn't stir as I lifted her and carried her back to the lounge. I laid her next to me under the covers and we slept, waking as the new day was unwrapping itself. The rain and wind had settled. I lifted her, blanket and all, and she smelt of warm urine. I crept back out to the bathroom and placed her in her bassinette.

Each night, I did the same. I couldn't bear the thought of a sleeping baby by a cold copper. I could do little else.

The rest of the week was the same. Nora unhappy, Alf trying to keep the peace, the kids in trouble. But I saw Nora, too, in those unguarded moments, when she stood at the sink gazing out of the window, staring at grass lush with rain, before blinking and plunging her hands back into the suds and continuing with the scouring. I saw her watching Grace as she suckled, a tear welling in her bottom lid and escaping down her cheek and onto the milky skin of her breast.

I knew what she was thinking. I knew her dreams had never been given breath. I saw a woman so caught up in her own hurt that she was hurting everyone around her and she didn't even know.

We were both powerless to change how our lives had turned out, and all I could do was be there to pick up the pieces. I'd always hoped that Nora might one day see her children for the gifts they were, but I was slowly realising that she wouldn't.

It was dawning on me that not all women were built for child-rearing, even if they'd been built for childbearing.

Chapter 21

The time came for me to go home. The night before I was to leave, as I tucked the boys into their beds, Ted said, 'Can you stay, Aunty? Forever?'

Yes, Yes, I wanted to say. *I won't ever leave.* But I had to shake my head.

'Why not?' he said.

'You already have a full house.'

'You can sleep on the couch.'

I smiled, despite myself. 'Besides, I have to look after Grandma. And Uncle Len misses me.'

'We miss you more.'

'I'll miss you more than you'll miss me.' I'd miss his exquisite face, the feel of him on my lap, and his little-boy smell of mud and food and perspiration.

'If you live with us, then you won't have to miss us.'

I sat on the bed and forced myself to smile. 'But then I'd miss Uncle Len. The trouble is that I want to be in two places at once, Teddy. Out here with you and in town with Uncle Len.'

His eyes widened. 'I know! I can come and live with you and Uncle Len!'

Yes, yes! Come! But I shook my head and swallowed. 'Your Dad and Mum would miss you too much.'

His eyes were dark and troubled.

'But while I'm not here, I'll think of you and what you're doing. At school, or reading, or learning to kick a football,' I said. 'And you do it, too. Think of me while you're doing those things and we'll know we're both thinking of each other at the same time.'

'That's not the same as you being here.'

'No. But if you try really hard, it might almost feel real.'

As I left the room, I turned back. His eyes blinked in the dimness, and I knew as well as he did that it wasn't real and we would only be pretending.

Our house looked still and lonely when I climbed down from the truck the next day. The iron lace drooped like a torn petticoat. One of the downpipes at the side had come loose and had fallen outwards like the broken stalk of a flower.

The gate whined as it opened and I walked up the steps onto the verandah. The boards were grey with age and the geraniums in their pots all wiry. I fumbled with the key, opened the door and stepped inside. It smelt of a cold fire and last night's dinner. Everything was still and coolly familiar.

I walked down the hall, past our bedroom door, where the crocheted cover stretched unevenly over the bed. Past Mum's closed bedroom door and past her hats on the hall stand. Past the baby's room and the lounge. Down to the kitchen where unwashed dishes sat on the sink and Len's hat was perched on the kitchen table.

I spotted him through the back window, sitting on a stool by the fence, mending a fishing net strung up on nails. His hands worked in and out, in and out, as they hitched and knotted the twine.

I opened the door and he turned. His face softened when he saw me. He set the needle down beside him and stood. I stepped outside and we moved towards each other—over the grey stones of the path, over the clods of dirt, under the empty clothesline—until his arms were around me and his rough skin was against mine.

'Don't leave me for so long again,' he said, his voice a croak. I looked into his eyes, the same colour as the soil where I'd just been, and shook my head in a silent vow.

I made afternoon tea and took it into Mum. She grabbed my arm and started to cry. 'Oh, Ida, I've missed you.' She looked frailer and older. 'Len just doesn't care for me like you do.'

I kissed the top of her head. 'It's good to be back, Mum.'

She wiped her tears with an embroidered hanky and sniffed. Then she peered into the cup of tea I'd just poured. 'And this cup's a bit weak. Could you make me a stronger one?'

It was more than seven years since I'd given birth to the last of my children, but there were still nights when I couldn't sleep. Sometimes I slipped out of bed and did something useful, like darning or knitting; other nights I crept into the spare room and closed the door so Len didn't hear me. I stood by the bassinette in the dimness and let my tears come, hard and fast like water from a burst river bank. Until I was empty, with no more tears left to cry.

I crept into that room and cried more times than I care to admit, sitting in the rocking chair until the sky was lightening and the rooster was crowing. Then I'd pull myself together and head out to the kitchen to stoke the fire for breakfast.

It was hard seeing Nora pregnant time and again, watching her tummy distend, then looking on as she birthed a living, breathing baby she didn't want. It was like going into Mr Gourlay's sweetshop and watching all the lollies being given to someone who didn't like sweets.

I kept my tears from Len, because I knew he'd say, 'C'mon, Ide. Pull yourself together.'

And I knew I couldn't.

⚬≈⚬

On the last Thursday of each month, Mum and I waited outside on the verandah. Mum would settle herself against a pile of pillows, her embroidery or felt in her lap, while I clicked away on my knitting needles. Every now and then, one of us would glance up the street towards the corner, willing Rex and the lorry to come. As soon as we heard the familiar growl, Mum would sit straighter and I'd dash down the steps towards the gate. I'd be standing on the verge before the truck had even stopped. Nora would open the door to my outstretched hands and I'd take baby Grace, swaddled in soft wool.

This was an exciting time for their family and Nora always had lots of news. Alf and Rex were doing well, buying more leases on plots of forest, or setting up another mill, or appointing a new manager for their business.

All of this impressed Mum. She'd nod and say, 'I'm not surprised. I knew he'd do well in business.'

Then Nora, Grace and I would catch the tram to town. I'd push Grace in the pram around the city, while Nora paid her bills and bought her groceries. If the boys were with us, we visited Mr Gourlay. He always wore his crisp, white apron, and would slide a few extra boiled sweets into the bag for the kids.

The boys grew taller, but their personalities didn't change. Ted was always precise and neat, his socks pulled up to his knees, the buttons of his shirt done up to his neck. Always quiet, always polite. Ben, on the other hand, grew fast and it soon became evident he'd be much taller than Ted. He was all wide, gappy smiles, hair sticking up and socks around his ankles.

Each time before they left, Ted would stand back, drawing on the ground with the toe of his boot while the others clambered into the truck.

'When are you coming to stay? 'Cos dreaming you up doesn't always work.'

I'd pat his shoulder. 'As soon as I can . . .'

Grace grew, too. Soon she was big enough for me to carry on my hip, then her legs were long enough to clamber down from the lorry all by herself. She'd become a little girl, with soft, red curls and pink cheeks and eyes the colour of gum leaves.

'Aunt Ida, Aunt Ida,' she'd call as she tumbled out of the truck, securely buttoned into a woollen coat. I'd gather her up and feel her arms slide around my neck.

'Careful, Grace,' Nora would say, 'Getting your sticky fingers all over Aunty Ida.'

I'd squeeze Grace more tightly to let her know I didn't mind at all.

Grace would chat all the way to town, her tongue rattling as hard as the tram. Her face was eager and alive as she pointed out the river and the hall and the town clock. There was so much for a little girl to see—cars, crowds, colourful shops and, in the windows, all those mannequins that looked like real people. Nora would call, 'Stop dawdling', each time the town clock chimed. In the end, she'd grab Grace by the arm and haul her along behind.

One day as we were passing through the toy section of Cox Bros, Grace was dallying, her feet sticking to the lino as if it was covered in treacle.

'We haven't got time for that,' said Nora, tugging her arm as she tried to wriggle free.

'I'll stay with her,' I said. 'We'll look at the toys and you can shop in peace.'

Nora glanced at her wristwatch and nodded. 'I'll meet you in an hour at the tea rooms.'

Grace and I ambled up and down the aisles, gazing at the shelves of toys—teddies, balls, trucks, cars—until we found the dolls. Shelves of them: baby dolls in their cribs; little girl dolls with pink cheeks; and bride dolls, rising above the others like tall orchids. Their locks shone and their lips were as kissable as rosebuds.

Grace picked one up and stroked her hair, then pressed her nose into its face and inhaled. She held the doll out to me and I lifted it to my nose and sniffed, too. The clean scent of a new doll reminded me of Polly.

Grace laid her down and the doll's eyes closed. 'She's asleep!' she said, squealing. 'Just like real!'

I knew exactly what she meant.

'Oh, Ida!' Nora said over the din of the tea rooms. 'She's three years' old. She's too young for a porcelain doll.'

'There are certain things little girls are meant to have, and a doll is one of them,' I said, and kept eating my egg and lettuce sandwich.

'You and your dolls.' Nora sat down and placed her bulging basket beside her. She leant forward over the table. '*You're* the one who wants it.'

'No. Grace should have a doll. Every little girl needs a doll.'

She raised an eyebrow and shook her head. '*I* didn't.'

Grace named her Penny. From that time on, whenever they came to town, two little faces peered out of the window of the truck: one freckled with dancing, green eyes, the other silky and serene and smooth.

The kids still asked when I'd come out and visit. 'Soon . . .' I kept saying. But I couldn't bring myself to ask Len.

In early 1951, Alf bought a big, old warehouse in Tinsdale, as well as a kiln and a lathe. *Hill's Joinery* he called it. He employed a furniture maker and began sculpting fine blackwood furniture.

Not long after that he purchased a plot of land in the foothills of Ben Craeg, not far from where we'd lived when Dad was alive. On this, he started building a house.

On the day Nora told us, she was wearing a red blouse and dark-grey slacks. She'd put on lipstick and brushed her hair up into a roll. Her hair was darkening as she aged, which only made her look more dignified and imposing than before. She held her head up as she walked through the gate, and there was confidence in her step. She sat on the wicker two-seater with Mum, her face the most lively I'd seen it for many, many years.

'It's brick, red brick,' she said. 'And it'll have a porch at the front and a concrete driveway.'

Mum listened intently. 'Will it be two-storey?'

'No,' said Nora. She glanced aside at Mum.

'But double storey is so majestic,' Mum continued.

'It sounds fabulous,' I cut in. I was sitting on a chair beside them, Grace and her doll on my lap. I smiled at Nora. 'Please keep telling us about your beautiful new home.'

Nora glanced askance at Mum, then continued. 'There's going to be wall-to-wall carpets and built-in wardrobes and venetian blinds. And the laundry will be indoors, too. I can furnish it throughout with whatever I like, Alf said.'

'I can't wait to see it,' I said.

Mum peered at her legs. 'Oh, how I wish I could. If only I wasn't crippled.'

'I'll tell you all about it, Mum,' I said.

Mum looked at Nora again and sighed. 'Let's just pray for a miracle.'

Laughter curled up the steps to the verandah and we lifted our eyes. The day was warm and a couple were strolling past on the other side of the street. They were young—the girl in a light cotton dress that flared from her waist and the boy in loose trousers, his sleeves rolled up. He slid his arms around her shoulders and they stopped to kiss before walking on, their heads still close.

I turned back to Nora, but her eyes were still on the couple, the liveliness gone from her face.

After Nora and Grace had gone, Mum and I took our tea outside. Mum started sewing a flower to a hatband, a couple of pins between her teeth. 'That turned out all right in the end, didn't it?' she said through gritted teeth.

'What do you mean?' I said.

She removed the pins. 'Nora and Alf. It's worked out. I had my doubts, I must say, but at the time we couldn't be choosy. We had to take what we could get. Nora wasn't happy, I can tell you. She told me she wouldn't get married and definitely not to a sawmiller. But I said to her, "I know of no other man would take on another fellow's child. Especially the child of a foreigner. You have no choice."'

I felt fury rising as she spoke and didn't know what to say.

'But look at her now. She could have done a lot worse.'

'Mum, I don't . . .' Then I sighed and waved my hand in the air. 'I'm not even going to bother talking to you.'

'I know what you think, Ida,' said Mum as she pushed the needle through the felt. 'But life's full of sacrifices.'

We were quiet again.

'I do wonder what might have been,' I said.

'You can't wonder about that,' said Mum, as she tugged on the needle, pulling the thread tight. 'You make a decision, the one you consider best at the time and that's that. Ruminating over choices made a long time ago won't change them and will only make you unhappy.' She picked up the hat and studied it, pressing the petals of the flower flat with her hand. 'Nora'll be really happy in her new house. It's all worked out for the best.' She set the hat on the wicker beside her and smiled at me. 'C'mon. It's time to take me inside.'

The next day, I heard shifting and scraping coming from Mum's bedroom. I crept down the hall and stood outside the door for a while, listening to the grunting and groaning coming from within. Gently, I nudged the door open. The bed was empty, so I pushed the door further, and there was Mum, standing by the end of the bed. Yes, standing. Wobbling about like a puppet on a string but upright and holding onto the bed knob.

She turned to me and beamed. 'Miracles do happen after all.'

I was speechless.

That night, Mum showed Len how she could stand up.

'How long have you been able to do that, Mum?' he said.

'Oh, I don't know. A little while. A few months. Maybe a year . . .' she said.

'A year?' I said. 'And you didn't think to tell us?'

'It didn't happen overnight, and I wanted to wait until I could walk well to surprise you. But now, with Nora's new house, I thought I'd better hurry myself along.'

That night as I undressed for bed, I muttered under my breath to Len. 'I've never heard of anyone getting over a paralysis just like that before.'

'Me, neither,' he said. He climbed into the bed and it creaked.

I flicked off the light and padded over in the darkness. The covers rasped as I lifted them and climbed in. 'I wonder if there was anything wrong with her to start with. I reckon she's decided to walk again because she wants to see Nora's new house.'

I felt Len's arm slide under my shoulders. 'Look on the bright side. You won't have to do so much running around for her.'

'No,' I said. It hit me, then, that no one would need me anymore.

Doreen from next door gave me an old walking stick. Each morning as I took in Mum's breakfast, I'd clang the tray on the bedside table and flick up the blind so the sun would stream in on her face. Mum would squint and hold her hand over her eyes.

'Is it morning already?'

'Half the morning's gone,' I'd say, and peel back the covers. 'C'mon, you've got to practise your walking.'

I laced her shoes and helped her to standing. She shook and trembled as she leant on the walking stick and tried to lift her foot.

'Oh, oh, oh. My hip's clicking. I don't think I can do it.'

'Yes you can, Mum. Remember, the quicker we can get you moving, the quicker you can see Nora's new house.'

So she dragged herself up and down the hallway on her stick, and all the while, I said encouraging things like, 'Imagine you're walking over those wall-to-wall carpets, Mum', and 'I wonder what those built-in wardrobes look like'.

One brisk morning, when she'd mastered a few laps of the hall without stopping, I wrapped her in her coat and helped her into her gloves and hat. Together, we walked up Pearson Street to the main road and back. We repeated the distance each day until she got used to it, and then I let her walk up and back on her own.

I watched from the verandah as her hunched figure hobbled up the footpath. She set the stick down, then leant forward until her feet caught up. Her dress hung loosely and nearly reached her ankles. She'd always been small, but she seemed to have shrunk even more over the five years she'd spent in bed. It took her the best part of an hour to walk the couple of hundred yards.

When she came back, she was panting and beads of perspiration dotted her forehead.

'You made it, Mum,' I said.

She heaved a sigh and smiled. 'Now we can visit Nora.'

Chapter 22

They moved into the new house at Ben Craeg in October of 1951. Just before Christmas, Alf came into town to pick us up. He turned up in a new fawn-coloured truck, with *Hill's Joinery* painted on the door. Although he was only my age, thirty-three, his hair was already thinning and greying. He stopped on the footpath when he saw Mum hobble out the door on her stick. Then his eyes crinkled and he bounded up the steps, bending to kiss her powdered cheeks.

'By Jeez, it's good to see you up and about,' he said. 'Nora's bursting to show you the house.'

I helped Mum down the steps and through the gate.

'Watch where you're going!' she said as I led her over the uneven grass on the verge. When we finally reached the truck, Alf gathered her into his arms and lifted her up as if she was a child.

'Be careful! Be careful!' she said, her knuckles blanching on his shoulders as he slid her onto the seat.

'What's that?' I pointed at a rectangular-shaped object covered in a white sheet and tethered to the tray of the truck with ropes.

'It's a surprise,' said Alf, and winked.

I climbed up next to Mum and shut the door.

'Let's be off, then,' said Mum with a smile.

We drove through the Sideling Range and on to Tinsdale, Mum chattering all the way: 'Oh, Mrs Flanagan's closed her shop . . . And they've painted the hall . . . There's Harry Logan's house. I wonder how he's managing. He lost his legs in the War, and I know how hard it is being a cripple.' She was silent for a while. 'I know that for a fact.'

We turned off the main road and drove past patchwork hills. On through the familiar, maternal landscape towards Ben Craeg. I held my breath when I spotted her, still and unmoving on the horizon. The forest climbed halfway up her slopes, then the brown ridges of her rocks rose to the peak. She looked like a kindly mother watching over the valley.

The new house was one of a smattering in a gully in the foothills. Alf bumped over the gutter as he drove into the concrete driveway and creaked on the handbrake.

Mum inspected the house—the orange brick of the walls, the concrete path lined by rose bushes, and the neat lawn sprouting in the front yard. She smiled at Alf. 'You're doing very well for yourself.'

He nodded. 'I'm doing my best.'

Ben and Grace flitted about behind the venetians at the window. They burst through the screen door onto the front porch and tumbled down the steps.

'It's Dad and Aunty Ida,' Ben hollered as he ran, bouncing up and down. He was seven years old and built like a truck, the image of his father.

Grace followed, her four-year-old legs scuttling as fast as they could. Her hair was longer and sprayed about her face, the tips glowing gold in the evening light. Penny, her doll, dangled from her hand.

They launched themselves at me, little missiles of arms and legs, both talking at once and plunging their hands into mine.

'I bowled Ted at cricket,' said Ben. 'Then he quit when it was my turn to bat.'

'I wear pants now,' said Grace. 'No nappies.'

Behind us, Alf helped Mum down from the truck and set her feet on the ground. She wobbled and held the door of the truck. 'Where's my stick? I need my stick.'

'Mum!' The screen door swung open and Nora stood at the top of the steps. She wore dark-navy slacks and a yellow floral blouse. Her hair was short, trimmed so it framed her face, and she'd dyed it dark. She looked like Elizabeth Taylor. She bounded down the steps and over to us. As she kissed me, I smelt her perfume—fresh, like daffodils. We all floated back over the green lawn, as weightless as a cloud. We were laughing and chatting and babbling as we climbed the steps.

'I'm roasting a chicken in the electric frying pan,' said Nora.

'Oh, you young ones,' said Mum. 'You're a lot braver than me when it comes to electricity.'

Ted slouched against the wall of the porch. He was nearly ten but smaller than Ben. He wore long trousers and his shirt was buttoned neatly to his neck. He was reading a book, as if he wasn't interested in us. I let go of Ben and Grace and went to him. He didn't look at me as I squeezed him, and he felt slight and fragile.

The others ran inside through the screen door; it banged against the wall and again as it slammed shut. *Bang-bang. Bang-bang.*

'Oh, look,' came Mum's voice from just inside the door. 'It's a telephone!'

'I've missed you so much,' I said to Ted.

'Isn't it intrusive?' came Mum's voice a bit further away.

Ted kept his eyes on his book. 'Why didn't you come sooner?' His chin was pointed, his nose fine, his skin olive and smooth.

'I couldn't . . .'

'Aunty Ida! Aunty Ida!' Grace called from inside the house.

'Yes, you could've,' he said. He sounded angry.

'I couldn't, Teddy. I'm sorry.'

'You left us out here on our own.'

Footsteps pattered down the hall. Grace appeared at the doorway, Penny in her arms. 'Come on,' she said, pushing the screen door open.

I took Ted's hand. 'Come inside. We can talk later.'

He yanked his hand from my grasp and his caramel curls bounced, thick and wavy.

'You're sleeping in my room, Aunty,' said Grace.

I kept my eyes on Ted. 'Come inside with us.'

He didn't move and his eyes bored into the novel in his hands.

Grace took my hand and pulled me towards her. 'Come and see my room. And Penny's cradle.'

'In a minute, Gracie. Let me talk to Ted.'

'No, now,' she said, and tugged at my hand so I stepped towards the door.

Ted's eyes were still on his book, his lashes lowered so they looked as if they were resting on his cheeks. 'Gracie, just give me a minute with Ted.'

'One minute,' she said. 'That's all.'

The screen door slammed behind her. *Bang-bang.*

'Stop banging that door,' called Nora from down the hall.

'Ted, I'm sorry. I don't know what to say, except that I couldn't leave Uncle Len and Grandma on their own.'

'You love them more than us.'

'It's not that. Not at all. I just can't leave them. They need me to look after them.'

He glanced at me. 'We need you, too.' His face was pained.

I rubbed my chin. 'I wish I could be in two places at once. In town with them and out here with you.'

He screwed up his face and returned to his book.

Grace's face came to the door again. 'It's been one minute.'

Ted was still slumped against the wall with his book.

'I'd better go in,' I said. 'Are you coming?

He stayed where he was.

Grace skipped ahead down the carpeted hall. Just inside the door, a green telephone sat on a low table with a vinyl-covered seat. On the right, was the main bedroom. The door was ajar, and I glimpsed an ornate wooden bedhead and a ribbed, maroon bedspread. On the left was the formal lounge. It, too, had new furniture—a lounge suite of maroon velvet with blackwood arms, and a buffet with sliding glass doors.

We headed down the hall, towards the sounds of sizzling and laughter. The house smelt of new paint and new carpet and roasting chicken.

In the kitchen, golden light streaked through the venetians. It flashed off the stainless steel and striped the wall and laminex.

Nora spread her arms wide. 'What do you think?'

Mum leant on her walking stick and gawked around like a nosy neighbour. 'I like your hall carpet, Nora,' she said. 'I like olive green. But I can't say the same for this wallpaper. All of those yellow and orange semicircles. I feel as if I'm surrounded by sunrises.' She limped through a doorway off the kitchen and into the dining room.

Nora watched Mum disappear through the door, the smile gone from her face, as she finished tying her apron around her waist.

'Nice dining table,' came Mum's voice, then she reappeared in the doorway. 'But those venetian blinds. It would drive me batty peering through stripes all day.'

'Isn't anything I do good enough?' said Nora.

Mum stiffened. 'I'm just giving my opinion.'

'Well, don't. Keep it to yourself.' Nora turned to the frying pan, lifting the lid. The fat spat and sizzled.

'Don't worry, Nor,' I said. 'Mum loves your house, don't you Mum?' I glared at Mum, but she was still looking at Nora, her eyebrows together and her brow furrowed.

'I can't say I like something when I don't,' she said.

Nora turned the chicken roasting in the centre of the pan with the tongs. It sizzled more and she replaced the lid. Then she faced us again and shook her head. 'No, and you never have, so why would you start now?'

Mum's hands fidgeted on the walking stick. 'Well, I do like it. Very much.' She glanced at the walls and window. 'Except for the wallpaper and venetians.' She looked at Nora again. 'And I *am* looking forward to eating chicken cooked in an electric frying pan. That will be interesting.'

'Come and see my room now,' said Grace. She took my hand and led me down the hall to a room at the back, opposite the bathroom. Its floor, too, was carpeted. The walls were covered with wallpaper patterned with lilacs. Lace curtains hung either side of the window, caught at their middles and tied like pigtails. The room had a built-in wardrobe and two blackwood beds, side by side.

'That's yours,' said Grace, pointing at one of the beds. They were both covered with matching lilac bedspreads. 'And this is where Penny sleeps. Dad made it especially.'

In between the two beds was a wooden doll's cradle. Grace set Penny on a pink blanket inside the cradle and rocked it from side to side.

Heavy footsteps thudded down the hall, then Alf appeared in the doorway. He was panting, but his eyes were smiling. He wiped the perspiration off his face with his hanky, then beckoned. 'Come and see what I've bought!'

Grace followed her father down the hall, her footsteps light and fast. When I walked out onto the porch, Mum and Nora were already there. Ted still stood in the shadows. Clouds sponged the sky, the sun was low in the west and the air smelt of the mountain.

Nora, Mum and I waited at the top of the steps, while Ben and Grace bounded down behind their father, nearly tripping over their feet in eagerness.

Still covered in the white sheet, the big, rectangular object that I'd seen on the back of the truck now sat on the concrete path in the front yard of the house. Grassy seedlings sprouted in the lawn beside it. Alf smiled, then bent and lifted the sheet on one side. The object underneath peeked slyly from below the sheet. It was brown and shiny and looked warm in the late afternoon sun. Alf lifted the sheet higher and tugged so it slid off. I felt Nora stiffen beside me.

It was a piano. A tall, walnut-brown piano, which stood lopsided on the uneven turf. It had intricately carved sides and three shiny brass pedals.

Nora didn't move.

Alf let the sheet fall from his fingers onto the path, then returned to the truck. He came back with a round stool with four feet that splayed daintily. He set the stool in front of the piano, then took a key from his pocket and opened the lid. The black and white keys glowed like a mouthful of teeth. *Renardi* it said, in gold gothic lettering.

Alf faced us with a grin that lit his whole face.

'A piano!' I said, clasping my hands together. I turned to Nora. 'He's bought you a piano!'

Nora's profile looked sharp—eyes ahead, chin pointed, lips pinched.

Mum was staring at the piano, too.

Alf beamed at us again. 'Come and see, Nor. Come and play it.'

Nora was trembling now, red blotches forming on her chest and neck.

'Go on, Nora,' I said.

Her lips opened and shut without sound.

Mum stepped forward until she was beside Nora. 'Don't do it if you don't want to.'

'Mum!' I said. 'Alf's bought Nora a piano. To play.'

Mum ignored me. 'Don't play it, Nor. Don't. It'll just remind you. And look at all you have now. A beautiful house. A family. A husband.'

'She can have both, Mum. Music and a family.' I took Nora's arm. 'Come on. You can do it.'

Nora stared at the ground, then up at the piano. Everyone waited, holding their breaths, eyes on Nora.

'Ida, leave her alone,' said Mum. 'Don't make her do something she doesn't want to. Can't we all just go inside and not ruin a perfectly good evening?'

'Be quiet, Mum,' I said. I held Nora's elbow and pressed her forward.

Nora froze. 'I can't do it.'

'Yes, you can.'

She shook her head.

Mum patted her arm. 'Good decision.'

'Come on,' I said. 'I'll come with you.'

She shook her head again.

'Do it, Nora,' I said. 'Find that girl again.'

She hesitated and glanced at Mum, but I kept the pressure on her elbow and her feet shifted forward.

Mum exhaled loudly but said no more. I kept urging Nora on, down the steps and along the concrete path towards the piano. The kids and Alf stepped aside to let us through. I stayed beside her all the way. She reached the stool and stopped, exhaling through pursed lips. She sat and brought her hands together, then raised them so the tips touched her forehead. Her lids were closed and we waited while she prayed. Then she straightened and placed her fingers above the keys.

The bird sounds faded and the wind eased. It was as if the earth hushed, readying for this moment.

She began. Hands close together, they crept up the keys, one soft, slow note after the other. There was no other sound except for hers. The notes joined and became a gentle rhythm. Debussy's 'Clair de Lune'. The tempo quickened and the sound built. I felt a familiar warmth rise inside of me. It was the thrill I always felt when I heard her music. I hadn't heard it for a long time, more than a decade, and it was as welcome as a warm drink on a cold day.

Her hands moved up the keys, rippling in waves right to the top of the piano where the notes sounded like the tinkling of crystal. She paused between each wave, momentarily teasing us, making us wait until she played the next one. Then her hands came back down again, rippling wavelets, corrugations of sound, one after another, falling, falling.

She barely moved as she played, but she didn't need to—the music moved for her.

I stood behind her, watching and listening, barely breathing. My chest and belly tingled and I never wanted it to end.

But it did, and when she'd finished, she sat with her back to us, still except for the gentle rise and fall of her shoulders. The wood of the piano gleamed, the sheet crumpled beside it.

'Oh, it's good to hear you play again,' I said.

Grace ran forward and beamed at her mother's back. 'Play something else.'

Nora didn't move and Grace stepped closer to the gleaming keys. She reached up and touched one. Tink. Then another. Tink. Tink. Then a jangle of notes.

Nora's hands went up and covered her face, then she fell forward until her elbows hit the keys with a clang.

Grace stared at her mother. Slowly, her hand reached up and stroked Nora's back. I laid my hand on Nora's shoulder. She felt bony beneath her shirt. Then Alf was by her side, his arms around her, his big head against hers.

They stayed like that until eventually Nora turned towards us. She wasn't smiling, but she looked alive, as if a veil had been lifted and she was herself again. I could see it in her bright eyes and her reddened cheeks.

'All right,' said Mum. 'That's over with. Let's go in to dinner.' She turned and opened the screen door. It whined and Mum let it bang shut behind her.

Alf kept his arm around Nora's shoulder as she stood. The kids went inside, and Nora and Alf followed.

I stayed outside in the settling dusk. Her playing still moved me, even after all this time. Her music spoke, and it told me everything about her without the need for words. In those notes, I heard the musical child from the concerts in Grandma's lounge. I heard the gifted girl who'd won the Eisteddfod and the joyful girl who'd been swept away by love in Melbourne.

I heard, too, the grieving girl who'd been forced to give it all up. I heard the longing for relinquished dreams. I heard everything she'd gone without all these years.

The blackwood table was set with a lace cloth, ivory-handled cutlery and delicate crockery with an aquamarine fleur-de-lys pattern around the edges. Alf sat in an ornate wooden chair at the head of the table and Mum took the chair at the other end, while we took our seats along the sides. Nora carried the roast chicken in and set it in front of Alf, before sitting down next to him.

'Thank you, Lord,' Alf began, his hands together and his eyes closed. 'For all Your gifts, all of whom are here tonight.'

'And thank you for the piano,' said Grace.

Alf and I laughed. Nora even smiled—her eyes crinkled and looked lucent. Mum kept her face bland and Ted just glowered.

Alf picked up the carving knife, brandishing it like a sword and rasping it over the sharpener. The chicken rose from the plate like a trophy, and he looked confident as he carved it and placed the pieces on an oval platter. As Nora took the platter from Alf, their fingers touched and he smiled at her. Her gaze lingered before she turned away to dish up the roast potatoes and peas, and ladle the gravy over the top. As she passed his plate to him, he said, 'Thank you.'

'No,' she said. 'Thank you.'

Nora served the meat, vegetables and gravy as fluidly as she'd played the piano. The plates passed around the table like batons in a relay. There was a new lightness in the air. Everyone's spirits seemed lifted as we sprinkled pepper and salt from the crystal shakers and began to fill our empty bellies.

'I caught a frog,' said Ben. 'And a lizard. In the ditch. But Mum wouldn't let me bring them inside.'

'Oh, it's good to be back at Ben Craeg,' said Mum. 'I never thought I'd see it again.'

'Can I play the piano, too?' said Grace.

Nora looked at her daughter. Grace's eyebrows were raised, her eyes pleading. 'When you're older,' said Nora.

Beside me, Mum had tensed. 'I think it's best to leave the lid down on that thing,' she said.

'Why?' said Grace.

'To prevent any . . . heartache,' said Mum. 'I remember the trouble it caused last time.'

Nora had stilled. Alf reached for Nora's hand, but she brushed him away.

'Be quiet, Mum,' I said, shaking my head and glaring at her. 'Don't say any more.'

'Let's just enjoy being all together again,' said Alf. He smiled.

Nora was glaring at Mum.

'Yes,' I said. 'Let's just enjoy our meal together.'

Mum picked up her knife and fork and began to eat. 'It's an ill wind,' she muttered under her breath.

Nora glowered at Mum a while longer, her neck and cheeks blotched, and the tips of her ears pink. Then she resumed her meal, too.

After dinner, Mum went to the spare room where Nora had set up her bed. While Nora and I washed up, the boys helped Alf heave the piano up the steps and into the lounge, where they set it against the wall on the other side of the chimney.

Nora stood by the sink beating the soap dispenser under the hot water, while I scraped the leftovers into the bin. 'This was meant to be a nice evening,' she said. The cutlery jangled as she slid it into the soapy mountain in front of her. 'She's visiting for the first time in years and you'd think she'd be happy. But all she can do is pick my house to pieces and bring up old, dead memories.'

'I know,' I said. I returned to the sink, set the plates down beside her and picked up a teatowel.

Nora washed the cutlery individually, clanging each one down on the sink after she'd cleaned it. 'She's never liked me much, even when I was a child.'

'She didn't like either of us much when we were children,' I said. I wiped the knives and forks as Nora set them down.

'I used to try so hard to please her, but I was never good enough.' Nora moved onto the glasses, sponging them and setting them upside-down on the stainless steel. 'I was a good girl. I prayed, said the rosary, went to mass. But it was never enough.' She quickly slid the plates into the water and began scrubbing them, her hands moving faster now.

'She's a hard woman to please. Always has been.' I picked up one of the glasses, wiping inside the glass and popping the glinting soap bubble.

Nora finished washing the plates and set them on the sink with a clang. She lifted the pot and slid it into the water, then took to it with the scourer, scratching at its bottom and rasping around its sides with urgency. 'I was so looking forward to this night and she had to ruin it.'

'She *is* proud of you, Nor. She just has a funny way of showing it. Don't forget, your new house was incentive enough to get her on her feet again.'

Nora stopped, her hands still in the suds. A flush had appeared on her cheeks. 'It'd be nice to hear her say she was proud.' She lifted the pot and sat it on the sink. It gleamed. Soapy suds ran down its sides, along the grooves in the sink and back into the water. 'But I won't hold my breath.'

Before I went to bed, I slipped along to the lounge, just to view the piano again. It appeared warm in the light of the dying embers, a spidery glow flickering on the whorls in the walnut. The brass pedals glinted, unscratched. I placed my fingers on the lid, and it felt cool and smooth. But when I tried to raise it, it was locked.

When I passed the spare room, the door was ajar. Mum was sitting on the bed rubbing Pond's cream into her hands. She beckoned me in and signalled to close the door.

'Of all things to buy her—a piano,' she hissed under her breath. She was frowning and the ruts either side of her chin looked deeper.

'I thought it was the nicest gift he could have given her,' I said.

'What?' She had a look of horror on her face. 'A ghost from the past come back to haunt her?'

'That's a bit melodramatic.'

'You saw what it did to her.'

'And you saw how she was afterwards. It might be just what she needs.'

'Fiddlesticks. No good'll come of it, that's for sure.' She finished with the cream and screwed the lid back on. She gestured for her walking stick and I handed it to her. 'And they'll have to keep an eye on young Grace,' she said as she pushed herself to standing. 'I saw her watching and listening. She's got it, too. That musical streak of your father's and grandmother's.'

I moved to the head of the bed and began folding back the quilt. 'It's not a bad thing to have,' I said.

'Well, you can think yourself lucky you took after me.'

I finished plumping the pillows and straightened. 'Mum, why can't you be nice to Nora? Let her know you're proud of her and her house.'

She limped towards me, suddenly looking little and tired. 'Seeing that piano today frightened me. I haven't forgotten what happened the last time Nora got involved with music. It made her run away from home and then . . . a shotgun wedding.' She sank down onto the bed.

I removed her slippers, lifted her legs onto the mattress and slid them under the covers. 'It wasn't music that did that,' I said.

'No, it was passion.' She looked up at me. 'You're better off without it, then you don't get let down and you don't do anything stupid,' she said as she smoothed the quilt over her. 'You know that and I know that, and Nora needs to learn it as well.'

That night I lay in bed in the darkness. Grace was already asleep in the bed beside me. The moonlight darted in between the edges of the venetians and made scalloped patterns on the walls. I pulled the quilt around my ears and lay awake, watching the jagged lines of light on the walls sway in the draught.

Mum was wrong: I did have passion. I'd just learnt to hide it.

The following day as I was packing to leave, I heard a sniff. Ted was leaning against the doorframe.

I set the clothes I held in my hands on the top of the bed and turned to him. His eyes were so dark, the same colour as his pupils. He was turning eleven, still slightly built, and his skin as smooth and olive as always. 'Are you all right, Ted?'

He shifted his weight on his feet. 'Can I come live with you?'

'Oh, Teddy . . .' I felt the familiar twisting of my heart and stepped towards him. He was the height of my shoulder, but I could still see the baby I'd bathed and fed and held.

'Please?' His mahogany eyes didn't leave mine but grew wider and sadder, more pleading. I wanted to fold my arms around him and say, *Come. Come live with me.* I wanted to pack him in the suitcase with my clothes and scoot out the door. But with a tiny, almost imperceptible movement, I shook my head. 'I can't.'

His brow furrowed and his eyes kept pleading. It took all of my self-control not to turn away so I couldn't see his face and how much I was letting him down.

He kept staring and his lip quivered. 'You don't really care about us.' His voice was sharp.

'Teddy . . . I care so much, more than anything.' I reached for his arm.

He pulled away, still staring at me. His brows lowered so he was frowning, glaring at me. 'That's not true. If you did, you'd let me live with you. You'd look after us.'

'I can't Ted. I'm . . . I'm not your parent.' I stood with my hands by my side, not moving. A bird cawed outside. 'But I do know how unhappy you are.'

He kept glowering at me. His eyes were glistening and his lip trembling, then he turned and walked out. His feet trod hard on the boards up the hall, and the door to his bedroom slammed shut.

I sighed and turned back to my suitcase. I finished packing my clothes inside and closed the lid. It felt heavy in my arms as I hauled it off the bed and carried it down the hall. Outside, Alf was already waiting by the Ford.

As we backed out onto the road, I gazed at the neat red brick, the trimmed lawn and the path lined with rosebushes. Through the window of the front room, behind the venetians, I saw the sad face of the boy I loved but couldn't help.

Part III

They came from the mountain,
and to it they returned,
to sleep.

Chapter 23

Back at home, life was easier with Mum hobbling about. She got herself in and out of bed and down to the table for her meals, although she refused to use the outhouse and didn't help with housework, except occasionally to shell the peas. In the afternoons, she took herself out to the verandah and sat there for a couple of hours making her hats, although there was less of a demand for them by then.

'Tell you one thing I don't miss,' said Len. 'The tinkle of that bell.'

Nora and Grace still came to town each month. Every time Nora stepped off the truck, she seemed to stand taller and look more confident. It was as if she'd been reinflated. She dressed fashionably—in slacks and blouses with precise creases. The patent leather of her shoes was always polished and her handbag always matched. She kept her hair short, cropped around her face. Her face filled out and became less angular, less sharp. Her cheek even felt softer to kiss and she smelt of jasmine.

After the trams stopped running, we caught the bus to town each month. Grace sat on my lap while Nora told me about the new things filling their house—a new wardrobe with a built-in dressing table and a new chenille bedspread with a ruffled flounce—and I heard the pride in her voice.

In town, Nora strutted about the shops, examining the chalky plums and telling Mr Wong they were too soft, or smiling and laughing with the shop assistants when they told her how gorgeous she looked in her new patent leather shoes.

At the end of the day, we always went home laden with parcels and boxes.

～◆◇◆～

Life continued like that for the next few years. It was a relief to me that Nora didn't have any more children. Pregnancy and childbirth seemed to unsettle her, make her anxious and angry. But during those years, I didn't see Nora lose her temper once, although the kids told me they copped the switch on their behinds from time to time.

Over that time, Nora and I talked more than we ever had. We chatted in the kitchen as we prepared the meals or washed up, and late at night, after everyone had gone to bed, we sat in the lounge by the fire, talking until well after the mantel clock struck midnight.

One night, I asked her about the piano. 'Do you play it much?' I said.

She shook her head, then glanced over to where it stood against the wall. It shone like a mirror, reflecting the dancing firelight. 'I can't,' she said. She still dyed her hair dark and the skin of her face looked bleached. Creases crept from the edges of her eyes and she looked tired.

'I'm sure it'd all come back to you,' I said.

She shook her head. 'It's not that.' She picked at some fluff on her slacks, then brushed it away. 'I can't play the piano because it reminds me of the girl I was.' She looked up. 'Whenever I play, I want to go back there and be her again.' She sniffed and went quiet.

'You still are that girl,' I said. A log spat a red-hot ember onto the hearth and I stood and picked up the fireside shovel. 'And you could go back and be her again. It's not too late. You could still play. Even sing again.' I scooped the ember back into the fire and set the shovel back on its holder before taking my seat again.

'Don't be ridiculous,' she said. 'I'm thirty-three years old, and I have a husband and three children.'

'It mightn't be at the same level, but you could sing again. Even locally . . .'

Her eyes flashed with anger. 'I couldn't do that. As if I'd want to sing at the Ben Craeg Memorial Hall when it could have been Covent Garden. Every time I got up on the stage and sang to farmers, I'd be reminded I wasn't in London.' She went quiet again. A log shifted in the fireplace, softly crunching against the coals.

'Do you want to know what I think?' she said. I nodded and she went on. 'I think that when you're a woman, you don't have a choice. There are certain things you're meant to do and that's that. Too bad if you don't like it.' She glanced at me before continuing. 'It seems to suit most women. I'm just the odd one out.'

'I'm sure there are others like you,' I said.

'I haven't met anyone.' She rubbed one hand with the other, then fingered her wedding ring. 'I've tried to want what everyone else wants, but . . .' She shrugged. 'I'm not made that way.'

I rested my chin on my hand and watched the crackling flames and spitting coals. 'Each time you got pregnant, I used to feel so jealous I could barely look at you.' Smoke hissed as it coiled its way up the chimney. 'I tried not to show it, after what happened when we were kids. You know, when I was jealous.' I rubbed my chin before continuing. 'But every time you complained that you were having another baby, I wanted to say, "How can you not want a child? You have everything I ever dreamed of." I couldn't understand how you couldn't want a family.' I turned to her. 'I'm not sure I'll ever really understand. But I'm trying to.'

'I think God got it muddled,' said Nora after a while. 'He meant to put my head on your body, and your head on mine.' She scratched her elbow, then rested it on the arm of the chair again. 'You say you're jealous of me. Well, sometimes I'm jealous of you.'

'What for?' I said.

'Your freedom. You can come and go as you please.'

'I have my restrictions. One of them is in your spare room.'

'You have more freedom than me.' Her eyes flitted around the room. 'It's not just freedom. It's not wanting any of this. Not really. The house, the kids, a husband. None of it. I could get up and walk out of here tomorrow.'

I rubbed the back of my neck and let my hand rest there. 'I reckon you'd miss them,' I said.

'I don't think so,' she replied and shrugged again. 'I don't think I'd look back.' She sat back in the chair. 'I feel as if I've been given a hundred-pound weight to carry around with me. For life.'

I kept rubbing the back of my neck, massaging the muscles that were tightening.

'I know I should feel grateful and not the way I do,' Nora continued. 'But that's the honest truth. That's how I feel.' She looked at me. 'I know what you're thinking. I know I have a family and you don't. I know I have a beautiful home and Alf's a good man, with a good heart.' She shook her head. 'But this isn't what I'd have chosen. If I'd had a choice.'

I nodded, albeit stiffly. 'I know, Nor.'

A rustle out in the hall made me turn. Through the crack between the door and the frame, I glimpsed red curls and two glistening eyes. They disappeared, and soft, quick steps raced down the hall and away.

Later that night when I went to bed, Grace was quiet. She was lying still and facing away from me towards the window. I undressed in the darkness and slithered between the sheets.

'I hear her play sometimes,' Grace whispered.

'Pardon?' I said.

She sat up in the dark, the jagged strip of light from the edge of the venetians striping her face. 'Late at night, when she thinks everyone's asleep, she plays the piano and I hear her. I tiptoe out and sit in the hall by the telephone so I can listen better. She plays really sad music. Then I sneak back into bed before she catches me. Which she did once. And told me off.'

'She used to play all the time when she was a child. And sing.'

She shifted closer towards me and her face was in darkness again. 'I'd love to hear her sing.'

'Oh, she was something else,' I said. 'She was really, really good. I never heard better.'

'Why did she stop?'

'She . . . married your Dad.'

'But why did she have to give it up because she got married?'

'Because that's what you do when you get married,' I said.

'Then I'm never getting married,' she said. The bed creaked as she slipped back between the sheets. We were quiet for a while. 'Why did she marry Dad if she didn't love him?'

I didn't know what to say. 'She does love him,' I said eventually. 'I'm sure of it.'

Grace's sheets rustled again as she rolled over. I lay still, thinking about what Nora had said that night. We were different, Nora and me, and we wanted different things. I had no idea what it was like to desire the things she wanted. But I did know how it felt to long for something and not get it.

Each time I saw the kids, they'd grown and changed. Grace was always the first to greet me, scrambling down the steps as I arrived and whisking me inside. I laughed as I followed her, all long legs and red-gold hair, down the hall to her room. That hair! It looked as if it moved all by itself and had a personality as vibrant as the girl who owned it.

Ben was more like his father, in looks and personality. He never said much and never complained, just did as he was asked. He grew bigger and sturdier, a clone of Alf. He seemed happy enough going to school and spending his weekends playing sport or fishing with Len.

Len sometimes came with us to Ben Craeg. He'd bring his fishing rods, and we'd pack a picnic and Alf would drive us all out to the Ringarooma River. Nora didn't come, but sometimes Mum joined us. Ted and Grace would soon lose interest in the fish—Ted preferring a book and Grace her doll—but Ben and Len would sit all day with their rods in their hands. They sometimes went fishing on their own, just the two of them.

Ted became a teenager. His voice deepened and his face lengthened, but he stayed small and slight and looked as if he'd been hewn from fine-grained wood. He spent most of the time in his room, only coming out for dinner. When he did emerge, he stayed in the shadows and barely uttered a word, but his dark eyes watched everything that was going on and never lost their depth.

Ted was the only one who didn't seem happier during those years. Rather, he seemed to withdraw even more. He never looked directly at me, or at anyone. Sometimes I felt him staring at me, but he'd look away if I turned. It made me wonder, though, if he really did want to be so alone.

A few times, I knocked on his door and tried to start a conversation. But he wouldn't look up from his book or he'd answer with a look that said, *Leave me alone*. I'd ask how he was or how was school, and wait in silence for a few minutes before turning and walking back out again. As much as I wanted to reach him, I didn't know how to break through the intangible wall he'd built around himself. I felt as if I was letting him down.

I used to lie awake at night wondering how much Ted sensed. Alf treated Ted exactly the same way he treated Ben and Grace, and anyone watching on would never have guessed he wasn't Ted's real father. Apart from their looks, of course. But Nora acted differently towards Ted. She wasn't affectionate with any of her kids, and she kept Ted even further away than the others. I tried to remember the last time I'd seen her hold him or even converse with him, and I couldn't. Not since he was a baby, and even then it was only out of necessity.

I wondered if it was because he was a reminder of her first love. If it was too painful and that's why she couldn't let him in. But I would never have asked her and she would never have said.

When we visited Ben Craeg, Mum and I would catch the bus and wait outside the post office in the main street for Alf to pick us up in the fawn truck with *Hill's Joinery* painted on the door.

One day as we were waiting, Mum turned to me. 'Remember when you were little and I'd bring you into town, and Mrs Monteath in the bakery would cut the crusts off the day-old bread for you girls?'

I nodded and smiled. 'And Mr Douglas would give Nora and me a candy cane at Christmas.' I looked out over the old street. I remembered those happy days in this tiny town, back when Dad was alive and everyone was older and bigger than me. When the street seemed wide and bustling. When there were horses and traps and piles of dung in the middle of the road. And, if a car came, we all stopped to watch it pass. When a shop seemed big and bright and full of delicious and enticing treats.

I looked around me at the now-small street and wondered if my memories were real or if they were only in my child's mind. Then I saw that Mum was smiling, too, and knew I hadn't imagined them.

Ted finished school at the end of 1956. He wasn't quite sixteen, but the Commonwealth Bank in Tinsdale employed him as a junior clerk anyway. He cut his hair short, and wore a collar and tie and polished shoes and, suddenly, he looked older.

Alf was beaming as he told us about Ted's job over dinner. 'You'll be bank manager one day, son.' He shook his head. 'I can't believe a son of mine will be working at the Commonwealth Bank of Australia and wearing a suit.'

Mum stared at Alf wide-eyed for a moment before continuing with her meal.

Later that night as I passed the spare room, Mum called me in.

'I wince every time Alf brings up Ted's paternity,' she whispered.

'He *is* Ted's father,' I said. 'That's what it says on the birth certificate.'

'You know what I mean. Why even mention it? As if Ted gets his brains from Alf anyway.'

I rolled my eyes.

'Don't act like that, Ida. I just say what everyone else is thinking and too frightened to mention. Does Ted know Alf's not his real father?'

'Shhh! Keep your voice down,' I said. 'I don't know. And it's none of our business.'

'I wonder if Ted's ever questioned it. I wouldn't be surprised. You've only got to look at him and Alf to suspect *something*. And Ted's a bright boy and doesn't miss a trick.'

'Does it matter who Ted's biological father is? Alf's brought him up as his own.'

'It just makes me uncomfortable whenever Alf mentions it,' she said. 'I'd avoid the topic altogether if I was him and let sleeping dogs lie.'

For a couple of years, the piano stayed locked and we didn't hear Nora play it again. Grace told me she still heard her mother sometimes, at night when she thought no one was listening. Nora kept the piano pristine; there wasn't a fingermark or speck of dust on it. I couldn't help but admire it—the sheen of the walnut and the way the knots in the wood formed whorls on my reflected face. I always felt the urge to open it up and let its music out, free the ghosts hidden inside. But it was always locked.

Grace kept asking Nora when she could start piano lessons, but Nora kept delaying.

'Grace's ten now,' I said to Nora on one of her visits to town without the kids. 'You'd been learning piano for years by her age.'

It was spring 1957, and Nora, Mum and I were sipping tea on the verandah. Pearson Street was quiet, just the distant hum of traffic on the main road.

Mum coughed. 'Yes and look at all the good that did,' she said. I shot Mum a stern look. 'Well, look what it caused,' Mum continued. 'It made Nora run away from home. As a mother, I can't describe the anguish of not knowing where your daughter is.'

Nora was staring at her hands and didn't look up.

'And I haven't forgotten what happened on the mainland, either,' Mum continued.

'Shut up, Mum!' I said.

'No, I will not shut up,' said Mum. 'Those memories are still very much alive. For me, anyway. It's not nice to see that happen to your daughter.'

Beside me, Nora hadn't moved, her head was still down.

Mum started coughing again.

'Are you all right?' I said.

Mum's face was red and her eyes were watering, but she nodded as she took out her hanky.

'No, I think Nora's making the right decision,' Mum went on after a moment. 'I see Nora in Grace and, well, I'd be keeping her away from that piano if I was her.'

I stood. 'C'mon, Nora. Let's go to town and leave Mum to contemplate how to keep her mouth shut.' I turned to Mum. 'And while Mum's at it, she might also want to ponder how to stop dredging up the past.'

Mum looked affronted. Nora and I collected our hats and coats and walked up to the bus stop on the main road. I waited for Nora to mention Mum's outburst, but she didn't. She didn't speak for the whole bus trip but looked out the window, her face pensive in the reflection. She stayed quiet while we did our errands and even during lunch. On the bus on the way back, she turned to me.

'Does Mum think I've forgotten all of that? Does she think I don't regret everything I did? Can't she find it inside her to forgive me? To let me forget? As if I'm not surrounded by enough reminders already.'

'She's getting mouthy in her old age,' I said.

'It's why I keep stalling and not letting Grace take piano lessons. In case she loves it like I did. I don't want her life to turn out like mine. I just keep hoping she'll lose interest and want to grow up and do something normal, like be a nurse or a teacher. And one day get married.'

I didn't answer her. Later, after Nora had left, I said to Mum, 'I think it's about time you forgave Nora.'

'I've tried, Ida. But there's a constant reminder, don't forget.' Her voice went quiet. 'Every time I look at Ted I'm reminded of that day in Mrs Flanagan's store and Nora's petrified voice down that telephone wire.' Mum closed her eyes. 'It was the most heart-stopping moment of my life.'

'Nora knows that, Mum. And I think she's waiting for you to forgive her.'

Mum glanced over at me. 'She doesn't care what I think and she never has.' She started coughing again and brought out her hanky.

'I'll fetch the Senega and Ammonia,' I said. I brought it out and trickled some of the medicine onto a teaspoon. 'I think Nora cares about what you think more than you realise.'

Mum took the teaspoon from my hand, taking care not to spill any. 'We all must do our penance, Ida.'

'Don't you think she's done enough?' I said. 'Isn't it about time you forgave her? Before it's too late?'

Mum didn't look at me, but winced as she swallowed the medicine.

Chapter 24

Mum's cough worsened. The doctor diagnosed her with bronchitis and prescribed penicillin and bed rest. Mum took weeks to improve, and although she still looked pale and wasn't her usual self, she insisted on visiting Ben Craeg.

It was early November and the wildflowers were still out, dotting the roadside all mauve and pink and yellow. When we arrived, I set Mum up on the new couch and draped a knitted rug over her legs. Then Nora wanted to show me some samples of velvet for a new bedroom chair she was having made at the factory.

'I quite like this dusky pink,' she said. 'Goes with the maroon bedspread.'

Drifting across the hall came the glass-like high notes of the piano. Nora and I both looked at each other, then hurried out the door.

In the lounge, Gracie was sitting tall on the piano stool, her red-gold hair tumbling down her back. The piano was open and her fingers were creeping over the keys like spiders, touching each note lightly. The music that came made me think of water droplets from a fountain.

Mum was sitting behind her on the couch, one hand on the arm tapping the rhythm of the music. She turned as we stepped into the room and put a finger to her lips.

Unaware of her new audience, Gracie kept playing. Her two hands were together, then apart, and then she began to sing.

Somewhere over the rainbow

Her voice was as sweet as a chaste kiss and I was taken back to another time and another girl sitting straight-backed at an old piano.

Mum glanced over at us, and although her skin was pasty and wan from her illness, she was smiling and her eyes were bright.

Nora didn't move. Her eyes were intent on her daughter, but her face was soft, her mouth slightly open.

As soon as Grace finished, she spun around to face Mum, beaming proudly. Mum clapped and so did I. Grace startled and looked over. When she saw Nora, she stopped smiling and sprang off the stool, her face flushing.

'I'm sorry,' she said. 'I'm sorry.' She stood with her head down and her arms by her sides.

Nora was shaking her head, her brow furrowed. 'You know you're not allowed to play the piano.'

Grace's cheeks reddened even more.

'Now, Nora, Grace isn't to blame,' said Mum quickly. She coughed and cleared her throat. 'It's my fault. I asked her to play.'

'Who taught you to play?' Nora was still looking at Grace, her head shaking and her mouth still open. She looked stunned.

Grace shifted her weight on her feet but didn't answer.

'Don't be angry with her,' said Mum. 'It was my doing.'

'But, Grace, who taught you to play like that?' said Nora.

Grace fidgeted and lifted her eyes. 'I played when you went out. I knew where you kept the key. Under there.' She pointed to the statue of the Holy Family on the mantelpiece. 'So I used to sneak in—' she looked down—'and play.'

Nora kept looking at Grace as if she couldn't comprehend what Grace had said. 'But someone must have taught you?'

Grace looked up and shook her head. 'No, no one's taught me. I just kept playing until it sounded right.'

'You taught yourself?'

Grace nodded.

Nora rubbed her forehead, the frown still on her face.

'You'd have done the same thing, Nora,' said Mum. 'You'd have done anything in order to sing. You *did* do anything in order to sing. Remember?'

Nora turned to Mum. 'Why are you encouraging her?'

'I know what you're thinking,' said Mum, nodding and smoothing the blanket over her lap. 'I know I've not been a music lover in the past, but I want to correct that. I want to encourage Gracie—' she looked up, her face kind, '—in a way I never encouraged you.'

Nora and I both stared at her. We wanted to believe her, but didn't dare after so many years of hearing the opposite.

Mum coughed and cleared her throat. 'Why don't you sing for us, Nora?'

'Yes,' said Grace and clasped her hands together. 'Please, Mum.'

Nora rubbed her forehead again. She still looked perplexed.

'It would make my day,' said Mum.

Nora shook her head. 'I can't. I couldn't . . .'

'Please, Nor,' said Mum, interrupting her. 'It would mean a lot to me.'

'Go on,' I said and tapped her elbow.

'Just give me a minute,' said Nora. She put her hands together and brought the tips of her fingers to her lips. She closed her eyes for a moment and seemed to pray, then she stepped towards the piano. Grace moved aside to let her pass.

Nora sat on the piano stool and the house fell silent. She laid her hands on the keys and began to play. It was like a caress, her fingers stroking the notes, and the sound was soft, like the brush of a cat's tail against your calf as it passed.

Then she started to sing. Her voice was quiet, soft, dreamy. It gently unfurled and wound its way around the room.

Silvery moon in the velvet sky
Your light shines far in the heavens
Over the world, wandering
Gazing in human dwellings

I recognised the melody: Dvořák's 'Song to the Moon'. Nora's back stayed straight as she sang, her eyes on the music. The song rose higher and her voice rose, too, and became richer and smoother, thick as blood-red velvet. Grace was standing to the side, her face open, her eyes not moving from her mother. Mum leant back on the couch, her eyes closed.

Oh, moon, once in a while, stay with me
Tell me, oh, tell me, where is my lover?
Tell him, please, tell him
I am here, waiting . . .

Nora's voice swelled as she pleaded with the moon to tell her lover she was still waiting. I could hear the longing and the love, and just as it did in childhood, her voice reached inside of me and moved me in a way no other could. I felt the emotion stirring and almost had to turn away.

Moon, oh, oh, shine for him
Shine for him
Shine, shine, oh shine for him.

She sang the climax, her voice reaching high before dropping to the final notes, which were so low and full they seemed to come from the depths of her belly. The sound faded and we remained still and silent. Not a rustle, not a creak. She'd reached all of us, wrapped us all in her beauty. It was a jewel for our memories, never to be forgotten.

It took a while for the spell to break and then we clapped, all three of us, but Grace the most.

'There you go, Grace,' said Mum. 'You have something to aspire to.'

Nora swivelled on the stool and faced Mum. 'What made you change your mind?'

'I've watched you and Grace,' she said. 'I've seen what music does for you, both of you. And I've realised you can't change the way people are made.'

'But that's not what you've said before,' said Nora. 'Why change your mind now?'

'Oh, something Ida said about forgiveness. Before it's too late.' She paused. 'There's a lot that's happened I can't change, but there are a few things I can.'

Nora was still for a long while, her eyes on Mum's. 'Thank you,' she said, her words barely audible.

From then on, the piano stayed unlocked. Grace began piano lessons and her hands were soon chasing each other up and down the keys, giving life to those dots on the page, just like her mother. It was a joy to witness.

Despite the warmer weather, Mum's cough progressed over the summer and she lost weight no matter how high I piled her plate. In May, she took to her bed and she was too weak to even tinkle her bell. If it was sunny, I took her out to the verandah, but she stopped taking an interest in that, too. The doctor started coming every day, but she didn't improve and by June she was sleeping most of the time.

As Mum grew more frail, I took the rocking chair into her room and sat with her during the day. When Nora visited in July, we didn't go to town but spent the day sitting by Mum's bedside as she slept. We didn't talk much, both of us just sitting with Mum, occupied with our memories.

'I remember her before Dad died,' I said, 'when she was happy.'

'I don't remember that,' said Nora.

A bit later on, she said, 'That day she asked me to sing, do you reckon she already knew?'

I nodded. 'She really does love us, Nor, in her own way.'

A few weeks later, Mum stopped eating and I stayed with her all night, giving her sips of water and sponging her. She passed away in her sleep in August, just before dawn, a couple of months after her fifty-eighth birthday.

In the quiet light of the pre-dawn, I washed her hair one last time. I trickled the water over her long tresses, still not completely grey but streaked with brown like the trunk of an ageing gum. I grated Lux flakes and rubbed them into her scalp, then rinsed it all out. As the sun rose and the room filled with light, I wrapped her hair in a towel and rubbed it dry, then brushed it out, still soft after all these years.

I dressed her in a mauve silk dress and laid her out for the undertakers. Then I called Len in and we stood by the bed looking down at her. She was pale and even smaller in death. I kept wanting her chest to move, or her eyes to open and for her to sit up. But she stayed still.

I chose a hat with violet flowers, and when I took it in, Len said, 'She doesn't need to wear a hat to her grave.'

'I want her to take one with her,' I said. I fingered the flowers decorating its brim and the tiny stitches she'd sewn, then I placed it on her breast. Her hand felt heavy and swollen as I lifted it, the blood already pooling and darkening her skin like a bruise, and laid it across the felt brim. 'Her hats were a part of her, a beautiful part of her, and I want one to stay with her always. I want to remember her like that.'

Mum's funeral was in the church at Ben Craeg, the same church in which she'd married, and she was lowered to her final resting place in the cemetery beside our father.

Nora and Alf and the kids started walking back towards the pine trees, but I lingered. I stood by their graves, the two of them side by side again, and it gave me solace to know that Dad was already there and waiting for her, ready to greet her when she arrived. He'd waited a long time to see her again.

Sometimes when I was alone in the house, I sensed her presence, as if she was still in the room. I'd close my eyes and whisper, 'Mum?' Around me, the air would move. I'd wait so I could feel her, hear her voice, smell her hand cream and hairspray. I wasn't frightened—it felt nice; she felt close.

I talked to her in those moments and told her about Nora and the kids, Len and the garden, and the weather and the passers-by. I talked to her until I felt ready to open my eyes and face an empty room. For as soon as I opened them, she was gone.

Once again, I felt the weight of emptiness pressing down on me. The hollow house, the silence, the stillness. After having Mum around for all those years—in her bed, sitting on the verandah, eating at the table, even filling her chamber pot—I didn't appreciate the tranquillity.

Dinner times were quiet, just the sound of our cutlery scraping against the plates.

'Never thought I'd say it, but I miss hearing that bell,' said Len.

I smiled, but I felt like a tiny marble rattling around in a tin without a corner in which to lodge. While Len was at work, I turned on the wireless for company and, after I'd done my jobs, I sat out on the verandah knitting and hoping the gentle succour of the sun and the sky would cheer me up.

I put off cleaning Mum's bedroom. I tried a few times, but it felt as if she was still there, like the room had absorbed her and she was part of it. I waited until a few months had passed, then made a start, slowly, so it didn't hurt as much. I peeled back the bedspread and untucked the sheets. As I slid the pillow from its case, I smelt the Lux flakes from her hair. I held it to my nose and I didn't know if I could wash it because then the last of her scent would be gone.

I took her dresses and coat from her wardrobe, and her shoes, barely worn, and packed them in a box to give away. I wrapped the set of pillowcases and the tablecloth she'd embroidered in tissue paper, and placed them in the memory box on top of my wardrobe. I couldn't give Mum's hats away, so I left them hanging on the hall stand. Every week when I dusted them, I felt as if a part of her was still with us.

When I'd finished, I closed the door on the neat room with the empty bed and wardrobe, and I felt hollow inside.

I'd neglected the garden and it needed tending. The ivy had lost its leaves and resembled a shaggy, untrimmed beard draped over the side of the house, so I cut it back. The weeds were flourishing, and I took to the soil with my hoe and rake and dug them out. I fertilised the earth and planted more bulbs and seedlings.

Being out under the sky and amongst a living garden helped, but the house still felt claustrophobic with memories.

In December, Len and I went out to Ben Craeg for Grace's end-of-year concert. Grace had turned eleven in September, and as we pulled up, she was sitting on the steps with her knees together. She saw us and jumped up and ran down the path. Her hair streamed behind her, the ends of her feathery curls catching the light.

She slipped her hand in mine, her face lively. 'Guess what?' she said as she led me up the path, past the letterbox and rose bushes full of blooms. She looked about to burst.

'I couldn't possibly,' I said.

'I've been chosen to sing tonight.'

'Oh!' I stopped, my hand involuntarily going to my chest.

'What's wrong, Aunty?' she said.

I shook my head. 'Nothing.' I blinked and slipped an arm around her shoulders. 'I reckon your grandmother's had a hand in that.'

Nora greeted us curtly.

'Are you all right?' I said.

'Of course I am,' she snapped. But she seemed quiet and distracted. I asked her three times if she wanted me to prepare the vegetables for dinner, before she sighed and said, 'Oh, for goodness sake, Ida, I don't care.'

I nodded and peeled potatoes and carrots anyway, and then I washed Grace's hair. Grace leant forward over the bath and her copper spirals tumbled down the mint green of the ceramic. I kneaded the shampoo into her scalp and rinsed the suds from her curls with the plastic hose. We sat by the rotary clothesline, under cottontail clouds and in a light breeze, while I dried her hair with a towel. I took each section and rubbed it from top to bottom until all her curls returned, soft and weightless. I brushed it, slowly, gently, the curls stretching and springing back in undulating shades of red and gold and copper.

Over dinner, Nora was sharp in her responses, and when Alf was tardy coming in from fixing the fence, she barked at him because they'd be late.

'What's wrong with you?' I asked her again as we were clearing away the dishes.

'Nothing. There's nothing wrong with me.' But her face twitched.

Grace changed into a frock the colour of emerald with a white Peter Pan collar and a bow at the waist.

'Oh, Gracie,' I said when she walked into the lounge, her skirt swishing and her hair tumbling down. 'You do look lovely.' She looked like a mirage, a moving ripple of green and red and gold.

The men all wore collars and ties, even young Ben. He was four-teen and had changed even in the three months since I'd last seen him. He'd shot up and filled out, all muscle and broadness, and his voice had deepened. A couple of pimples spotted his chin and forehead.

We stood around waiting for Nora. The mantel clock chimed the half hour, then the quarter to, and I went in to hurry her up.

Nora was sitting on the edge of the bed wearing a burgundy dress that was buttoned at her wrists. Her hands were clenched tightly in her lap. Her hat and bag waited on the bed beside her.

'Come on, Nora,' I said. 'We don't want to be late.'

She shook her head and her earrings glinted as they swung. 'I can't.'

'You can't miss Grace's performance.' My voice was sharp.

She twisted her hands together and shook her head. 'I can't go.'

'You can't let Gracie down.'

She shook her head again and her eyes began to fill. 'I just can't do it.'

'Why not?'

She looked gaunt and pale, and her lips were trembling. 'I'm too nervous for her.'

I felt my body soften and sat down next to her on the bed. I reached for her hand and she clasped it.

'What if she forgets the words?' she said. 'Or the tune?'

'It's 'Silent Night'. Everybody knows the words to that.'

Her brow creased and she kept shaking her head as her fingers squeezed mine. 'I'm so nervous. I've never been more nervous. Not even when I performed on stage myself.'

'Gracie will be fine.' I patted her arm and stood. 'Come on. Let's go.'

'I can't.' She shook her head. 'I can't go and watch her do what I did.'

I bent so our eyes were level. 'Nor, Grace isn't you. It doesn't have to end the same way.'

She held her hand against her chest for a moment until her breathing slowed. Then she gathered her hat and bag and looked up at me. She nodded, her face still pinched.

'I'll be right there beside you,' I said.

Chapter 25

Grace stood alone in the centre of the stage, the choir behind her in the dimness. The hall quietened and, hands by her sides, she gazed out over the heads of the audience towards the back of the hall, her face open and her eyes clear. Her dress gleamed and the white of her patent leather shoes shone below her hem. The fluorescent light overhead caught the tips of her hair and they shone copper and gold.

The piano played the slow opening chords. Next to me, Len straightened and looked ahead, and I felt his arm press against mine. On the other side of me, Nora was gazing down, her hands clenched in her lap.

Silent night, Holy night.

It was a bud of a voice, soft and filled with innocence. As soon as she began, everyone sat forward; all eyes were on her.

All is calm, all is bright.

Her voice grew stronger and clearer, a pure sound. I let it pass over me, soft as a breeze and, oh, so soothing.

Round yon virgin, mother and child.

My memory stirred, for I was hearing another young girl. I could see her fingers flitting over the piano keys and hear her voice reaching out and wrapping itself around all who were listening.

Holy infant so tender and mild.

The two girls mingled, and the girl on the stage became the girl in my memory. I turned to that other girl sitting beside me. Her head was bowed and her hands were clasped so her knuckles were white. Her mouth was forming the words as Grace sang, and together they inhaled before Grace sang the final line.

Sleep in heavenly peace. Sleep in heavenly peace.

Her voice trailed off and the rest of the class joined in.

Silent night, Holy night
Shepherds quake, at the sight.

Some were looking up, others down. Some wriggled and some scratched their heads. But their mouths opened as one, and their voices came in unison.

Glories stream from heaven above,
Heavenly hosts sing Alleluja.

The hall seemed to lighten as their innocent voices rose.

Christ the Saviour is born! Christ the Saviour is born!

No one moved until the sound had faded. Then slowly, one by one, we began to clap. The front row stood and applauded, then the second, and down through the rows all the way to the back, until everyone was standing and clapping.

On the stage, Grace smiled and bowed. The nun who'd been conducting beamed and motioned to Grace to keep bowing.

Len and I were on our feet and cheering, our grins broad. Grace kept bowing, and I doubt if the old hall had ever heard so much clapping. The applause went on and on. Nora stayed seated, her head down and her hands clasped against her forehead. She was the only person in the hall not standing.

Eventually the applause settled and we sat back down.

Len inclined towards me. 'That went well, I thought.'

I leant closer to Nora and whispered into her ear. 'It wasn't just Grace up there. You were there, too.' She didn't look up.

Afterwards, we headed out into the warm night air. The clouds were grey in the black sky, like spumes of smoke, and a crescent moon shone just above the dark shadow of Ben Craeg. Outside the hall, we jostled our way through the crowd of people offering their congratulations and commenting on Grace's beautiful voice.

Alf stayed by Nora's side, acknowledging everyone who greeted them. Nora didn't smile or stop to talk. She kept her head down and pushed her way through the throng in silence.

'Oh, you must be very proud,' came an Irish voice. It was the small nun who'd conducted the choir.

Alf stopped, but Nora kept walking, a statuesque figure striding over the lawn towards the car, the burgundy dress swishing about her calves.

'Grace did very well,' the nun said, smiling. Then she turned to Grace and her face became serious. 'I hope you do something with your gift. God has given it to you for a reason.'

Grace freed her face from her father's side and looked at the nun. 'Thank you, Sister.'

Nora was silent in the car on the way home and when we arrived, she swept inside without a word. The rest of us filed into the kitchen, and I filled the electric jug and switched it on. The others sat around the table in the dining room, while I cut fruit cake and made a pot of tea.

'How did it feel?' Alf asked Grace. 'Standing up there in front of everyone?'

'Good,' she said.

'You weren't nervous?' he said.

'I loved being up there. I wanted to stay there and sing all night.'

'No one would get me up on a stage singing in front of people,' said Len.

'No one would want you up there,' I said as I carried the teapot and cups into the dining room. I left them on the table and went to find Nora.

The front door was ajar. Nora was outside on the porch, her elbows resting on the brick balustrade. She'd kicked off her shoes and they were toppled on the ground beside her.

I opened the screen door and she glanced up. We stood side by side. I could just make out the fence on the other side of the road and the dark shape of a cow. The wind rustled through the grass and the only other noises were the crickets and the occasional groans of the cattle.

'Grace was exquisite tonight,' I said. 'Mum would have enjoyed it.'

Nora nodded. She unclipped her earrings and they jangled in her hands.

'I'm sorry I didn't go to your concert,' I said. 'When we were kids.'

Nora sniffed. 'That's long forgotten, Ida.'

'I've felt bad about it ever since,' I said. 'But seeing Gracie tonight, well, now I feel like I was there . . . in a way.'

We fell silent, then she said, 'I saw myself up there tonight, too. Young and innocent and full of dreams.' She spoke slowly, pausing between the words. 'Sometimes, I wish I could undo it all. Go back and not make the mistakes I did. I wonder what I might be doing . . .' She looked out towards the paddock.

'You were young,' I said. 'And in love.'

'And stupid.' Every now and then the shard of light from the doorway caught a bauble on the earrings in her hand, and they glinted.

'You can't torture yourself forever about what you did when you were a girl,' I said.

'I'm not torturing myself. It's just always there.' She wiped under her nose with the back of her hand. When she turned to me, her eyes were sadder than I'd ever seen them. 'Every day I live the consequences of that decision. And the shame. Getting pregnant and having a child to a man who's not your husband is like having your shame written in big letters across your forehead. The whole world can see. Anyone who looks at Ted and then looks at Alf can see it. Every time I look at him, I see his real father, and I'm reminded—'

We were interrupted by the whine of the screen door. When we turned, Ted was standing in the open doorway.

'What the hell are you talking about?' His voice came loud and echoing. He was trembling and his face was ashen.

Nora dropped the earrings. They rattled as they hit the cement.

'Ted . . .' I tried to move towards him, but my legs were shaking and the ground was tilting.

'What are you talking about?' he repeated, staring at Nora. He was standing on the doorstep, holding the screen door open with one hand.

Nora was frozen, her hands to her cheeks.

Ted stepped out, letting the door bang shut behind him. 'Tell me what you were talking about?' His face was snarling, his voice sharp and loud.

Nora shook her head and swallowed.

He stepped closer to her, the air whistling through his nostrils. Nora kept shaking her head, her eyes unblinking.

Ted kept moving closer, until he stood right in front of her, glaring up at her, his hands clenched at his sides. 'Who is my father?' He spat the words, droplets of saliva spraying in the air.

Nora shook her head again.

Ted raised his finger so it was close to her face. It was trembling. 'Tell me,' he said through gritted teeth. 'Who is my father?' He said each word slowly and clearly.

'I'm your father.' It was Alf. He pushed the screen door open and stepped out onto the porch. Ted whirled around to face him. Alf inhaled and stood tall. He kept his voice even and straight. 'I'm your father,' he repeated.

Ted snarled. 'Stop lying.'

Grace appeared at the screen door, Ben behind her. Their eyes were wide and frightened. I could see Len down the hall, scratching at his temple.

We all waited for Ted to move or speak. He looked from Nora to Alf, his breathing still audible.

'Stop lying, both of you, and tell me who my father is.' Ted's shoulders were heaving.

Nora shook her head again. Her face and neck were blotched and mottled.

'As far as I'm concerned, it's me,' said Alf. He swallowed and his mouth trembled. 'You're my son.'

Tears welled in Ted's eyes and he looked about to crumple. He inhaled and pulled himself taller again. 'I'm sick of asking for someone to tell me the fucking truth. Can someone tell me who my fucking father is?'

We waited, holding our breaths.

'His name was Marco.' Nora's voice was low and deep and sounded as if it was coming from far away. She kept herself composed, as if she was talking about an acquaintance she barely knew. 'Marco,' she repeated in an Italian accent.

Ted was still and not breathing. He looked as if he'd been hit and was about to fall. Alf stepped closer, his arms out, but Ted pushed him away. 'Don't come near me,' he hissed.

Alf stayed where he was.

Ted stood in the middle of the porch. His breathing grew even heavier, and ugly sounds rose from his throat, gurgling noises as if he was about to choke.

I went towards him. 'Ted . . . Ted . . .'

Alf tried to reach him, too, but Ted pushed him away, punching and kicking.

Grace screamed and flung open the door. 'Stop! Stop!' She ran to Ted.

'Go away!' Ted screamed, flailing out at Alf and Grace and me. 'All of you. Go away!' He shoved us out of the way, trying to reach the door.

Grace kept reaching for Ted, crying, 'Stop! Stop!'

Ted jostled past Alf and Grace. He reached the screen door, pulled it open and ran down the hallway towards his room.

We stood on the porch in a daze. None of us knew what to do. Alf stood by the door, his hand in his hair. Nora was by the balustrade, rocking to and fro, her arms wrapped around her waist. Ben and Grace stood by the doorway, tears in their eyes, their faces ghostly pale.

Then Alf took off after Ted. I followed. Ted was in his room shoving clothes into a duffel bag.

'Ted . . .' said Alf from the doorway.

He didn't look up but grabbed a shirt and shoved it into the bag.

'The fact you're not my biological son has never meant anything to me,' said Alf.

Ted finished packing the bag and pulled the drawstring closed. He shrugged on a coat and swung the bag over his shoulder.

'I don't care who made you,' Alf continued. 'As far as I'm concerned, you *are* my son and always have been.'

Ted wiped his face with the back of his hand and sniffed before looking up at Alf. His eyes were dark and heavy and his face was pale. 'Don't you think it might have been important to me to know who my father is?'

Alf's face puckered. 'Doesn't being your father for the past seventeen years count for anything?' His voice was hoarse, pleading.

Keeping his eyes downcast, Ted walked to the doorway. He paused for a moment, then said, 'Let me through.' His voice was a growl.

Slowly, Alf stepped aside, his shoulders drooping.

Ted's face was small and scared as he walked past us. He strode up the dim hall, opened the front door and stepped outside. I followed him with hurried steps. Len's anguished face looked up as I passed the lounge. Ben, Grace and Nora were still waiting on the front porch. We watched Ted stride down the steps and up the path. When he reached the gate, Nora gasped and ran inside.

'Ted!' called Grace. She hitched up her frock and bolted down the steps. The crickets were still chirping as she ran after him. She flung her bare arms around his waist as he crossed the road, struggling to keep up with his long strides. They reached the other side and the green of her skirt dragged through the long grass. Ted kept walking, bag over his shoulder, Grace stumbling alongside, still clutching him with her arms.

When they were a hundred yards or so down the street, they looked up as they heard a distant hum. It grew louder, and Ted turned and waited. Grace's arms still clasped his middle. The car's headlights flashed into view and blanched their faces, and Ted stuck out his thumb. He shielded his eyes and when the car pulled in, he bent and spoke to the driver through the passenger window. Then he opened the door and threw his duffel bag onto the seat. Before he climbed in, he looked back at the house. We were all still watching. I stepped forward, but he climbed into the car. Grace stood alone in the long grass as it pulled out, her face in her hands and her skin as pearly as the moon. The red tail lights disappeared around the bend and the smoke from the exhaust faded into the night.

He was gone.

Then the noise began. Like a siren squeezing through a pinhole. Soft at first, then rising in volume and pitch until it burst, like water from a dam, into an open wail.

I went to her and sat beside her on the bed. She was curled up, still in her burgundy dress, wailing with wet grief. Alf came in, his face desolate. He crouched beside Nora and his big hands lifted her shoulders and held her close as her cries rose and fell, rose and fell.

I left. Grace was in her room, sitting on the edge of her bed, her eyes rimmed red, her curls soft around her face. 'It's not true, is it?' she said.

'Yes, it is true.'

'How do you know?'

I sat on the bed beside her and took her hand. 'It's true, Gracie.'

'Ted's still my brother, isn't he?'

'Yes, he's still your brother,' I said. 'It doesn't matter who your dad is, or who your mum is for that matter, we're all still family.'

That night I lay in Len's arms in the spare room and wept. I wept for the boy who'd left, the boy who'd just lost a father. I wept for the father who'd just lost a son. And I wept for the mother, too.

All night the house felt restless and filled with the sighs of the sleepless. Occasionally, I heard Nora's cries, like a cat mewling into the night. Outside, the wind gusted and the house creaked, and every now and then a window rattled as if agitated, too. Somewhere in the distance a bird cawed and kept cawing, again and again, punctuating the lonely night.

Len eventually drifted off, but I couldn't sleep. I felt as sombre as if there'd been a death. If there was one night I wanted to unravel and start all over again, it was that one. I wanted to pull Nora's words out of the air, take the conversation back, so Ted would never overhear us and the joy of the night could continue.

Yet, I knew it was inevitable that the truth would come out, as truths do.

Just before dawn, I rose and walked into the lounge. The mantel clock ticked, regular and soft as always, and I walked over to the statue of the Holy Family beside it.

Mary held the child Jesus in her arms. Her lids were hooded as she gazed lovingly upon her son. Beside her stood Joseph, also admiring the child. The child who wasn't his.

I stepped closer and blessed myself, and for the first time in many years, I prayed.

I prayed to Mary to look after the young man who, this morning, was alone. My eyes didn't stray from hers as I mouthed the words, '*Ave Maria, Gratia plena . . .*'

I prayed to her as a mother who knew what it was like to lose a son. '*. . . Nunc et in hora mortis nostrae. Amen.*'

'Keep him safe,' I whispered. 'He is my child, too.'

Chapter 26

The next morning, I cooked breakfast. The sizzling eggs and bacon made the house smell busy and cheerful, but my eyes felt puffy, and my chest and limbs felt boggy and sore.

Len looked weary as he ate his scrambled eggs. Alf emerged, dressed and shaven, but with a stoop to his gait. His shoulders sloped and, between mouthfuls, he paused and rubbed his forehead. When he'd finished eating, he carried his plate over to the sink.

'I'll go searching for him,' he said.

'I'll come with you,' said Len.

I could think of nothing else but Ted as I made the beds, especially when I passed his empty room. The bedspread was unrumpled and his books were stacked neatly on the bedside table.

Later in the morning when Nora didn't appear, I made a vegetable broth and took it to her along with some buttered bread. I stood outside her door for a minute and braced myself before I knocked. She didn't answer, so I twisted the door handle. The venetians were closed and the room smelt stuffy. She was lying on her side in the dimness, facing away from me.

'Nora . . .'

She stayed as she was.

'I have some lunch.' I crept in with the tray. 'It's soup.'

'I don't want anything,' she said.

'You need to eat,' I said.

'Leave me alone.'

'What if I just put the tray by your bed?' I said.

'No. Take it out.' She didn't turn. 'Just leave.'

I retreated. I busied myself in the kitchen, scouring the stainless steel of the sink and sorting the cutlery drawer. Then I sat at the dining table and drummed my fingers against the wood as I gazed out of the window at the driveway and the paddocks beyond. The clock chimed one o'clock, then two o'clock, and, finally, I heard the car.

Len appeared at the doorway to the dining room.

'You didn't find him?' I said, standing.

He shook his head. I heated up more broth for Len, then went to find Alf. He was down by the back fence chopping wood, stripped to his singlet, a cigarette dangling from his lips. He was working quickly, picking up a log, steadying it on the stump and bringing the axe down with a loud crack. The wheelbarrow behind him was half-filled with a jumbled pile of split wood.

When he saw me, he let the axe head drop to the ground and pulled the cigarette from his mouth.

'I'll run you in to catch the bus soon,' he said.

I nodded. 'I've made some lunch.'

'Thanks.'

'Len said you didn't find him.'

He shook his head. 'I'll go into the bank tomorrow when it opens.' He drew back on his cigarette and the tip glowed orange, then he exhaled a thin stream of smoke through pursed lips. 'I don't know what else to do. I keep telling myself he's seventeen, he's old enough to look after himself and he'll be all right.'

I brushed my hair from my eyes. 'Let me know as soon as you hear anything.'

Alf took his hanky from his trouser pocket and wiped the sweat from his forehead. His hair stuck to his brow, and he looked drawn and tired. He puffed on his smoke again. 'He's my son, Ida. I've never thought of him as anything else.'

'I know.'

'From the minute I laid eyes on him, that day on your verandah. I know he's not, well, he's not mine by birth and he looks nothing like me, but that doesn't count for anything as far as I'm concerned.' He finished his smoke and stubbed it out with the toe of his boot. He kept his eyes on the ground for a while, then sighed and looked up. 'We were just getting on our feet. Nora was, well, she was the best I'd seen her since . . . I don't know when. Since those days dancing at the hall. Everything was falling into place, and I thought things were looking up. I thought . . .' He shook his head and shrugged his shoulders. 'I thought we might be happy.'

I rubbed my forehead. 'I'm sorry if this embarrasses you . . .' I paused, and when he looked up, I went on. 'But there aren't many men who'd do what you've done. Bring up another man's child as his own. I just wanted to say that.'

He kept his eyes on mine and they reddened. He turned away and took a few steps towards the fence, pulled his hanky from his pocket and blew into it. When he faced me again he was trying to smile. 'You're a good woman, Ida.' He looked big and sad.

'And you're a good man, Alf.'

'I'll unload this wood and then I'll come in,' he said. He swung the axe so it stuck fast in the chopping block, then picked up the handles of the wheelbarrow and wheeled it into the woodshed.

Later that afternoon, we packed our suitcase and Len carried it out to the car. I went into Nora. She hadn't moved, and the room was even dimmer now the sun was lower in the sky. I stood at the foot of the bed and rested my hands on the polished bed knob.

'Len and I are heading home now,' I said.

Her hair scratched against the pillow as she nodded.

'If he's not at the bank here, I'll go around all the banks in town looking for him.'

More scratching.

'I don't know what else to say . . .'

She pushed herself up to sitting and the bed springs squeaked. She looked wretched. Her hair was sticking up except where it was flattened on one side. Her face was swollen and her eyes red-rimmed, the whites shining in the dimness. 'I wish I could wind back the clock and take the words back,' she said. 'I'm berating myself for being so careless, for not seeing Ted there . . . '

'For what it's worth,' I said. 'I think you did the right thing by telling him when he asked. We've just got to hope he'll . . . get used to the idea.'

She lay back down on the pillow and covered her eyes with her arm. 'I just want him back.'

My heart lurched. 'I don't think he knows that, Nor.'

'I didn't know it myself,' she said.

We were silent for a while. 'I've got to go now,' I said. I kissed her and left.

Len held my coat and I slid into it, then I pulled on my gloves and hat, and said a reluctant goodbye to Ben and Grace.

'Will Ted come back?' Ben asked.

'I don't know,' I said.

His face pinched and his eyes filled. He was growing taller and broader and turning into a man, yet he was still a boy.

'You'll see him again,' I said. 'We all will. I'm sure of it.'

Outside, the day was waning. The sun was low on the horizon, a hollow circle of light that brought no warmth. Suddenly, I felt heavy and tired. I dragged my feet down the steps, up the path and over to the car. I didn't want to glance back at the house as Alf drove out—at the red brick and grey cement, and the trimmed lawn and pert roses. It looked lonely and terribly sad.

Alf dropped us off in Ben Craeg and we boarded the bus. I rested my forehead against the window as the bus rattled into town and watched the edge of the road whiz by underneath like a pottery wheel. By the time we reached Pearson Street, the sky was dark and the streetlights were coming on. Len carried our suitcase up the steps. He fiddled with the key before unlocking the door.

I felt like a ginger-beer bottle all shaken up and needing to be uncorked, and I could barely contain the noises threatening to gurgle out of me. As soon as the door was open, I ran inside, straight to our darkened bedroom. I shut the door behind me and leant against it. I let myself cry, hard sobs that made me shudder.

There was a tap on the door. 'You all right, Ide,' Len said.

'Just give me five minutes,' I managed to say.

I pushed my sobs down again and wiped the tears from my cheeks. When my breathing had slowed, I went out to the kitchen.

Len was down by the back fence, surrounded by a yellow circle of light from the kerosene lamp. He sat on a stool, a wooden needle wound with twine in his hand, mending a hole in a fishing net. He shuttled the needle in and out, in and out, looping, checking, hitching, looping, checking, hitching across the breadth of the hole.

As I watched him, I imagined our three boys. They'd have been dark like him but taller. They'd be grown up now and working— one for Stan, maybe, the plumber next door; another for Max, the butcher; and the youngest, Leonard, he would have been sitting by the fence with his father, helping him mend the nets. I had a feeling those two would have been close.

I opened the back door and went over to Len, squatting down next to him. He set the shuttle down and slid his arm around my shoulders. With his other hand, he stroked my chin.

'We'll find him, Ide,' he said. The lamplight glowed yellow and made his face look warm.

'I hope so.' I rested my arm on his thigh and I could feel the warmth of his body through his trousers. 'I still miss our boys.'

'Me, too,' he said.

The following week, I kept myself busy dusting, sweeping, mopping and washing. I pottered in the garden, mulching the soil, trimming the apple tree and striking cuttings from the geraniums. I ran errands and cooked dinner, and Len and I ate while the town clock chimed six o'clock. After dinner, Len would sit out by the back fence, mending nets in the lamplight, or he'd stay at the kitchen table making fishing flies. Meanwhile, I'd sit in the lounge knitting a cable jumper with leather buttons for a boy I might never see again. In the distance, the town clock chimed the passing hours.

No matter how much I tried to keep busy, not for a minute did my thoughts leave Ted. I wondered where he was and if he was safe. My mind would flit back to that night and the conversation with Nora. I replayed it over and over, wishing it hadn't happened, that he hadn't overheard. But I knew, too, that he deserved the truth. Ted's paternity had always been there, following him like a wave on the verge of breaking. It didn't matter that the words had never been said; they'd hung in the heavy air around him, always.

On the Thursday when I went to town, I walked past all three Commonwealth Banks in the hope of spotting him. I peered through the windows and doors, then turned and wandered past again in case I'd missed him. I didn't find him.

The following week, I went to town to pay the electricity bill and do my own banking. I headed towards the stone building of the Launceston Bank for Savings, and as I put my hand on the chrome handle of the door, I glimpsed him through the glass. My heart started pounding as I pushed on the door—it was heavy, so I had to push hard until it opened. It *was* him. He stood behind one of the glass partitions, all business-like as he served a customer.

The door closed behind me with a soft 'whoomp' and muffled the sounds of the cars and pedestrians outside. Inside, the bank smelt of polished wood and brass. I kept my eyes on him as I walked over to the counter against the far wall, and my chest felt fluttery. I picked up a form and filled it out, glancing back at him every now and then.

He wore glasses with thick, dark frames, and his hair was cropped and neat. He wet his fingers on a sponge beside him on the counter, then flicked each note in the pile and secured them with a rubber band. When he'd finished, he stamped a book and slid it across the counter to a young lady with dark hair and eyes. His lips smiled, but his eyes looked sadder than ever.

When it was my turn, I stepped forward and smiled at him through the gap in the glass. 'Hello.' My throat felt dry and I had to clear it before I spoke again. 'Look at you . . .' That was all I could say because my face crumpled at how good it was to see him again.

He came over a couple of nights later. When I kissed his cheek, I noticed it had hollowed, and that his trousers were baggier than when he'd left home. He was smiling, but his eyes had grown even more sombre.

Len was outside mowing the lawn, the blades whirring and grinding as he pushed the mower. I called out to him, 'Quick, Len, Ted's here!' He hurried in, the bottom of his old trousers flecked with green. He clasped Ted's hand and shook it hard, as if Ted was the most important person in the world.

'Good to see you, mate,' he said. 'Good to see you.'

I piled Ted's plate high with mince stew and asked where he was staying.

'At a hostel in town.'

When I offered more stew, he declined, and when I said we had bread and butter pudding, he shook his head. 'I'm sorry, Aunty, but I can't fit any more in.'

'I'm trying to fatten you up. You're looking peaky.'

Len frowned at me, so I returned to eating my dinner. The sounds of scraping cutlery and chewing continued for a minute or so.

'What's it like,' I asked, 'the place you're staying?'

Ted shrugged. 'It's a bed.'

'There's always a bed here if you want,' I said.

He shook his head. 'I'm all right.'

'Well, you know it's here.'

'Thanks.' He nodded.

There was another silence.

'Can I tell your parents where you are?' I said.

Ted shook his head. 'No.'

'Can I at least let them know you're safe?'

'Ida,' said Len, frowning. 'He said no.'

'They're worried, Len. I just want to tell them he's all right,' I said.

'Ted's given his answer and you've got to respect it.'

'It's all right,' said Ted. 'You can tell them I'm safe.'

We were quiet again.

After we'd eaten, I made a pot of tea. Len stayed at the table reading the newspaper, while Ted and I took our cups and saucers into the lounge. I set them on the spindly mahogany table that used to be Grandma's and flicked on the lamp. Then I pulled a chair into the circle of light and motioned for him to sit.

I moved the other chair closer and sat, too.

'How're you faring?' I asked.

He shrugged again. 'I'm all right.' He sipped from his cup, then rubbed his forehead. 'How are Gracie and Ben?'

I shook my head. 'I don't know. But they weren't good. No one was.'

Ted's brow wrinkled and he bit his lip. He seemed fidgety and rubbed his forehead again. 'Can you tell me about him?'

'About who?'

He kept rubbing his eyebrow. 'My father. My birth father.'

'I . . .' I squeezed my eyes shut before opening them again. 'It's not my place.'

He stopped fidgeting. 'I need to know.' His voice was steely and his eyes drilled into mine. Those dark eyes. 'I deserve to know.'

'I know you do.'

'Please . . . '

I inhaled. 'Your mother was happy in those days. Really happy. She was doing what she'd always wanted to do, which was singing.' I heard my voice change, become lighter. It was nice to tell this memory from when our lives still stretched ahead of us, full of hope. 'It'd been a battle for your mum to sing,' I continued. 'Mum didn't want her to, thought it was a waste of time, but Grandma encouraged her and secretly paid for her singing lessons. Then she won the Melba Scholarship to the Conservatorium in Melbourne, had a part in an opera . . .'

He sat unmoving and his eyes didn't waver from mine.

'And she fell in love.'

'With Marco?'

'Yes.'

'What was he like?'

'I don't know. I never met him.' I paused. 'He was Italian, from the north of Italy, the same town as Verdi. That's all I know.'

'So why didn't they marry?'

I could see how much he was hurting, but I knew he deserved the truth. 'He was already married.'

He was quiet for a while. 'It all makes sense now. Why I felt different. Why I always felt like an outsider.' He sniffed. 'Because I am.'

'No, you aren't. Not to me. Not to your Dad. Not to anyone.'

'To her I am. I ruined her life.' His eyes narrowed. 'There were times I saw her looking at me, just staring. And I could see the hatred in her eyes. I used to stare back at her, trying to work out what I'd done wrong.'

'I know you mightn't understand, but it wasn't hatred. It was love. You reminded her of love, of everything she'd loved. And lost.'

He looked down again.

'She's realised how much you mean to her—' I went on.

'Don't . . .' he cut in, glancing up again. 'Don't. I don't want to know. I don't want to see her again. Ever. Or . . . him. They both lied to me.'

We were quiet for a long time after that. I heard Len's footsteps in the kitchen, and the back door open and shut. 'Len and I tried for a family,' I said. 'A long time ago. Before you were born. But we lost our boys. Stillbirths. Three of them.'

Ted looked up, surprised. 'I never knew,' he said.

'No. It's not the type of thing you're allowed to talk about, no matter how much you might want to.' I paused before going on. 'When I lost my babies, I didn't think I could keep living anymore.' I spoke slowly because these memories were harder to put into words. 'Each morning, I could barely drag myself out of bed. I didn't want to get dressed. Didn't want to eat. Didn't want to do anything.' I looked at him. 'When you were born, I didn't want to see you because I thought you'd remind me of the babies I couldn't have. But when your Dad was sent to Darwin, you came to live here, and I started waking up each morning and thinking, "Oh, Teddy'll be awake soon so I'd better get up." I started jumping out of bed and going in to where you slept, watching you and waiting for you to wake, so I could pick you up. Then I'd bathe you and sit with you on my lap until you fell asleep. I started looking forward to the days again. You got me going again.' I paused as I swallowed. 'You were the reason I kept going, Ted.'

His hands were over his eyes and they were man's hands, with ropey veins and taut tendons. His fingers pressed against his lids and his shoulders began to shake.

I went to him and pulled him against me so his head burrowed into my belly. He felt like a child. I held him and rubbed his cropped hair and his bony, muscular shoulders. His arms slid around me, and I felt them tighten as he pressed into me. I found his hand, and even with its man's shape and size, it felt smooth and gentle, and just as it did when he was a soft, pudgy child.

I leant down close to him so my mouth was against his ear and I could taste the salt of his tears.

'You're very special to me,' I whispered. 'And don't you ever forget it. If ever, ever you need to hear someone say that, come and find me and I'll tell you just how special you are. And I'll keep telling you as many times as you need to hear it.'

We stayed like that for a long time.

'I did nothing wrong,' he said when we separated. 'Except be born.'

'You did nothing wrong, full stop,' I said.

Chapter 27

I wrote to Nora and Alf and told them Ted was in town and had a job, and that he was safe. That's all I said because he didn't want me to say any more.

After that first visit, Ted started coming for dinner every Monday. I looked forward to his company—it was the one night of the week when our house wasn't silent, when Len and I didn't sit on our own as the distant chimes of the town clock counted down the night. Mondays were a bright spot in our week, even though seeing Ted reminded me of Alf, Nora and the kids.

Sometimes, I broached the subject of seeing his parents again. 'I bet your father's missing you.'

'Aunty . . . Don't,' Ted would say, and keep eating his meal.

Len would glare at me and after Ted had gone, give me a talking to. 'He's just found out everyone's been lying to him for all of his life,' he'd say. 'And that he's not who he thought he was. Give him time, Ide. Give him time.'

When I went to town to do my banking, I saw Ted then, too. I felt proud when I entered that old stone building with its wood and brass and smell of prestige. As I waited in the queue to be served, I watched him counting the money, stamping the bank books and signing the forms. Each time I saw him, he seemed more adept and confident, more professional. He even looked taller.

Nora didn't come into town that first month, but I didn't think too much of it because she'd missed visits before. She missed the second and the third months, too, and then one Friday when I answered the door, Alf was standing on the verandah.

'I wasn't expecting to see you,' I said.

His hand was running back and forth along the brim of his hat and he looked stooped and worn. He was freshly shaven, but his cheek felt dry when I kissed him.

'Is everything all right?' I said.

He cleared his throat. 'Not really,' he said. He dropped his hat and bent to pick it up. When he straightened, I waited for him to say more, but he didn't.

'Come in,' I said, and stepped aside.

He didn't move.

'Come in,' I repeated, and waved my hand. 'I'll make us a pot.'

He followed me out to the kitchen. I opened the back door and called out to Len, who was down by the back fence mending a fishing net.

Len and Alf shook hands. They were the opposite of each other in appearance—Len was short and wiry with eyes as dark as raisins, and Alf was tall but wilting, and with eyes as grey as rain clouds. The only feature they shared was the steel colour their hair was turning.

I popped the kettle on the stove and stoked the fire underneath. The men sat at the table and lit their smokes without speaking. Alf usually shrank a room when he entered it but, that day, he seemed barely noticeable. Finally, the kettle bubbled, and I made a pot of tea and took it to the table.

As I poured, Alf fidgeted with his hat, which now sat on his lap. 'Nora's not good,' he said, glancing at me. 'She's, umm, having a hard time of it since Ted left.'

I sipped from my cup.

'She spends a lot of time in her room with the curtains drawn.'

Len's forehead creased.

'Some days she cries and cries until she makes herself sick. Retching sick. And Grace has to stay home from school to look after her. And other times, well, there's no telling what she'll do.'

I glanced at him. 'What do you mean?'

He sighed. 'Angry. Flying off the handle.' He rubbed his chin and shifted in his seat as if his trousers were too tight. 'You know what she gets like.'

I felt goose bumps crawl over my skin and my tea tasted bitter.

'I was wondering . . .' Alf said. He glanced down as if to compose himself, then looked up. 'I was hoping Ted might . . . come out and see her. He doesn't have to move home again, just . . . come and see her. I thought it might perk her up.'

I glanced at Len, but he was looking down. 'I'll ask Ted,' I said.

'We can't make him, though,' said Len, looking up.

Alf nodded. 'Thanks.' He straightened his hat on his lap. 'How is he?'

'He's good,' I said. 'Doing well at the bank.'

Alf nodded.

'It flipped his world upside-down,' I said.

Alf nodded again. 'Tell him I said hello.'

'I will,' I said.

'And that I miss him.'

I nodded.

'I'll get out of your hair then.' He stood.

I followed him down the hall. His shoulders were sagging, and his coat no longer pulled tightly across his shoulders.

At the door, I said, 'Come and visit next time you're in town.'

Alf nodded. He didn't smile and his eyes held mine for a moment. 'Thanks.' He put his hat on and lumbered down the steps and over to the Ford, his stride shallower and slower than before. He looked like a broken man.

I felt too sad to wave as he left.

'No,' said Ted. He didn't hesitate. His face was stern, as solid as concrete. 'I've got a job here and I like it. I'm not leaving.' He squeezed a wedge of lemon over his fish. Len had been fishing at the weekend, so we were eating salmon I'd fried in a pan.

'You don't have to live there again, just visit,' I said.

Ted shook his head. 'No.' He picked up his knife and fork.

'Your father would like to see you, too.'

He cut in. 'He's not my father.'

'And Gracie,' I added.

He stilled at that. 'How is she? Gracie, I mean.'

'She misses you.'

Ted's face strained and he shook his head. 'I can't go out there again. Not ever.' He stared at his plate, then set his knife and fork down. 'They lied to me. Both of them. They should have told me. They let me think I was someone I wasn't.' He was breathing heavily. 'And now I don't know who I am.' I reached for his arm, but he shook me off and picked up his knife and fork again. 'I don't want to see either of them.' He separated some flesh from the bones of the fish. Then he looked up. 'Why's she making a fuss now? She never acted like she cared before.'

'She's realised how much you mean to her.'

'No.' He picked up a piece of the fish with his fork, then shook his head again. 'No,' he said, still shaking his head as he took a mouthful.

'It's too soon, Ide,' said Len later that night. He shook his trousers straight and draped them over the chair by the bed.

I slid under the bed covers. Len flicked the light switch and his shadowy shape came silently towards the bed. The springs squeaked and I felt his warmth beside me. In the distance, the town clock chimed eleven times.

We were both silent for a while.

'I should have realised something was wrong. Nora hasn't come to town for months,' I said.

'You weren't to know,' he said.

'I've got an uneasy feeling. As if something bad's going to happen.' I propped myself up on my elbow. I could just make out his shape in the darkness. 'I should go out to Ben Craeg.'

He sighed. 'If you must.'

'You don't sound very happy about it.'

'It's just that it's not the same here without you. The place feels crooked when you're not here.' I felt his hand on my arm. 'But you've been lying here every night, tossing and turning and snorting like a bull. So, go to them, Ide, because I know you're worried.'

I lay back down and fitted myself alongside him, letting my hand rest on his chest. 'I don't like leaving you, either.' I found the gap at the top of his pyjamas and touched the bony prominence of his collarbone. 'I don't know where I'd be without you, Len. You might be a little bloke, but you've got the strength of a mountain.'

The following Saturday, I went out to Ben Craeg. Alf picked me up at the bus station and dropped me off at their house, but he had to nip out again.

'I've got a meeting with the mayor today. We're furnishing the boardroom at the council chambers,' he said, before driving off.

It was late on a Saturday morning in April. The sun was nearly at its zenith, and the sky was cloudless except for a thin layer of clouds streaking the horizon. The grass in the front yard had grown long and shaggy and was dotted with weeds. The leaves were turning and the concrete of the driveway was littered with debris. Weary roses, their petals faded and curling, hung limply from the bushes lining the path, barely clinging to the branches. There were no faces at the windows, no one rushing down the steps to greet me.

The front door was unlocked and I let myself in. 'Hello?' I called.

The house was dim and silent and smelt of old ashes. Although the weather was mild, the air felt chilled. Nora's and Alf's bedroom door was ajar and the bed was unmade, the chenille bedspread in a lump on the floor. In the lounge, a scrunched up sock poked furtively from under a chair, the cushions on the velvet couch were awry and a mountain of ashes had gathered in the fireplace. The piano still stood against the far wall, looking serene but lonely.

The whole house felt eerily still and cold, and as I walked down the hall, it chilled even more. It seemed to seep from the walls and the floors, eking from the very bones of the home. I left my suitcase in the spare room, then poked my head into the kitchen. It was deserted, too. The venetians were crooked and a jumble of dirty pots and plates were piled in the sink. An empty milk bottle sat on the bench beside a stained teatowel.

I headed out towards Grace's bedroom. Her door was ajar and I pushed it open. Nora and Grace were inside.

'Here you are!' I said, and smiled.

They turned towards me and I saw the tension. Their faces were unmoving, their muscles rigid. They were standing at the foot of Grace's bed, Grace with her back to the window. She'd grown taller and even more like her mother. Her eyes were wide and frightened, and her hands were behind her head, pulling her hair back off her face. It fanned out from her fingers in fine red-gold curls. Nora looked severe and stern. Her grey roots were growing out so a peppery line framed her forehead. She looked older than her thirty-nine years.

Nora faced Grace again. 'Come here,' she said. She held her hand up, and the silver blades of a pair of scissors flashed in the light. 'I need to cut your hair.'

Grace shook her head and lifted her chin. 'No.' She stared defiantly at her mother.

'What's going on?' I said, but neither of them seemed to hear.

Still holding her hair behind her head, Grace backed away from Nora towards the window. Her copper curls looked wispy and fine in the light.

'Come here,' said Nora again. She raised her hand, the black handles thick around her fingers and the metal blades glinting.

The back of my neck prickled and my heart throbbed in my ears. 'Can someone tell me what's going on?'

Nora didn't look at me but lifted her hand higher, the scissors rising with it. Grace retreated further until she stood in front of the window. Nora advanced towards her, holding the scissors high. Grace leant back and the venetian blinds bent and crinkled behind her.

'Nora, what are you doing?' I said, stepping into the room.

Without answering, Nora leapt forward until she loomed over Grace, who inclined even further back until the blinds were flattened against the window, scraping against the glass. Nora reached out and grabbed Grace's hair. Grace screamed as Nora yanked her head and jerked it towards her. Quick as a flash, Nora whipped the scissors across and cut through a chunk of hair. Grind-snip. The blades sounded crisp and metallic as they ground through her tresses.

Grace screamed.

'Nora!' I raced towards Grace, my hands outstretched.

Grace started to cry and grabbed at the back of her head, screaming again when she felt the blunt ends of her hair. She pulled the remaining locks to the front and shrieked at the sight of the sparse auburn waves in her hands.

I reached Grace and slid my arm around her. 'What have you done?' I yelled at Nora. 'What have you done?' My voice was a screech.

Grace's shoulders were heaving and tears coursed down her cheeks. I held her tight, feeling the back of her head and the blunt ends of her hair. 'Why?' I said. 'Why?' I was shaking and I could feel the heat rising inside of me.

Nora was holding the long skein of Grace's hair in her hand, the scissors in the other. She was trembling and the hair shook, the copper-gold spirals rippling in the light. A few wisps escaped and fluttered to the floor. Nora was staring at her hands, unblinking. She opened one hand and the scissors fell, landing on the carpet with a dull thud. Then she uncurled the fingers of her other hand and the hair floated to the floor, long ringlets scattering over the carpet and forming wavy copper lines over the olive-green.

'I *hate* you,' said Grace through gritted teeth. 'I *hate* you.'

Nora said nothing. She was still holding her hands out, palms open, shaking violently.

'Why?' I repeated, glaring at Nora.

Nora didn't answer but kept staring vacantly at her empty hands.

'You've cut off my hair,' Grace cried. 'My *hair*.' She was howling.

I glared at Nora. 'For the life of me, I can't understand why you'd do this.'

Nora was still staring at her open palms, her face blank, her eyes distant. Her shoulders slumped forward and she began to rock on her feet. Back and forth, back and forth. She clasped her hands together and clutched them to her chest, her eyes downcast. She twisted her fingers around each other and rubbed them together so her skin rasped. She kept rocking and rubbing, all the time staring down at the floor.

She'd lost weight since I'd last seen her, so her bones were almost visible through the cream of her blouse and the navy of her slacks. Her skin was pasty and sallow. She was still rocking and rubbing, and she looked pathetic and forlorn.

I watched Nora for a minute or so, then Grace's cries lulled and she raised her head, too.

'Nora?' I said. I let Grace go and stepped towards her.

Nora's mouth was gaping and she was still staring at the floor, rocking back and forth, her fingers writhing and rubbing. She no longer seemed aware of us or of her surroundings, as if she wasn't inside her skin anymore. Her chin quivered and, slowly, she turned. In small, shallow steps, she left the room, her shoulders lowering with each step.

When she'd gone, Grace began to cry again. 'I hate her. I hate her.'

I waited with Gracie until she'd settled, and then she told me what happened: Nora had found a note in the pocket of Grace's school uniform. It was a letter from a farming boy, saying that he liked her hair because it was the same colour as their cows and shone in the sun. Nora had raced into Grace's room and ripped the note up in front of her. She said she needed to protect Grace, that Grace shouldn't be drawing attention to herself like that, that it would only get her into trouble. When Nora left, Grace heard her rummage about in the cutlery drawer before she returned with the scissors, sleeves rolled up and perspiration on her brow, and said she needed to cut Grace's hair off.

'And now I'm ugly,' Grace sobbed.

I bent so I was level with her face and ran my hand over the jagged ends of her hair at the back. 'No, you're not. You're still beautiful, Gracie. Nothing will ever take that away.'

'But it was my *hair*. She cut my hair.'

'I can fix it,' I said. 'Make it so you'll be just as beautiful.'

She shook her head. 'You won't be able to.'

I picked up the brush and ran the bristles through the blunt, frizzing strands, and the remaining russet spirals. I held the long auburn locks in one hand and the scissors in the other, and I cut. Grind-snip. They were gone. The long locks drooped from my hand like used festive decorations.

'Hold them, please,' I said to Grace and draped the wavy skeins across her palm. She stared at them, sobbing quietly while I trimmed the rest of her hair all the way around.

Out in the hall, a cupboard door opened, then slow footsteps faded away.

When I'd finished cutting Grace's hair, it sat just below her ears. It was blunt and cropped but neat and even. I ran my fingers over it and smoothed it down. Grace turned and she looked fragile and elf-like, her eyes bright with tears. Her hair framed her face and it unveiled her, making her look even more beautiful than before.

'No one can take your beauty away, Gracie,' I said.

She lowered her lids and shook her head.

I took the copper curls from her hand, then stooped to pick up the ringlets littering the carpet at my feet. One by one I gathered them and draped each tress over my palm. When I'd collected all I could, I went into the lounge and extracted an old newspaper from the wood box. I spread one sheet of the newspaper out and laid the strands along the crease, then I folded the paper around them and slipped the package into my bag. I stood for a minute or two, slowing my breathing and swallowing the bitter taste at the back of my throat. Then I went to find Nora.

The cupboard at the end of the hall was open and I shut its doors as I passed. Nora wasn't in her bedroom or the kitchen. I couldn't find her in any of the rooms of the house. 'Nora!' I called as I searched the bathroom, then Ben's room. I opened the door to Ted's room, but it was untouched since I'd last been in there. My footsteps quickened as I darted through the house again, opening doors to rooms I'd already searched. 'Nora! Nora!'

Grace crept from her room, her face still puffy and red. She didn't know where her mother had gone, and Ben was out playing footy with friends, she said, so he wouldn't be back for a couple of hours. I checked the front yard and the road. The cows in the paddock opposite raised their heads but the street was otherwise deserted.

The backyard was also empty. I walked its length, past the empty rotary clothesline, over the uneven ground and through the long grass. I checked inside the woodshed. It was big, with a pitched roof and rafters, and it smelt of woodchips. The firewood was stacked along one wall, and Alf's lawn mower, a couple of spades and a hoe on the other. A coil of thick hemp rope hung from a nail on the wall. I closed the door and made my way to the back fence by the incinerator. I leant against the wooden railings, gazing towards the forest and Ben Craeg. All was still.

Alf returned about an hour later and I told him what had happened. 'She's probably just gone to visit a friend,' he said, but he looked worried and kept glancing at his wristwatch. His face sobered when he saw Grace, her hair blunt and cropped, and her eyes puffy and red. He pulled her close and combed his fingers through her hair. 'It'll grow back,' he said, and kissed the top of her head.

Ben came home not long after that and ran to see if the neighbours—the O'Reilly's on one side and Myrtle Fisher on the other—had seen Nora. But no one had seen her, not for weeks. Alf drove along to Rex and Beryl's, but they hadn't heard from her either.

Rex and Beryl returned to the house with Alf, and I made a pot of tea. We sat around the dining table, restless and agitated and wondering what to do. Beryl checked Nora's wardrobe to see if she'd taken any of her clothes, and Alf looked in the hall cupboard to see if any of the suitcases were missing.

Alf returned and stood in the doorway, rubbing his hands against his sides. His face was white, his eyes on mine. He cleared his throat. 'My rifle's missing.'

My stomach dropped. 'No!'

'I keep it in the hall cupboard,' he said. 'And it's not there. I haven't touched it for months.'

I started shaking. 'No, no, no . . . She wouldn't . . .'

'We'll find her, Ida,' said Beryl. She took my hand and her arm went around my shoulder. 'Don't fret. We'll find her. I know we will.' She kept patting my hand and squeezing my shoulder.

'We need help,' said Rex, and he stood. 'I'm going to get the sergeant.'

'Good idea,' said Beryl, as she rubbed my arm again. 'The police'll know what to do. They'll find her.'

The house filled after that. Neighbours came and Sergeant Price. They huddled in the front yard and decided on a plan. They set out in twos and threes in all directions—over the paddocks, into the forest and down towards the river. Ben went with Alf, while Grace and I stayed at the house. Beryl sat close, still patting and squeezing my arm.

The sun sank lower over Ben Craeg and its craggy tips glowed golden. Dusk came and then darkness. The searchers ate before setting out again with their lamplights.

I couldn't eat but kept myself busy heating soup, slicing bread and making cups of tea for the searchers. Beryl sat at the table wringing her hands, and every time she saw me, she said, 'They'll find her, Ida. Don't fret. They'll find her.'

In the lounge, the mantel clock chimed each hour that ticked by. Every now and then I went out and stood by the back door. The air was brisk and I pulled my cardigan more tightly around me. The sky was brilliant with stars and the moon was rising over Ben Craeg. The crickets were chirping, the owls hooting, and I could smell the forest. It was like any other night, except for the torchlights ricocheting across the paddock and the searchers calling Nora's name.

The whole time my ears were pricked for the sound of a gunshot.

Then someone came running across the paddock, calling out something I couldn't understand. I pushed the door open and ran outside, through the backyard, over the dips and mounds and clods of dirt. I clambered over the back fence and kept running towards the searchers clustered in the middle of the paddock. I was panting when I reached them, and they separated to let me through. I slowed my step, eyes ahead, then I stopped. A wonky lamplight was swaying and slowly making its way towards us.

As it neared, I saw Ben holding the kerosene lamp high and Alf on the other side, the rifle slung over his shoulder. Between them was Nora. Alf was holding her hand and elbow, half-carrying, half-walking her as they moved gently forward.

'We've found her!' he called.

When they reached me, Nora looked up. 'I couldn't do it,' she said. 'I didn't have the guts.'

'Thank God,' I said.

Chapter 28

They took Nora to the General Hospital in the city for treatment. Alf went with her and I stayed out at Ben Craeg with Grace and Ben until he returned.

While he was gone I set to work. In the kitchen, I washed the dirty pots and scoured the stainless steel of the sink until it shone. I scrubbed the stains off the laminex, cleaned the crumbs from the toaster and ordered the canisters on the bench. Then I swept and mopped the floor.

In the lounge, I cleaned the fireplace and plumped the cushions. As I dusted the mantelpiece, I lifted the statue of the Holy Family to clean under it. The piano key was no longer there. I turned to the piano. It was coated in a thin layer of dust and its brass pedals were beginning to tarnish. I tried to open the lid but it didn't budge.

For some reason, I felt overcome with sadness and had to sit down. I didn't like the piano being neglected and the music being locked inside, and I had to sit for a few moments. Then I pulled myself together and ran the cloth over the wood, down the carved sides and in between the curls and ridges. I found the Brasso in the laundry and polished the pedals until they glinted like mirrors.

That night, the three of us sat at the blackwood table and ate shepherd's pie. No one ate with relish, not even Ben.

'Will Mum get better now?' he said.

'I hope so,' I said, shaking salt and pepper over my dinner.

'I don't think she'll get better,' said Grace. She shook her head and her cropped hair swung about her ears as she spoke. The haircut had given it even more life. 'Not 'til Ted comes home again.'

'Will he come home again?' said Ben.

'I don't think so,' I said.

'I wish he would,' said Grace. 'It's not the same here without him.'

'I don't blame him for leaving,' said Ben. 'It's horrible here.' He took a mouthful.

'It's because your Mum's sick,' I said.

He finished chewing, swallowed and shook his head. 'No. It's always been horrible.'

When we'd finished dinner, Grace helped me clear the table and wash up, while Ben made a fire in the lounge. Then, Grace and I joined him. We sat in the velvet chairs and I picked up my knitting—a pair of mittens for Grace, in bottle green wool.

'Can I ask you something?' said Ben. He was squatting by the roaring fire.

'Of course,' I said.

'Can I come to town and live with you?' he said.

'What about school?' I said, setting the wool and needles in my lap.

'I don't care. I want to leave here as soon as I can.'

'You've got to finish school,' I said.

'Then can I come?' he said.

'If you want.'

He turned back to face the fire. The flames were high and made wild patterns on his face.

'I want to leave, too,' said Grace. 'Because I want to be a singer.' She felt the crude ends of her hair. 'When my hair's grown back.'

I smiled. 'You don't need long hair to be a singer, Gracie.'

The next day while the kids were at school, I stripped the beds and washed the sheets in the twin-tub and hung them out. I spent the rest of the day in the garden, weeding the dandelions and the prickly thistles. Then I cut some of the remaining roses and set them in vases in all the rooms. Except for Ted's bedroom. It hurt to go in there and see his bedspread unrumpled and his books still neatly stacked by his bed. I inhaled and the air smelt like a room, not like him.

Alf returned the following day. Rex had been minding the factory while Alf was away, but he needed to return to the sawmill.

'She's had a nervous breakdown,' said Alf. 'And she's going to be in hospital a fair while.' Then he faltered. 'They're going to give her shock treatment.'

He explained that it could take weeks, even months for her to get better. That she'd have a couple of treatments each week until she was stable enough to come home.

As he spoke, I felt a growing dread. I tried to hide it, but obviously I didn't because Alf said, 'No, I didn't like the sound of it, either, but the doctor said this is the best treatment. It'll fix her the quickest, and hopefully for good.'

Alf drove me into Ben Craeg to catch the bus. Just before I climbed from the car, he said, 'Can you keep an eye on Nora?'

'I'll visit her every day. You didn't even need to ask.'

As I was unpacking, I found the parcel of Grace's hair and unwrapped it. The long skeins lay over a page from the Personal Notices. The waves were flattened but the hair still shone red and gold and all shades in between. I folded them back up, then placed the parcel inside my box of keepsakes, on top of the babies' layettes and shawls,

Mum's embroidery and the photos of Ted. All the reminders of children and people who were no longer with me.

That night as we lay in bed, Len said, 'Do you reckon the shock treatment will fix her?'

'The doctors think it will,' I said.

'I dunno if anything will fix her,' he said.

I rolled onto my side and I could make out his profile against the window: the curve of his forehead, the peak of his nose and chin. 'I know what you think of her,' I said. 'And I know what she's like and what she's done . . . But she's my sister. I've known her the longest of anyone on this earth, since she was a child. And once you've known someone as a child, that's how you always see them. I saw what she went through. I was there, and I know. I know, too, if circumstances been different, what might have been.'

'But it doesn't excuse what she does.'

'No,' I said. 'But I can't leave her on her own.' I shifted closer to him so I fitted alongside his arm and hip and legs. 'I tell you, Len, that night she took the gun . . . It scares me to think what she might have done with it.' I rested my arm on the flannelette of his pyjamas. 'I don't know what I'd do if I lost her.'

'You're good at forgiving, Ide.' He slid his arm under my head and I caught the faint odour of his underarm as I settled into his shoulder. 'Too forgiving sometimes.'

'Family is family,' I said. 'It's more important to me than anything.' Then a bit later. 'I'm not giving up on her.'

The next day, I caught the bus to the General Hospital at the top of Charles Street. It was high on the hill and big and white, with a long, curving balcony along each of its three storeys. The wind was gusting, blowing the leaves along the gutters, and the clouds hurried across the sky. I had to hold on to my hat as I walked towards the doors of the hospital.

Inside, I combed my hair with my fingers and smoothed my coat before I asked at the counter for Nora's room. Then I walked down the long corridors that smelt of waxed linoleum and antiseptic, past nurses with clipboards and stainless steel dishes, until I found her.

There was another woman in the room, skinny and young with limp, brown hair. She had a visitor, an older woman. They were both smoking and the ashtray sitting on the tray by the bed was full of butts. They looked up as I entered and watched me walk over to Nora and stand by her bedside.

Nora looked ghostlike. Her eyes were shut, her mouth open and her face appeared bloodless. Her hair looked wiry and clung to her cheeks in jagged strips.

I laid my hand on her arm and her skin felt dry. Her eyes opened at my touch and her head wobbled as she turned, as if her neck couldn't hold it up. The sheets scratched as she shifted. It took her a while to focus, then she said, 'Aww, gawd,' in a slurred, low voice. 'Fancy seeing you.' Her arms shook as she pushed herself up on the pillows and the bed rattled. Then she lifted an unsteady hand, which trembled. I grasped it and bent to kiss her.

'Hello, Nora,' I said, trying to keep my voice bright, so she wouldn't notice my shock at the sight of her. 'How are you doing?'

She lay back on the pillows and shut her eyes. 'Not too good.' She exhaled as if exhausted and lay motionless on the pillow. Her eyes opened and she beckoned me closer. 'I don't know why they're keeping me here. It's like a jail,' she whispered. 'I just want to go home.'

I squeezed her hand. 'Soon, Nor. You'll be home soon.'

The next day when I visited, Nora's bed was empty, so I sat down and pulled out my knitting and prepared to wait.

The other patient piped up, 'I don't know where they take her, but she never looks too good when they bring her back.'

I nodded and kept my eyes on my knitting.

'The doctors here aren't any good,' she continued. 'They keep us here when there's nothing wrong with us.'

'Oh,' I said, glancing up and back down again.

She lowered her voice to a whisper. 'I know about the Russians,' she said. I looked over at her. She was only young. She lit a cigarette and began telling me how the Communists were sending messages to her through her wireless. I focused on the garment growing beneath my fingers, on the softness of the wool and the gentle waves of the cable, as she went on.

'I keep trying to tell the Premier and the police, but they don't want to know. They just keep sending me back here.'

Outside in the corridor, heels tapped up and down and trolleys rattled past. I sat in that austere room with its anaemic walls and bare linoleum, listening to bizarre stories of Russian spies, all the while trying not to imagine what the doctors were doing to Nora.

About an hour later, they wheeled Nora in. She was lying on her back, with her mouth half-open. She was still and barely moving, and her skin looked grey. As soon as the nurses left, I sponged the goo from her temple, and cleaned the hair that was stuck to her face. She groaned, and I patted her arm and told her I was there.

When she woke, she ached, in her head and jaw and limbs. She didn't know where she was or why she was there, and I had to remind her. Her memory returned over the next couple of days, just in time for them to take her off and do it all over again.

We were getting into winter and the frosts had started. The following Monday when Ted came, I'd set a fire in the lounge and the kitchen was warm from the stew I'd cooked. I told Ted about Nora while I was dishing up. He sat at the table, his face tense and his jaw muscle twitching.

When I told him about Grace's hair, he thumped the table so the cutlery jangled. 'How could she do that?'

I set his plate in front of him. 'She thought she was protecting Grace.'

'Protecting her?' His voice was raised. 'What sort of mother cuts her daughter's hair off to make her ugly?' His nostrils flared as he exhaled.

I served Len and then myself. 'She was protecting Grace from what happened to her.' I explained about the letter from the boy.

'That's just insane,' he said. 'She's gone off the deep end.'

'Yes,' I said. 'She has. She's had a breakdown and she's not thinking straight.' I told him about the gun, and the hospital and the shock treatment.

He folded his arms as I spoke, staring at the steam rising from his plate. His shoulders rose and fell with each breath. He didn't look at me and I wasn't sure he was even listening.

'Stop,' he said after a while. 'I don't want to know any more.' His eyes looked cold, but his knee was jiggling.

'I'm sorry,' I said.

Ted ran his hand through his hair. 'It's not my fault. Even if she had killed herself, it's not my fault.'

I waited until he glanced up. 'No, it's not your fault.'

He swallowed. 'I don't want to hear about her ever again.'

I bit my bottom lip and nodded. 'Righto,' I said.

He wiped under his nose and sighed, then reached to the middle of the table and picked up the tomato relish. He spooned some onto his plate.

'What about your father?' I said, and felt Len's sharp glance although I wasn't looking at him. 'Do you want to hear about him?'

Ted stilled. He shook his head, then replaced the relish in the centre of the table.

He was quieter for the rest of the evening and every time I glanced at him, his eyes were dark and sad. When he was leaving, Len and I went outside to say goodbye. The night was cold and foggy, and the light from the hall didn't penetrate far into the darkness. Ted hovered by the door. He pulled the collar of his coat up and thrust his hands into his pockets. 'There was something I was going to ask you tonight.'

'Yes?' I said.

'But maybe it should wait.' He was fidgety and his breath puffed in the air.

'You don't have to wait,' I said. 'Just ask.'

He kept his eyes on the coir mat by the front step and brought the pockets of his coat closer together, gathering the wool more tightly around him. 'I was wondering if I could . . . bring someone to meet you.'

'Oh,' I said. My hand went to my chest.

'Course you can,' said Len.

'Yes,' I said. 'Of course you can.'

'Her name is Clara,' he said, glancing up.

'Clara,' I repeated. 'That's a lovely name.'

'Bring her around whenever you want,' said Len.

'Next week even,' I said.

We said goodbye and, as soon as the door clicked shut, Len said, 'I once knew a dairy cow called Clara.'

'Anyone called Clara has to be nice,' I said. 'I don't care what she's called anyway. I'm just glad he's got someone.'

'Yes,' said Len. 'That is nice.'

'I won't have to worry about him so much.'

'You don't have to worry about him now,' said Len. 'But you do anyway.'

Alf came into town to see Nora at the weekend. Ben and Grace stayed with Rex and Beryl because the doctors didn't think it would be good for Nora to have too many visitors.

We went up to the hospital together. The room smelt of cigarette smoke and stale food. Alf stood stiffly on one side of the bed, while I sat on the chair on the other side. I chatted about the garden and the weather and anything that came to mind. Between us, Nora lay silently, her eyes staring without blinking, as if they were stuck and couldn't move.

Alf was quiet on the walk back to the car. The clouds were low and the air felt heavy. He didn't speak for the whole drive home, and when we reached Pearson Street, I had to ask him twice if he wanted to come in for a cup of tea before he heard me. His face stayed bland as he shook his head.

I collected my bag and opened the door.

'I thought she'd be back on her feet by now,' he said.

I turned. 'The doctors know what they're doing.'

He scratched his chin, the engine still idling. 'I hope so,' he said.

I stepped out, and Alf put the car into gear and drove off. I waved, but he didn't look back.

Towards the end of the following week, I was walking down the corridor of the hospital when I spotted a familiar figure. I hurried my step and caught up to her.

'Dr Godfrey-Smith?' I said.

She turned and her face crinkled. 'Oh, Ida!' She recognised me straight away. She wore glasses and her hair was a soft grey, but she looked just the same, her skin only lightly etched by time. Even wearing a white coat, she still looked as gentle as the cashmere for which I remembered her.

When I'd first left work, I used to see the Godfrey-Smiths once or twice a year, but we'd drifted out of touch and it had been a few years since we'd caught up with each other. She asked me how I was and what I was doing at the hospital. I told her I'd been to see Nora.

'Oh, I hope it's nothing serious,' she said.

I hesitated, but she was a doctor, so I told her about Nora and the breakdown. I told her, too, about the shock therapy.

'It's been over two weeks and she's not getting better,' I said. 'She seems to be getting worse, in fact. Barely moving or eating or talking.'

She nodded as I spoke.

'And she forgets everything. Where she is and what happened the day before. She can't even remember what she did on the night she had the breakdown.'

'That can happen,' she said. 'Electro-convulsive therapy can cause short-term memory loss. But her memory will return. Sometimes it takes a while to notice an improvement.'

I sighed. 'It's hard to watch. It's like she's disappearing before my very eyes.'

She took my hand. 'She *will* get better.'

She felt warm and still smelt of lavender, and I believed her.

I asked her about the girls. They were all grown up. Elizabeth had moved to America to study naval architecture so she could design ships.

'Naval architecture?' I said. 'I didn't even know such a thing existed. But of course they'd have that in America.'

Mary had become a doctor like her parents. She'd gone to the mainland for her training, and it didn't look like either of the girls would return to Tasmania.

'You must miss them,' I said.

'I do,' she said. 'But they're out in the world, pursuing their dreams. What more could a mother want?'

Ted brought Clara di Bertoli for dinner the following Monday. She was dark and petite and smelt like musk. Her hair was short and wavy and teased high on her head, and her eyes were as black as midnight. She worked at a bakery in town and had met Ted when she did the banking.

'Everyone in the queue in the bank probably thought I was polite letting them go first,' she said. 'But I wanted to wait to make sure I could go to Ted's window.' She giggled.

She was exactly the sort of girl you'd want to serve you vanilla slice in a bakery.

Ted had booked a taxi to take them home, and they walked down the steps in their coats and hats with their arms around each other.

'Told you someone called *Clara* had to be nice,' I said to Len after they'd gone.

'Yes, you did,' he said. 'And you were right.'

'Yes,' I said. 'And don't you forget it.'

'You won't let me,' he said.

It took four weeks before Nora began to improve. She started eating more, first dessert and then a small meal. Then she got out of bed and sat on the chair. The following week, she began taking short walks along the corridor. She'd lost so much weight, it looked like the bones of her body were about to break through her skin. Alf came in at the weekend and his face brightened when Nora asked about the kids.

The doctor reduced the medication and frequency of the shock treatments. Nora became less drowsy and her memory started to return. The events of the night she was admitted came back to her. She remembered cutting Grace's hair and taking Alf's rifle. As she was telling me, her legs writhed under the sheets and her hands twisted themselves into knots.

'What have I done?' she said. 'What have I done?'

'Nor, go easy on yourself,' I said, stroking her arm. 'You had a breakdown. Don't give yourself another one.'

One afternoon, we went outside for a walk. It was the heart of winter, and the sunlight was muted and the air frosty. I felt the cold through my coat, but although Nora was dressed only in a dressing gown and slippers, she didn't seem to notice. The lawns were green and lush and a few lonely leaves still clung to the branches of the birch trees.

'I don't like it here,' Nora said quietly.

'I reckon you'll be able to go home soon,' I said.

'I don't like the doctors,' she said. A nurse was wheeling a patient in the opposite direction, and Nora waited for them to pass before she continued. 'Or the nurses. Everyone here treats me like I'm . . . a lunatic.'

I shifted a little closer to her.

'But I'm not a lunatic.' There was an edge to her voice even though it was quiet. 'I've just made so many mistakes.'

'Grace has forgiven you,' I said.

'It's not just Grace. It's everything. I wish I could undo everything and start again.'

'Nor,' I said, taking her hand. The skin on the back of her hand was mottled by a big purple bruise. 'You have to forgive yourself.'

'I can't.' She said the words under her breath.

We reached the end of the path, so we turned and headed back the way we'd come.

'I can't forgive myself for what I did.'

'But you must,' I said. 'Or you'll never be happy.'

She shook her head. 'Then I'll never be happy.'

'Nor, you're serving a lifetime penance for a mistake you made as a young girl.'

'I deserve it.'

I shook my head. 'No, you don't. It's time you gave yourself a bit of mercy. How can I make you believe that?'

She shook her head again. 'You can't.'

After nine weeks in hospital, Nora was discharged. I helped her pack and make her way down to the entrance of the hospital, while Alf drove the Ford up to the doors. Her face was the colour of ice, and as I held her arm, I could feel her bones and sinews through her coat.

Outside, the air was sharp with cold. The fog was so thick, the birch trees on the lawn appeared like ghostly outlines.

'Thank you, Ida,' said Nora when the Ford appeared. She took my hands in hers. 'I don't know what I'd do without you. I mean it.'

'I don't know what I'd do without you either,' I said. 'And I mean it, too.'

She slid inside and Alf closed the door. Nora raised a gloved hand to the window, and they drove off, the two rear lights swallowed quickly by the fog.

Chapter 29

Tinsdale had grown over the years and now had all sorts of stores, so Nora didn't come into town very often to shop. I visited Ben Craeg as often as I could, every few months or so. Whenever I went, Nora was tired and listless, but at least there was no sign of her anger.

It felt to me, though, that she'd lost more than her rage. She was disinterested in the food on her plate, and was as thin as a stick insect. She didn't talk much, either. If I asked her a question, she answered, but it never sparked a conversation, not like we used to. She seemed to be disappearing, becoming as translucent as her skin.

'It's a good thing, Ide,' said Len, 'that she's not flying off the handle. She mightn't be happy, but at least she's not angry.'

'I s'pose so,' I said. 'But it's like she's lost her motor. She might have lost her anger, but it'd be good if there was something to replace it.'

The piano stayed locked, and the key hadn't been replaced under the statue. Grace told me she never heard her mother play at all anymore, not even late at night when everyone was in bed.

'And you, Gracie,' I said. 'Do you ever play? Or sing?'

She shook her head. 'It doesn't matter.' Her hair was growing back, long curls about her face, even more vibrant than before. Still, she looked wistful and sad.

≪≫

Life went on much the same for the rest of that year and the next. I still worried about Ted, Nora and Alf, and how to reconcile them, but I kept my promise to Ted and never mentioned his mother to him.

It kept me awake at night. While Len snored, I lay in the dark, watching the light patterns move across the ceiling change as a car drove by. If I couldn't sleep, I got up and stoked the fire in the lounge, and sat with my knitting and my thoughts, listening to the town clock strike the passing hours until the rooster started crowing and it was dawn.

≪≫

At the end of the following year, 1960, Ben finished school and moved to town to find work. He came to live with us. Before he arrived, Len and I packed up the baby's room. I took the coverlet off the bassinette, fingering the embroidered teddies before folding it and wrapping it up in tissue paper. I did the same with the sheets and the tiny pillowcase, and I packed them all away in the box on top of the wardrobe. Len took the bassinette and pram out to the shed, and I dusted the mantelpiece and made up the bed ready for Ben when he came.

He arrived on our doorstep with his duffel bag over his shoulder. He looked muscular and handsome and just like his father. He even walked with the same loping gait.

'Thanks, Aunty,' he said when he saw the room. His arms were folded across his chest, his biceps bulging from under the short sleeves of his shirt. Then he bent and pulled me close.

I rubbed his back, up and down, so broad and firm. 'It's yours for as long as you need.'

The next morning, before I woke him, I paused in the doorway to the bedroom, savouring that someone was sleeping in that room again. Not a baby but a young man with tousled hair and strong body odour. I tiptoed in and tapped him on the shoulder and told him his eggs and toast were ready.

After breakfast, Ben went next door to see Stan, the plumber. Stan agreed to take him on as a labourer and told him he could start work the next day.

Ted and Clara came for dinner on the Monday night. Ben and Ted hadn't seen each other since Ted had left home three years earlier. They clapped each other on the back, and Ben embraced Ted so hard he lifted him off the ground. Then Ted introduced Clara. She offered her tiny hand, but Ben seized her around the waist and picked her up, too.

The five of us squeezed around our little table, with Ben almost folded double. Our tiny kitchen, with its peeling paint and worn lino, was overflowing with young people and laughter.

'You two are so different,' said Clara, her face creased with amusement. 'If you didn't know, you wouldn't believe you were brothers.'

We all stopped, our cutlery mid-air as if we were caught in a photograph.

Then Ted continued eating, ignoring Clara's words. Clara glanced from Ted to Ben and back again, before taking a mouthful, too. The rest of us followed their cue, the untold story hanging in the now-weighted air.

At the end of the evening, we made our way outside into a night that was clear and warm. Clara tucked her cardigan under her arm and turned to Ben. 'It was so nice to finally meet you.'

'You, too.'

'I've been wanting to meet you for ages. All of your family, in fact,' she said.

Ben scratched behind his ear.

Ted jingled his keys. 'We'd better get going,' he said.

As they made their way over to Ted's car, a new white Morris, Clara looked back once, twice, before giving us a final wave and opening the door.

A few months after Ben had moved in, I was out pruning the roses at the front of the house when Stan backed out of his driveway in his plumbing van. I waved and went back to pruning, but he braked and climbed out.

'He's a good kid, your Ben,' he said, as he swaggered over in his navy overalls.

'I know he is,' I said, and wiped my hands on my apron. The sun was directly behind him and I had to shield my eyes to see him.

'A real good worker,' he continued. 'Does whatever we need him to do, no matter how shitty the job, pardon the pun. I was talking to the foreman last night, and we thought we'd ask him to stay on. Give him an apprenticeship as a plumber.'

The roses suddenly smelt sweeter, and even the odour of the geraniums became as fragrant as perfume.

Ben living with us brought our old house to life. It swelled my heart to see a living, breathing boy sleeping in the baby's room, and having family filling our house every Monday brought joy back into my day. I felt needed, as if I had a purpose.

The house became noisier, not that I minded. Except when Ben bought a television. He set it up in the lounge room, and we could hear him shifting boxes and furniture about. Then he called us in.

'Sit down,' he said, and motioned to the armchairs he'd arranged so they were facing the television.

It was a weird-looking thing. A big, brown box, with *General Electric* written along the bottom and a spiral antenna on the top.

'Looks like it's from outer space,' I said.

Ben didn't say anything but kept clicking the dial at the front until it made a buzzing noise.

'Be careful you don't electrocute yourself,' I said.

He kept clicking and, finally, the screen lit up like a shaken snow-dome, and then he shifted the antenna about until a phantom shape formed on the screen. He kept twisting the antenna until the ghostly form became a woman. She had black hair twisted high on her head and inky, exotic eyes. She wore a dusky dress that covered one shoulder. But, oh, her voice! She could sing.

I sat forward, my eyes not moving from the screen. It was as if we had a concert right there in our lounge room. When the lady had finished her song, I started clapping. Ben looked at Len and smiled. He knew he had me hooked.

Oh, I loved that telly. To be able to watch the news and the serials, even the advertisements, anytime I wanted.

A few months later, Ben came home and said, 'Aunty, there's something else we need.'

'Hurry up and tell me,' I said, barely glancing up from the telly. 'Maria Callas is coming back on in a minute.'

'I've organised for the telephone to be connected.'

'No,' I said. 'We don't need any more machines. One's enough.'

'But I need it for work,' he said.

'What?' I said. 'You just work next door.'

'For when I'm on-call,' he said.

I sighed. 'More disturbance of my peace and quiet.'

He laughed. 'You don't seem to mind the telly.'

'I like the singing,' I said. 'But a telephone ringing is a different matter.'

'You'll like it when you can talk to someone without leaving the house,' he said.

But I didn't. It had a tinny ring and I jumped each time I heard it. Ben set it on the hall stand, and I didn't go near it except to dust it. I left Ben to answer it, and if it rang when he was out, I let it ring until it stopped by itself.

We'd had the telephone for a few weeks when, late one afternoon as I was out at the clothesline, Ben called me inside. I followed him down the hall. The handset of the telephone was off the hook, resting beside its base. Ben picked it up.

'Here she is,' he said into the mouthpiece, then held it out to me.

I stepped back. 'I'm not using that.'

'There's someone you might like to talk to at the other end,' he said.

'No.' I eyed it warily and shook my head. 'That thing frightens me.'

He smiled. 'Nothing to be frightened of.' He stepped closer to me and the squiggly cord on the telephone pulled taut. 'C'mon, Aunty.' He caught my arm, pulling me towards him. When I was close enough, he held it to my ear.

I tilted my head to listen.

'Say hello,' he said.

The mouthpiece was warm from his breath. 'Hello,' I said, timidly.

'Hello, Aunty,' came the voice down the line.

I turned to Ben. 'It's Grace!'

'Speak to her, not me,' he said, and held the receiver against my ear again.

'I'm talking to you, Gracie,' I said, grinning at Ben. 'You're out there and I'm in here, and I can talk to you.'

Ben leant closer to me. 'You don't have to yell,' he whispered.

From then on, Gracie telephoned every couple of weeks, telling me what she'd been up to at school and with her friends. She could talk and talk, and whenever she rang, Ben brought one of the kitchen chairs down the hall for me to sit on while we chatted.

I was enjoying life again, and I stopped worrying about Nora and Alf so much. To tell the truth, I forgot about them. Looking after the boys kept me busy.

Actually, that's not the truth. The truth is that I avoided thinking about them. It hurt. I knew there was nothing I could do to resolve the situation, to bring us all back together. Ted had made that clear.

I began to dread visiting Ben Craeg. Although the lawn was mown, the beds were made and the canisters all lined up on the kitchen bench, the house felt different. Empty. I could see it in the neatness, in the unslept beds and the cold fireplace.

And in the locked piano. Each time I saw it sitting on its own against the wall, I felt sorry for it.

Nora was in her early forties. She hadn't regained the weight she'd lost when she had the breakdown. She no longer kept up with the fashions or dyed her hair, and it had turned the colour of the scourers I used to clean the pots.

Alf had changed, too. He was my age, but he looked older. His hair was turning the same colour as his eyes, and his years of hard work were etched onto his face. He'd never been one for talking, and now he spoke even less. He didn't smile, and his shoulders slumped as if they were about to cave in. Although he was still tall, I wouldn't have called him 'big' anymore. It was as if he was shrinking, tucking himself away.

It hurt to witness.

While her parents seemed to fade a little more each visit, Grace appeared to flourish. One day, she was a girl with a flat chest and a tangle of curls, and the next she was a graceful and elegant young woman. When we visited in the spring of 1962, just after she'd turned fifteen, the sight of her stopped me in my tracks.

'What's wrong, Aunty?' she said, her voice gentle and bell-like.

'You!' I said. 'You're not a little girl anymore.'

She was holding the door open and wearing an olive-green dress that made her eyes look softer than moss. It nipped in at the waist and the skirt flared to just below her knee. She was taller than me, possibly even taller than her mother. Her hair was pulled back and her neck was long and elegant, her shoulders slight and slim. Her face was as fine as a pixie's, her skin unblemished except for a smatter of childhood freckles over the crest of her cheeks.

She leant down and embraced me, and I felt her long fingers on my shoulders. I held her, her skin fresh against my cheek. She smelt youthful.

'I can't believe my little Gracie is a young woman,' I said.

She laughed and it sounded like a cluster of piano notes.

Ted and Clara still came for dinner every Monday evening. Towards the end of that year, we'd just sat down for dinner one night when Ted cleared his throat.

'I've asked Clara to marry me.' He exhaled and smiled. Clara held out her left hand. The electric globe above the table caught the tiny diamond on her finger and made it sparkle like a water droplet in the sunlight.

Len and Ben jumped out of their seats. 'Congratulations!' They shook Ted's hand and kissed Clara. When they sat back down, everyone was looking at me, but I couldn't move. I was overcome. It seemed like no time since I'd been standing in this room at this table bathing a baby boy. Now here he was, a young man with a girl by his side, telling me he was getting married.

'Ida,' said Len and nudged me.

I stood and kissed both of them. As I sat back down, my lips were quivering and I had to keep blinking away the watery film from my eyes.

'Aren't you happy for us?' said Clara.

I nodded, but I couldn't speak. 'I'm happy for you, I really am. Just give me a moment.'

'We want you there, of course,' said Ted. 'And Uncle Len, would you make a speech?'

'What about your father?' I said.

'Aunty, don't start.' Ted glared at me.

'We're only having a small wedding,' said Clara, but she glanced at Ted and back at me, then lowered her eyes.

I couldn't eat much of my dinner because my throat felt dry and my belly felt leaden. Later, Clara and I cleared up while the men went outside. They were down by the back fence, Len holding up the kerosene lamp, while Ben strung up a fishing net on nails along the fence. The golden light was swaying back and forth and their shadows on the fence were moving with it.

Clara took the dirty plates and cutlery over to the sink and set them down. 'I want Ted to invite his parents to the wedding, too,' she said.

I turned away from the men, and went over to the table. I collected the glasses and they chinked together as I carried them to the sink.

'But I've tried and tried to bring him around and he won't budge,' Clara continued. She picked up the salt and pepper shakers and the bottle of tomato sauce, and took them over to the cupboard. 'There's nothing I can do to change his mind.'

I nodded and ran the water in the sink.

'I've never met them. I'm marrying him, and I've never met his parents,' she said as she put the condiments away.

I started washing up. Clara returned to the table and gathered the tablecloth to shake it outside.

The men were still down the back. Len was smoking and the orange tip of his cigarette bobbed about as he spoke. Ted was standing by his side, hands in his pockets. His profile was earnest as he listened to Len.

'I don't understand why he's so angry with them?' Clara said. She was standing next to me at the sink, the teatowel in her hands. 'Family is the most important thing to me.'

I nodded and kept washing up, sponging the glasses in the suds and placing them on the stainless steel.

'I know he was very hurt,' she continued. 'So hurt he can't get over it.' She sighed. 'But I just wish he would.'

'You need to tell him how much it means to you,' I said.

She nodded. 'I won't give up. Not yet.'

We finished cleaning up. 'Oh, and before I forget,' she said, 'we'd like Grace to sing at the wedding.'

I went out to Ben Craeg alone. I wanted to tell Nora and Alf in person. We ate a quiet dinner, then took our cups along to the lounge. Nora poured the tea and sat in the chair opposite me. Alf stood by the hearth and lit a cigarette, flicking ash into the empty fire grate. Grace had already gone to her room.

They both looked tired and neither of them spoke. I didn't know how to say the words, so I sipped my tea. The clock on the mantel ticked slowly, as if to remind me of its passing.

'There's something I need to tell you,' I said.

They looked up. They didn't look frightened, just resigned.

'Ted's getting married.'

They were still, so I went on. 'To a lovely girl. Clara di Bertoli.' I waited, but neither of them spoke. 'She's Italian.'

Alf nodded. Nora rubbed the side of her neck with a hand. 'When's the ceremony?' she asked.

'Next year. End of April.' I paused. 'There's something else I should mention.' I rubbed at the worn varnish on the blackwood arm of the chair. 'They want Grace to sing.'

Alf glanced at Nora, but her face remained impassive. We sat for a few more minutes and I took another sip of my tea. Then Nora stood and left the room. Alf finished his cigarette. 'We appreciate you coming out to tell us,' he said, his hands in his pockets.

'I thought I should tell you in person.'

He nodded. 'Thank you.'

We could hear Nora shuffling about in the bedroom, opening and closing a drawer. The door creaked and she returned. She didn't look at us but moved quickly towards the piano. One hand on the lid, she jostled the key in the lock until it clicked. She lifted the lid and rested it against the back of the piano. The keys beckoned, the ivory as shiny and smooth as new china, and the ebony as dark and deep as night.

Then she straightened. 'If Ted wants Grace to sing, she'll need to practise.' She looked at me, then at Alf. 'I've been wanting Ted to forgive me, but I've never given him a reason to. There's so much I want to tell him, to explain to him, but I'm not good at talking about it. I've kept that part of me boxed up, and I've been too frightened to open it up, for fear of what would come out. But this is the start.'

Alf was by her side, reaching out, his hand on her arm.

She looked up at him. 'One step at a time,' she said.

He let his arm drop and it hung loosely at his side. 'I can wait,' he said. 'Take as long as you need.'

Chapter 30

I tried one more time to talk to Ted. Over dinner, I told him that Nora was helping Grace prepare a song for the wedding.

'She wants a chance,' I said. 'To show you . . .'

'Aunty,' he said and put up his hand. 'Stop.'

Clara eyed him. 'Ted . . .'

'Please leave it alone,' he said, turning to Clara.

Her shoulders sagged, then she pulled herself straight. 'No,' she said. 'I'm sick of this. When are you going to get over it?'

The muscles of Ted's jaw clenched and unclenched.

'You know I'll marry you, no matter what,' Clara continued. 'But I really want your parents there, too. You've told me what happened and from what I can see, your father did nothing wrong except bring you up as his own son. And I know your mother made mistakes, but she wants a chance to make it up to you, and you won't let her. I think it's time you did.'

'Just leave it,' he said. He was looking down at his dinner, hands either side of his temples. 'Please.'

Clara bent her head and blinked a few times. 'I'm just saying, Ted, that I really want a nice wedding . . .'

'It will be a nice wedding,' he said, looking up. 'The family I want will be there.'

Clara sighed again. 'Why can't you . . .'

'Stop!' Ted rubbed his temples. 'Just stop! Please. All of you.' He turned to Clara. 'I'll do anything for you . . . except that. I can't face seeing them again.'

Clara looked down at her dinner, then picked up her fork. She sat for a while before she started to eat again.

Later, when we were on our own in the kitchen, she said, 'I guess I'll have to accept it. And try not to let it spoil our day.'

I turned to her. 'I wish it was different, too.' I shook my head because there was nothing else I could say.

The night before the wedding, Alf dropped Grace off at Pearson Street. Grace wore a new hat with a brim and a woollen coat, and carried a small suitcase because she was staying for the weekend. The two of them stood on the verandah, and behind them the sky was darkening. I could just make out the silhouette of the birch tree on the verge.

'Do you want to come in?' I said to Alf.

He shook his head. 'It's getting dark and I'd better get home. Nora's a bit, umm, well, she's not too good.'

I nodded.

Alf set his shoulders and cleared his throat. 'I've made a gift for Ted and Clara.' He stepped aside. Behind him was a low table with sculpted edges and turned legs.

'Oh, Alf,' I said as I stepped outside to inspect it more closely. It was made of blackwood, its top streaked all different shades of brown—blonde, tawny, umber. 'It's beautiful. It's the nicest gift. Ben'll take it up to them first thing in the morning.'

'I have a card, too,' he said. He fumbled in the pocket of his jacket, extracted a stiff envelope and held it out.

I took the envelope. *TED AND CLARA*, it said in block letters.

'It's from his mother, too,' he said. 'If you get a chance, tell them we wish them all the best.'

'I will,' I said.

His posture was stooped as he walked down the steps, and his jacket and trousers hung loosely from his frame.

'Alf,' I called. He looked back, one hand on the gate. 'You deserve to be there.'

He closed his eyes for a moment before opening them again. He looked wounded and weary as he nodded, then continued on through the gate, his footsteps slow and dragging. I waited until his tail lights had bumped all the way up Pearson Street and turned the corner before I went inside.

Grace stood in the doorway to Mum's old room and I flicked on the light. The room looked dark and old-fashioned, but I'd aired it and dusted, and set roses in the vase beside Mum's statue of Our Lady.

'It's lovely,' said Grace. She sniffed the air. 'I can smell the roses.' Her voice sounded resonant and mature. 'Your house never changes, Aunty. Nothing about you ever changes.'

Later that night, Len brought the coffee table inside. As he lifted it, I spotted the engraving on the underside of the wood.

> *FOR TED AND CLARA*
> *ON THEIR WEDDING DAY*
> *28th APRIL, 1963*
> *Made by A.L. Hill*
> *Ben Craeg*

We readied for bed, but before he turned out the light, Len sat on the edge and pulled a crumpled sheet of paper out of his pyjama pocket. He smoothed its creases.

'It's my speech for the wedding,' he said. 'I'm a bit nervous.'

I climbed under the covers and waited while he studied it for a few minutes, his lips moving as he read. Then he set it aside and turned out the light.

We lay in the dark for a while. 'I'm not the one who should be saying it,' he said.

I reached over and took his hand. 'Just do the best job you can.'

The day of the wedding dawned clear. Ben looked handsome, his hair neat and slick, and he wore a dark suit and a slim tie. He'd bought a car a few months beforehand, a second-hand Holden, and he took the coffee table with him when he drove off to meet Ted.

Grace dressed in a bottle-green sheath frock that made her look even taller and slimmer, and turned her eyes the colour of mint. She wore a tiny hat that had a sprig of netting, and from under it her curls splayed out over her shoulders and down her back.

I'd bought a new outfit for the wedding, too. A pleated skirt and matching jacket in powder blue with a white trim, and a white pillbox hat, gloves and shoes. Len whistled when he saw me and took photos of Grace and I standing by the front fence. As Len clicked, the breeze blew stray wisps of Grace's hair into her mouth, and she giggled that tinkling laugh of hers.

The church bells were tolling as we walked up the steps and the organ was playing softly. The church smelt of candle wax and incense. We walked down the aisle, the pews already filled with people.

Ted and Ben were seated at the front on the right, and we slid in behind them. As soon as he heard us, Ted turned. He was pale and twitchy, wiping his nose and wringing his hands.

'I've made a mistake,' he said.

'What?' I said, feeling my forehead start to perspire.

'You can't back out now,' Len hissed, his eyes wide.

'It's not that,' he said. He looked frightened. 'The table Dad made.' He looked about to cry. 'I should've . . .' Ben shifted closer to him so their arms were touching. 'I should've asked him.'

Then the organ played a loud chord to signal the entrance of the bride.

'Oh, Ted,' I said.

'I should've . . .'

I shook my head. 'It's too late.' I gave his arm a squeeze. 'We'll work something out. You go and get married.'

Ben took Ted's elbow, and they stood and walked to the front of the sanctuary. Two brothers, side by side, together. Then Clara was beside them, too, tiny on her father's arm, her face concealed behind a fine, white veil.

I don't remember much of the mass or even the exchange of vows. My mind was on the two people who weren't there. If I'd known how to drive, I'd have driven out to Ben Craeg and brought them back myself.

One thing I do remember was Grace singing 'Ave Maria'. I remember every note. She sang all that couldn't be said, all the joy and all the sadness.

The reception was busy and noisy. Platters of olives and calamari, thin slivers of salami and cured meats, and dishes of fish and pork. Course after course of food. Len was having a rollicking time, helping himself to beer and wine and fried pastries dipped in sugar.

The wedding cake was huge and tiered, and then a three-piece band started playing.

'If this is a small wedding, I don't know what a big one is,' said Len as we waltzed.

Ben and Grace took to the dance floor, too. Poor Gracie didn't get a chance to sit all afternoon as young men lined up to sweep her onto the floor.

Towards dusk, Clara changed into her going-away outfit. We stood in a circle and sang 'Auld Lang Syne', and the newlyweds went around everybody and said goodbye.

'We're going out to visit Ted's parents now,' said Clara when they reached us, 'as soon as we leave here.' Her eyes shone in the light and she looked sweet in a salmon pink skirt and jacket.

'Oh,' I said. 'I'm so relieved to hear that.'

'Ted says the coffee table is beautiful,' said Clara.

'Oh, that reminds me,' I said. 'I forgot to give you their card.' I dug in my handbag and found the envelope.

Clara watched as Ted prised the card from the envelope without tearing it. It was white, with two embossed hearts wrapped together by a ribbon. When Ted opened it up, a slip of paper fell out and onto the floor. He bent and picked it up and the blood drained from his face. He held it out to Clara with a trembling hand.

Clara inhaled. 'One thousand pounds,' she said in a half-whisper. It was a cheque for a thousand pounds.

Ted's lip was quivering. He looked at me, his eyes filmy. 'We can't accept this.'

'It's their gift,' I said. 'They want you to have it.'

Still holding the envelope in his hand, he moved on to Gracie, who was standing next to me. 'Thank you for singing,' he said.

'That was *my* gift to you,' she said. 'And from Mum, too.'

They left in Ted's Morris, lip-sticked and toilet-papered, the tin cans clanging on the road as they drove off down the hill. We waved until they disappeared.

We dragged our weary bodies home, and a bit later, into bed. Before I fell asleep, I had just enough time to think about a future that might remedy the past.

We were awoken by a rap at the door. I pushed myself up onto my elbow and rubbed my eyes, straining through the dimness to see the hands of the mantel clock. It was just after midnight.

'Who could it be at this hour?'

Len was already out of bed, clawing his way through the clothes draped over the bedroom chair. The knock came again.

'Coming!' Len called as he slipped his dressing gown over his shoulders and tied its cord. He closed the bedroom door as he left. The front door clicked open and I heard low voices. They quietened and I waited for a few minutes, sitting up, fully awake now.

When Len didn't come back, I climbed out of bed and shrugged on my dressing gown. The front door was ajar and I pulled it wider. Len was standing at the top of the steps, and on the step below, were Ted and Clara. They were still wearing their going-away outfits. Even by the dim light, I could see their eyes were red-rimmed and their faces were grey.

I knew something bad had happened. As I looked from one to the other, from the bottom of my belly, a dread began to rise.

Len started coming towards me, his arms outstretched. 'I'm sorry . . . I'm so sorry to do this to you . . .' he was saying. When he reached me, he took my shoulders in his hands and opened his mouth, but no words came.

My stomach was churning and my skin felt chilled. 'It's Nora, isn't it?' I said quietly.

Len shook his head. 'No, it's not Nora.' Everything slowed, like in a movie, and Len's voice seemed to come from a distance so I could barely hear him as he said, 'It's Alf. It's Alf . . .'

I was shaking my head. 'No, not Alf. Not Alf . . .'

'He hanged himself yesterday morning.'

The colour left the world and there was only light and dark. I tried to turn, to walk away from it, but my legs were shaking and wouldn't hold me up. I could hear my voice clanging inside my head as I kept repeating, 'Not Alf. Not Alf . . .'

Len's arms were around me and his mouth was moving, but his voice was coming from so far away. 'Ida, Ida . . . Can you hear me?'

I tried to tell him I could. I opened my mouth and moved my lips, but nothing came out.

Then Clara was beside him, saying, 'Lie her down. Lie her down before she passes out.' They laid me on the floor in the hallway. 'I've got you. I've got you. It's all right, Aunty,' they kept saying. A hand was in mine, and a voice was saying, 'Can you hear me? Squeeze my hand if you can hear me.' I grabbed it and tried to squeeze it, but the voice was still saying, 'Squeeze my hand.' I tried to tell them that I was, and to ask them where Grace and Ben were, but I couldn't get my mouth to speak.

Then the blackness came and when I came to, they were there, the three of them hovering over me, and the colours were coming back into the room. They tilted me up, and Len tried to make me sip water from a tumbler, but I pushed it away and kept repeating, 'Where's Grace? Where's Ben?'

They helped me up and led me back to bed and lay me down. I kept trying to get up because I had to check on the kids.

'Shhh, Ide,' said Len, pushing me back down and patting my arm. 'Stay still. Stay still.'

Then Grace came in and we lay on the bed. I put my arms around her and squeezed her and we cried. Afterwards, we were quiet and in the lounge next door, I could hear them talking. I got up off the bed and walked down the hallway to the lounge.

They turned when they saw me. Ted and Clara were sitting on the fireside chairs, and Ben and Len were standing in front of the fireplace where the last of the embers were glowing.

'Tell me what happened,' I said.

Len came over and rested his hand on my arm.

Ted started to speak. 'Dad told Mum he was going outside. And Mum thought he was going to chop some wood. She saw him enter the woodshed, but after about an hour, when she hadn't seen him come back out, she went looking. And found him . . .' He paused and shook his head. 'The O'Reillys heard her screaming and went running over. They called the ambulance, but it was too late.'

None of us moved.

'It was just after eleven o'clock, apparently. The time we were getting married.'

In the distance the town clock struck once. We were all quiet as we remembered a man who'd never done a thing to hurt anybody else. Then I wept. I stood there in the doorway, my shoulders heaving and all of me shaking. I just stood there and cried for the man who deserved a lot better than what he got.

Ted and Clara left, but none of us returned to bed. We stoked the fire and all night we boiled the kettle and drank tea and sat with our thoughts. I couldn't help but think of Alf, alone in the wood-shed, slinging a rope over the rafters and tying a noose while Ted and Clara were saying their vows.

I waited until the sun had risen, then I looked up the number and picked up the telephone and made my first ever phone call.

Her voice sounded weak at the other end.

'It's me, Nor,' I said. 'Ida.'

She cried. Her breaths came in bursts, before she said, 'Don't blame Ted. It's not his fault.'

'I know,' I said. 'He went out to see him.'

'If you want to blame someone,' she said, her voice quieter. 'Blame me. I should have loved him more than I did. In the way he loved me.' She started crying again, softly. 'But I couldn't.'

I waited until she was quiet, and then I said, 'Nor, can't we be done with blame? Isn't it time we found some forgiveness? Including for ourselves.'

Chapter 31

We returned to the little church at Ben Craeg. Rex and Alf's other brothers waited outside in their sombre suits. I felt their prickly chins as I kissed them and they smelt of mothballs and aftershave.

The hearse drove in and they slid him out, packaged in shiny wood.

Nora and Grace and I walked in together and sat in the front pew of the church.

Alf's brothers, and Ted, Len and Ben carried him up the aisle as the organ played 'Abide With Me'. They set his coffin down just before the altar. The morning sun streamed through the stained-glass window, lighting a dove in the leadlight and falling onto the wood so it gleamed.

The little church was bulging, filled with people from around the district whose ancestors had known the family for five generations and had come to farewell one of their own. They spilled out through the doors and onto the steps outside.

They carried the casket out to 'Be Thou My Vision' and we gathered around the grave in that little cemetery in the valley, where so many of those I loved now rested. They lowered him into the ground beside his mother and father.

Nora went up to the grave and stood at the side. She was dressed all in black, tall and erect. She bowed her head and brought her hands together at her lips. Then she wasn't alone. Beside her stood Ted. She turned. He was smaller than her, but when he reached for his mother's hand, he looked big. They held each other's eyes momentarily and the looks on their faces said, *I forgive*.

I looked out and up, over the pines, over the green of the forest, and up to Ben Craeg, watching over Alf forever now. 'Goodbye, dear Alf', I mouthed. Because I knew that's where he was—up there on the summit of Ben Craeg, greeting God.

I was only forty-six years old, but my bones were weary and the world felt heavier and sadder. I didn't enjoy cooking or getting out in the garden. I couldn't even knit. Len couldn't be bothered doing much of anything either. He didn't go fishing and, by the back fence, the pile of nets waiting to be repaired grew higher.

Of an evening, Len and I would sit in front of the television until they'd played 'God Save the Queen', then we'd switch it off and sit in the silence. We didn't speak, but I knew Len was thinking of Alf, too. Some nights I couldn't sleep at all, and I got up and sat on my own until the sun rose.

I telephoned Ben Craeg each Sunday and spoke to Grace. Most weeks, Nora came to the phone, too. I waited for her to crumple, like she had after Ted left, but it seemed as if the opposite was happening. As if Alf's death switched something on in her and she was opening up, emerging from the hazy half-life she'd been living.

She learnt to drive, and drove the Ford to the Ben Craeg shops and to mass on a Sunday. Then she began playing the organ for the church. When I next visited Ben Craeg, I went with her. She played the hymns with a reverence she reserved for music and God, the two things she respected above all else.

'You play so beautifully,' I told her as she drove home afterwards. 'You always have.'

She sighed. 'They needed someone to do it after Myrtle had a stroke.' She was dressed in slacks and a matching jacket. She kept her eyes focused on the road. 'I was only going to do it until someone else came along, but I quite like it.' She changed gears without looking down, turned the corner and then we were on the road home. 'If I tell you something,' she said, 'promise you won't breathe a word of it to anyone else.'

I promised I wouldn't.

'I couldn't stand the way Myrtle played,' she said. 'She made the hymns sound like funeral dirges. I used to think that if she didn't hurry up, we'd be dead before she finished.'

She glanced at me and we laughed.

We drove in silence for a bit. 'We've got to do what we were put on earth to do,' she said. 'I've been a mother. And a wife. And I've not done well at either of those.' I opened my mouth to speak, but she went on. 'Don't try to be kind, Ida. I know my faults. And I know you would have been a better mother than me.'

I looked down at my lap.

'But my family's nearly grown now. They're their own people, living their own lives, and now I have time to do something for myself.'

Sometimes, Grace went with her mother to mass and sang the psalm. Grace would stand in the pulpit and as she inhaled, Nora would start playing. They were together, perfectly in time, connected by something that went beyond the present and back to the womb. The mysterious connection between a mother and her child. And music.

Grace had one more year of school, then she wanted to start formal voice training at a Conservatorium. That, too, seemed to inspire Nora, and the two of them practised together, working hard to perfect Grace's repertoire.

During a telephone call around that time, Grace mentioned she'd seen an Audrey Hepburn movie.

'Oh, which one?' I said.

She hesitated. 'I didn't mean to tell you that, because I haven't told Mum.' Her voice hushed even more. 'I went with a boy. The same boy who wrote the note about my hair . . . You won't tell Mum, will you Aunty?'

'No,' I said, without hesitating. Nora was doing so well, I didn't want to upset her again. 'Your secret's safe with me, Gracie.'

Meanwhile, Ben worked his way through his plumbing apprenticeship. He was a ballast for us all, safe and reliable. Even if he brought more bloody gadgets into the house.

'This is the last one,' I said, the day he arrived with a vacuum cleaner, a blue Electrolux. 'After this, no more machines are allowed in this house.'

He just smiled at me as he wheeled it into the kitchen. I watched as he connected the chrome tubes and attached the hose onto the machine. Then he unwound the rubber cord from the top and plugged it in.

'I don't see what's wrong with my broom and dustpan,' I said. 'I won't be using it.'

'That's what you said about the telly,' he said, and flicked the switch.

The vacuum burst into life and I jumped.

'You should see the look on your face!' he yelled over the roar of the vacuum.

'And you should see yours!' I yelled back.

Then we laughed. From our bellies, real laughs, and I couldn't remember the last time we'd done that.

Ted and Clara still visited once a week. Each time I looked into Ted's dark eyes, I saw his guilt. One Thursday when I went into the bank, as I was packing my bank book away, he said, 'Can I come and see you after work?'

'Of course,' I said.

I was outside potting pansies when he arrived. 'I'll just finish this,' I said, 'then I'll put the kettle on.'

'Don't hurry,' he said. 'I'd rather stay outside anyway.'

'I won't be long.' I kept digging a hole with my trowel. 'So, how've you been?'

'I . . . I . . .' He stammered and I looked up at him. 'It's all my fault. Dad would still be alive if it wasn't for me.' His shoulders bowed and he covered his face with his hands.

I set the trowel down and went to him. I didn't speak for a long while, just let him cry.

'I wish I hadn't been so pig-headed,' he said.

I waited until he'd finished and then I spoke. 'Listen to me, Ted. There was a lot more behind your father's decision to do what he did. It wasn't just your wedding. It had been years in the making, if not decades.'

He looked at me, his eyes and cheeks swollen and red. 'What do you mean?'

I shook my head. 'There's no point going over it. There's no point blaming anyone. The thing is, every single person who's ever lived has regrets, things they wish they'd done differently. You made the best decision you could at the time, and you can't twist yourself in knots over something you'd change if you had your time over.' I paused. 'Look what it did to your mother. You've managed to forgive her. Now it's time to forgive yourself.'

The year ticked over into 1964. Summer and autumn passed and we were into winter. It was July, just before Len's forty-eighth birthday. The night was squally and I couldn't sleep, so I got up and sat by the fire with my knitting. Ben was away for a couple of weeks, on a job down the coast. The wind gusted and shrieked down the chimney, and the rain battered the roof in waves that sounded like cannon fire.

It was well after eleven, maybe even getting on for twelve, when I thought I heard the gate whine, followed by a thud on the verandah. I set my knitting on my lap and pricked my ears, but it didn't come again, so I turned back to the fire and picked up my knitting once more.

The thud came again, against the wall. *It's probably just the wind*, I told myself, but I laid my knitting on the table under the lamp. The roof was rattling in the wind, the tin sheets chafing against each other and the fire was hissing.

Another thud and a scrape.

I stood up and stepped out of the ring of the lamplight and over to the fire. I picked up the poker, all the time telling myself, *Surely, it's the wind. No one would be out on a night like this.* Nevertheless, my heart was pounding in my chest.

I crept to the door of the lounge and peered out into the hall. It was dim and still. Nothing had moved. The mat was on the floor. The dark shapes of Mum's hats were silhouetted on the stand. Shadows and light swirled with the wind in the stained glass of the door. I held the poker out, ready to swipe, and as I stepped out into the hall, the lounge room window rattled.

I swivelled.

A tap against the glass and a bump against the wall.

My heart thumped louder again and my hands on the poker were slippery with sweat. I stared at the drawn curtains. They hung straight and motionless.

Shuffling and a scrape.

I crept back into the room and towards the window, one foot and then the other, the poker high. The mat softened my footsteps, but my heart pounded loudly in my ears and I could feel it in my throat. I gripped the poker more tightly.

Another tap.

The hairs on my neck rose and slowly, slowly, I tiptoed towards the window. My hands trembled, my throat felt tight and my breaths were ragged. I raised the poker with one hand and eased the edge of the curtain away from the window frame with the other, peering into the murky darkness. Rain gushed from the gutter and splashed to the ground. Shadows lurched in the wind. The tree from next door scraped against the fence. The water had pooled in the mud and formed a big, murky puddle in the middle of our tussocky driveway. I could see down to the front gate and out to the street, and there was no one there, only the streetlight trying to shine through the rain.

I heard a crunch and a shuffle and tightened my fingers around the poker as I pulled the drape out further.

'Who is it?' I called. 'Who's out there terrorising people in the middle of the night?'

Shuffling and scraping. A flap of something dark. A hand, reaching towards the window. Then a face, so pale it was almost transparent.

Grace.

She stood just outside the window in a heavy coat, her hair straggly and wet and dripping down her face. She was staring at me with clear, green eyes. Behind her, the shadows swirled and whooshed.

'Grace!' I was too shocked to move straightaway. 'Hold on, I'm coming.' I dropped the poker onto the chair and ran. Down the hall to the door. My fingers knotted and fumbled as I tried to undo the safety chain, and I wanted to rip the damned thing out. I opened the door and the wind gusted in and the cold air hit. I ran onto the verandah, slicked with rain, down the steps, and up the sodden driveway at the side of the house.

She was almost hidden in the shadows except for her face. The rain teemed and the wind howled around her, but she was as still as a marble sculpture. If she hadn't been standing, I'd have thought she was dead.

When I reached her, I took her elbow and slid my other arm around her shoulders and pulled her towards me.

She was wet and cold, and shivering so her teeth rattled. Rainwater dribbled from her hair down over her lashes and cheeks in long, wet tracks. Her coat was open and her dress underneath was wet and stuck to her body and legs.

'Quick! Let's get you inside or you'll catch your death.'

I tried to move her forward, but she stayed where she was.

'It's all right, Grace. I've got you. Let's go inside.'

I pressed on, and she came with me. 'That's it,' I said. 'Keep going.'

She lifted a boot and took a step through the grass. The hem of her dress was muddied.

'Good girl,' I said. 'And another one . . .' I tugged her elbow and she stepped forward. Each step, she leant closer, letting herself sink into me. The wetness of her seeped through the fleece of my dressing gown and felt cold against my skin.

I kept talking to her as we moved. 'Come on, Gracie. There's a warm fire inside.'

At the steps, she stopped and held her breath, and placed one hand on the wall beside the down-pipe and the other on her belly. As her hand pressed in, I saw it—the tight mound of her abdomen. It wasn't big, in fact, it could have easily been missed under her loose dress, but in the wet, her clothing clung to the contours of her body and I knew straight away what it was.

My breaths quickened and everything else slowed. I didn't feel the rain beating against us or the wind whipping our ears. I no longer heard the water gushing from the spouting. All I could see was Grace, standing by the wall with dripping hair and a bulging belly, and all I could hear were her slow breaths in and out through her pursed lips.

I felt chilled through my clothes and skin and into my bones, and it wasn't because of the weather.

The contraction passed and she glanced up. I took her arm and she held her belly as we climbed the steps. We crossed the verandah, past the shifting shadows of the wiry geraniums. When we reached the front door, Len was standing in the light. He was wearing his pyjamas and slippers and squinting.

'It's Grace,' I said. 'And we need a doctor.'

He looked frightened as he stepped aside to let us in. 'What's the matter?'

Grace scrunched her face and clutched at her belly as her breathing quickened.

'She's having a baby,' I said.

'I'll call Dr Williams,' he said.

'No,' said Grace. She glanced up and shook her head, her eyes alarmed.

'We have to get the doctor, Gracie,' I said.

She shook her head, gripping her belly and breathing through pursed lips.

'I can't deliver a baby on my own,' I said.

Her hand grabbed mine. 'Don't. Please.' Her nails dug in. 'I don't want anyone to know.' She started to breathe faster, grimacing and squeezing my arm, her fingers pinching my skin. 'No one at all.' Her face was ghostly pale, even her lips. Her hair, wet and an even deeper auburn, was the only part of her with any colour.

The wind and the rain still beat against the roof, and I waited until the pain eased.

'All right,' I said. 'We'll go into Mum's room.' Len closed the door on the storm outside, and I led Grace down the hall. Her boots left muddy prints on the mat and rainwater dribbled onto the floor in squiggly lines. Len flicked on the electric light, and I led her to the bed.

Grace clasped the bedpost. Legs apart and one arm across her belly, she turned to me, her eyes big and wide. 'I'm sorry.'

'You've nothing to be sorry for,' I said.

Len stepped closer. 'Just tell me what you want me to do.' His face looked worried.

'Can you fetch some towels and make a fire?'

He left the room.

'Let's get you out of these sodden clothes, Gracie.' She slid her arms from her coat without speaking and I hung it on the hall stand. When I returned, I unlaced her boots. She rested a hand on my shoulder as she raised one foot, then the other, and I slid them off along with her stockings.

Len came back with some towels and a dish of warm water. He set the kindling and wood in the grate and lit the fire. 'I'll be in the kitchen. Call me if you need anything.'

I wiped Grace's face and rubbed her hair as she breathed in and out through pursed lips while another contraction passed. Then I bent and lifted the muddied hem of her dress. It was heavy with rain and dirt and leaves, and I hauled it up her legs and over her round, taut belly. I lifted it up over her chest and her head and extracted her arms one at a time.

She stood naked except for her underwear. She was pale and shivering and her belly stuck out over her knickers. Shiny striae like the tracks of a snail crept up from the line of her pants.

I wiped her shoulders with the towel. She let me take her arms, and I dried them and each of her limp fingers. Then I towelled her breasts, full and taut, and ran the cloth over the tight skin of her belly. I rubbed her legs and cleaned away the flecks of dirt and mud. When I'd finished, I found one of Mum's old flannelette nightgowns and helped her into it. Then she sat on the bed. I lifted up her legs and lay her on her side and pulled the sheet over her.

She grimaced again and brought her knees up. I stroked her shoulder as she lowered her chin to her chest and clutched at her middle. When the contraction had passed, I lit two candles and set one on the mantel, beside the statue of Our Lady, and the other on the dresser. Then I switched off the electric light.

I sat on the faded fabric of Mum's old bedroom chair and wiped Grace's hair from her face. The rain and wind were still pounding the roof. Len boiled the kettle and filled the hot water bottle.

Grace's breaths were coming shorter and faster. I wiped the perspiration from her skin with a towel.

'Don't leave me,' she said. The light of the candles and fire flickered in her eyes.

'I won't.'

She held my hand and breathed through another contraction. 'I don't want to do this.'

'I wish I could do it for you, Gracie.'

'I'm scared.'

'I'm here, Gracie,' I said. 'And so is Len, and we won't leave you.' I bent and kissed her and tasted the sweat on her face. Her cheeks and lips were pink again.

I stayed beside her, swabbing her face and stroking her hair, and giving her sips of water. I took her hand as each contraction came and let her squeeze it white. She didn't utter a sound, just the rush of air with each breath.

Outside the wind and rain beat against the house, but inside we were warm and safe by the fire and its flickering light.

I looked at the statue on the mantelpiece and prayed. *Please, Mary, take care of her and the baby that is coming.*

'I want to push,' she said.

I helped her roll onto her back and lifted up the nightdress. She closed her eyes as I pulled down her pants and parted her legs.

With the next contraction she held her breath and pushed in silence. Then she exhaled and breathed quickly, before tilting her head back and pushing again.

I peered between her legs; she was widening and bulging. 'You're doing good, Gracie.' I reached for her hand and she didn't let it go.

She stared at the ceiling and panted as the next contraction came, then she held her breath and pushed again.

I peered between her legs once more. She was opening and I could see the top of the baby's head. 'It's coming, Gracie. The baby's on its way.'

The contractions were coming in waves now, rolling one after the other. She pushed and breathed and stretched as more dark scalp appeared.

'I can see the baby's head. Keep going.'

I turned to the statue on the mantel and prayed one last time. *Please, take care of them. Don't let them die.* I'd never prayed such a heartfelt prayer.

I held her as she pushed and held my breath as she held hers. I mopped her brow and let her squeeze the blood from my hand. It was as much as I could do, just be there and hold her hand.

'Gracie,' I whispered, stroking her forehead. 'I'll look after you, I promise. You and your child.'

She squeezed and pushed and I promised her and kept promising that I'd look after her, after both of them.

She lifted her head and squeezed. I crouched between her legs and her insides stretched until her skin was opaque. The top of the child's head appeared, then more, and slowly, sliding, sliding, a little more with each push, its head slid fully from her womb and into the world.

'It's here,' I said and my words caught in my throat.

She breathed slowly, then silently began to push again. One shoulder nudged out, then the other. I held the head while the baby slipped into my hands in a gush, and I held it in my arms, all purple and limp.

Then it cried. The baby cried. It was a girl and she was crying. She was alive! Grace's child. She was here. I held the baby against my chest and inhaled the scent of newborn again.

The storm and everything else were outside, but inside that room, it was just us, together, and at that moment it didn't matter where this life had come from or how it had come to be—a baby had been born.

Chapter 32

I wrapped the baby in a towel and gave her to her mother.

Grace pushed herself up to sitting. Her hair clung to her forehead, her eyelids were tinged blue, and smoke-coloured crescents ringed her eyes. She looked drained and weary, but she took the baby in her arms as if she'd done it before, as if she'd been doing it all of her life.

The baby moulded against her and fitted into her, like it was still part of her. The baby's eyes were open and the colour of mud. Her face was purple and pudgy, and the mucus of birth still streaked her skin.

I called Len in. He kissed Grace and took the baby in his arms, and when he turned to me there was wonder on his face. I committed that night to my memory—all of it. The smell of new birth, the feel of the baby in my arms and Len's wonder. I never wanted to forget it.

After Len left, I sat back on the old chair and Grace lay on her side with the baby tucked alongside her. As she watched her child, her breaths slowed and her eyelids closed. Her face was unlined and her hair fanned out across the pillow, a rich colour even in the dark. She was sixteen, little more than a child herself.

The rain ebbed away and there was no sound except for the crackle of the fire and the gurgle of the stormwater running down the pipes. Then the birdsong came, the night was wrapped in light and it was gone.

I must have drifted off because I didn't hear anything else until the baby stirred. When I opened my eyes, Grace was sitting up with the baby, still wrapped in the towel, in her arms. The baby began to cry. Her mouth opened and shuddered, and her gums were smooth and glistening pink.

Grace looked alarmed.

'She's hungry,' I said.

'What do I do?' she said.

'You feed her,' I said. I went over and sat on the side of the bed. 'She won't stop crying until you do.' I held the baby while Grace unbuttoned her nightgown, then she held her to her breast. The baby's nose bumped against the nipple and then her mouth was around it and she began to suckle. She knew what to do without being taught. They both did.

Grace looked up at me, her face lighter.

'I'll have to call the doctor to come and check you're both all right,' I said.

Grace looked down at the baby at her breast.

I leant forward and stroked the back of the baby's hand. 'And then I'll have to call your mother.'

Grace looked up. 'I don't want Mum to know.'

'Oh?' I said. 'But she'll be worried about you. We need to let her know you're safe.'

'Tell her I'm here, but that's all.' Her lip quivered. 'I don't want her to know about the baby. I can't do it to her.'

'But . . . she'll realise . . . when she sees . . .' Grace was shaking her head, and my words trailed off.

'No, she'll never know,' said Grace, 'because I've decided to give her up for adoption.'

I held my breath and tried to stop my head from shaking. *No. No. You can't.* I looked at the baby nestled into its mother and tried not to hear the words coming from Grace's mouth.

'I've made up my mind,' she continued. 'I've lain awake every night for the past few months thinking about it. That's why I haven't told a soul. Not my mother. Not . . . the father. No one. Because I don't want anyone to know.'

'The father might want to know, Gracie,' I said quietly.

Grace shook her head, glanced back at the baby and adjusted her against her breast. 'He needn't know.' She looked up at me again. 'It's not his baby. It's mine. That's why I came to you, because I know I can trust you with my secret.' Her face was long and her eyes were serious.

The baby made squeaking noises and soft murmurs at Grace's breast.

'Are you sure about this, Gracie?' I said.

She nodded. 'I know what I want, and I know what I don't want.' She stared at me without blinking. 'I don't want a baby.'

Tears wanted to burst from my eyes. 'Len and I would help,' I said, 'so you could still do whatever you wanted. You could live here, you and the baby.' Grace was shaking her head but I kept talking. 'We wouldn't mind, Len and me. We'd look after her while you studied . . . or worked.'

'My mind is made up, Aunty.' Her face was determined.

'But what if you change it?'

'I won't. I can't do what I want to do with a child.' She slowed her breathing. 'I want to sing.'

'But you can still sing.' I was pleading now. 'You can do anything you want.'

She shook her head again.

I slowed my breaths before I spoke. 'What if Len and I . . . What if we adopted her?'

She looked at me and her eyes filled. 'I can't . . . I couldn't. I'd have to see her . . . and I'd be reminded.'

I stared at her and then at her baby, the baby she wanted to give away. *How could you? How could you give away your child? Your living, breathing child.* I stood and collected the dirty towels from the floor and walked out of the room. The floor and the walls of the hallway were swimming in front of my eyes. I took the towels to the bathroom and left them on top of the basket. Then I jammed the plug in the basin and ran the cold water. I splashed it on my face and tried to cool it, tried to stop my eyes and cheeks from stinging. I kept splashing and then I picked up the flannel and soaked it in the cold water and held it against my skin.

I caught sight of myself in the tiny mirror propped at an angle on the windowsill. My hair was an untidy frizz, my eyelids were red with extra creases and the whites of my eyes were shot with blood vessels. The flannel felt cool against my cheeks.

When my breaths had slowed enough, I left the bathroom.

Len was sitting at the kitchen table when I came out. 'You all right, Ide?' he said.

I didn't answer him but went straight to the hallstand and rummaged about in the drawer until I found the telephone directory. In the W's, I found Dr Williams' number and wrote it down on Ben's notepad sitting by the telephone. I heard Len's voice, distant and echoing, asking me again if I was all right. I didn't answer him but lifted the telephone receiver off its hook. I dialled the number I'd written on the paper. A woman answered. She sounded close. I told her I wanted Dr Williams. She called out to 'Ernest' and there was scraping on the other end of the line and then Dr Williams' deep English voice.

'You need to come to 15 Pearson Street,' I said. 'My niece has had a baby.'

He asked me questions, but I can't remember what they were or how I answered, and then I hung up.

I paused and then I picked up the receiver again and dialled the number I knew by heart. When Nora's voice came on the line, I had to quell the quiver in mine.

'It's me. Ida.' I grappled to find the words. 'Gracie's here with me and she's all right.'

She said, 'What?' There was confusion in her voice. 'She's not here? How did she . . . ?' She stopped and in the silence down the phone I could detect a change in her. 'Ida?' she said.

'Yes.'

'What's happened?'

I was silent while I thought of what to say. 'Grace is safe,' were the only words I could find.

'I think I know . . .' said Nora.

We were both silent, and I rubbed my forehead and looked at Mum's hat hanging on the hook. The band was decorated with a red hibiscus with an orange stamen.

'Ida . . . Are you there?'

'Yes.'

'She . . .' She struggled to say the words and her voice sounded as if it was about to crack. 'She's had a baby, hasn't she?'

I didn't answer. 'I can't say . . .' I said.

'You've told me the answer.'

'I'm sorry . . . I can't say anymore . . . I'd better go,' I said. I hung up and waited for a moment, before walking down the hall, through the kitchen and out the back door.

I crossed the muddy grass to the shed. The bassinette was under Len's fishing rods and an old table. As I shifted them, I heard Len behind me, asking what was the matter. I just shook my head and lifted the wicker carry basket from inside the bassinette. I carried it back into the kitchen, Len following me, asking what was going on.

I set the basket on the table. It needed a good clean, so I found a rag in the bathroom and dusted down the wicker of the basket and its handles, then I washed it with Velvet soap and warm water and wiped it dry.

I walked along to our bedroom and Len followed, silent now. He watched as I dragged the bedroom chair to the wardrobe.

'Let me get that,' he said, and climbed up. The box scraped the top of the wardrobe as he pulled it towards him. Then he climbed down and carried it to the bed. It fell with a 'whoomp'.

I wiped the dust from the top and opened it up. The packages were inside, wrapped in tissue paper. I took out the tiny coverlet, sheets and pillowslip, as well as a knitted layette and shawl.

I went back down to the kitchen and unwrapped them and made up the carry basket. Over the top, I laid the coverlet with its embroidered teddies. From the laundry, I fetched the basin in which I'd bathed Ted twenty-three years earlier. I filled a jug with hot water and poured it in, followed by cold water, until it was body tempera-ture, and then I found a clean towel and a soft flannel and pin.

I looked at it all laid out on the table and blinked the watery film from my eyes.

'What's going on?' said Len.

My mouth trembled. 'She's . . . She's . . . not going to keep the baby.'

'Oh, Ide,' he said, and his face filled with kindness.

The blinds were still drawn in Mum's room and I crept over to the bed. Grace's eyes glistened in the dimness, and the baby lay still and silent alongside her.

'I've called the doctor.' My voice was hoarse. 'He's on his way. I let your mother know you were safe. And I've run a bath for the baby.'

Grace nodded, folded back the covers and climbed out of bed. The nightie reached just below her knees and her legs were skinny and pale. She scooped up the bundle in the towel and turned towards me.

'Can you bathe her?'

I took the baby and held her against me. She felt limp in my arms and fit perfectly against my chest. Her scalp was covered with tiny hairs, and I kissed it and tasted her soft, newborn skin. She was familiar—everything about her I'd seen before.

In the kitchen, I laid her on the table, gently so her head didn't bump. Her eyes opened, but she didn't cry. I unfolded the towel and lifted her up, naked in my hands—her tiny arms moved as if in slow motion and her legs looked like a frog's. I lowered her into the water. Her tummy bulged above it, the umbilicus clotted and dark. Her arms and legs moved just below the surface, splashing the water softly, like music. I trickled it over her head, over her cheeks, over her tummy.

Len stood beside me as I soaped her skin. As gently as I could, I cleaned all traces of her birth from her body with the flannel, then lifted her out and laid her on the towel. I patted her dry, dabbing her doll-like nose and lips, and her scalp where her hair was already curling.

I used a dry flannel for a nappy and pinned it. Then I pulled the singlet over her head and tied the booties on her feet. Finally, I wrapped the knitted shawl around her and picked her up and cradled her in my arms.

'You're ready,' I whispered. Her dark eyes gazed up at me as if she knew she was going away.

Dr Williams had aged. His hair had silvered, his cheeks had hollowed and his eyes were so grey they were almost clear. I took him into the front room where Grace sat up in the bed and the baby lay in the carry basket on the floor beside her.

'If you don't mind leaving us,' he said in his mellow voice as soon as he stepped into the room. He waited until I'd left, then he closed the door behind me.

I walked down to the kitchen and sat at the table. Len took the chair opposite. Neither of us spoke. I wrung my hands and rubbed my arms, then I got up and stoked the fire. I walked to the doorway and peered down the hall. It was still and the grey morning light shone through the stained glass, lighting the dust motes. I returned to the table, then stood again and paced, then sat.

Len stayed seated and his fingers drummed on the table.

Then came a knock at the door.

'Send them away,' I said to Len. He got up and left, then murmurings drifted down the hall, followed by footsteps. Nora stepped into the kitchen. She was buttoned into her coat, her handbag primly at her side. Her face was ashen, her lips tight and she looked as stark as a winter tree.

I stood. 'Do you want to sit down?'

She shook her head. 'I don't think I could.' Unfastening her handbag, she extracted a hanky and clipped it shut again. She scrunched it in her hand and, with a sigh, seemed to brace herself. 'Where's Grace?'

'The doctor's with her,' I said.

We were silent for a while. Nora's gaze flitted around the kitchen and she scrunched the hanky in her hand. 'I knew.'

'Knew what?' I said.

'That Grace was . . . pregnant. I told myself she was just gaining a bit of weight, but I knew. I just didn't want to admit it to myself. I couldn't deal with it. Not after everything that's happened.'

Then I said it, the thing that was really troubling me. 'Grace wants to adopt the baby out.'

Nora didn't miss a beat. 'She's making the right decision.'

'I know why you say that,' I started. 'But to take a baby from its mother . . .'

'And to make a mother keep a baby she doesn't want,' she said quickly. She stared at me. She looked as unyielding as flint.

'But, Nor . . . I'd look after her. After them both. Or Len and I could adopt her . . .'

I was about to continue, but the bedroom door clicked. Footsteps came down the hall and the doctor appeared in the doorway. The wicker basket hung stiffly from his hand and, inside, I could just see the mound of the baby. Nora stared at the basket, too, and the bundle wrapped within. She held her hanky under her nose and her breaths were serrated.

The doctor cleared his throat and nodded at Nora. 'Good morning, Mrs Hill,' he said. Nora nodded in return. 'I've checked Grace and the baby, and they're both in good health.' His vowels were posh, his consonants clipped. 'Grace doesn't wish to come to the hospital. I've tried to talk her into it, but she's adamant.' He looked at me. 'She says your care, Mrs Bushell, is just as good.' He tried to smile. 'I won't force her to come as there are no problems health-wise and someone her age should make a speedy recovery.'

I nodded but my lip trembled. Nora hadn't moved.

He set the basket on the floor. The baby looked like a doll, too still and tiny to be real. Her eyes were closed and her lips were together with a neat pleat in the centre. Nora was staring at her, too, and wiping under her nose with the hanky.

The doctor opened his Gladstone bag and extracted a brown bottle. 'These tablets will dry up the breast milk. One tablet, twice a day.' He held out the bottle and its contents rattled. My feet wouldn't move, so Len stepped forward and took it. He placed it carefully on the dresser.

The doctor opened his bag again and extracted some papers. He cleared his throat. 'Grace has signed the papers for the adoption.' The sheets rustled in his hand as he peered at us. His eyes were a bottomless grey.

I saw the top of the page: 'Adoption Consent Form'.

'No,' I said. The word escaped before I could stop it.

The doctor frowned at me, and I felt Len's hand on my arm. I clasped my fingers together so tightly I thought my knuckles might burst through my skin.

The doctor was still glaring at me. 'As you're aware, Mrs Bushell, illegitimacy can have disastrous consequences. For mother *and* child.'

I pressed my fingers hard against my lips. My teeth cut into my gums and I could taste blood.

'She's making the right decision,' he went on. 'Adoption is in everyone's best interests.'

My eyes returned to the pink, warm baby I'd just bathed and dressed.

'This is best for your daughter, Mrs Hill,' the doctor continued. 'She won't have the shame and stigma. She'll be able to forget about it and move on with her life as if it never happened. And it's best for the baby. Keeping the child would give it a severe handicap.'

I kept rubbing my mouth and my lips hurt. The blood tasted metallic on my tongue and I swallowed.

'We have many childless couples on our books. Married, financially well off. This baby will go to a good home.'

'I don't care about any of that,' said Nora. Her voice was clipped and abrupt. She paused and lowered her voice. 'I have only one request.'

'Go on,' said the doctor.

She kept her words even and slow. 'Please give her to someone who wants her.'

'I guarantee it,' said the doctor.

'I—we—want her,' I said, looking at Nora. I felt Len's hand on my arm again. 'We would look after her. After both of them.'

Nora regarded me with her cool green eyes. 'It's not about what *you* want. It's about what *Grace* wants.'

'But Grace could still do what she wants. I'll bring the baby up. I'll look after her—'

'Ida,' Nora interrupted and shook her head. 'I know what it's like to be forced to keep a baby you don't want and I'm not going to let history repeat itself.'

I stared at her, my head and body shaking. I had no answer to that, nothing to counter it. She was right. She was right. I nodded, then turned to the doctor and swallowed. I pulled myself up to my full height, eye level with him. 'All right. Take her,' I said, and I felt as if I was tearing in two.

The doctor opened his Gladstone bag and replaced the papers. 'She needs a couple of days of complete bed rest and then she'll be ready to go home. I'll visit each day and if you have any concerns, telephone me.' He bent and picked up the carry basket, wrapping his hand stiffly around the handles, as if the bundle it contained wasn't a precious baby. Our precious baby. 'And don't forget, every cloud has a silver lining.'

Len walked him to the front door, but Nora and I stayed where we were and watched them walk down the hall. Len opened the door and their figures were silhouetted against the grey light angling in from outside—little Len and the tall, dark shadow of the doctor with the bassinette dangling from his hands. The doctor spoke to Len before he stepped out into the sunless gloom. He trudged over the boards and down the steps, and his footsteps grew fainter along the path. My muscles flinched, but I stayed rooted to the spot. I wanted to follow, to whip the bassinette out of his hands and carry it and its precious cargo back inside our house.

The gate ground open, more footsteps. A car door opened and shut, and another. The chug of an engine.

He was taking her. She was going.

I ran.

Along the hall. Past Len in the doorway. Down the steps. I heard Len call my name, but I kept running along the path to the gate, my hands waving in the air. 'Stop! Bring her back!' The grey car was reversing into the street. I fumbled with the latch on the gate and flung it open. The car was straightening. I ran across the footpath, stumbling because my feet couldn't carry me fast enough. The car was off up the street. I raced across the muddy verge and onto the road, trying to catch up to the car. 'Stop! Stop! Bring her back!' But the car kept moving, faster and faster, bouncing through a pothole, clear water spraying from its wheel.

I was still running, still crying, but they were drawing further and further away. They reached the main road. I kept running, trying to reach them, but my legs were slowing, and my cries were growing fainter. At the break in the traffic, they turned the corner and were gone.

They were gone.

I bent over, hands on my thighs, panting and heaving, shaking my head and crying. 'No. No. Not our baby. Not our baby.' I stood hunched in the middle of the road. My chest hurt and I couldn't breathe. I wanted to fall down where I was and lie there and wait for a car or a truck or anything to drive right over the top of me and squash me flat.

Then Len was by my side, taking me in his arms and pulling me to him. I lowered my head to his.

'I would have looked after her,' I said. 'I would have. I would have.'

'I know you would have, Ide. I know.' His voice was dry and raspy and he rubbed my back and kept rubbing it. He was there. I needed him and he was there.

We trudged back down the street. The grey clouds and the heavy air pressed down upon me, and my heart was so low in my chest, I could feel it in my belly. My head was aching and my eyes felt gritty. My arms hung by my sides and my feet were leaden as I walked along the footpath and climbed the steps into our house.

Nora was sitting in the chair beside Grace's bed. She and Grace looked up as I entered. Grace's eyes were ringed by smoky crescents, but they shone glistening green.

'I'm sorry,' she said. Then she turned to her mother. 'I'll make it up to you. To you both. I promise.'

Nora sat forward on the chair, her eyes steely. 'Grace, look at me,' she said. Grace turned. 'You have nothing to make up for,' she continued. 'Just go and live your life. Do what you want to do. Then none of this, giving up the baby or . . . anything, none of it will have been in vain.'

That first night, I crept in to check on Grace a few times. The light from the hall gave her face a sheen. Her breaths were even and slow and her hair splayed across the pillow. She was still the same—still the baby I'd watched sleeping in the bassinette. She would always be the same to me. Because I loved her.

Grace stayed with us for a couple of days while she recovered, then she went home to Ben Craeg.

Each night when I lay in bed, I remembered how it had felt to hold the baby, to bathe her, to dress her. I would never forget her.

Chapter 33

Many times over the next few years, I thought of Grace's baby. I wondered where she was, who might be caring for her and what she might be doing. Sometimes, I'd walk slowly past a schoolyard, searching for her. Or I'd scrutinise the kids on the bus, or a group of girls walking down the street. I kept looking out for her, hoping to see her, but I don't know if I ever did. I never found out to whom she'd been given. I just hoped they loved her as much as we would have and that she had a good life.

Not long after that night, Ben said, 'Let's go fishing.' Clara and Ted came, too. The night before, Ben and Len spent the evening making new flies and the next morning, we were up before the sun. They checked their tackle, and we packed the fishing rods and a hamper of sandwiches and scones and a thermos of tea. Then we set off for St Patrick's River.

Len and Ben strapped on waders and made their way out into the middle of the river where the water eddied about Len's middle, but only came up to Ben's thighs. They held their rods in one hand and the web-like line in the other. They flicked the rods to and fro so the thread caught the light and landed in a wiggly line on the water.

The rest of us sat on the riverbank and watched as the two men waded up and down, their rods springing back and forth. Now and then, a fish broke the surface of the water gulping at one of the flies. Then Ben's rod bent and he'd caught one. He pulled on his line and the fish flipped and writhed and splashed towards him.

'That's it, mate,' called Len.

The fish twisted and jerked and glinted in the sun as Ben kept pulling it closer. He caught it in the net and lifted it out of the water, still flipping and splashing and trying to escape. It was shiny and silver. A trout.

I picked up the camera and took a shot of him in his waders with the water eddying around his legs. His rod was in the air, his mouth open, and he was laughing at the fish splashing in the net in front of him.

I sat back down and watched them fish and then I heard the thrum of a car. It was Nora and Grace in the Ford. They joined me on the rug and Nora had brought blackberry tart.

I took many pictures that day—of Len and Ben fishing; of Ted and Clara sitting together on the blanket, Ted's hand brushing back one of her stray curls; and of Nora, looking all shy and waving me away.

As the sun began its descent, I photographed Grace. She's facing the water, her hands hugging her knees. The light is falling on her face, just on her and nothing else. I called her, and as she turned I took another photo of her, sitting on the blanket with the river swirling about the rocks behind her. She's not smiling but her hair's still moving because she's turning. She looks as natural as the breeze, but I can see the sadness in her eyes.

My favourite photo is one of all of them. Len's in the middle, on tiptoes to make himself look taller. His arms are around Grace and Ben, and he's grinning like a king. Ben's holding up his trout, and Grace is standing tall and looking into the distance. Nora's beside Grace, squinting and not smiling, her mouth pursed because she's telling me to hurry up. Crouching in the front are Ted and Clara, their knees touching.

A few years later, I was in the waiting room at the doctor's surgery when a young female doctor came out to call her next patient. I glanced up as a young woman stood to go with her and then looked back at the magazine on my lap. I felt the room still, so I raised my eyes again. The doctor was coming towards me.

'Ida?' she said.

I nodded and smiled. 'Yes. I'm here to see Dr Williams.'

She tilted her head and smiled. 'You don't remember me?'

I racked my brain trying to place the fair face, the beautiful accent, the groomed appearance, but I couldn't and shook my head.

'I'm Mary. Mary Godfrey-Smith.'

My mouth fell open and I was speechless for a moment. 'I can't believe it. I can't believe it,' I kept saying. 'After all these years. Fancy running into you.'

She'd returned to Tasmania with her husband and children because her parents were ageing and she wanted to be with them.

'They're enjoying having family around them again,' she said, 'especially their grandchildren.'

She leant down and took my hand. 'You must visit.'

'I will,' I said.

'It would mean the world to me,' she said.

Ben, Ted and Clara still came for dinner every Monday night, even after Ted and Clara started their own family. They had a girl and then a boy. Len brought the bassinette out of the shed and I cleaned it up once more. It brought back memories, happy ones, of the babies that had slept in it over the years.

Once again our house was filled with the sounds of children. Nora started visiting more often, and each time she brought an exquisite gift—a smocked dress from England for Sophia or a soft toy for Alberto. She seemed to be enjoying this next generation in a way she couldn't enjoy her own children, much like Mum had before her.

Nora stayed out at Ben Craeg, even after Gracie left. We spoke on the telephone every week, sometimes more. I asked her a few times if she wanted to move in with us, but each time she declined, which was probably good because I don't know how Len would have coped. She liked being on her own, she said, and besides, they needed her at the church.

Ben finished his apprenticeship and bought a house in Richards Street, around the corner from us. When Stan retired, Ben took over his plumbing business and every day when he was between jobs, he popped in for a quick cup of tea.

We lost Len in 1984. He was all right when I climbed into bed that night, but when I woke a couple of hours later, he was making gurgling noises. I tried to rouse him, but his colour changed and his breathing slowed.

'Len . . . Len . . .' I shook him and kept shaking him, but I could see in his eyes that he knew he was going, so I told him what a good man he was and how much I loved him, and I kept on telling him as his breathing slowed.

'You're a good man, Len Bushell. You're the best man a woman could have hoped for. I've not regretted a single minute of my time with you.' I said it over and over because I wanted it to be the last thing he heard.

Then I waited for him to take another breath, but he didn't.

We had forty-five good years together and I couldn't have asked for better.

Epilogue

The doors are the same—glass and wood and polished chrome. Ben pushes one open and I step inside. The foyer is full of people. I turn to Ted and Clara behind us. 'There's a big crowd here. This is lovely.'

'Yes, Aunty. It's lovely.' They smile at me and then at each other.

People are wearing fawn jackets and calf-length dresses, and some of the men don't even have ties. 'Once upon a time, people dressed up for a concert,' I say, 'in long gowns and furs, and men wore dinner suits. It was quite a palaver.'

We make our way through the crowd, across a carpeted floor. 'The parquetry's gone,' I said. 'It's all changed since I was a girl.'

We reach the stairs and Ben grasps my elbow. He takes the steps one at a time with me.

'You go on ahead,' I insist.

'I'm not in a hurry,' he says.

As I step, I'm whisked back in time, back to when I was a young woman and came here with the Godfrey-Smiths. We saw—what was her name again? 'I've forgotten the name of that singer,' I say. 'What was her name?'

Ben shrugs and shakes his head.

'Dorothea Schwarzkopf. That was her name. She had a beautiful voice.'

He smiles.

It was a long time ago, but it's still so vivid in my mind, as clear as one of Len's photos. Her silver dress, her curls, her voice. The first time I'd ever heard magnificence.

We reach the halfway landing. There's the circular hollow in the wall, and is that a vase of gladioli and hydrangeas? I blink and they're gone. There's no recess and no vase. It must have been a memory flitting by.

Ben holds open the heavy door to the theatre and I step inside. It's the same—red seats, all in rows—but it smells different, of old wood and dust. 'It used to smell of fresh paint and new carpet.'

We walk down the steps of the aisle and then along the front row to our seats. A couple stand to let us pass, and I smile and say, 'Thank you.'

She's already seated in the centre of the row and I sit down next to her and we kiss. Then I crane my neck and gawk around. My word, there are a lot of people. Every seat is filled. I lean over the balcony to look down into the stalls. Ben catches my arm and pulls me back.

'It's full,' I say. 'There isn't an empty seat.'

He smiles at me again.

'She must be very famous.'

Everyone's chatting around us and they seem as excited as I am. I look up. The dome's still there and the pressed tin's still painted blue. There's no gold on the leaves, though.

The orchestra's already in the pit. They're tuning up. 'It's a bit rich on my ears,' I say, and Ben pats my arm.

The lights dim and the theatre quietens. The concertmaster plays a note—a single note, long and thin, and the musicians all tune to the sound. The conductor strides on, in tails—it's nice to know some things don't change. We clap, all of us, even the musicians.

Here she is. She's walking onto the stage. My heart somersaults inside my chest. She's wearing a deep green off-the-shoulder dress and her skin is the colour of milk. Her earrings dangle like chandeliers and the bracelet around her wrist shines, too. Oh my, she's beautiful. Her hair is pulled back so it's off her face. It's loose at the back and spirals out like an auburn fan. She's smiling and her face is open. That unblemished face.

She bows and the audience claps.

My Gracie.

She's here. She's been gone so long. Twenty, twenty-five years. I've forgotten. She was nineteen when she went to Melbourne and did her training. And then she went to London and lived there for a good many years. She was living in Germany for a while after that, then Italy. She's even lived in America. All over the world.

When she left, she never said she was going for good, but I knew she was. I knew when we waved her off at the airport that the world was beckoning and she was leaving us. And so she should. Our children aren't really ours. We like to think they are, but they're not.

She comes home about once a year, whenever she has a gap in her schedule. She slips in and out on the quiet. And she writes. Every couple of weeks an aerogramme arrives from wherever she's performing—London, Paris, Milan, Vienna, New York. An almost transparent sheet of paper crammed with tiny writing telling me all her news. And there's always something about her in the papers. I've kept them all—all the articles, including that one in the *Women's Weekly*. I keep them in the box on top of the wardrobe.

I have all her records, too. Ben bought me a record player—he loves his noisy gadgets—and I was hooked as soon as I listened. I even learnt how to work it so I could play her records over and over. A few years ago, he bought one of those compact disc players, but that was too much for me to learn and I leave that one for him to operate when he visits.

She's started. She's singing.

Ave Maria.

Oh, that voice! Soft and high and ever so gentle.

Ave. Ave. Ave Maria.

Ben takes my hand. It's calloused from his work, but there's a comfort in its roughness.

Sancta Maria. Sancta Maria.

Her voice rises. It's full and resonant and fills this old theatre. I close my eyes so all I can hear is her.

Sancta Maria.

I can hear more than the melody and the music. There's pain in her words, and pain in her voice. Her pain and my pain. Our pain. I can hear it. She's singing for all of us.

Ave. Ave. Ave.

Her voice is higher now. This is the voice I've heard all of my life. It sang all through our house, throughout my childhood, and then it was lost, for many years. But here it is again. It's come back.

It's been a long time coming and there are things that could have been that will never be. Sacrifices made that can never be regained. I hear them, in the silences between her words.

But what's here now is here. This sound. Her.

Finally, it's all been worth it.

She finishes singing and the audience claps. Clara and Ted and Ben stand. They're smiling and applauding. Everyone is standing and smiling and applauding.

I stay seated. Nora, beside me, takes my hand. Our gnarled old fingers wrap around each other's. She smiles. She's hearing her daughter sing, hearing her beauty, and her tears tell me she's hearing her dream.

Nora and I stay seated, our hands still joined. I want to stand and clap, too, but I can't move. All I can do is sit. For I can hear them all. They're all back with me. Dad. Grandma and Mum. Alf. And

Len. I'm not in the theatre anymore, but back in an old house filled with people and children and the tinkling notes of an old piano. I'm back by a kindly mountain, sitting on my father's knee. I'm back and I can hear them again, all of their sounds, coming from the floor, the walls, the ceiling, and it's not just Nora and me in this old theatre, but everyone is back with us and all is how it's meant to be.

The audience have sat down again and she's preparing to sing once more.

Bist du bei mir. If you are with me.

Geh ich mit Freuden. Then I will go gladly.

Zum Sterben und zu meiner Ruh. Unto death and to my rest.

Ach, wie vergnügt, wär so mein Ende. Ah, what pleasant end for me.

Es drückten deine shönen Hände. If your dear hands will be the last I see.

Mir die getrauen Augen zu. Closing shut my faithful eyes to rest.

Notes

I have squandered many hours researching for this book. The delicious archives of 'Trove' educated me about many things, including: train journeys in northern Tasmania in the early part of the twentieth century, the design of the Queen Victoria Maternity Hospital in Launceston, Dame Nellie Melba's concert tours and the winners of the vocal sections of the Launceston Eisteddfods in the 1930s.

In Chapter 8, I quoted from an article published in the Hobart *Mercury* on Thursday, 21 April, 1938. In the article, the adjudicator, Mr L. Curnow, criticised the Government for the paltry sum it had donated towards the running of the Eisteddfods. He is quoted as saying, 'Governments also should realise that art is essential, as it lifts persons from the humdrum groove of existence.' I was so impressed with this quote and that it still holds true eighty years hence, that I have quoted his words almost verbatim.

Apart from 'Trove', I also used a number of books as reference guides:

The quaint *Handbook of Garden and Greenhouse Culture* by J. Walch and Sons (Printed by John Davies, Hobart, 1870) gave me a gorgeous insight into old-fashioned gardening techniques.

The unique and personal anecdotes and stories in *Tasmania's North East—A comprehensive history of north eastern Tasmania and its people* by Hon A.W. Loone (First published by The Examiner and Weekly Courier Offices, 1928; Republished 1981) gave me an insight into Tasmania's regional history.

Jinkers and Whims—A pictorial history of timber-getting by Jack Bradshaw (Vivid Publishing, Fremantle, 2012) and its companion video, *Timber Getting in Western Australia* showed me some of the logging and sawmilling practices of yesteryear. I also found many helpful historical images on 'LINC' at linc.tas.gov.au.

I've used a combination of actual and fictional towns in the story. Hobart and Launceston are real cities in Tasmania. *Tarney's Creek* is, or perhaps I should say *was*, an actual place, but I've never found it on a map. It's where my maternal grandfather and grandmother lived when they were first married, and the living conditions described in the book are similar to those my grandmother described to me during a series of conversations I had with her in 2010. *Tinsdale* is fictitious, and the name alludes to the tin mining that was once prevalent in the northeast of Tasmania and the farming that continues there to this day. I borrowed the name *Milaythina* from the Palawi kani word for 'country', and chose it as a means of paying respect to the original inhabitants of Tasmania. I made up the name, *Ben Craeg*, from the Scottish term for mountain and Craeg is an anagram of Grace.

In the novel, I mention a concert performed in Hobart by Dame Nellie Melba in 1903. Melba did come to Tasmania in February, 1903, and was scheduled to perform in Launceston, but the concert was cancelled.

I've taken licence in using cervical cerclage as a treatment for cervical incompetence in the early 1940s. This procedure didn't come into medical practice until over fifteen years later, after it was described by Dr Ian McDonald in the *British Journal of Obstetrics and Gynaecology* in October 1957.

Finally, I acknowledge the short story, 'The Yellow Wallpaper', by Charlotte Perkins Gilman. This story was first published in 1890 and the fact it still resonates today is a tragedy and a sign that nothing much has changed when it comes to defined gender roles for women. My novel pays homage to Charlotte Perkins Gilman and to the countless intelligent, insightful and courageous women throughout the centuries, who, through no fault of their own, have been prevented from achieving their potential and following their dreams.

Acknowledgements

Publishing a novel takes a long time and it also requires a village. Over the past six years, many wonderful people have helped to bring this story to the page:

I couldn't have asked for a more understanding, insightful and knowledgeable team to work with than my publishers, Allen and Unwin. I thank them for their guidance, for being prepared to take on an older beginner, and for giving me the time I needed in order to make this book the best it could be. I particularly thank Annette Barlow for seeing the potential in my book, understanding what I was trying to say and enabling me to realise that vision. I'm also indebted to Siobhán Cantrill for her editorial guidance and for being at the other end of a telephone. I thank Jeanmarie Morosin and Christa Munns for their insights and attention to detail in the copy edits and proofreading.

Going back to the earliest origins of this story, I thank my first writing tutor, Rosemary Stevens, for her gentle wisdom, support and encouragement. I'm also grateful to my first writing group—Emily Paull, Kristen Levitzke, and Glen Hunting—who read my early, and terrible, drafts without complaint and still managed to give encouraging feedback.

I thank Iris Lavell, who helped me sharpen the first 50 pages of my manuscript. Without her guidance, I'd never have been awarded a 2014 Varuna Residential Fellowship. I'm indebted to the Eleanor Dark Foundation for awarding me that fellowship, which gave me time to continue working on my novel away from the distractions of home. I also thank Carol Major, who read my manuscript during my residency and gave me the crucial feedback that enabled me to transform a clunky series of events into a story.

I thank Fremantle Press and the Judges of the 2014 City of Fremantle-TAG Hungerford Award—Susan Midalia, Richard Rossiter and Delys Bird—who shortlisted my manuscript for the award. Even though I didn't win, the shortlisting gave me hope that my story had potential and motivated me to keep going.

I thank my friend, Natasha Lester, who has always been at the end of a telephone or email, and who has freely and generously shared her writing knowledge and experience.

I feel overwhelming gratitude to my fellow writing group members, Michelle Johnston and Jacquie Garton-Smith. These ladies read and re-read countless iterations of this novel, pointed out its flaws in the kindest of ways, and never gave me anything but encouragement and support. I thank Jacquie, too, for her expert gardening advice.

I'm obliged to Marlish Glorie, Lily Malone, Monique Mulligan, and Emily Paull for reading my book and giving me considered feedback. Dear Emily deserves a medal for reading my novel three times.

I thank Lyn Tranter from Australian Literary Management for representing me, and particularly for her generous feedback in 2015, which made me return to the drawing board and rewrite my story, turning it into a much better one.

Lastly, I thank my family because I couldn't have written this novel without their understanding and patience. My children—Isabelle,

Alexandra, Timothy and Samuel—have shared their mother with a fictitious family for the past six years largely without complaint. My husband, Scott, has taken up the household reins and generally sustained us all over that period. I thank him, too, for his steadfastness, for listening and encouraging, for believing in me and, most of all, for giving me the confidence to believe in myself.

I also want to thank everyone who's encouraged me along the way—every reader of my blog, every follower on Facebook and anyone who's offered advice, shared their writing story or written to me. Your support has been invaluable and helped keep me motivated. I thank you all from the bottom of my big, swollen heart.